I0749276

INSIDE DISTANCE

A NOVEL

Konrad Karl Gatien & Sreescanda

INSIDE DISTANCE

Published by IRP (USA)

For information, contact: irpnovels@gmail.com

2021 HARDOVER EDITION PUBLISHED BY IRP (USA)

ISBN 978-0-9845730-3-5
FICTION
1st Printing
2nd Printing

http://www.irpnovels.com

Library of Congress Cataloging-in-Publication Data

Gatien, Konrad Karl. Sreeescanda.
Inside Distance: a novel / Konrad Karl Gatien & Sreescanda.
ISBN 978-0-9845730-3-5
1. General Fiction 2. Suspense- Fiction 3. Thriller-Fiction. 4. Sports-Fiction
5. Boxing/Mixed Martial Arts-Fiction. 6. Crime Fiction 7.Crime-Police Procedural

"No groin attacks, no head butts, eye-gouging," Referee Ray McAlister, 61, 5-9, 175, ex-fighter, and a company man to the T, droned out the no-nos above the crowd hollering to get on with it.

I tuned him out when I noticed Nigel Hansom, 43, 6-0, all 323 lbs. of him sliding into the front row, ringside seat. He was fat but nobody dared call him that. Nigel dressed like a Wall Street shark for this fight—red tie, blue shirt underneath one of his many specially tailored Italian suits, and shoes shined into mirrors. He called it his 'occasions-only' look. Otherwise, he usually wore jeans and and an open shirt that never went through the wrinkle-free cycle.

Nigel stroked his completely bald head, which he shaved every morning religiously, then opened his thumb and forefinger in opposite directions over his 'stache all the way down to his goatee. An unconscious ritual. He was usually never without a cigarette either. The man had to light up every half hour. But there was no smoking in the arena. He chomped tobacco gum instead and greeted me in a voice as rough as leather soles crunching across gravel, "Dusty."

"Nigel," I greeted back.

We'd known each other some twenty years, give or take, ever since Nigel was a freshman at LSU—Louisiana State University. He was born and raised in New York's Hell's Kitchen—an unfriendly place to grow up, considering his parents were Brits without an iota of Irish in 'em—and why he was such a tough, mean mothafucka. Being acquaintances two decades didn't mean shit, not with Nigel. If he looked as if he had a temper like a grenade, you were right on. Naturally followed then that he turned into a human two-by-four if you fucked him over. No matter you were his kith or kin. I still sometimes scratched my head how and why such a nasty piece of work never made it in the cage.

Ref Ray finished up. "Any questions?"

Both fighters shook their heads, no. There been enough

chirping leading up to tonight.

"OK," Ray pointed them to their corners, "let's have a good, clean fight."

The fighters walked away. The full house crowd roared.

I straightened as Jenny, 20, 5-8, 133, sauntered over. A stunner of a face without a blemish. Sky blue eyes, wide mouth, perfect teeth, full lips. B-cup above a six-pack stomach. Cut all over like 'em black athletes, but there was a softness to the lines. Think of her as the kid that come outta Jennifer Lawrence and Chris Helmsworth. She had big hands at the end of arms that stretched almost to her knees, giving her deadly reach. Girl like Jenny never had to work for nuthin'. Guys, dough, nuthin'. At least not until she got outta school, at which point, the real world mugged her. That didn't change her one bit, though. Jenny remained a loudmouth, Class A bitch who knew she was smoking hot, with skills and smarts. That's a triple helping of entitlement.

Her opponent tonight, Bella Haroon, 26, 5-9, 134, was from Ethiopia by way of Atlanta. Clearly not much thinking went into nicknaming her 'Black Widow.' She was good. *Damn good.* Many called her great. Not me. She didn't belong in the pantheon 'cause she never reached the summit. Great in regular fights, but choked in the ones that mattered for a record of 6-3. Actually, this was the closest she'd gotten—one match away from the title, making this fight such a big deal, made even bigger with Jenny's almost-daily shitting on Bella on Tik Tok, Twitter, Facebook, Youtube, Instagram, Snapchat, you name it. Calling her Ma Bell and old and on the downside of her career, which nobody'd proved. *Not yet.*

Jenny arrived at the corner of the Octagon, acknowledging Nigel with a cocky grin, "Hey, boss."

Nigel nodded. He wore a thin, tense smile. We'd both been waiting a long while for this, you know, to fight for a shot at the title. *God knows I've paid my dues.*

"I can't believe they let you back in the corner," Ref Ray, remarked, all snide, when he walked by.

"I served my time," I snapped. "So fuck you." *OK, so it was a year long suspension.*

I saw Nigel's jowls jiggle, tighten. They jiggled and tightened some more when the three judges took their seats. Every one of them stared at me unfriendly. *Shit, the odds are already pilin' up, the fight ain't even started yet.*

Jenny tossed her robe over the top of the cage railing. Wolf-whistles erupted, appreciative of the eye-candy that she was head to toe. Not half as many were directed at Bella, who you'd call good looking if you were into the stocky kinda black chick.

Puma Song, 68, 5-7, 161, wiry, plucked the robe outta the air with his cane. He was one-legged, half-black, half-Korean, with as expressive a pair of eyes you ever seen, a practically lipless mouth, and a wide, flat nose. All set in a skull perfectly spherical with his white hair tied into a pony tail like 'em Ninja fighters. Puma had cut his teeth as a Flyweight on the fringe, then moved to the corner as a trainer for third stringers. In the 1990s, he saw MMA—mixed martial arts—as the next big thing and switched over to scouting on account of his right leg being stolen by gout. Instead of dragging around a stump, he had it amputated thigh down and got himself a high tech steel leg. I didn't ask him how he could afford it 'cause, I believed, if you asked no questions, you got told no lies. Puma and I went back a ways—as much friendship as it was business, both built on just enough trust to make it work.

"Listen to them!" I said through the chainlink,

"Jailbirds! Jailbirds! Jailbirds!" That was my past and Puma's time served being dredged up. The name callers been outshouting supporters from the start. Now, with the fight about to start, it grew louder.

"They don't much like us, lil girl!" Puma said "Shove the hate back in their face!"

Jenny grinned, gestured for the detractors to get louder.

"Look!" I continued. "Bella's the fighter with the sponsor's name on her shorts." As if her hatred for all things Bella needed more motivating, it rankled Jenny no end, the big Cali internet company's name appearing above this match, passed on hers truly, a girl born and raised in LA. Hardly surprising then, also, a pro-Bella partisan crowd filled Texas Stadium. "The ref'll be on her side. Crowd on her side. Judges on her side. You ain't gonna get no decision goin' your way out here, you got that?"

"Yeah, lil girl," agreed Puma, lurking behind the chainlink "You KO the muhfuhin bitch, y'hear me." He was born and raised dead center of South Central Los Angeles in Compton. Gang of record he dealt with were the Crips. So, Puma been raised around knives and guns and hurt. A nasty mothafucka you'd regret antagonizing in a one-way dark alley.

"Yeah." I added, "A win here put you into the title fight. That's your motivation."

A bleached blonde bombshell in a Coors's thong pranced around along the painted line with a 'ROUND 1' card. They'd really pulled out the stops. It felt like a boxing match at Caesers Palace in Vegas. Like it or not, Jenny responsible all her own for hyping this as the Saturday night fight to watch with her confident—OK, arrogant—yap. On my way in, I heard the UFZ—Ultimate Fighting Zone—brass crowing that PPV—Pay Per View—had recorded the most buys for a non-championship MMA fight. *Ever.*

Ultimate Fighting Zone became the world order in MMA when the big bad wolves of the sport plundered the smaller local and international leagues to create a global behemoth. They won antitrust exemption. Meaning they were a monopoly in the US, Brazil, England, Germany, Russia—you know, countries which mattered.

"Pay attention!" I yelled, when Jenny's attention drifted. "So what you gotta do?"

"KO the bitch," Jenny grinned.

TingTingTing! Coors's perfect ass sashayed out the gate.

"Stick to the plan," I fed Jenny her mandatory mouthpiece.

Jenny bit down into the plastic, threw a jab, and mumbled, "Yeah."

I retreated and dropped into the vacant seat between Nigel and Puma. Not before I saw Trevor Ross, 58, 5-6, 153, a pasty-white, grim-faced suit, slip into the seat behind us. An ex-ref, he voted against my reinstatement. He glared back, disapproving like the rest of 'em. Funny, how notoriety works. You don't have to know the person at all but you can hate him with a passion nonetheless purely on gossip and rep. I was guilty of it, and now found myself at the receiving end. I could do nothing but be all philosophical, 'I made my bed. Now I'm bein' fucked in it.'

Pow!

Jenny landed the first significant strike—an MMA metric of power strikes that caused damage—into the middle of Bella's midsection like a wrecking ball. Bella staggered. Surprised. As she should be. The tape on Jenny—a scant two fights—showed her in love with power head strikes. She was good at it, with an insanely elite 40% accuracy, putting her in upper 90% of fighters. I knew Bella'd be defending her head. The crowd was caught off guard too and went awful quiet. Bella was their favorite, thanks to the media being on her side and the way she conduct herself, all lady like, through Jenny's negative personal attacks. Before Bella could react, Jenny got in, hit hard, and stepped straight back outta the way of Bella's wild swing. Jenny made the Widow pay with a short right to the chin. Followed it with a whammo to the head. Bella staggered again.

Nigel yipped happily. I reserved my jubilation. It was just the first thirty seconds. Jenny stole being the elite boxer that Bella been to open bouts. The crowd went boo. Judges none too pleased neither. Nothing they could do, though. Bella clinched—hugged—Jenny, who didn't let up. Continued to land blows. Dirty boxing, it was called. Fair game in MMA. Bella held on. Stayed on her feet. Threw weak punches. Jenny started to set up for a lower body takedown, going against what the pundits been predicting—a stand-up war 'tween two of the best upright strikers.

"Yeah!" Puma hollered.

"This could be over in the first round," Nigel gloated.

A little too early for that kind of pronouncement, but I was feeling good too. I caught the judges glaring at Ray. Before Jenny could lock Bella around the knees and plunk her down, Ray stepped in and stood them up—MMA lingo for separating the fighters and resetting the fight.

Puma jumped to his feet hollering, "What the fuck! Did you see that?"

"Next time improve your position," said Ray evenly to Jenny, who didn't like it neither.

"That's bullshit!" Puma jabbed his aluminum crutch. "Dusty?"

There was no point crying foul. I muttered, "The fix is on."

"We knew that coming in," Nigel replied sharply.

As much of a sensation as Jenny'd become, her bad girl image didn't find universal approval. Particularly purists. Even if they come to terms she was anointed to the main event this night, they felt some of Jenny's rants against Bella on social media went too far. Orchestrating the ol' credo, 'any publicity is good publicity,' UFZ smartly engineered the global interest into that time-tested battle cry.

Good vs. Evil.

Translation—Bella'd get borderline calls. Still, you couldn't excuse your way out with Nigel. So, I said nothing more. Ray motioned the girls to resume. Jenny, all square, came right at Bella, fists flying.

"No, no, no," I groaned.

Jenny tossed out the playbook. *Typical.* That was her problem. A know-it-all. Just 'cause of the early success with her fists, she figured she'd continue throwing punches. Bella was no moron. Onto Jenny and over the early wrinkle in our tactics. Jenny played into Bella's hands. Literally. Bella backpedaled, ducking, weaving, blocking. Escaping easily and landing the first of her blows.

My eyes leapt. I shot up, pointing, "Watch out!"

Jenny didn't hear, or just plain ignored me. Probably the latter.

Whabam!

Bella arced in a left that everyone in the arena, but Jenny, saw coming. You could hear Jenny's teeth and thoughts rattle all the way to the standing room spectators way up in rafters of Jones Mahal—the nickname for this 80,000 seat megastadium—in Irvin, Texas. A colorful maverick, Jerry Jones, who'd amassed a fortune in oil, built this billion-dollar home field for his team—America's team—the Dallas Cowboys. UFZ'd never hosted a match in an arena bigger than 30,000 fans. Thanks to additional seating from the Octagon to the stands, there were 15,000 more. UFZ made all standing room seats available for free. First come, first served. That brought in another 30,000. Making this the biggest audience ever for an MMA match in the fucking galaxy. Yep, this fight was that huge and anticipated. Rightly reflected on the world's biggest HDTV, where most of these fans' eyes were riveted. Suspended from the roof, seven stories high, and hundred and sixty feet long.

My girl was rhino strong. A lesser fighter's feet would've left the canvas. Jenny just rocked on her heels. Couldn't believe she just got hit.

"Be mad!" Puma rose. "Sheeuh, lil girl, make her pay!"

Puma's motivation only made it worse 'cause Jenny believed it. A prideful hesitation got her deeper in the hole. Bella unloaded a multiple punch combo that was hell on fists and just too much. *The Widow's found sumthin'*. Bella connected on strikes with her left hand going at Jenny's right. The crowd got back into it, seeing their betting hopes revived.

Judges smiled too.

"What the fuck?" Nigel reacted. "She's getting beat by a *left* hand!"

As a southpaw, Jenny naturally defended against an orthodox fighter's power hand. So Bella went to her jab hand for power head strikes. Jenny shoulda been able to ward them off. Fact—an orthodox fighter's left was 10% weaker than the right, unlike southpaws, who packed almost equal power in both hands, on account of living in a right-handed world.

Clang! Jenny crashed into the chainlink.

The crowd came to their feet, roaring.

Bella advanced, fists swinging. Jenny ducked, escaping

another direct hit to her head. She grabbed Bella, tried to upend the Widow. *Crack!* Bella landed a knee into Jenny's crotch. Don't matter girls didn't have balls, it hurt just as badly. Even vaginas concuss, so Jenny told me.

I rose, "Low blow! Low blow!"

Ray ignored me and danced away. I waved my arms in disgust. Jenny staggered, clinched Bella, who dirty boxed Jenny over the back. Jenny's knees crumbled. She tried to use her upper body strength and unbalance the Widow into the canvas.

"That's it! Drop her!" Puma yelled.

Bella would have none of that. *Whack!* A wicked uppercut. The contact between Bella's knuckles and Jenny's chin sounded like a gunshot. Jenny's face snapped up toward God. Blood sprayed outta her mouth. *Clang!* Her head had a violent meeting with the fence.

Bella walked in. *PowPowPow.* Left-left-left. All significant—make that devastating—strikes to the right side of Jenny's head. Jenny didn't react to even one of them, but stayed upright, I don't know how. Clinched Bella once more.

I glanced at the clock. *Shit.* Still two minutes to go—an eternity in MMA's five-minute per round format. I knew the fight was now back on track for Bella's corner. Going the way they wanted. Being a former pugilist, who'd won and successfully defended her welterweight boxing belt not once, but twice, Bella was showing she was better than Jenny on her feet. I suspected that, when we were training. So I increased Jenny's reps on the ground, where she had a shot at flourishing. But Jenny hadn't even come close to taking Bella down.

Bella clocked Jenny. Somehow, Jenny hooked her ankle around Bella's. The Widow's foot slipped and her eyes darted for no more than a split second. The press of bodies eased for an instant. Enough to break the rhythm of Bella's relentless punching.

Fighting at this level was all about an instant here, an inch there. This was both.

"Plant her!" I shouted, then, without taking a breath, "No!"

'Cause Jenny crooked her elbow into the gap and shoved off. Bella staggered back, still on her feet. *Goddamnit!* Jenny did that every time—show incredible strength, then incredible stupidity. The right transition, when she created that hole in space and time, was to tackle Bella to the canvas. Known as a takedown—single or double, depending on how many legs you grabbed. MMA 101.

Nigel sat back angrily. Puma rolled his eyes. As any good trainer must, I put Jenny's blunder in my rearview.

Whabam!

Jenny paid for it. Courtesy of Bella's trunksize left leg roundhousing into Jenny's temple. To move from boxing to MMA, way back when, Bella took a year off to first train at a Shaolin Temple in China. Then, she'd gone down to Thailand and studied the national sport, Muay Thai, or "The Art of Eight Limbs," so known on account of the fact that you struck from eight points of contact, not just two fists like boxing. As thick as Bella was, she demonstrated the quickness of a gazelle. A fiend standing up.

Jenny staggered.

PowPow! A ruthless one-two into Jenny's belly. Jenny's mouth opened, coughing up red spit and all the air in her lungs in two installments.

I heard a TV commentator snicker, "Welcome to the real big league, young lady," this being Jenny's first legit UFZ fight, "where your fists have to do the talking, not your Tweets."

The other commentator piped in, "Jenny doesn't even look like she belongs. Bella is taking her behind the woodshed."

"Angle yourself!" I shouted.

Somehow, Jenny heard me over the crowd on its feet yelling for Bella to drop the hammer. Jenny swiveled and ducked and avoided Bella's next punch, which if it had landed, would've laid even Tyson out cold. Bella packed everything into it. When she missed, she stumbled. This time Jenny didn't make the same mistake. She lowered her head.

Boom! Jenny plowed skull first into Bella's rib cage. *Slam!* The two women hit the canvas hard, Jenny on top of Bella.

"You got this now!" I hollered, having trained her for what must come next.

The triangle. MMA lingo for a chokehold using either arms or legs to force your opponent to tap out—concede defeat. Nobody'd done it better and more wickedly in her previous two fights than my girl. Bella's corner had seen film on Jenny and Bella jacked up her hands. Not letting Jenny get into any type of mount or guard—dominant positions to force a submission.

The two girls grappled viciously. Neither was getting TIP—Time in Position—points. Scoring that judges used for maintaining your Offensive position. While Bella tried to free her legs, which Jenny had pinned with ankle locks, Jenny was doing her darndest to get her left forearm down on Bella's throat for a push or a choke—as simple a submission technique as there was. The Widow knew if she let that happen, this fight was over.

I glanced over at the judges. The anxiety did an encore on every noggin.

Right now, Bella's clobbering of Jenny was earning her nothing 'cause close range strikes had numbers but not injury. Worse, this'd be as shocking and ignominious a defeat as there was for Bella, the prohibitive favorite.

Ref Ray circled the fighters, looking for an excuse to stand them up. But he couldn't, not with Jenny using her right elbow to pound the side of Bella's head. Meaning, it wasn't a case of two fighters lying on the canvas with neither gaining ground.

Plus, this played on TV, being watched by millions. Not to mention the behemoth overhead HDTV that magnified the women a hundred times. A blatant fix would bring down the wrath of everyone, from UFZ brass to the fucking federal government. Unlike boxing, which never quite lost the taint of being dirty, UFZ'd gone the extra mile to keep the sport clean. Ironically, Vegas made sure of that, what with all that betting money at stake. Gamblers'd flee if they saw a fix the public recognized.

'Sides, UFZ brass saw the big picture beyond just this fight. Even if the price was accepting Jenny, who was a whole another category of 'bad girl.' She mocked good manners and sportsmanship. Her arrival and antics had reignited the women's league, firing up fans more than Rhonda Rousey and Amanda Nunes combined—still the most famous female MMA fighters.

Bella couldn't spare a second hand, seeing as she needed both to hold Jenny's forearm off her throat. This allowed Jenny to keep pummeling the side of Bella's head. I could see the Widow's eyes. They were turned toward me and squinting and dilating with each blow from the bony tip of Jenny's elbow. Another thing you could do in the MMA that you couldn't in boxing—elbow the crap outta your helpless opponent.

"Don't stop!" I hollered 'cause another minute of pounding should do it.

"Yeah!" agreed Puma at the top his lungs.

Nigel was on his feet too, as was the third of the crowd rooting for Jenny.

TingTingTing!

"Goddamnit!" I exploded, having lost track of the clock, which been crawling when Jenny was getting beat, but raced, the other way around. *Great, Bella has God, UFZ, and luck on her side.*

Jenny being Jenny remained atop Bella after the bell with a devilish grin, which looked quite evil on account of the blood dripping off her teeth onto the Widow.

"Get off! Round's over," Ray yelled. "To your corner!"

I headed into the cage with a stool. One of Nigel's lackeys followed me in with a bucket and towels. I couldn't help sparing Bella a glance. She looked dazed. But that didn't mean shit. They'd have her good as new for Round 2. MMA was all about limits and testing them, finding your breaking point and pushing past it.

Jenny flopped onto the stool. I palmed the mouthpiece she spat out and shoved it in ice. Held up the spit bucket. The lackey began to wipe her down with an ice pack.

Jenny bloody grinned, "I had her, Dusty. I fucking had the bitch."

"Don't worry about it." I left out the part that Round 1 went to Bella free and clear.

A 10-point system governed these rounds. The three judges scored each round and the winner got 10, the loser 9, 8 if one was markedly dominant. Rarely were there even rounds—that happened if a point was deducted from the winner for something illegal. It'd be a cold day in hell that'd occur here in this fight. 'Cause Bella dominated four-some minutes and Jenny only came on in the first and last thirty seconds, I wouldn't be shocked if the judges scored the round 10-8 in favor of Bella. Though, as long as it didn't change the fact that their girl won, they probably stayed with 10-9 for appearances sake.

I proceeded to Endswell Jenny—that's pressing bruises and swelling with this hockey puck with compartments inside containing frozen water. Despite the beating, she showed only slight bruising's all. No major cuts. "She's orthodox, so why's she getting to you with her left hand?"

Jenny blew her nose into Dusty's hand cloth. "Don't worry, Dusty. I got this."

"No, you don't, not unless you win your transitions."

"The ref ain't letting me."

"Speak of the muhfuh," Puma pointed.

Ref Ray approached with Dr. Ned Gillian, 65, a beanpole thin old hand—the cutman slash physician on UFZ's payroll. He serviced both corners, not like boxing, where each fighter brought his own guy. It ensured nothing illegal was administered. Secondly, the thinking was he'd be neutral in his assessment of injuries. UFZ wanted to stay away from the black eye boxing had gotten, with guys passing out in the ring 'cause a cutman, beholden to his corner, kept a damaged fighter fighting knowingly. That didn't mean Ned couldn't play favorites. Come down to it, it was the same shit, different pots is all. I trusted nobody not part of Team Jenny anyways, and definitely not about to start now, not here, not after I'd seen the shenanigans that go down already.

"Don't say a word," I baited. "We know who side he on, and just looking for an excuse."

"I heard that," snapped Ray.

"Good," I snapped back. "I made sure at least two rows back heard it too."

Ray didn't say nothing more. Last thing he wanted was more talk that could go viral.

"Nothing looks too serious," Ned pronounced after he bent down and checked her out. I'd smeared Vaseline on her cuts. It took him five seconds, less even, to plaster some additional ointment and leave.

I waited till Ray and Ned moved outta earshot. "OK. Look. As good as you are on your feet, she's better. So, stop squarin' up, 'cause every time you do, she turning her jab into a power strike. This time, go back to what got you here."

Jenny nodded.

"Bella been fighting patsies," Puma piped in. "She ain't fought nobody like you, lil girl!"

"Yeah!" I added, even though that wasn't at all true. To make this headline, Bella'd come through some quality opponents. But nothing pumped up an athlete like an ego boost. I whispered something for just her ears only before I quit the cage.

TingTingTing!

Bella advanced, flummox in her eyes, 'cause Jenny crouched deeply as if she was taking a dump on her toes. Jenny sprang to her feet, catlike. Bella backed a step, still trying to figure out this tactic. Commentators didn't know quite what to say. Jenny grinned, bowing tauntingly. I cringed. This was when she got into trouble, trying to rile up the crowd, who roared with equal boos and laughs. That was the curious thing about Jenny. As much as they hated her, the audience loved her too. Or loved to hate her, more rightly. I reckoned it was jealousy that someone so pretty could be given all this talent—a DNA jackpot, some reporter called her gifts—and not be the least bit thankful for either.

I held my breath, wondering if she'd heed the last thing I'd whispered. *First, avoid contact.* She did. She danced and stanced for a good quarter minute. Distancing, it was called in the MMA, when fighters stalked and reassessed reach and range. Thanks to the unorthodox way we started the first round, I wanted to psych Bella's corner into wondering if we were going to pull something new this round too.

I gave Jenny the nod. *Then, go for the legs.*

She dove. Nigel snapped toward me, "What the hell?"

Jenny'd misjudged her distance for the double-leg takedown. She was so impatient for contact, she forgot where she was. I shoulda waited before I signaled, even though it made common sense Jenny should know her own fucking range. But I couldn't say that wasn't all my fault to Nigel. Puma shook his head too.

Anyway, only results mattered, that now being enough time for a fighter with Bella's experience to easily stuff Jenny. We all knew what this mistake'd lead to—full guard. Bella got under Jenny, wrapping and clamping her legs around Jenny's hips. It might sound odd to the novice, but in this MMA position, you had the upper hand being at the bottom 'cause then you had a shit load of options, with joint locks, chokeholds, and the like. It forced Jenny to try and pass the guard—squirming into a better position. Easier said than done when you got a fighter of Bella's experience and massive muscled thighs. She might like fighting upright, but to get to this far, she had to win from the ground in prior matches.

WhamWham! Wham! Body, body, head.

WhamWham! Wham! Body, body, head.

Bella went about her business like Bella usually did. The TV commentators began kissing her ass. I could see why. She was putting on a clinic of the MMA mantra. Body, body, head. *WhamWham! Wham.* She kept them compact so she could maximize the number of strikes per minute—another metric judges used to score. Each hit had Jenny look a little more helpless, vulnerable. To her credit, even under siege, she didn't give up trying to actively advance guard—that's attempting to switch from Defense to Offense.

"Coach her!" snapped Nigel, seeing me fold my hands like a neutral spectator instead of getting all worked up.

"She knows what she has to do," I retorted.

Weather this vicious maulin'. I checked the clock. We were ninety seconds into the round 's all. The crowd rose to their feet in a feeding frenzy, chanting, "Bella! Bella! Bella!"

Then, the Widow did something I didn't expect. She released Jenny to pass guard.

Oh, shit.

Her corner reacted with the similar shock. Here was a level headed fighter, her flawless technique keeping her in the upper echelon of MMA fighters, even getting her to this point, but now, suddenly, Bella was abandoning all that for a low percentage but spectacular victory. Clearly Jenny, with a habit of risking everything for a highlight reel, had gotten into Bella's head with the prefight sniping about how boring the Widow was as a fighter. So, now Bella wanted to show the upstart she was capable of going into the history books too.

Puma rose from his chair, recognizing what was about to happen.

Japanese invented it in judo. *Ashi Hishigi.* The deadly Achilles lock. In a perfect world, you locked the opponent's leg, trapped that foot in your armpit, then leveraged your forearm against the Achilles tendon with a heel hook. Since trying to escape it could tear the ligament, it was as deadly as it was breathtaking.

But you'd better be damn sure of success 'cause it was helluva gamble. Especially where Bella had to get to from where she was. When Ryo Chonan did it to Anderson Silva, in that memorable takedown, they were on their feet, sparring. It was perfectly executed—a total fluke, everyone said. I understood why Bella risked it. If there ever was a moment in the bout for her to open her guard—unlock her legs from around Jenny—this was it. Blood poured outta Jenny's nose. She looked beat and beaten down.

Bella pivoted in a matter of a second for the heel hook.

Pow! Jenny's fist came outta nowhere!

Think of a cobra you thought dead suddenly rear its head and strike. Jenny's vicious right came at Bella packing that kind of venom and surprise. The contact of knuckles and skull reverberated with that crunch you didn't just hear but felt all the way down in your gut. Bella's head swung halfway around the Octagon, her expression equal parts astonishment and jarring pain.

I leapt, so did Puma and Nigel. Elated as one, our identically worded yells came out as a perfectly synchronized chorus, "Fuck yeah!"

In that moment you saw the beauty of MMA. The immediate next moment could be the memorable one. *You see, what Bella didn't count on?* Jenny could act, and acting was a tactic. There was no shame in playing dead, I told Jenny during training, and whatja know, she remembered. The other quality my girl had, more than any fighter, male or female—recovery speed. Jenny could shove aside and forget agony as if it never happened.

Bella lost her position.

PowPow! Jenny unleashed two more significant strikes and threw Bella off. Jenny just got started. *Wham!* Straightening off the mat, Jenny blasted a frontkick square into Bella's chest, right where the heart enjoyed its coordinates. Bella tossed backward, her last two minutes of domination instantly forgotten. Jenny's fans roared. I could've sworn we picked up supporters, or they were just bloodthirsty spectators with no allegiance, who just wanted to see the girl-on-girl go more than just a couple of rounds.

Bella had just enough time to get to her feet before Jenny straightened and flew into her. The back of Bella's close-cropped skull smashed into the cage. Jenny pinned her to the chainlink and began throwing power head strikes with a non-stop southpaw.

"Keep at it!" I hollered, circling to where they were.

Jenny quickly got into a rhythm with her strikes. Bella's corner screamed instructions. *What can they tell her to do?* I couldn't help glancing over to the judges, who sat there helpless. If Jenny could draw enough blood outta Bella's nose and ears, Ref Ray would have no choice but to call the fight. But this wasn't Bella's first rodeo. I saw her underhook in place. I opened my mouth to warn Jenny the same time Bella delivered a knee.

Bam! Right into Jenny's privates.

Another low blow Ray conveniently missed.

Even though she was the first female I trained, this was our third fight together, and I made it a point to educate myself on a woman's pressure points. The clit's got a lotta nerves and a blow like this one probably crushed it against the pubic bone. No wonder Jenny's head rocked and she almost puked out her mouth guard.

"Low blow!" hollered Puma before I could, but his lone voice was drowned out by the crowd that went off like a terrorist bomb. The Jones Mahal actually shook with cheers.

"You owe us five minutes!" I shouted to Ray, who circled to my corner. "It's the rule after a low blow!"

Ray paid me no heed. Jenny staggered. *PowPowPowPow.* Jenny crashed into the chainlink under a rain of the Black Widow's fists. I lost hope until I checked the clock.

"Ten seconds!" I emptied my lungs. "Ten more seconds! Stay on your feet!"

Jenny elbowed off the next swing and clinched Bella. Not only that, she stomped down hard on Bella's foot, forcing her to reset, which gave my girl a moment to catch her breath.

TingTingTing!

I pumped my fist. The round was over. Jenny limped back. Blood dribbled down her forehead from a new cut along her hairline. Bella walked away upright, all cocky. I could've have sworn the usually stone-faced bitch was smiling. *Why not?* The way the judges were grinning and talking, they'd given her this round unanimously.

I climbed into the cage, slid a stool to the corner. The lackey began his routine. Nigel headed over, that's how worried he was. But first, I had a beef with the ref.

"Ray!" He tried to dodge me and we danced back and forth. "Don't tell me you didn't see that?"

"See what?" Ray shot back.

"The second low blow!" I directed that toward the judges. "There oughta be a deduction." But they weren't even looking my way, laughing among themselves, guzzling from the soda company sponsored cups in front of them.

Ray gestured angrily, "Get back to your corner!"

From the other side of the chainlink, Puma taunted. "When they begun hirin' blind referees?" Then turned toward the front row and played it up, "Who else got that memo?"

"Dusty," Ray warned, sticking his face up against mine, "get back to your corner and get your girl ready to fight at the bell, unless you're throwing in the towel."

"You'd like that wouldn't you?" I shot back.

Ray didn't wanna get into it, again wary of being overheard saying somethin compromising. He pivoted, strode off.

I headed to my corner. Jenny had a bag of ice pressed into her crotch. "You OK?"

"It's fucking painful. She got me twice. It isn't going to affect me in the sack, will it?"

"Not that I know of." I pulled out the Vaseline, Endswell, the usual.

"I got to fuck to function, Dusty," she grinned through the agony.

Coors's ass circled the Octagon one last time with the 'ROUND 3' card. I shoved my face in front of Jenny. "OK. If you thought the first two rounds were a battle, this one's going to be a fucking war. Bella's prideful that nobody's gotten her into the third round in all her years as a pro. So she's pissed you did'n gonna come after you hell for leather!"

Ned sauntered over. There were bruises all over Jenny but that was normal. He applied extra first aid on the bleeding along her hairline. He nodded, satisfied, and left.

"Fighters wait a lifetime for a match like this," Nigel spoke up, surprising me and Jenny. He'd never done this before, come over, for one, and speak up, for another. A stern crispness to his tone made Jenny pay attention. "Fighting to be one match away from a title shot barely six months into your UFZ career, that's unprecedented. Don't waste it."

The timekeeper rattled the cage. Jenny tossed the ice pack

into the bucket. The lackey scampered off with it, sweeping up the spit bucket, towels, and sponges along the way. I shoved the mouthpiece in, took her hands in mine, and warned her again, "I notice her jab with her right, so can she can fool ya with her left." Orthodox boxers jabbed with the left, to land a right. "So, pay attention to her left!"

I returned to my seat beside Nigel. He leaned over, "The ref's got it in for you."

I shrugged. *Nuthin' I can do.*

The Black Widow clearly arrived in no mood for sparring. She wanted nothing less than a KO and unleashed a volley within the first ten seconds. Quit cautious distancing and landed three, missed three. Each time she connected, Jenny shook her head and laughed. The crowd erupted. And on each miss, Jenny got in some hard leg kicks and taunted Bella some more. I hated it, but that was Jenny. Always showing up the opponent.

"Jenny has to be careful," I heard the TV announcer say. "Bella doesn't come to play ego games. She treats every fight like a business trip." I didn't buy that. Bella had her chance to end the fight from full guard. But Jenny'd broken into the Widow's brain and burglarized rationale with goading smiles and gestures.

Oh, shit no! Bella switched power hands and got her left fist to the right side of Jenny's skull. Nigel leaned back, exasperated, "Has she forgotten Bella has two hands?"

"I can only teach. I can't do nuthin' if she don't learn."

"Bullshit. You're the trainer, Dusty. That's on you."

Puma looked over, concerned. I didn't say nothing, and as much I didn't like neither Nigel's tone nor accusation one bit, he wasn't entirely unjustified in saying what he said. It was my job to prepare Jenny. Not like her lack of discipline was something new. I been battling it since Day 1. That, and squaring up. It was maddening. Of course, Bella had seen tape of Jenny's two previous fights and picked up on all of Jenny's bad habits. So, Nigel was right. On me for not ridding her of them.

Bella went orthodox. Faked a left hand power strike. It never arrived. Instead, Bella's right hand careened in. To my feet is as far as I got.

Whabam!

One moment Jenny's head faced straight, and in the next, wrenched almost a full one-eighty with Bella's mitt attached to it. *How the hell did her spine not crack at the neck?*

With that punch, Bella took the fight to Jenny, first kicking the legs out from under Jenny, then landing on top like a WWE goliath. There was no mistaking Bella's intention—winning a submission in a way that looked like vendetta for pushing her into Round 3 for the first time.

Jenny tried to wrap up Bella. Failed. Then tried for a butterfly guard—hooking the ankles against Bella's thighs to lift her off balance; frankly her only way outta this—and failed again. Each gambit weakened Jenny's position another notch, intensifying Bella's assault into a relentless ground and pound. An animal on her feet, Bella was doing a damn fine job with the weakest aspect of her game —grappling.

It began to look bleaker and bleaker for Jenny.

The crowd got louder and louder. Jones Mahal quaked again with chants, "Bella! Bella! Bella!"

Jenny's blood smeared the canvas.

Ray leaned in.

Shit.

Nigel said out loud what I feared, "He's going to call it."

The judges leaned forward, waiting for Ray to exert his discretion and shut it down. Bella hammered away with a single-minded concentration. Her knuckles picked up more blood with each blow. I didn't know when I got up and got to the edge of the cage. Ray started to reach out to Bella to lay off and end this. His finger came within an inch from ending the fight, when—

Bella's belly buckled upward!

Same time, her spine at the neck bent her head up and back like someone yanked her by the hair—which she had none, having crew-cropped it all. But you know what I mean.

Her eyes bulgéd. Her cheeks blowfished.

Regardless, in the matter of a split second, Bella's dominance vanished. She tumbled off Jenny, who lunged like a tigress that just spotted red meat.

"Back off!" hollered Ray, stopping Jenny cold by grabbing her hand.

I shot to my feet, "What the fuck!"

"Illegal hit!"

I was speechless. "What? Where!"

Nobody saw what exactly occurred. I looked up at the megascreen. The replays showed the girls clinched too tight to tell. Ray, being so close and down on his knee, knew it was his call to make and made the most of it. "Low blow!"

Payback knee to Bella's clit is what he was pointing and saying he saw.

I responded, "Bullshit! This is fucking total bullshit!"

It wasn't humanly possible to deliver a debilitating low blow without a long enough swing starting in the other direction. The way the Black Widow was gasping, she was outta breath more than pain. Somehow, someway, Jenny'd rammed the bony part of her arm into Bella's solar plexus. Not her clit.

"I saw it!" Ray said, knowing his was the final word.

Jenny's side of the arena knew his word was worth shit, considering the judges, Bella, her corner, and he were sucking the sponsor's dick. Boos rained down amidst the applause.

"You're a damn liar!" I answered hotly.

"Jailbirds! Jailbirds!" chanted Bella's fans, but with none of that prior unity or volume.

Ray ignored me and pointed to the judges, "That's a deduction!" He crouched over Bella, "You got five minutes, if you want it."

"And a room for both of you?" Jenny smirked, all disdain.

"Back off!" Ray snarled at her.

Jenny shrugged and played to the crowd. As bloody and bruised as she was, she stretched out her hands, palms up, urging the crowd to bring it. They did, now with more cheers than jeers.

"Sheeuh," Puma observed. "Seems like you're winning 'em over, lil girl!"

Jenny laughed.

"This is a fight, not a club!" Ray put the kabash on the party Jenny had started.

I looked over. Being prideful, Bella dismissed her trainer from accepting the break. She saw what was happening—this crowd turning. Sitting down for five minutes'd come off as a pussy-move.

"You sure?" Ray asked.

Bella nodded.

Ray could do nothing, said, "Let's go."

There was but a minute left in this round.

The girls began launching strikes, Jenny choosing kicks to unbalance Bella. But if Bella was going to get a submission this frame, she wasn't showing none of the earlier urgency.

I dropped down into my chair.

"Maybe for the championship," Nigel leaned over to me, "you should sit it out."

"Who's going to run the corner on fight night?"

"Someone."

"Else?" I clarified.

Nigel raised his eyebrows. Yes. "I was thinking, Kevin."

Kevin was the grappling coach I'd brought in. I was shocked. "You're demoting me in my own corner?"

"Just for appearances." Nigel distracted. "Goddamnit!"

Bella effectively used her left to go savage to the right side of Jenny's skull. Jenny's ears bled. Blood sprayed outta her mouth too.

"There she goes forgetting Bella has a left hand!" Nigel moaned.

Sensing she had Jenny on the ropes again, Bella charged in with a big hook. But Jenny ducked and stopped Bella dazed and dead in her tracks with a right-left combo. Bella not only withstood the power strikes, she slammed one home. Jenny stayed on her feet. Bella pummeled her heel into Jenny's chest, then used Jenny's recovery time to roundhouse in from the right. Jenny didn't react to the oncoming threat. The crowd gasped before Jenny felt the full force of Bella's massive foot.

Whabam! Jenny's head ripped around. Fell.

Bella went to the canvas and wrapped her thighs around Jenny's neck.

"The clock's at zeros," noticed Nigel.

As did Puma. "Hey! What the fuck?"

I shot to my feet shouting and pointing at the giant digital timer. The timekeeper darted his eyes for permission from whoever and then slammed his palm down. In the nick of time too, 'cause Bella's thighs were tightening like a vice, choking the life outta Jenny.

TingTingTing!

Bella didn't release Jenny clean like she was supposed to. *Bam!* Deliberately cracked my girl's head on the canvas before unhooking her legs. If it affected Jenny any, she didn't show it. Not satisfied she'd exposed an ugly mean streak in Bella, Jenny audaciously planted a bloody kiss on the Widow's cheek!

The 125,000 folks, crammed from the Octagon all the way to the top tiers, went nuts.

Bella shoved Jenny away. I couldn't resist smiling, but I could see Jenny shaking off cobwebs as she came back to the corner. Even with Bella winning this round, everyone in the arena recognized this fight be far from over. In fact, the way they cheered with nary a boo, they reckoned a classic shaping up. There hadn't been one on the women's side. Not ever. Rhonda Rousey vs. Meisha Tate been a lot of hoopla and bragging, then Rhonda whupped Meisha's ass without much contest or suspense about the outcome.

Deciding there's no point harping on her squaring up, I lauded, wiping her down. "You did it! You did it, Jenny! You survived three rounds! Now Ma Bell's in even deeper uncharted territory. Trust me when I tell you, I don't know if her corner even planned for a fourth round!"

Meantime, Puma and his cane was all over Ref Ray. "Now you fixing the clock, you crooked son of a bitch!"

"That ain't my jurisdiction," defended Ray.

"What else you got cooked up to deliver this fight for the Black Widow?" Puma kept jawing like the dogged mothafucka he was. "Now that the bettin' line don't mean shit!" 'Cause Vegas had Bella winning by submission in three rounds.

I noticed Nigel come over yet again. But he shut his trap this time as I preached to Jenny. "She's still trickin' you, switching up."

"I just wasn't looking last time."

"Well, start. Because the more she connects, the more confident she gonna get. Getting you guessing which hand is coming with the power head strike's gonna be their strategy since it's working."

"I got it."

"Then fight like you do! You can't win on your heels facin' up against her. On the ground, you're the beast!"

Ned appeared. "How you feeling?"

Jenny grinned, "Like kicking some ass."

Ned wasn't amused. "There's blood on your teeth."

"No shit."

"Open your mouth." Ned entered her mouth with a Q-tip and smeared ointment. He looked at the other cuts and bruises. "Nothing serious." And trotted outta the Octagon.

"How we been trainin' for this fight?"

"Chokes and locks."

"How you get there?"

"Ground'n pound."

"You come out fight clubs, so you been to war and back more times'n most fighters done their entire careers," I hyped. Jenny nodded vigorously. I shoved back the mouth piece. "Blood'n' guts! You got both in spades and spilled 'em in buckets!"

"Yeah!" Jenny mumbled, jacked up.

"Don't worry about no points! Don't worry about no submission!" I grabbed her by her wrists. "You get outta the fourth and I'll show you how to fuck her up in the fifth!"

TingTingTing!

"There ain't no room for error!" I warned her sternly.

"Why the fifth?" Nigel asked angrily. "Why not end it now?"

"So you and me are clear," I retorted. "I brought her this far, I can end it right here."

Round 4 got under way, the crowd fully into this one now.

Nigel yelled in my ear, "What if Jenny dropped you?"

I stared at Nigel. He was ruthless Mr. Money Bags. Jenny had no scruples. But I was no angel either, shouted back, "She can try."

CASE FILE: 010146888
Reporting Officer: Detective Bostwick Oswald

Boz, 38, 6-3, 190, stared down at the burned human remains.

His NOPD shield, clipped to his belt between the 9mm Browning and cell phone, caught the rising sun and glinted. *Whoosh!* A wind kicked up as if City Park realized it had early morning company, didn't much care for the intrusion, and spat wet odors at them. Bayou St. John flowed nearby. No matter how long you lived here—and Boz had been born and raised in these parts—you never ever got used to that shitty smell of stagnant moisture. Especially when temperature and humidity ran about even throughout an unseasonably hot February.

The body was unrecognizable. Skin and flesh burned almost entirely to the bone. You could see right through where the lungs used to be, the heart a pan fried tomato. Pieces of blackened stomach, guts. Muddy brown shore water of the artificial creek rippled back to reveal only a skeleton, pelvis down.

"The leg bones below the knee," Officer Hyatt Lincoln, 25, 5-10½, 175, pointed, before the water rolled back up, "see how they are striped?"

Like the victim felt the fury of a cane.

Not a tatter of clothing—they'd completely burned away.

"But then," Hyatt pointed to the cracks in the skull, cheekbone, and ribs, " that looks like the killer took a baseball bat."

However, the first thing that caught Boz's attention—a

crumpled newspaper stuffed between the victim's exposed teeth in a skull laid bare. Not charred. *So, inserted post mortem.* Boz carefully extracted and unwrinkled it.

"Holy shit!" gasped Hyatt, rocking onto the balls of his feet beside Boz, who ignored him and stared at the snapshot from the fight of Jenny's agonized face turned to camera with Bella's fist connected to her right temple. The huge type across the top asked: 'NEXT-JEN?'

Hyatt's eyes leapt to the corpse. "Jenny Sharp!"

Sure, the headline suggested the victim's ID in no uncertain terms, but Boz checked his emotions and snapped, "We don't know if the victim is female."

His Adam's apple, with a mind of its own, rolled the slightest. As too, his lips, which drew into a thin line. Since he kept his head down, Hyatt couldn't see either.

Boz played detective. Worked his eyes down the cadaver.

His admonishment seemed to have no effect on Hyatt, who prattled on, "She was in an epic fight just a week ago. Five rounds of awesome. And how it ended? Fans and pundits haven't stopped talking."

Boz held out a clear plastic Ziplock. "Hold it open, please?"

Hyatt did, without shutting up. "Supermodel hot, always talking smack. Everyone said Jenny was a real bitch for real too. You loved her or hated her, there was no in-between."

Boz gently stuffed the newspaper in.

"Pretty clever, huh? The headline?"

"Yeah, genius," Boz scowled because there'd been no reason to smile of late. He didn't look at the young uniform who coulda walked straight off the force's recruiting brochure. Bright-eyed and bushy tailed. Clean shaven. *Reminds me of me.* Growing up in the lily white suburbs, playing soccer, and eating apple pie. You could tell. The good diction. How Hyatt carried himself.

Yakked on, "Tossed over the side, looks like, huh, Detective?"

Nobody knew to call him Boz—short for Bostwick Oswald—except for the Commander and the squad room, city's lawyers, and of course, family and friends, but there weren't many of those left.

"Whoever did this," Hyatt went on, "figured the skeleton'd hit water and sink without a trace."

Wrong. This was Louisiana, the bayou state. Acres and acres of swamp, most of it swirling through and around impenetrable wet forests. Easy peasy to lose a body. *That's not the intention with this victim.* Leaving it along a deserted stretch of Harrison Avenue, which cut through City Park, right where it bridged over flowing water, was no accident.

Boz caught the murder because he was meant to.

It fell within the jurisdiction of the Third Police District—Boz's beat. Whoever dumped the victim here knew he'd signed up to take the overnight shift. Nobody fought him for it. Why would they? It was party night last night in New Orleans. Neither were they surprised he'd want it. Perhaps the most disliked cop in his squad room, Boz did nothing to rehab his rep. In fact, he tried to live up to it at every turn. "If anyone is 'dick' for detective, it's him," Boz once overheard a couple of uniforms trashing him across urinals while he was in the crapper unbeknownst to them. Just to prove their point, he opened the door, pants around his ankles, and said, "Dick is criminal slang of Romany origin for dik, d-i-k, meaning, to see. And what I'm dikking is a couple of flatfoot dumbasses."

"You didn't touch or move anything, did you?" asked Boz with allegation in his tone.

"No, sir," Hyatt sounded almost offended. "This is exactly how I found her." He couldn't help carrying on, "This is going to blow up."

"Again, we don't know if it's her. Not until a positive DNA match."

"Of course." The kid'd already made up his mind, Boz knew.

Being Ash Wednesday—that annual morning when most of New Orleans woke up hung-over to kick off forty days of Lent—nobody'd gotten out of bed yet. Not even a jogger had trotted by. Yesterday, Fat Tuesday, marked the end of Mardi Gras, when the parades and partying orgasmed after more than a week of of escalating foreplay.

"What's that?" Hyatt pointed.

The creek receded the furthest it ever did since they got here. The current dragged a clear plastic grocery bag, handles tethered to the hip bone, into view. Boz lowered himself back down, as did Hyatt, all eager-beaver.

"Are those hands?" Hyatt caught his breath loudly.

Boz darted his eyes. *How did I miss that?* The bones had been severed—shattered, whatever you wanted to call the untidy lop—at the both wrists. "Amputated."

"Genitals are missing too," Hyatt breathed the words out.

"Hacked out," nodded Boz. Loose, cooked flesh, crudely cut out, clung via scraps of cartilage and vessels around the pelvis.

"Is that it sloshing in the bag with the hands? Ughhh!" grimaced Hyatt.

Boz returned to the skull. Peered past the cracked cheekbone. "Tongue's gone too."

"Jesus," Hyatt reacted, distressed. "You think she was alive?"

"No point to torture if it's post mortem," Boz said, matter of fact, refusing to let rising emotion get the better of him. "Being burned alive may've been the merciful part."

Like every other uniform, the kid obviously had aspirations to become a detective. He maybe could. Sounded bright enough. Made all the right prelim observations. Boz remembered when he had everything going for him. Then it'd all unraveled into a life of woulda, coulda, shoulda.

"How did you find the body?" Boz waved off the feasting flies. His palms, trapped in the blue-plastic crime scene gloves, began to sweat.

"City Park is my beat." Hyatt explained eagerly. "Saw birds on the railing, circling." They were still there, some perched, the rest hovering overhead. "They took turns swooping down and coming up. I knew right away something was dead. Looked over the side, saw the skeleton, and called it in. Didn't go down till you got here, just to be sure I didn't destroy evidence."

"OK." Curt. Boz couldn't help it. That'd become his manner,

even when he was being cordial. Eyes to expression, manner to words, he came off as a ball-busting asshole—worse of late—because it was what his decisions in life had turned him into. He wondered if Hyatt expected a compliment. Kid wasn't getting any. His job was to report the body and he'd done that. The rest, the Detective 101 shit, well, he'd taken it upon himself to go above his pay grade. Boz wasn't about to acknowledge that.

Boz stood, as did Hyatt, who exclaimed warmly, "What sick motherfucker would do this to her?"

"Listen," Boz looked him in the eyes and said in no uncertain terms, "you don't breathe a fucking word about what we have here. If I as much as hear a whisper that the victim's identity may be—just even may be—Jenny Sharp before an official positive ID from DNA, I will know only one other person could've leaked it. You. Any part of what I said you don't understand?"

"No, sir," gulped Hyatt.

"Say nothing to nobody, not even CSI when they show up. Or, I will have your badge, Internal Affairs up your ass, and personally bury your ambitions in law enforcement."

Hyatt nodded, a showroom model of a bobble-head.

Boz went at him again, "Any part of *that* you don't understand?"

"No, sir," Hyatt repeated and swallowed and shook his head from side to side, gabby no more.

"Tape off the crime scene." Boz left him guarding it.

CSI turned in as Boz turned out of Harrison Avenue. Kid did not dare question—maybe because he was shitting his pants, he didn't notice—that Boz took the Ziplock bag with the newspaper, the only evidence pointing to the identity of the victim. He did not return to the Third Police District HQ on Paris Avenue to file a report or log the headline as evidence.

Instead, Boz, made one stop, then headed downtown to *Tremayne*, an obscure deli—the spot he and the Orleans Parish District Attorney, Arlen Taylor, 46, 6-1, 178, used to meet to avoid prying eyes. Again, this being early and the morning after Mardi Gras, none of the other tables were occupied. Still, he took their usual booth, way in the far back corner.

Arlen arrived shortly after Boz did. Lean, angular—five parts slick, three parts shark, two parts shady—Arlen removed his jacket and dropped down into the seat across. The rest of his attire—pinstriped shirt, gold tie, navy blue trousers, and brown belt, shoes—all screamed 'politician!'

Boz held up the Ziplock. "It's done."

Nigel Hansom: Hearsay from Heroica Caborca

Nigel drove through the street called Calle 8. Locals stared at him and his car, a shiny black Lincoln. A cigarette drooped from his lips. To those inhabiting Mexico's underworld, looking for Americans they could scare, snatch, rob, or blackmail, he'd earned the rep as someone you fuck with at your own peril. Caborca wasn't lawless like Juarez used to be, but it could be dangerous if you acted like a Bambi-eyed tourist. About 52,000 people lived in the city proper and almost as many in the surrounding towns of the municipality. Suppose you were headed from Mexico City to Tijuana on Federal Highway 2, you'd drive through Caborca, the town nested up in the hilly desert of Sonora, immediately south of Arizona's Pima County, on the Mexican side of the border.

Clouds rarely showed up in the sky over these parts. So, at 10 AM, the ground was already roasting. If you believed in hell, this heat—dry, scalding, around 120°F—probably had you repenting your sins. Dust devils scampered around the arid landscape. Sometimes—not today—they reached over a hundred feet and looked like a full blown twister, but even at that size it was harmless if you kept your head down and just let it go by. Kids in front of a school stopped playing to look at the Lincoln go by. Few people here owned a car with fresh paint let alone the latest luxury model.

Nigel spared the tykes a glance. He turned at the hospital,

worked his way to the outskirts. Rusted out pickups dotted the curbs and driveways. The homes reeked of working class occupants. The occasional house elder, sitting under a sombrero and a covered porch, watched the Lincoln go by with the same idle curiosity as the school kids. An irregular trench snaked alongside the road—carved out by a flashflood from that rare downpour Caborca received.

The neighborhood changed, going from homes to more sprawling, industrial structures called *maquiladoras*, or factories that received raw materials and turned them around into finished products with cheap labor. A product of the free trade agreement between Canada, the US, and Mexico—which Americans never stopped complaining about. Not Nigel. His payroll was almost entirely Latin. The thinking around these parts was that *gringos* would have those jobs if they got off their high-wage horse and worked like the illegals—without any bullshit.

The Lincoln pulled up outside the local police station, a flat roof cement building that was once probably a bright lime yellow. Now just patches of fading ochre remained. The further away you got from Mexico City, the less money municipalities received from the central government. So, public buildings looked like shit.

Nigel climbed out. Stamped out his smoke. Emerging from the air-conditioned comfort of the car, he reacted to the heat as if it was a physical thing. Sweat sprung out of his pores like water out of a showerhead. Nobody, not even the locals, ever got used to the intensity of this dry heat. He reached in and grabbed a stylish Panama. Donned it. Headed past the only official Jeep—another aging vehicle—climbed unhurriedly up the steps, and then shoved open the unvarnished door. It creaked loudly.

It wasn't much cooler inside. A fan turned as fast it could, but it just recirculated the heat. The whitewashed walls faded in wide swatches. Rusting, ajar gates led to two empty cells.

A constable, 40, 5-5, 202—gut overflowing out of his belt—swept the floor. Sunlight blasted in as a single shaft through the window and fell upon the only desk, where the Captain,

50, 5-8, 210, just as fat, yellow teeth, medium build, pork belly, had his feet up on the desk, reading a newspaper. Hearing the front door hinges scrawl, he bent down the top corner of the page, lazily leaned his head, and looked sideways at Nigel. The constable stopped sweeping, swung his eyes around as well. He showed some curiosity, unlike the Captain, who displayed all the symptoms of a jaded lifer. Regardless, neither cop's demeanor gave any indication justice could be gotten here. Utter indifference could almost be the third entity in the room. Nigel wasn't unfamiliar with this kind of attitude.

He lifted his hat an inch, dropped it back down, and greeted. "*Buenas tardes. Mi nombre es Nigel Hansom.*" Good afternoon. My name is Nigel Hansom.

"*Hablas español muy bien,*" drawled the Captain. You speak Spanish very well. In a tone that suggested he felt obligated to say something. He folded the newspaper, tossed it down on the table. The constable leaned on the broom.

Nigel laughed. Continued in Spanish. "My mother insisted I learn a second language that is relevant."

The Captain tilted his chin upward a fraction. OK. Indifferent.

Nigel reached into his coat and removed an envelope. "I'm not going to waste your time and mine with bullshit."

"I've heard of you."

"Then you know I'm a coyote. But for fighters only. I take them across the border at my expense, pay them well—free rent, free food. They fight along the I-10, California to Florida. Three fights, six weeks. The big boys come and watch. Take on those they think can cut it. Those who don't, I give them a choice—thousand dollars to return to Mexico, where I found them, or take their chances in the US. Every now then, I hire a fighter to work for me. I get them a Green Card." Nigel paused, looked at the constable, then back to the Captain, then placed the envelope on the table, then pushed it across.

The Captain lazily reached forward, parted the flap. There were hundred dollar bills, but also the edge of a photograph.

"Do you know him?" asked Nigel.

The Captain opened the flap some more to see the entire picture. Nodded. "Jorge Vargas. I watched him grow up. I knew his parents too. Farmers who crossed the border every harvest season, but Caborca was their home and they always came back. Jorge, he didn't have that loyalty. I remember when he went drinking all night, what, three years ago, maybe? Boasting that he was going to America to fight and get rich."

"He didn't make it."

"Not according to him."

"Lousy reflexes, slow feet. But he was a good teacher. Being Mexican, I thought he'd relate well to other fighters from here. So, I made him a full time trainer. Then I found out he was making deals with them, fixing fights, throwing some, winning some. I promise everyone who comes to scout or just to place bets, that my fights are honest. He threatened my integrity and my business. He discovered I found out. Ran."

"He's been behaving like a big shot since he got back a couple of weeks ago."

"A smart thief would lie low."

The Captain said nothing. The constable waited.

"I just want what's mine," Nigel finally said. "Nothing more, nothing less."

The Captain shrugged. "I don't know how much he has left."

"I expected that. I know what will make up the difference."

"It seems you know where he is. So, why did you come here?"

"It's the way I do business—I don't want to be accused of disrespecting authority."

"It's your business how you do your business."

Nigel stood up. "So we are good?"

The Captain shrugged. He didn't care.

"I'll come back for my car. I am going to walk there." Nigel tipped his Panama and left. Returned half an hour later. "He had only half the money."

The Captain and the constable stared at the clear plastic grocery bag Nigel carried in and put down on the table to light up. Whatever was in there, floated in bloody goo.

"He lied and wasn't man enough to own up to his mistake." *SloshSlosh.* Nigel wiggled the contents. "So, I took his tongue, his cock, then I killed him. And I believe traitors must burn in hell."

Their eyes lifted to the window.

Thick black smoke swirled skyward.

According to Dusty Saldana

'GRAMMY'S BBQ' looked across a swamp. That be your view. But if you grew up in New Orleans or Baton Rouge or anywhere in between, and was a confessed whore for baby back ribs, you really didn't care. Folks came here for the food, not the scenics, which, if you liked endless swampy desolation, was fucking spectacular. This evening, though, I came here looking for work. Having been here before, I knew which way to turn my head. Regulars sat at the tables on the outer edge. Rightly enough, there sat Nigel, alone, with empty chairs around him. He saw me just as I saw him. We both waved at the same time.

"Good to see you," I said when I got there.

He's put on a shit ton of weight. He'd always been big and heavy—had to be as a lifter. He'd just bloated every way since. Sported a goatee now. He wore a wrinkled white shirt, open at the collar, stretched tight over his oversized body and hanging over pale blue jeans. He did nothing to hide the fact he weighed close to three hundred pounds. His head looked bigger too, having devoured his neck. The Hulk minus the green color. He didn't get up. Nigel was never one for manners, especially if he was the one holding the cards. I didn't care. I was just glad he took my call.

"How long's it been, coach?" Nigel stretched his hand out.

I shook it. "Ages."

"I never pass up a meal at Grammy's, especially since I haven't been back in years, what with the kids now teenagers who won't be caught dead in public with their parents."

I laughed. Nigel had married the reigning Miss Louisiana—a part-Honduran hottie like you wouldn't believe. They had three daughters, last I heard. "Add a son to those three girls?"

"No. One of them would've been a boy if God intended." He poured me a glass with just the right amount of froth. "I didn't forget you liked dark beer. I ordered a pitcher."

We clinked our glasses and said together, "Cheers.

Then he pulled out a cigarette. I remarked, "You smoke."

"Started to in high school, gave it up in college and when I was fighting, and now I can't stop."

"You still runnin' your dad's trucking company."

"We have a fleet of over a hundred trucks now, that run from literally the north pole down to the southern tip of Mexico, and of course sea to shining sea."

Meaning the length of the I-10 freeway. *Genius.*

For the last half dozen years or so, a string of unsanctioned fight clubs—UFZ's dirty little secret that no one quashed or confirmed—started operating along this interstate highway, which stretched literally along the belly of the United States. Mostly illegals, looking for a way into legit leagues, fought on these cards. One made it in fifty, probably even fewer.

"So, to say you're doin' well," I smiled and nodded, "would be an understatement." A bonafide multi-millionaire. Maybe a billionaire.

Never shy, Nigel nodded, "You could say that." Matter of fact. "So, I can't complain. You?"

"I got nuthin' but complaints. Stringin' life paycheck to paycheck, harder now that I'm on a one-year UFZ suspension."

"I heard about that."

"But I ain't letting my guard down 'cause misfortune's always waitin' around the next corner with a loaded gun."

Nigel did not laugh, and sounded sincere saying, "I think you are one of the best trainers who never got his due."

"I should be greasin' your ass, not you mine."

The waitress, 20, if that, 5-6, 135, college student written all over her, buxom, in a low cut blouse that showed most of her cleavage, arrived with a plate load of ribs. Filled out a little more than she should be around the parts that mattered, she caught Nigel staring at her tits and smiled. "Anything else I can get you?"

"We are good," Nigel smiled back with quick wink. "Maybe later."

The waitress smiled back. Say what you want, even now, as big as he was, he could charm the panties off chicks. Age hadn't mellowed his libido—still the same hound he been in college. Don't get me wrong, Nigel loved his wife and girls to death, but never could keep his dick exclusive. Screwing around's a habit hard to shake, especially since he'd always known he had something that drew honeys to him like sheep to slaughter. Plus, they probably did stuff his wife didn't or he didn't want her to. Nigel fit the stereotype. The woman you married wasn't the girl you kinky-fucked.

"More rack on her," I remarked, "than this plate."

His wife had to know about his infidelity—or at least suspect. Women were intuitive. She probably ignored it, figuring his cheating was a small price to pay for a lifestyle most chicks only dreamed about. Plus, no way in hell she'd get half of everything Nigel had, even if she had the best counsel in town.

"Corner opened up a couple of days before you called," Nigel said, dumping a chunk of ribs on his plate. "So, your timing was perfect."

"Finally." I said, unable keep the acid outta my voice, then quickly changed my tone, "But I'm glad for the opportunity."

"This isn't some favor I'm doing you," Nigel said, biting into the ribs and talking with his mouth full. "You can get someone ready better than anyone I know."

"Talent is most of the battle and I run into some good ones you picked," I complimented 'cause it was the polite thing to return kiss his ass. He'd offered me a job before I even asked. "Raúl and Luis came outta the I-10." And about a dozen others over the past five years, but they languished in B & C leagues—you know, those MMA fights in Riyadh on some shit cable channel in the upper 400s on your dial in the middle of the day.

"Being MMA's underground farm system is good money," said Nigel. "I'm not going to give that up, but the dream is always UFZ."

"Ain't it for everybody? Only findin' that fighter to take you there is as elusive as winning the Powerball. You have a better chance of being struck by lightning. Twice."

Nigel snickered. "Still, that's why you are in it, I'm in it. Trying to find the end of that rainbow." I joined in with him and we chanted together. "Where fame nor money is no longer important or relevant. It's all about your place in history."

We both cracked up.

"I can't believe you still remember the swill I sold you."

"Hey," smiled Nigel, "it worked. We won Olympic Gold and two world titles. Haven't won a damn thing worthwhile since."

"Me neither," I sighed nostalgically.

The buxom waitress returned. "How's everything?"

"Terrific." Nigel's eyes held hers a moment longer than needed. She flashed a smile and left. "I'm hitting that tonight." He was dead serious even though he said it with a lascivious grin.

"Nigel," I dropped my voice with gratitude. "Thanks. Not many'd give a man my age a second look, let alone a second chance. I turned fifty this morning. Five-fuckin' oh."

"Hell. Happy birthday, coach."

"I woke up this morning and realized I'd successfully pulled off a life of minimal achievement."

I didn't come from nothing, I came from less than nothing. We lived in a double wide. Calling us or my neighbors white trash would've been a step up. I perched myself on the front fender, knowing since I was three, when it rocked, my redneck parents were fucking. Mom jumped jobs—always a cashier or grocery clerk, never aspired higher, bringing home more weed than food. Dad was a fuckup too. Worked as a framing contractor between stretches of drinking, but did make time to beat the crap outta me. When Mom and he went at each other, who was abusing whom became a tossup.

Dad, though, was a huge boxing fan, having grown up during the golden age—the gift and the curse he passed on to me. I made it my escape outta my personal hell. I just quit high school one day and never went back home. I already had a job at a boxing gym, allowing me to work and work out. Cobbling together chores and other part time jobs, I survived. Grew into a Welterweight, 5-10, 145, who showed promise to weasel onto a few cards, but not enough to get much further.

Boxing was dying anyway too, and this brutal, gladiator-style, anything-goes thing called Mixed Martial Arts was catching fire. I thought this could vault me into prime time, added Muy Thai to my skills, but flamed out like I did boxing. Since I was little, whenever he was sober and gave his belt a rest, Dad reminisced about fighting history and talked shop, arousing my curiosity and interest to cram like I was up for a quiz from books, films, watching fights. In the ring and Octagon, I loved picking brains.

I turned thirty and woke up to an overdue epiphany—knowledge and passion ain't worth shit if not accompanied by talent and luck. If I was gonna find glory, it had to be vicariously. So, I moved over to training. Lo and behold, twenty years later, I traveled not an inch further than my fighting career.

"When you called," Nigel said, "I had a gut reaction that maybe we can recreate our Olympic magic."

"Only I'll be training illegals."

The meat, half way up to my mouth, froze 'cause I saw Nigel's eyes turn into dark, depthless holes. The goodwill and friendliness vanished as if someone unplugged the light. Nigel's tone sounded like a serrated saw. "The I-10 may not be legit, the fights are."

"Sorry," I retreated at once.

"I kill to keep it that way."

The corner'd opened up mebbe 'cause he'd done just that. The rumors about him leapt to the front of the line. Also, I wasn't naïve or deluded, and 'sides, I'd come to him. He was doing me a favor. I should know my place and capitulated right away, "Didn't mean anything by it."

"You did," Nigel replied bluntly.

I knew his philosophy about this sort of thing. "If I'm saying sorry, it's too late 'cause I've already told you what I really feel."

"Yes, and it's OK. I understand. This isn't what you saw yourself doing at this stage of your career." I knew I shouldn't take any comfort. He never forgot slights. "You have the skills, I have the money. Let's make it work."

"Redemption's all I got left to live for."

Nigel's eyes narrowed, cold and sober. "You have any prospects?"

"I stopped looking once they suspended me," I confessed. "Being old as I am don't exactly make me a magnet for talent, even if I discovered one."

"Old is when you can't tell your dick from your balls."

"Welcome to my world."

Nigel threw his head back and roared.

I just smiled, suddenly second guessing myself.

That notion never left me. Kept me on edge and wary. I always knew never to look where I shouldn't, and I figured if I didn't listen, I would never hear what I shouldn't neither. These two simple rules'd kept me outta jail, and I never saw a reason to do anything else. I had never worked top tier fights where integrity mattered. They'd all been C, D, and fucking E and F leagues, where the outcome needed to satisfy the line. There was money riding on these fights, just hundreds, but could as well've been millions to these promoters, who sometimes fixed fights to fund their next stop.

Nigel didn't need the money. I done my research before taking this meeting. There wasn't even a whisper of hanky-panky about his fights or fighters. The cops, judges, and politicians Nigel was paying off trusted him at his word. Any blowback would never be about cheating or screwing the poor shlub wagering his Friday paycheck on one of his illegal I-10 fights. Ironically, this honesty was achieved with dark shit nobody knew or saw. Which kept me awake nights, 'cause that flip side was my beat, where I was very much aware that Nigel was a clear and present danger to my good health if I didn't keep a LID, as he put it—loyalty, integrity, discretion. It'd be tested, I knew. *Just a matter of time*. Sure enough, when my cell rang, my gut tightened.

"Hello?"

"Dusty Saldana, please." Male. No nonsense. Not Nigel.

"That's me."

"Detective Bostwick Oswald, New Orleans PD."

Damn those chickens. They always came home to roost.

CASE FILE: 010146888
Reporting Officer: Detective Bostwick Oswald

"She can try, you said." Boz sat across from Dusty in the trainer's second floor apartment. The late afternoon sun streamed in through the blinds. The humming air conditioner mitigated the temperatures the city experienced around May, not late February. "Recall saying it?"

"Maybe I did, maybe I didn't," Dusty replied, wishy-washy.

"You did. It's been confirmed by a credible source."

Dusty didn't flinch. "What's all this about?"

"Have you spoken to Jenny?"

"Not since the fight."

"So, was it a threat?" Boz asked.

Until he could pull a warrant, which needed probable cause, Boz had to go to the suspect. Dusty lived in the Warehouse District. Blockades for Mardi Gras turned two-way streets to one, creating detours that didn't exist before. Throw in gawking tourists—a couple of million nearly—who weren't here the week before, the drive from his Third Police District address took half an hour longer. It soured Boz's mood, doured his demeanor, and sharpened his tone—all good symptoms for an interrogation. Especially if, as a matter of rule, he also disliked all perps. Little doubt lingered in his mind about Dusty's complicity.

"I don't recall. So, in my mind, I guess it didn't mean much." Dusty shrugged and leaned back, crooking his elbow around the backrest of his chair.

"What did you do after the fight?"

"We got on the plane and come home. Mind tellin' me what's goin' on?"

"Nigel Hansom,' Boz sidestepped. "You work for him."

"I train his fighters," Dusty nodded.

"Your comment came after he threatened to have Jenny fire you on the brink of your first title shot."

"Exactly why what he said and what I said back never stuck with me. You say lotsa things when emotions are running high., especially if you left everything you had out there in the Octagon. So, you gotta take it in context."

"I am. In the context of two bodies, one in Mexico, and now, one here, both murdered, both belonging to Nigel Hansom. I checked other trainers and promoters. No one else's had a single employee die on them, in or out of the ring, not in the past six months, not in the past year, not in the past five, actually, not ever."

Dusty said nothing. Boz tilted his head, expecting a response. Dusty shrugged, "Far as I know, no fighter die on my watch."

"You sure about that?"

"I'd know, don't you think?" Dusty twisted his lips sarcastically. "I'd notice a missing fucking fighter. As far as I know, they all accounted for."

Boz jumped topics. "You started out as a cutman after you failed as a fighter."

"It was a way to break into the corner and work up to training."

"When was the last time you worked as a cutman?"

"A year'n a half ago, give or take. I only do it if trainer work dry up."

"So, you are good with a blade."

Dusty didn't shrug or nothing.

Is he wondering how he should react? "Don't you need a careful, steady hand and an intimate knowledge of fatal points on the body?"

"Yep, but for the opposite of what you're implying. I fix cuts. Stop the bleeding. Not the other way around."

"Still you must have a book on which blood vessels can keep you alive through hurt and pain."

Dusty blinked. "I don't know what you're gettin' at. For one thing, I ain't touched a blade in eighteen months like I said. For another, do you mind tellin' me what this about? Is this about Jenny?" Dusty's forehead crinkled with vertical, anxiety lines between his eyes, "Is she OK?"

"Why shouldn't she be?" Boz asked pointedly.

"Mebbe 'cause you accused me of threatening her, then implied shit from me being a cutman, and now you're asking questions that sound like you checking for an alibi."

Perps. They always pack a shovel. "Why would you need an alibi?"

"I don't know. Shit, I don't even know why you're here?"

Boz circled back. "Who's we, when you said we got on the plane."

"Nigel, myself, Puma."

"Interesting, you didn't include Jenny," Boz leveled a piercing gaze.

"Yep. Sure. 'Course." Dusty hurried his response. "She was there."

"What was the mood?" Start digging, asshole.

"What do you think? Us three ol' men started drinking right off. Jenny—she already put the fight behind her and expressing serious concern she had no guy lined up to fuck." Dusty smiled, then stretched it one side into a taunting grin. "Which, as you know, for Jenny's as important to her as—"

"Can I see your blades?" Boz cut him off.

"Why?" Dusty sharpened. Wiped his grin clean off.

"I can get a warrant to search your whole apartment."

"I keep some in my tote." He got up, left the room.

Boz looked around. The clutter in the living room contained everything you'd expect with a well traveled, fifty-year-old fuckup. At least Dusty was tidy. Every piece of furniture looked second hand. *Frugal bastard.* Several unopened cartons—presumably pulled out of storage—stacked against one wall. *So, he thinks he has job security with Nigel.* A credenza. Atop it, a trifold frame from way back of Nigel standing on the top tier of the Olympic pedestal, kissing his gold medal, hand over chest in another, and arms raised in the third. Other pictures of Dusty in his fighting days, some from corners he worked, couple of them with Nigel as a pro. Posters tacked on the wall—legendary fighters from boxing and MMA. A ceiling high glass case contained tightly packed books—mostly all to do with one kind of fighting or another. Autographed boxing gloves—Boz counted four pairs—hung from their laces around nails on the wall.

Dusty returned with his corner tote—a fanny pack. "There's nuthin' in it."

Boz unzipped it. "Why not?"

"It'd be like saving used toilet paper."

Boz picked through swabs, gauze pads, medical gloves, medication bottles and tubes of adrenaline hydrochloride, avitene, Endswell, Vaseline, Thrombin, Surgicel, and Gelfoam—all brand spanking new. So too the pack of razor blades. Boz twitched his nose. Sniffed ammonia. "Inside's been bleached."

"Yep. After every fight, I toss out everything, sanitize the inside, and replace everything, even the medication. Can't be too careful. You could transfer infection from one fighter to the next and nowadays that's a lawsuit waiting to happen."

"You said you hadn't been a cutman in more than a year. Why am I smelling like this was bleached in the last twenty-four hours?"

"I take it to every fight, regardless, to clean off the blood or cuts between rounds. Usually after the fight too, until the ringside physician shows up."

"You have an explanation," Boz snapped his fingers, "just like that."

"It's the truth," Dusty shrugged.

The trainer was much too cagey. His kind lived life a half step away from crossing the line, especially working for Nigel. Boz had never not solved a murder that he'd been assigned. Only one walked, but eventually paid for the crime. Boz didn't believe in 24/24—the most popular police school of thought that the day before and the day after a crime were the most important. He was convinced of the opposite. *Perps are perps because they think they're smarter than the rest of us.* Driven by arrogance. So, the longer you went without an arrest, the bolder and more audacious they got. Finer details of the iron clad stories they'd prepared right off the bat inevitably faded because memory was a flaky bitch. They didn't keep detailed notes like a cop—Boz, at least—did. Other lies from other shenanigans got entwined and the contradictions came back to bite them in the ass.

Boz liked to hover patiently like a vulture. *Why not?* Murder enjoyed no statute of limitations. So, there was neither a need to hurry nor reason to rush to judgment.

However, he did not have that luxury of time in this case.

Nigel had dogs in his squad room—every Police District in New Orleans, for the matter—and the instant they got scent Boz was sniffing around the man augmenting their pension, leads'd dry up and promising avenues of investigation'd wall up into dead ends.

"Nigel was a bust as a pro, wasn't he?."

"Four'n two ain't a losing record."

"How did you two meet?"

Helena Garcia-Thackery: Off The Record, Louisiana State University, Baton Rouge

Associate Professor Ms. Helena Garcia, 40, 5-7, 128, was attractive—beautiful, most would agree—but she followed a strict self imposed policy of not dating coworkers. Her light chocolate complexion, lush cascading raven-black hair, and distinctly sharp, dark, Latina features turned heads. She knew that and took additional precautions of never showing even the slightest passing interest toward anyone on campus. There were no whispers of a significant other, guy or girl. Just public facts—single, no kids. She kept her social media footprint minimal and populated her accounts with postings from her friends.

Then, one mid-Fall Semester evening, on a Friday of a hectic week of midterms, there was a knock on her office door. Rubberbanded bundles of papers from each of her classes piled high on her desk. Helena'd just stuffed the freshman stack into her bag to take home to grade over the weekend between watching romantic Hallmark movies on TV, serving herself tequila, and stove-top grilling the *pollo marinado* she'd left marinating in the fridge.

"Yes?" she inquired, looking up. She'd unclipped her hair. For class, she tightly pulled it back. Now, it now fell to her shoulders, the ends beginning to curl. She brushed a wisp that crossed her eyes.

"Ms. Garcia, Dusty Saldana."

The office of an assistant professor was tiny, about eight feet square. Cram it with a desk, two chairs, and a twelve-inch deep bookshelf along one entire wall, precious little personal space remained. When Dusty stepped in, they stood barely a couple of feet apart. She smelled a masculine musk as he held out his hand. Shook it, expecting calluses. Felt them grind her soft palm. In fact, Dusty's skin felt tough, weathered like a farmer's. Veins started at his knuckles, roped up all the way to his elbows, and wriggled out of sight under the sleeves of an LSU T-shirt, which stuck like a second skin to a frame that wasn't imposing physically. He was muscular, though that wasn't how she'd describe him. The right word eluded her. Nagged her subconscious.

"I'm the strength and conditioning coach," he said. "Hired only at the start of this semester."

Neither big nor tall. Freckled—likely brought on by the fact he had pale skin and never wore a hat. Around thirty, maybe. But he looked and carried himself like someone much older. A hard drinker, she surmised. Exuded a cocky confidence. Not the entitled, brat bravado kind, but one acquired by a hard life. Being unfazed by hurdles he'd had to overcome by whatever means necessary, and now took everything with a giant grain of salt.

Sinewy! Lean and strong.

"Don't figger you know me," he added.

Helena didn't, even though sports was huge at LSU, a national powerhouse for football, basketball, baseball, others. She never went to games, only peripherally aware even when they won some sort of big championship. She began to politely shake her head from side to side.

"No apologies necessary," he smiled crookedly and bailed her out, "*No supe tu nombre ni hasta esta mañana*." I didn't know your name neither till this morning.

Helena blinked, her lips curling up at the corners. Dusty's Spanish, like his English, was rough, uneducated. Learned on the streets. She shouldn't be surprised. He didn't hide his coarse edges. In fact, they gave him a hustler's charm. He would know Spanish. Other languages too, probably. At least enough to help him navigate that world on the margins, hand to mouth, somewhere in between black and white.

"Not the Spanish you teach in your class." It was almost as if he was reading her mind. "I learn mine on the fly listenin'n trainin' *cholos*." Gangsters.

"I grew up around them." She caught herself, not realizing she'd replied, until she already had. She was smiling too, without even wanting to.

"You?" His eyebrows arched in surprise. "A *chola*. Then, I must say, you clean up terrific!" Off her spontaneous laugh, "Where you from?"

"Puerto Rico." Again, she'd revealed more of herself with two responses to Dusty than she had to anyone in her three years at LSU.

"Some great fighters come outta there. Benitez, Gomez, Felix Trinidad." When Helena smiled politely, he grinned, "You never heard of them. That's OK. And thank you for not naming *gringo* poets and scholars 'cause I'd never've heard of 'em neither. As you might've guessed, I didn't get very far in my education,

English or Spanish. San Juan?"

"Yes."

"I been there a few times. Scoutin'. Not the parts you'd go to, but I was recruiting tough sumbitches."

"La Perla?"

Dusty jerked his head back. Impressed.

"I grew up there," she added like it was a competition. Feeling a need to prove she was more like him than he gave her credit for. She didn't know why. Dusty'd touched a nerve, but in a good way. Known as the most dangerous place in all of Puerto Rico, La Perla, or 'The Pearl' district in Old San Juan, was hard to miss. Flying in, this massive, decrepit, filthy slum looked as dangerous from the air as it was walking it. Cops only came at the invitation of the drug lords who ruled its streets.

"Jesus. I never knew nobody who got outta there, not unless 'twas in a body bag or paying off a scumbag. Now, I got just all kinda respect for you, Miss Garcia."

"Helena." *What the hell?* Why was she opening herself to him? Maybe it was his raw, unfiltered genuineness. *Unpretentious.*

Her mother, 16, 5-7, 125, gorgeous, got knocked up by a boy barely eighteen himself. Being Catholic, abortion wasn't an option. Lucky for Mom, the boy turned out to be an up-and-coming piece of shit who subsequently killed his way into becoming a gang leader of some significance. Cruel, but a fiercely selfish psycho too, he coveted the women he fucked and housed them across the several blocks he controlled. It also meant mother and daughter were off limits to preying assholes. Somehow, Mom convinced him to send Helena to school in Dorado, the richest part of San Juan. Luckily, Helena inherited all of her mother's common sense and none of her father's evil. Except his ruthless ambition.

Helena did not make the same mistakes other kids from her father did. Maybe because Helena had incentive to be good. Mom kept squirreling money away, promising her daughter they were getting out of not just La Perla, but Puerto Rico. The day after Helena graduated high school, they got to leave the ghetto unsupervised, using the excuse of a mother-daughter day at the beach to celebrate. Instead, a coyote waited. He smuggled them into the US. Mom found a job in housekeeping at a Motel 6 in Baton Rouge, where she met and married Jose Garcia, a Mexican-American cook.

A good father, decent, and kind, he treated Helena like his own because he couldn't have kids. He got them both Green Cards and remained devoted to Mom till the day he died. Both valued education and lived to see Helena finish community college and go to University of Texas in Austin, where she got her Bachelors, Masters, and Ph.D. in Spanish literature. So, they passed away proud. Helena knew of no relatives. Relieved she didn't, in fact. Being alone freed her from family ties and obligations that allowed her to be singularly focused on reaching milestones she set for herself.

"Anyways, it's Friday," Dusty apologized. "You probably got plans, I don't mean to hold you up. I came to talk to you about one of your students, Nigel Hansom."

"Yes. He's a freshman." Every undergrad needed to take a foreign language class.

"Then you know why I'm here."

As soon as Dusty'd introduced himself, Helena suspected some star athlete needed help. LSU belonged to the SEC, the fourteen-some-college Southeastern Conference. Except for Vanderbilt, which had a reputation as the Princeton the South, the rest of the schools were known more for sports than academics. "He should be doing better."

"He wants to," said Dusty. "Kid's bright enough to know to take Spanish instead of German or French, 'cause he realizes it gonna help him when he go into his father's trucking business."

"What does he play?"

"He's a weight-lifter. Nigel's good. World class good. To qualify for the Olympics, he gotta win the US Nationals first. But he need a C average to participate and he never done better than a D."

"Can he afford a tutor?"

"Oh, yeah. Like I said, his father's loaded enough to get him what he need."

"Ask him to start working with one and I'll give him make-up tests to improve his grade."

"You got it. This went easier than I thought. On TV, the coach's always selfishly looking to win with no concern for the kid's welfare."

"That's not entirely untrue." But she knew better than to fight the Athletic Department, which, at LSU, brought in tens of millions of dollars via donations from boosters who gave proportional to the university's wins. "*Los maestros pueden ser reemplazado. Los atletas estrella no pueden.*" Teachers can be replaced. Star athletes can't.

"*Entonces sabes cómo funcionan los deportes universitarios.*" So you know how college sports work. "Hey. If you ain't had dinner, I know a hole in the wall that serves the best *pollo marinado.*"

Helena laughed, "Actually, I have some marinating in my fridge that I was going to grill for dinner."

"Do you have enough for two?" Dusty grinned confidently. "I'll bring Tequila."

Helena laughed again. "I buy that by the case."

"Shit, Helena, *el destino está enviando un mensaje.*" Fate is sending a message.

She found audacity attractive. Dusty oozed macho. Her Achilles heel when it came to men. He went home with her and stayed the weekend. She hadn't been intimate in over a year, and if she was going to end her drought, a man ten years younger'd be the way to go. They couldn't stop kissing, coiling tongues, swapping spit. Then they went down on each other. Followed that up with fucking every which way possible. He didn't wear a condom—considering neither had sex on their minds when he walked into the office—and first thing following morning, she went down to the drug store for morning-after pills. She had no plans to have kids, now or in the future. It took celibacy the week following to get over the soreness.

Nigel worked with a tutor and made the sincere effort that

Dusty promised he would, and Helena kept her word. Gave him make up tests and assignments, some more for show than anything else, which gave her cover and justification to raise his grade. Nigel qualified. Named the number one weightlifter in the US as a freshman, he went on to win Olympic Gold, and followed it up with two more World Golds.

What started out to be a temp job between gigs, turned into a four-year stint for Dusty. Helena observed the friendship between Nigel and Dusty thicken. The university kept Dusty around because Nigel wanted him around. She felt Nigel thought he owed Dusty when he found out how and why it all began between Dusty and her. Nigel didn't tell a soul. Even if anyone suspected, nobody'd believe it possible. Dusty came off as an urban redneck, Helena entirely the opposite—an academic through and through, who dripped sophistication.

It lasted and worked between them because neither wanted it to be anything more than sex. He wasn't going to be in Baton Rouge forever and she sure as hell wasn't giving up her tenure track, which she wanted to end with her heading up the entire Department.

Once he graduated, Nigel decided to test the MMA circuit and asked Dusty to be his trainer. The announcement made a huge splash. Helena went to their first fight in the Superdome, where the New Orleans Saints pro-football team played. The media made it a huge deal. All those medals had elevated Nigel into a statewide Louisiana hero. Nigel's father put his clout on full display. The Governor showed up, LSU's Chancellor, Mayors of Baton Rouge and New Orleans, even the two Senators from Washington.

Helena, who'd never been to a sporting event, found herself enjoying the visceral brutality of the sport. The undercards were the real fights, she realized. Nigel's opponent was a cupcake, some white guy from Nebraska, handpicked to lose, but nobody cared. Nigel thrashed this big but slow opponent, and won it in two rounds. Nigel could have laid him out in one, Dusty later told her, but they wanted to put on a show. Give the newspapers something to fill at least half the sports page above the fold and have a long enough highlight on TV.

The following morning, Helena still slept when Dusty left. They'd spent the night fucking like there was no tomorrow. because there wasn't. Dusty hit the road with Nigel with no guarantees if and when he'd be back. They texted daily, then weekly, then just off and on. Helena's interest waned. She became preoccupied with her own career, relationships—all of them brief and forgetful. Headlines diminished because Nigel didn't win consistently to be a serious contender. That's what she overheard at alumni functions. Dusty's name never surfaced. Nigel's career turned out to be short lived. When he called it quits, the news made the college newspaper and the only reason Helena even knew about it.

9/11 happened right afterwards. Nigel enlisted. A Marine. By that time she'd lost all touch with Dusty. Didn't have a clue where he was, what he did, and frankly didn't care, consumed with her professional goals. Once she reached the final one—full Professor with tenure and Department Head—she married one of Louisiana's most eligible billionaires. She quit, became a full time wife, and wealthy socialite.

So, it came as a quite a shock when she received a call this morning. The caller ID listed the number as local. Very few people had her personal cell, even though the number had remained the same for as long as she had it.

She answered tentatively, "Hello?"

"Helena Garcia? District Attorney Arlen Taylor."

"Yes?" The uber elite circle Helena moved in now was rife with sharks, and salacious gossip, however ancient, would be blood in the water.

The DA's next question demanded an answer she did not want to give.

"You're saying you'n Nigel hooked up because you helped him pass Spanish by fucking his teacher?" Boz tried to sound skeptical but college athletics, being so sleazy, especially in the SEC, Dusty was likely telling the truth.

"Yep," Dusty nodded. "Nigel values loyalty—gives as much as he expects. When he graduated, WWE came after him. He knew I been around fightin' all my life and I'd steer him right. I told him if he wanted to be took seriously, he should try MMA instead. Asked me to be his trainer—giving me my break as one."

"So, why did he quit?"

Dusty shrugged, "Why are you asking me?"

Boz left it alone. "Did you know how influential he's in this city?"

"I ain't surprised, if that's what you asking. Mainly on account of his family calling New Orleans home forty-some years. Both his parents're dead now. Nigel said they always been in transportation. The family name, Hansom, be some sort of English cab."

"Nigel's great-grandfather served time," nodded Boz, "for smuggling moonshine across state lines. His grandfather went to prison too, peddling weed before it was legal."

"Not Nigel's daddy. He started a legit truck business when he move here from New York. Nigel inherited it and expanded it."

"Very quick, how that happened."

"Nigel have a shrewd business head. That how." Boz didn't interrupt. Dusty kept talking. "His mother been on the New Orleans City Council almost twenty years. Then Nigel himself done the city proud when he stayed home for college and win Olympic gold and two world titles one after the other. Fighting in the the big leagues with the MMA turned him into a name to reckon with in Louisiana, New Orleans particular."

"When did you and he become partners?"

"About six months ago."

"But you started working for him three months prior to that."

"Yep. He need a trainer. His guy died."

"He tell you how?"

"Ain't none o'my business"

"You never thought to ask?"

Dusty just shrugged.

Boz's lips curled up one corner in a skeptic smirk, "So, you know nothing about the way Nigel conducts business?" When Dusty shook his head from side to side, Boz opened the folder he brought with him. "Let me educate you then." He pulled out a graphic, gruesome picture. "Jorge Vargas. Burned, after Nigel cut off his tongue, then castrated him."

Dusty stared at the picture. Blinked. Boz'd shocked him. Tried as he might, Dusty couldn't stop the wrinkled skin folding and unfolding as he swallowed. "I don't know nothin' about it."

"So," Boz persisted, "you also never suspected you train illegals for Nigel to fight up and down the I-10?"

"Not my place to ask for their papers."

Boz switched up. "You've known Nigel now for, what, twenty years?"

"Give or take."

"Four and two, you said. If he had a winning record, why'd he quit?"

"You gotta wanna fight and he didn't."

If Dusty knew he'd answered the exact same question he'd refused to answer a few minutes ago, he didn't show it. Crooks, as a genral rule, were stupid, all of them. *You have to be, if you think you can get away with it against a relentless machine known as the Law.* "Why not?"

Dusty shrugged. "You keep askin' questions you should be askin' Nigel."

He realizes he slipped up. Boz didn't fret. Criminals and ankles—one inevitably tripped over the other when it came to truth and lies. Sometimes you caught yourself, like Dusty just did, but he'd fall on his face soon enough. "Funny, for two guys joined at the hip for almost two decades, you know very little about him."

"I never said we was close."

"No? You banged a teacher for him, he made LSU keep you, gave you your first shot as a trainer, then hired you in spite of your suspension. I'd've assumed you sucked him off regularly."

"He was seventeen, eighteen, when we met and saw me as a mentor. Look, all told, I worked with Nigel for about six years maybe—four in college, less than two in the pros. When he quit the MMA, he joined the Marines, went his way, and I went mine."

After being so short with his answers to start, when Dusty went on, Boz figured he'd rattled the cagey bastard. "But you kept in touch."

"Barely." Again Dusty stopped being brief and to the point, explaining, "I had my own living to make and was busy chasing paychecks."

"What brought you back to New Orleans?"

"I was looking for work and putting down roots, considering I was fifty. I remembered bein' happiest out here in the bayou. I enjoyed my time at LSU. Ain't so expensive neither, and having been Nigel's mentor and trainer, I figured it was a good fit."

"He could trust you, is that it?"

"I brought experience."

"You married?" Boz jumped topics again.

"Fuck, no. I hate kids. Hated myself as one."

"Family?"

"Just my fighters."

"That'd be touching if you'd said it with an ounce of feeling, even if it was fake."

"I don't wear feelings on my sleeve. I've been doing this too long to get weepy eyed. And cryin' don't help no one. I seen fighters who never got up again. I seen fighters who blew out their spine and couldn't piss or shit on their own. I seen fighters who hang their address around their neck 'cause they afraid they might forget where they live."

"You talk as if you trained A-level talent," Boz smirked. "You were a C-grade fighter, pickup cutman at best, and even in the MMA, you trained dogs."

"So it han't worked out for me like I hoped."

"That's an understatement." Boz noticed Dusty's cheeks tighten and his lips thin. *I'm getting under his skin.* "Nigel's operation is hardly a step up, is it? If anything, I hear the I-10 circuit's the sewer. UFZ's unspoken underbelly. Illegals fighting in ghost towns from California to Florida, and you'n Nigel counting on the law of percentages to sell, what, one or two out of fifty fighters to the next level, all the while hoping to find that rare talent."

"We did. Jenny Sharp."

"UFZ brought you up before their disciplinary board." Dusty did not answer. Just stared back. Waiting for a question. Boz didn't ask one. *No point wasting time on questions I know the answer to.* "So Nigel was the only one who'd hire you."

"I didn't get around to asking anyone else. You know, you still haven't told me what it is you're investigating."

"Murder, what else?"

Nigel Hansom: Uncorroborated Intelligence, Baghdad

Whoom! The rocket-propelled grenade whizzed inches overhead. Decapitating the gunner, who occupied the 'crew served weapon' atop the roof of the up-armored M1114 HMMWV. Nigel glimpsed, just for a moment, the gunner's head impaled into the missile tip as both drove into the desert.

Booom!

Nigel spat the cigarette between his lips to the floor as everything came at him at the speed of thought. He couldn't decide where to take his eyes and fear and shock. To the gunner's lower torso, spraying blood, falling back into the vehicle from the turret? To the erupting flame, sand, blood, brain, and bone? Or the shockwave lifting the two wheels on his side—he was riding shotgun—and starting to overturn the Humvee?

The screams of the other two men with him in the vehicle hardly broke through the combined noise of the explosion, revving engines, and rattling of a vehicle on the verge of tipping over. The all-wheel drive's steel frame was tied by five crossbars and box rails. The independent suspension and helical gear-reduction hubs attached to the top of each wheel, not the center. The drivetrain shafts were raised, which lowered the overall center of gravity. This prevented a rollover, which would have signed their death warrant.

"Fuckfuckfuck!" screamed Tavon Cole, 24, 6-2, 238, African American, and came audible in a window of comparative quiet so fleeting, it snipped off the back end of the first expletive and he might as well've been mouthing the third because the Humvee slammed back down onto all four of its specialized, radial, low-profile, 37x12.5 tires. The underbody armor, inserted as part of an upgrade these past few months to give added protection against mines and roadside bombs, retained the integrity of vehicle.

There wasn't a soul on the Route 1, the oldest and longest highway in Iraq. Seven hundred and fifty miles long, it ribboned across the country from Umm Qasr Port in Basra to Ar Rutba in Anbar, and toward Syria and Jordan. Most of the violence remained north of Baghdad, and one of the reasons they were heading south. Travel time to Kuwait City, their destination, when they left the Green Zone in Baghdad shortly after dawn, was estimated at six and a half hours. They'd been on the road about two.

WhoomBoom!

A second RPG streaked into the road in front of them. Fiery fragments of blacktop blasted every which way. One foot-square chunk struck the vertical windshield. The bulletproof glass didn't break, didn't crack, but bent inward like plastic and popped back. Asphalt shrapnel struck the hood, sides, and rattled off the roof with the metallic clatter of a berserk nail gun. The smoke thinned, the dust cleared, and the road ahead came visible.

"Shit!" Tavon screamed again, his eyes widening, and slammed on the brakes!

Double wishbone suspension. Portal gear hubs on all four wheels. All-around brake discs, not conventionally mounted at the wheels, but inboard of the half shafts outside the front and back Torsen differentials. The mechanical features enhanced for military combat came into play. Including the center, lockable differential. Only one wheel required traction for this torque-biased system to lock the four tires. They tattooed the decades-old asphalt with remarkably straight black lines that detailed every tread. Smoke from burning rubber rose around the Humvee, which stopped a foot shy of the 5x3-foot gash the second RPG carved into the road.

The head of a large white individual, his face ruddy from the heat, leaned forward from the back seat. Nigel knew him and the dead gunner only as Tom and Jerry because that's how they'd introduced themselves. By choosing cartoon characters to not even attempt to hide the fact they were aliases was symptomatic of the level of arrogance and corruption plaguing every aspect of this US invasion and occupation of Iraq. *Operation Iraqi Freedom, my ass. More like Operation Iraqi Shakedown.* This war, triggered and run by special interests—hawks in Washington, who in turn were owned by the defense lobby—wasn't about the welfare of a country, but the biggest money making opportunity, or scheme, depending on your point of view.

Covered in blood from the gunner's decapitation. Tom screamed, "What the fuck was that?"

"Rainbows and roses, what do you think?" Nigel snarled. "An ambush!"

Tom, and his dead partner, Jerry, worked for Blackwater—the private security force hired by the US Department of Defense to 'assist in matters of enforcement' where the US military couldn't get involved. Deliberately vague to cover a broad swath of shit they could do without oversight. To them, the Geneva Convention could've been a Vegas shindig to get away and drink and fuck. How Blackwater scored a multi-billion dollar contract wasn't even a secret—nepotism. They were in bed with Halliburton, a multinational, megabillion company with a zillion subsidiaries, which received a 'sole source' contract. Meaning, nobody else could bid. Got the whole fucking pie—daily logistical support, construction, operating the oil fields, you name it, all the way down to installing portable crappers and supplying toilet paper.

Halliburton landed this sweet ass deal, thanks to its ex-CEO, currently the Vice President of the United States. Yeah, Dick Cheney, widely regarded as the one calling the shots in Washington. Taking down Saddam Hussein—unfinished business, he said somewhere—was an obsession that went back to Operation Desert Storm in 1991, which liberated Kuwait but left Saddam in power because that was the deal then-President George Bush Sr. made to forge an international coalition. Pissed, Dick never stopped having a hard-on for taking out Saddam. 9/11 gave him the excuse to expand the war from Afghanistan to Iraq. In addition to this war being a personal jerk-off, he and his cronies were lining their pockets too.

Gears ground as Tavon pedaled down. Reversed.

WhoomBoom! WhoomBoom!

RPGs 3 and 4 destroyed the road behind and any escape along the driverside. Tavon pumped the brakes. The Humvee careened to a halt, trapped between four giant smoking holes in the ground. The attackers had launched four missiles and missed all four times. Deliberately. *They want us out of the vehicle.* Barely did the thought cross Nigel's mind—

BangBangBangBangBang!

Machine-gun fire strafed the Humvee. It came only from their left. Dust clouds from the RPGs and the Humvee tires still billowed, giving them a tiny window to bail.

"Out, out, out!" hollered Nigel, wrenched his passenger side door open, and tumbled out.

Easier said than done from behind the wheel for Tavon. Raising the drivetrain into the cabin area created a massive chest-high transmission hump separating passenger and driver side seats. So, Tavon had to squeeze his big frame over. Rounds pummeled the bulletproof doors and windows on his side and ricocheted. Nigel had Tavon's gun and tossed it to him as they darted across and slid down the shallow embankment on the side of the road away from the attackers. They had to lay flat on their bellies to stay out of the line of fire.

"Why the fuck is he still in the car?" asked Tavon in a hoarse whisper.

Blackwater Tom could've gotten out the back door but chose to stay in the Humvee.

"He's figuring his odds are better inside?" Nigel shrugged, but a suspicion began to take shape in his head.

The shooting stopped. Silence screamed down as suddenly as the attack began.

Nigel surveyed the mess. Bloody bits to entire chunks of skull belonging to Jerry, the gunner, were strewn all over. A full eye, with capillaries strung out, stared back at them.

"How many do you think?" asked Tavon.

"Three," Nigel replied, having had a few seconds to figure it out by reaching into his mind's eye and reconstructing the attack.

The four RPGs ping-ponged from the same two spots. Either they reloaded or they'd each brought two howitzers. Once they'd trapped the Humvee, machinegun fire came from the same two locations and a third in between. The attackers were all on the other side of the road behind a range rocky of outcrops—the only cover along this stretch of desert to spring an ambush.

Where Nigel and Tavon were crouched, the dip of the roadside embankment was it. The desert behind them stretched flat like a lake bed.

Absolutely no escape.

"Nothing's fucking easy here, is it?" Tavon shook his head.

"You didn't really think it would be, did you?"

"What's the plan?"

"We have the low ground, we are outgunned, but not really outnumbered. We have only card to play."

"What about Blackwater Tom?"

"He's chosen to take his chances alone." Nigel didn't elaborate on his suspicion about why Tom stayed behind. "Fuck him."

Tavon was down with that. After another couple of minutes of silence, where neither side moved, Nigel raised his weapon, a white piece of paper punctured by the barrel.

"How do you know they won't kill us when we stand up?" asked Tavon anxiously.

"One way to find out." Nigel climbed to his feet, dangling his M4 Carbine as far away from his body as he could stretch his arm. Barrel pointing down. He held his breath. His heart pounded against his chest, but only he knew that. The attackers did not fire. He let go of his weapon, which landed with a soft cushiony thud into the sand, and clasped his hands behind his head. Still, no shots.

"*Alakhir! 'ukhbiruh 'an yaqif!*" A gruff male voice. Arabic with a heavy accent. The other one. Tell him to stand up.

Nigel nodded down to Tavon, who rose, arms extended as he dropped his M4 and placed his palms behind his head.

Three men emerged from behind the rocks in *thawb*—the traditional long white tunic. They all had on *keffiyeh*—that square cloth tied around and over their heads. Checkered scarves covered their faces up to their eyes. The uniform of insurgents, because they could melt back into the population, dressed just like them, after an attack. Except, Nigel noticed trousers underneath their tunics. Military boots. All three held American made M4 Carbines exactly like the ones that Nigel and Tavon just dropped. A lighter and shorter version of the M16A2, these semi-automatic assault rifles, standard issue and the weapon of choice in this war, fired off direct impingement, gas-operated, air-cooled, magazine-fed 5.56x45 mm rounds. Meaning, designed to send you to your maker, no questions asked.

Nigel revised his previous assumption that RPGs came from four howitzers and then the attackers switched to machine guns. No, they probably just stripped the .203 grenade launcher that could be retrofitted onto the M4. He had the same attachment in the Humvee because it could flush Big Foot in a hurry.

When they didn't ask about Tom, Nigel knew his suspicion

was spot on. He coughed.

BangBangBangBangBangBang!

Bullets sprayed from M9 Barettas that Tavon and he'd tucked into the back of their collars where their fingers were curled around the triggers. Nigel and Tavon hit the ground as they unleashed the 9mm rounds.

The M9s each held fifteen rounds. They needed only a couple for each target but pumped half a dozen to be sure. Knowing the attackers would be wearing Kevlar vests, Nigel and Tavon aimed high, lopping off hunks of neck and face. The attackers went down violently, a couple instantly. The third, who had a few seconds before Nigel and Tavon turned their guns on him, had time for let off a volley before he went down.

"Aaaah!"

Nigel looked over. The agonized cry came from, "Tavon!"

Blood sprayed from around his neck where a random bullet went through and through. Unfortunately, it severed blood vessels.

"We got 'em!" smiled Tavon, and blood gurgled out.

"Don't talk and don't fucking die on me!"

"Not planning to."

"You survived hell for two years. You surely aren't dying from a stray bullet." Nigel hurried over, "Come on!" Nigel helped Tavon to his feet.

Tavon nodded his eyes ahead.

Nigel straightened, his left hand propping up Tavon, whose arm circled Nigel's waist. Blackwater Tom emerged out of the back seat of the Humvee. Shut the door behind him. He raised the muzzle of a Colt 45 toward them. "Sorry, but you were never going home."

"Yeah, well," replied Nigel flatly. Didn't flinch.

Nothing to forewarn Blackwater Tom.

As Nigel drew the M9 he'd tucked into the belt just above Tavon's back pocket.

BangBang!

Blackwater Tom spun. Grabbed by a giant hand—actually

two well placed shots, which wrenched him full circle. He was on his knees by the time he came around, flopping forward., half his head sheared off by the bullets. He fell face down into the sand.

Tavon chuckled and buckled, wincing in agony, uttering, "Motherfuckers."

"You think I was going to let us die today?" smiled Nigel. "On the last day of our tour? Fuck no!" The front passenger side door was still open from when they'd bailed. Nigel helped Tavon in and drew the seatbelt across. He pulled out a battlefield first-aid kit, wrapped the neck wound tight to contain the bleeding. "Sit tight. Live."

Tavon laughed and grimaced right after.

Nigel shut the door and walked around. Dragged Blackwater Tom's body unceremoniously to the back of the Humvee. Swung open the tailgate. Tossed him inside with the same distaste you reserve for dog shit. Tom landed across and atop Jerry, his decapitated partner. Nigel then walked over to the attackers and went through their pockets.

They were not insurgents, just as he suspected.

Blackwater Tom probably knew, most certainly tipped them off. But Blackwater Jerry wasn't part of the deal and expendable, like Nigel and Tavon. Nigel stripped every piece of ID. Took their cell phones. Messages on there could be evidence and a deterrent for later. He climbed over the rocky outcrop, knowing he'd find their vehicle. A pickup. Nondescript 1990 Toyota. Junky, like the ones insurgents used. He piled the bodies onto the flatbed.

The third attacker, the one who struck Tavon, came conscious with a moan. Bastard opened his eyes. *Good. Now he can pay.* Nigel grinned down, "Should have stayed unconscious, bro."

"I'm American," he stuttered.

"No shit," sneered Nigel, tearing a long enough piece of the guy's *thawb.*

"Please!" he pleaded. The guy squirmed, but there was a body across him, trapping his legs and an arm. He was too weak to free himself and stammered through the pain. "I won't say a word, I promise."

"You're lying and what's worse you know it too."

"No, man, please. No—"

"This war is one big heist. Larceny on a national scale. Even so, you gotta have a fragment of a code. Honor among thieves, you know." Nigel stuck the strip of *thawb* in gas tank. "If there's one thing to admire about this fucking place, it's the simplicity of justice. You steal, they cut off your hand. You lie, you lose your tongue. Betrayal is a dishonor deserving of a place in hell. So—"

"Jesus, no!"

Nigel lit the *thawb*, leaned down to fire up a cigarette, and backed up to the top of the outcrop. The man's scream got louder, getting to that death pitch and cut the air like a nail across a blackboard.

Kaboooom!

The pickup exploded, propelling the attackers into the air, and the inferno consumed them as they fell back.

Nigel headed back to the Humvee. Likelihood of anyone giving a shit about a burnt truck and charred bodies was remote, and even if they did, their deaths would be listed as KIA—killed in Action. Nigel needed the bodies of Blackwater Tom and Jerry. They were on the manifest of this trip, plus useful to sell his narrative.

He climbed in behind the wheel. Tavon was conscious. "Stay alive for four hours, OK?"

Tavon's lips curled. "I can't make that promise. But you need to make me one."

"You first." Nigel fired the engine.

"Nigel. You have to. Please."

"Of course. Anything, man." Nigel skirted the holes in the ground.

"My wife and little girl—"

"You're going to see them." Nigel got the Humvee back on the road.

"You gotta promise me you'll do the right thing."

"Jesus, Tavon. Goes without saying."

"And don't bury me here. Please."

"Then make sure you live."

"Demanding motherfucker, aren't you?"

"Lay back," Nigel said. "Rest."

Nigel met Tavon in boot camp. In fact, they arrived on the same day. Found themselves in line one behind the other, got to talking, and became friends instantly. Deployed at the same time in the same unit, they flew into Iraq together and served almost every mission together.

Born and raised in Cherry Hill, one of the most dangerous neighborhoods in Baltimore, where violent crime numbers averaged three times the national average, Tavon enlisted because he had a wife, a kid, and a past dangerously close to catching up like a tragic episode of *The Wire*. Nigel, on the other hand, joined like a lot of zealots hungry to scalp Muslims following 9/11.

He and Tavon were a fit, albeit like flame to kerosene—one sparked the other, tag teaming for the most kills in that first year. Tavon loved it, but the war wore on Nigel. Going into Afghanistan—now that was a justified, revenge tour of duty to get Bin Laden. The Iraq war, he soon found out, was a hoax. All about oil and money at the expense of misguided dumbasses, like himself, who enlisted thinking they were on a heroic mission.

Six months ago, Nigel had had enough. *Fuck if I'm going to stand by and watch everyone profit except the grunts in the trenches.* Tavon stayed in the field but Nigel peeled off to work behind a desk in the Green Zone with the CPA—Coalition Provisional Authority.

Spurred by a sixth sense, Nigel looked over. Tavon slumped forward. Eyes closed. Still. "Tavon?"

Nigel reached across and felt Tavon's neck for a pulse, knowing he would find none. He rested his hand on Tavon's shoulder for a long moment. Then blinked his eyes ahead.

Desolation enveloped Route 1. Normally, discharged soldiers flew home from Baghdad. This was different. They were getting paid to deliver Blackwater Tom and Jerry to Kuwait City. The plan had been to then take an US-bound military transport later tonight and never look back at these two dismal, wasted years.

Evidence of a war gone awry lay on either side of the

highway—abandoned, stripped, burned wrecks from jeeps and trucks to artillery and tanks. Four uneventful hours later, structures rose out of the desert on either side, scattered at first, and getting real dense real quick, most of them bombed out black shells. Nigel took the turnoff to Safwan, the border town between Iraq and Kuwait.

Named after its founder, Safwan bin Assal, who fought alongside Prophet Mohammed to conquer the region, this town was etched in Iraqi lore. Not for anything noteworthy, rather, a bloodbath. On the night February 26, 1991, during the first Gulf War, the US 3rd Marine Aircraft Wing-led coalition air and ground forces blocked the head and tail of this six-lane highway at Safwan. Then, for ten hours straight, lambasted retreating Iraqi forces trapped in between. About two thousand vehicles burned, some ejected into the air and thrown almost a quarter mile. Soldiers, eyewitnesses recalled, could be heard screaming, torched alive by the relentless allied carpet bombing. Not accidently, the US chose Safwan, still smoking in the aftermath, to have Saddam's forces sign the articles of surrender. Afterwards, loved ones were simply told to go to the 'Mile of Death' to claim the remains.

Fast forward to March 20, 2003, when, as the location of an Iraqi Air Force base, Safwan once again felt the brunt of the early US 'shock and awe' shelling that first night of the second Gulf war. Even with the careful targeting, you couldn't avoid taking out homes and other nonmilitary structures. How many of the 70,000-plus civilians died, no one knew. Hours later, the repaired highway became the main conduit for the invading forces. A major node and hub since, Nigel's Humvee fit right in with the other US combat vehicles.

Two years in, and it still looked like this war was closer to the beginning and nowhere near the end. "Mission Accomplished," President George W. Bush'd claimed, a few weeks into the conflict, from the aircraft carrier, *USS Abraham Lincoln*. What a load of crock that turned out to be.

Locals and military used different check posts. Nigel pulled up behind two army supply trucks.

"We were ambushed," Nigel told the MP, when it was his turn at the border crossing. "Three KIA."

The MP glanced in and saw the bodies. Didn't bat an eyelid, not even when he saw decapitated Jerry. "Sorry, man."

Nigel tilted his head, accepting the implied condolence. The MP directed him to a series of trailers netted over with camouflage. Nigel knew the drill, having filled out Casualty Reporting paperwork quite a few times before of the '5 Ws': Who (was involved?) What (happened?) When (did it occur?) Where? And Why (were victims at the location?)

The designated field grade rep pulled up Nigel's record and read about that first year he served with Tavon—they never left a man behind, not even a casualty. That they didn't receive commendations or any sort or recognition rankled the field rep, who smirked, shaking his head, "That's fucking stuff of heroes that's never mentioned."

"Still," replied Nigel. "I didn't have my buddy's back when it mattered. He has a wife and daughter. Should have been me. I got no one."

Nigel's guilt and regret impressed the field rep even more. He glossed over the paperwork for Tom and Jerry. There was no love lost between the military and Blackwater. Those bastards were mercenaries, making money hand over fist, while uniformed soldiers killed in action left bigger holes in the family they left behind and just got a measley pension, barely enough to cover rent or groceries, never both. The field rep wrote up paperwork to allow Nigel to fly with Tavon's body and even pulled strings to get them on the next flight to Dover AFB.

A bitter sweet couple of weeks followed after Nigel returned stateside—the funeral for Tavon and the hoopla of Nigel's return to New Orleans. His father got the *Louisiana Times* write a profile that made Nigel out to be an unsung hero. Nigel helped Tavon's wife, Makena, 22, 5-7, 130, with the arrangements. She was so fucking pretty. First generation Somalian. When Nigel met her, utterly wrong and inappropriate thoughts ran through his head.

"I gave Tavon my word I'd take care of you and your

daughter," said Nigel.

"Thank you," she smiled, "but we are good." Makena worked as a bookkeeper for a shipping company in Baltimore's inner harbor.

"Please. If you need anything, call me."

Nigel kept in touch, each phone call deepening their friendship. He took over more and more of his father's company, Easy Trucking, named for being founded in New Orleans, the Big Easy. Six months to the day Nigel returned, his father officially retired. Nigel added more trucks, quickly going from two to twenty.

A year later, he made a trip to Baltimore, and over dinner, told Makena he planned to go national. He'd placed an order for another twenty trucks.

"We'll be covering Canada to Mexico," he said, "and I want someone I can trust."

He made her offer, which she took home, then called him back that night, and said, "I'm in."

"There must be details to iron out."

They met the next morning in his penthouse suite for breakfast. There were sparks—they'd started as the calls became more personal—but, face to face, they were palpable. Nigel wanted her from the moment he saw her. Slammed his lips upon her. They got to third base. He stopped. *Don't shit where you work.* His pants and her panties were around their ankles.

She realized it too. "This is not a good idea, is it?"

In that moment, Nigel knew she'd be the type to understand the preciseness of what he meant and wanted without saying it out loud. But he was also dejected he may not meet another woman like Makena.

Nigel stopped looking, having forgettable hookups. Six months later, at a LSU dinner, he met another alum, Kamryn Bloom, 21, 5-9, 130, Miss Louisiana and first runner-up to Miss America. Something about her compelled him to walk over. Not bad looking, but no George Clooney, he compensated with his broad frame, huge arms, confidence, and overwhelming masculinity.

How and why Kamryn and he hit it off was one of those inexplicable 'instant chemistry' things. Maybe having blue collar parents? Her mother was a Honduran refugee, now a claims processor for an insurance company, and her father worked for Entergy, the widely despised power utility in Baton Rouge, as a field tech. They dated just three months, then he married her. Nine months later, they had a daughter. He knocked her up twice in the next two years, hoping for a son, and instead ended up with two more daughters. Kamryn tied her tubes—the work it took to get back into shape after each pregnancy wasn't worth trying again for a son.

Disappointed, he did have a conversation with Makena about his desire to sire a son, maybe with her. She was open to it, but both quickly realized there were no guarantees, and having a kid would be an even worse complication than just being lovers.

His gut instinct paid off. Kamryn turned out to be a good—no, great—wife. Not just classy arm candy at money flaunting shindigs, Kamryn created a home—a cocoon of warmth and security for his girls. She knew he wasn't faithful but left well enough alone. In return, Nigel kept his flings discreet and made sure his family wanted for nothing. Kamryn never asked questions about the business, and so he separated home and work into separate worlds—never to intersect.

Easy Trucking took off. Six years into the business, at a trucking convention in Atlanta, the same time a fight happened to be in town, he ran into, "Dusty?"

"Nigel?" They bear-hugged.

Sheer coincidence had brought them to the back street smokehouse they'd discovered during their brief stint in MMA. Nigel looked him up and down, "You haven't changed."

"Going nowhere does that to you."

Nigel roared. "Same ol' cynic."

"When did you go bare dome?" Dusty pointed to Nigel's clean shaven skull.

"Couldn't see myself sporting a horseshoe when I started losing my hair in Iraq." Nigel shaved his scalp every morning, too self-conscious to sport even noggin stubble. He compensated with an impressive moustache and goatee.

Dusty wasn't bashful about the fact that the fight was D-league. Experience, knowledge, and the need to make ends meet made him a jack-of-all. So, he accepted any work, from training wrestlers to working the corner as a trainer and cutman for fighters, MMA or boxing. "If you're here for the trucking convention, you must be in the family business."

"Yup," Nigel left it at that, seeing that Dusty hadn't fared so well and didn't seem aware how big Easy Trucking had gotten.

"As tough and thankless as the circuit can be, I can't see myself doing anything else," confessed Dusty, then said something that stuck with Nigel, "Don't you miss it? The adrenaline rush of winnin'. If anyone would, I figured you'd—considerin' we reached the mountain top."

It triggered memories of the euphoria of winning Olympic Gold and the world titles. Hard to describe. Understood only by those who stood on the uppermost pedestal of the victory stand.

It opened an emptiness Nigel could not shake.

Got him thinking more and more.

Easy Trucking was a machine, now running on autopilot. A transportation goliath, minting money. He had good people in the right positions. He could cannibalize other smaller truckers, keep growing, but none of that would compare to raising a trophy.

How cool'll it be to find the next world champion?

Puma Song: Recollections from Long Beach, Los Angeles

Puma's jaw dropped, not 'cause he suffered a stroke all of a sudden and the muscles on either side of his face quit working, but 'cause he was impressed. No, not just impressed, but *holy fuck* impressed. That'd happened only once before. Forty years ago, when he laid eyes upon Sonya Suh, 19, 5-2, 108, the KoAm—Korean American—cashier at Suh's Liquor Market on Western and Wilshire in Koreatown. Twenty-one at the time, he overwhelmed her in height plus weight. Born'n raised walking distance from gang infested South Central L.A., what Sonya lacked in stature, she more'n made up in spunk, a sailor's mouth, and kinky imagination in bed. Puma fell head over heels for probably the only Asian who didn't overachieve, barely graduated high school, and declared she wasn't going to college. Puma never stopped loving her, remained faithful and monogamous till she died a coupla years ago. It left him heartbroke.

This broad now—she be hot. Not just her looks, she nailed that category. No, Puma was smitten by what she done just now. Lifting and landing her opponent, who weighed about the same, spine first on the concrete floor. She ought notta been able to do this, not after absorbing at least a minute of relentless pounding that shoulda sent her to the ER. He looked over to the wall with hand-scrawled matchups for the night.

Jenny Sharp v Mercedes Corona.

Jenny Sharp. From white America, head to toe, and a name to match. The chick he overheard a coupla drunks gaga-ing in a sports bar he frequented on Vermont—one of the main drags that cut through the hood. Peaked his interest enough to drive thirty-one miles. Actually, he was looking for an excuse to get back in the game after a year away.

What strike him even more remarkable? She'd grinned insolently the entire duration of Mercedes's minute long barrage. Puma, who'd spent a lifetime hunting talent, rightly attributed Jenny's arrogance to her being keenly aware she was simply better. When Jenny got tired of taunting'n flaunting, she turned the tables on a dime with nine cents to spare. Half the crowd roared, half booed, depending where they'd put their money. Jenny deftly ducked out of the next punch, showing no wear. That testify to remarkable upper body strength.

Jenny clinched Mercedes around the belly, ran her into the chainlink, taking some serious kidney blows along the way without as much as flinching. Mercedes tried to wrestle Jenny to the floor, figuring strikes were doing nothing. Jenny released Mercedes, stepping back.

Then! Oh, shit!

Puma'd never seen anything so fast outside the UFZ, you know, the big league. Her lead foot came at a dead ninety. A Thai roundkick of beauty—making contact perfectly perpendicular to Mercedes's ribcage. That wan't what made him go, *oh shit. No, sir.* The follow up roundhouse did.

Puma needed to relive it his head, it came that fast. Jenny barely landed on the foot that'd delivered the Thai roundkick, when she twirled. Not spun but twirled. 'Cause she accomplished this on her toes.

Ballet, pure fucking ballet.

The roundhouse to the side of Mercedes's head dispatched the Latina ass over teacups. Jenny hailed belly blows with her foot. Mercedes tried to curl up. Jenny would have none of that, yanked Mercedes up by the hair, moved directly in front, and without letting go, made Mercedes's face her personal punching bag.

There wan't no ref to jump in and stop this A&B, this being underground cage fighting.

Hundred percent illegal.

A few years ago, a smart forklift op, kid by the name Gavin Lobo, 25, 5-11½, 156, saw a nighttime income opportunity offered up by this warehouse in Long Beach, the second biggest container port in all the US. During business hours, it served as a distribution center for brand new appliances'n shit in the unopened cardboard boxes stacked around the chainlink crudely fashioned to be a fairly accurately sized Octagon. The ambience came straight outta the movie, *Fight Club*, which'd been good'n bad for business. It created a sudden surge in fights and fighters, brought in more fans, bettors, and cash. Rules from the movie—secrecy, one against one, no shoes, bare knuckles, no ref, no rules, no time limit, match ain't over till a KO or tap out—became the norm. On the minus side, an utter lack of self regulation encouraged brutality and bloodiness, which ratcheted up another notch every year, caused some grisly injuries and even fatalities that ticked up in number and seriousness every year, which in turn put the whole circuit more'n more on the radar of cops'n feds.

Jenny stepped back, letting Mercedes stagger for a few seconds. Then Jenny advanced, wrapped up Mercedes and finished her off with that violent throwdown that so captivated Puma. Mercedes lay there dazed.

The crowd started to chant the ten count—the custom down here. Mercedes writhed, her groans inaudible. Not one bit shy, Jenny threw up her hands, unleashing a cry while doing a three-sixty, smiling from ear to ear, her even teeth smeared from a bleeding nose'n other cuts inside her mouth. The crowd lost interest around eight and the applause and cheering dried up. Folks here had money on one or more fights, so they were on to the next match.

A boyfriend, handler, whoever, 36, 6-0, 162, with a bit of a gut, hurried in to help Mercedes to her feet. In here, if you came alone and got laid out, don't expect sympathy or a Samaritan to help you up. A lackey hauled you to the locker and left you to your own devices. If you were unable to leave the premises at the end of the night, a cab company on standby, was prepaid to dump you off somewhere deserted.

Mercedes behaved like she had no clue where she was. *Bitch be concussed.* Puma remembered the back of her head bouncing off the concrete when Jenny threw her down. Oh, yeah, these illegal operations didn't have canvas on springs to soften a landing. You fought directly on cement, not even on a thin rubber mat. No protection from nothing, fist to floor.

"You'll be OK, baby," he comforted Mercedes. "Come on."

Halfway out the gate, Jenny paused, "If you're going to fight her again," she mocked, "ask her to pack more resistance or pack a Life Alert."

"Fuck you," snarled the guy. Jenny laughed and turned to leave. The guy poked, "Cunt!"

Puma was close enough to hear the whole thing, so he was close enough to see Jenny's evil smile be replaced by just evil. He could've sworn her blue eyes actually darkened. She never stopped moving, one moment leaving, the next returning. Her turnaround once again dancer smooth. She left the ground, legs scissoring in the air.

WhamWham! One after the other, her bare feet pummeled the guy's head and chest. He left the ground. *Clang!* Slammed into the chainlink, dropping Mercedes, whose head thudded the concrete again.

The crowd erupted, enjoying this more than her KO.

Puma fell deeper in love with this broad.

Gavin, the brains behind this whole operation, rushed in. "Hey, hey, hey! Jenny! Get the fuck outta here!"

Jenny offered no lip or resistance. Jogged off. Puma lost her 'tween the stacked cartons, but knew where he'd find her, and leisurely hobbled after her, thumping his cane.

No one else followed Jenny.

Hmm. Why the fuck not? Nobody see what I see? Mebbe 'cause Jenny showed off more'n she showed off any skill? *OK, she lacks technique, her footwork be crap.* Hell, Rousey and Nunes weren't born floating'n stinging like no butterfly nor bee. You went into a gym, worked with a trainer, learned good form. *What am I missing?*

Puma approached the ladies room, which he knew be the locker too. The door opened and a young fella, 24, 6-0, 183, staggered out, his face all screwed up in agony. Seeing Puma headed where he just come out of, he warned, "She's a psycho fucking bitch!"

The way the young fella walked, knees jammed together, the blood pouring out of his nose be the lesser issue. Well, that answered his other question. If nuthin else, shouldn't her looks attract low lives tryin' to get in her pants? It did and she wan't interested.

Puma didn't bother knocking. Used his cane to shove the door open and entered.

Jenny'd stripped off her fighting clothes and was bent over

the sink naked. Puma's mind ticked off details like a cop. Her skin wan't pale indoor white. She had an even tan. Cleanly cut muscled upper body. *So, she do weights regular.* No wrinkling around the waist even striking this '7' pose, showing off a bubble for an ass. Firm thighs, tight skin. *She crunch and run religiously too.* Keeping fighting fit wan't gonna be an issue. *She love her body too much.*

"Jenny Sharp?" Puma inquired.

She didn't answer, blowing her nose, discharging snot and blood into the sink. Took her time raising her eyes to look at him through the mirror, not at all caring she had nothing on.

Neither did he. "My name be Puma Song."

She felt no threat, him being an ol' geezer, and continued rinsing. The body blows she'd taken showed up as black'n blue bruises all over.

"I been scoutin' this circuit more'n twenty years," he continued. "In all that time, I never saw talent worth even flushing down the crapper."

"Until you saw me." She dripped sarcasm.

"I know. You hear that before."

"You probably lived the history I learned in school, old man, so I'll be polite." She reached into the small bag, grabbing Band-aid for the cuts on her face, none of which looked serious enough to be stitched. Even if one did, in this circuit, it went on your tab. Should you go to a doctor, it better be a discreet one, or you lie. Open your trap how it happened, you became a pariah. Worse, some of these motherfuckers, like Gavin, could put the hurt on you outside the Octagon. "I just dumped one leech. No fucking way I'm getting another to pimp me out and take a cut." She went full frontal toward Puma. "I fight when I want, where I want."

She tryin' to be outrageous. He didn't bite. "How come I never heard o'you?"

"I know, right?" Sarcastic. "I better fire my publicist."

"You must've started fightin' recently."

"A year, on and off. That probably feels like a tiny sliver of time considering how long you've been around, huh?"

He smiled wanly, pulling clues. *Well spoken.* She be educated higher'n many.

"Also, I haven't left California," she went on, surprising Puma, considering she started out being dismissive and short. "Not yet."

"You wanna hear what I gotta offer?"

"A medical marvel of a dick for a man your age?" She twirled her nipples with her thumb and forefinger, rolling her tongue around her lips like 'em porn queens.

"Looks like you wanna fuck me more'n me."

"Never done a geezer. It'll be over in, what, a coupla seconds?"

"Can you keep up and come that fast?"

Jenny threw her head back and laughed. "You made me laugh. Shit. That's rare, Puma Song."

"You wanna talk?"

"Nah." She squeezed straight into ripped jeans without first putting on panties. "Even rarer I'm this chatty. Consider yourself special."

"Shit. I think I just come."

"Two seconds. I was right." She slipped on a T-shirt. No bra neither. Commando be a matter of daily attire. That explain why he saw no undie lines breakin' up her tan. "Thanks for the interest."

The door opened. Gavin entered and recognized, "Puma! Puma Song!"

"Gavin," Puma smiled back. "You doin' good, kid. Bizness grown lot bigger from the last time I come here."

"You've been gone a while." Gavin reached into his pocket and pulled out a wad of cash. He counted off a bunch of bills. "Everything OK, healthwise?"

Jenny snatched them out of his hand and started counting.

"Needed a new hip. Soon my lower body be all robot."

Gavin laughed.

"You're fifty short, Gavin," snapped Jenny.

"Because you broke the rules, Jenny," Gavin raised his eyebrows. "You only hit your opponent. You don't touch anyone else. And he didn't start it. You did, for no fucking reason. This isn't the first time but it is your last warning."

"Stop," she mocked. "You know how easily I scare."

"You think you're special? You're nobody and I can make you matter even less!"

"Now look what you've done. I peed in my pants."

"This is funny to you? Fucking white trash whore!"

Her flash of temper came in the blink of an eye. Jenny's fist acted before her brain thought the better of it. Gavin never saw it coming. Definition of a sucker punch. Puma figured Gavin didn't think she had it in her to hit him.

Crack!

Her knuckles connected with Gavin's jaw. Bone to bone.

He wan't a small dude. Would be a Welterweight in the ring—three weight classes above Jenny. Still, he came off his feet. Falling to the floor would've been humiliating but he hit the wall and stayed erect. Also, she missed his lip, or he'd be nursing a cut that'd need stitches.

Jenny realized what she'd done, sensibly stepped back.

"You fucking, bitch!" Gavin exploded, lunging.

"Wo, wo," Puma intervened, stepping in between, waving his cane.

"You crossed a line!" Gavin peered around Puma and wan't done talking, when he saw blood on his fingers. "Goddamn bitch! Born that way! Probably came out of a bigger one."

"Calm it down, both o'you." Puma looked from one to other, and both backed off. "In her defense, Gavin, the guy call her a cunt. Now you call her a whore. Those days be gone when you could cuss out a woman."

"Puma!" Jenny grinned, her mood swinging the other way. "You may be a hundred, but you're current."

"You're done." Gavin wan't about to forgive'n forget. "Only thing you got going is your face. Show it around here and that'll be gone too."

"Fuck you too." She grabbed her bag. "You're OK, Puma. But considering you have one foot in the grave, so long and RIP as well, I guess." She left.

Puma smiled. If she thought she'd told him off and he would just walk away, she didn't know him. His in-laws, if they were alive, would attest to the dogged pursuit of their daughter, Sonya, forcing them to overcome their prejudice against his kind—half black, half Korean—and marry her. Turned out to be a good business decision too. Their store was one of few never robbed by Bloods or Crips.

"She's not worth it, Puma," Gavin warned, sensing Puma's interest. "I know, she's so fucking pretty and brutal, you immediately go, oh shit, do we have Rousey and Nunes in one package? You're not the first to think you hit the jackpot with her. A lawyer—but he was smitten—bankrolled her into a PFL fight." Profession Fighters League, which served marginal fighters trying to garner attention and a semi-legit résumé. "She got demolished—KO'd in eighteen seconds. Rumor is, the lawyer and she had a contract and she threw some kinda low blow to pull out of it. If you're wondering why there are no scouts and promoters looking at her, they have, she interviews them, not the other way around. Word travels fast, good or bad, especially bad. Consensus down here, she thinks she's Pretty Woman." Movie about a hooker—Julia Roberts—who gets swept off her feet by a millionaire—that'd be Richard Gere. "Problem is, she doesn't have a decent human bone in her body."

"Good to know," said Puma. Gavin opened the door. Puma limped out with him. "She's a kid, convinced she's all that'n more. Don't blackball her, OK? Life take care o'that if she carry on misbehavin'."

Gavin nodded. "I know."

"Good night, Gavin. Proud o'what you've built here."

"You take care now." Gavin hurried away toward the cage. From the groans and cheers, another match got underway.

Puma emerged outside the warehouse. A light mist and the night swallowed up most of the vehicles. He didn't have far to go, having parked his big, white Ford 150 close to the door. As he reached for his keys, he heard a footfall, and sharply swiveled his head around. Obviously, none of the lamps in the lot were on and Gavin'd turned off all the security cameras. His hand tightened around his cane. Rare you'd be mugged outside a fight club, but the world was full of crazies. Puma wan't deluded he'd win, but he'd sure as hell leave marks the attacker never be able to erase.

"Being mostly crippled," a silhouette formed, "I figured you'd have taken a handicapped spot," and melted into view. It was Jenny, one hand holding the bag slung over her shoulder.

Puma relaxed. "Wan't smart what you do back there. Gavin's got the pull'n muscle to fuck up your career."

"He won't. I fucked him to get in and he knows I will again." She placed her bag on top of the hood.

"So, not necessarily this is when'n and where you come to your senses."

"We've barely met and you already know me. Let's build."

Puma did not smile. "Seems you not likely to take to teachin' neither. Sorry, I wasted my time'n yours." *Beepbeep*. He unalarmed his truck.

"Gavin was almost, um, respectful with you. He never is. Toward anyone."

Puma opened the door. "He knows I've yet to pick up a prospect from a fight club. I ain't about to waste the time I got left bein' content just gettin' to the big leagues."

"Have you discovered anyone who made it?"

"Would I be scavengin' here if I did?"

"Sell me."

"I see potential."

Jenny snorted, "That's your pitch? As tired a line as there is in sports?"

"I ain't for wasting words." Puma tossed his cane into the truck, the ploy being to make believe she needed him more'n than the other way around.

"I believe nobody has good intentions. What's yours, Puma?"

"You more raw than fresh kill. You need trainin', lot of it." He made it like he was reluctantly dispensing wisdom and wanted to just get in and drive away. "But seem like you too stuck up to trust advice or take instruction." Puma climbed in.

Jenny took the couple of steps she needed to grab the handle to keep the door open. "What do I need to improve?"

"Every fucking thing. That begin by quittin' to fight in shitholes like this before all the wrong you doin' become bad habits you never be able to shake."

"You gonna feed me and pay my rent?"

"That be the way nurturin' talent works."

"I don't have to suck, fuck, or jerk you off?" She stepped inside of the open door, leaned against it, folding her arms and crossing her legs.

"Lil girl, I be too old fashioned for shitty shenanigans that affront decency. 'Sides, does it look a boner even happen if I pop a whole bottle o'em blue pills?" Evoked a chuckle from her. "An opportunity to win it all is what drive me now."

"When do you start collecting?"

"When my share big enough to buy more'n a taco. Everything will be laid down in writing. I don't believe in the misunderstandings of a verbal handshake. But none o'that even on the table without you commit to quit fightin' in illegal cages'n start trainin' full time."

"You can barely move."

"Trainer be someone else."

"I've been burned, so I don't buy promises."

"You hear me make one?"

"I trust people even less."

"And I always waiting to be screwed. So we cut from the same cloth."

"Maybe that's why my instinct has a hard on for you." She smiled and held out her hand. "OK. I'm in."

"Let's shake once we actually get this off the ground."

"I'm who I am. So, we should talk about a compatible trainer."

Puma reached out to a ghost from the past—Dusty Saldana.

They went so far back—thirty years, more or less—he'd seen Dusty move from the ring to the Octagon to the corner. On'n off, chasing paychecks, they found themselves in the same hell hole, more so after Puma started scouting for scam artists calling theyselves promoters and Dusty coaching up a nobody or has-been. Puma thought highly enough to recommend Dusty, who returned the favor, pointing Puma to prospects.

"Shit!" Dusty reacted. "Puma Song! You ain't dead yet?"

"My first call be to Hell and the Devil say you ain't done shitting on the world."

Dusty laughed. "How is Sonya?"

"She passed last year."

"Shit, Puma. I'm sorry. Rare, what you two had."

"Thanks. "

"What about the store?"

"Sold it. Couldn't run it like she done. But I kept the house. What you been up to?"

"Quit bein' polite. It ain't you. How many calls did you have to make to find me?"

"One." And, with it, Puma learned Dusty been punished by UFZ with a year-long suspension. Puma wan't surprised. Neither did he think any less of Dusty. If anything, it reinforced he'd made the right call. The ornery old coot he remembered hadn't changed. Dusty still took no guff, regardless of the consequences. "UFZ give me your number along with a statutory warnin', hiring Dusty Saldana may kill you."

Dusty laughed, "They ain't wrong."

"Anyways, remember we used to drink'n lament we'd never moved up? Never got a legit shot? Never seem to be on the right o' good fortune?"

"You sick bastard, did you reach out after all these years to make me pull out my 45 and stick it down my throat?"

Puma didn't chuckle. He went on. Serious. "We wondered what if ever we found a prospect?"

The coupla seconds of silence told Puma he'd caught Dusty's attention. Dusty finally croaked, "Go on."

"I think I found one."

"You never mention anybody even worth sniffing. This must be legit. Where?"

"Here. In L.A. Where are you?"

"New Orleans on a gig."

"We can come to you."

"Nah," Dusty said quickly. "I'll fly out this weekend. But I've to take the redeye back."

"No problem I'll set it up at Gilroy's."

"It still there?"

"Hasn't moved. In El Segundo, right by the airport. Cora 'third generation' Felix run it now."

Gilroy's came to be in 1939, when Gilroy Nishimori, 30, 5-5, 139, and his wife scraped up every cent they had to buy a brick building. El Segundo in 'em days was considered the boonies. So, they got it cheap. A Golden Gloves boxer, more passionate than talented, Gilroy carved out a small home in the back, a gym up front, with ten bags'n a pro-size ring. They rented the rest of the building to make it work. Up'n coming fighters more'n just trained here, it became like home away from home.

Then, on December 7, 1941, Pearl Harbor happened, dragging America into the World War II. Didn't matter if they were born here, President Eisenhower branded all Japanese as 'enemy aliens,' even Americans like Gilroy and his wife. They were rounded up and sent to, believe it or not, an American concentration camp in Rohwer, Arkansas. Instead of being forced to sell the place, pennies for the dollar, like a lot of other Japanese Americans had to, Gilroy's childhood and best friend, Cora Felix promised to watch over'n hold the place till they returned. Alas, Gilroy's wife fell ill, died in camp, and a month later, sorrow took Gilroy too. Cora took over and swore to keep it open, hell or high water, to honor Gilroy. He passed down that obligation to his kid, who did the same. Cora Felix III, 48, 5-6, 142, recognized MMA be the next best thing and smartly converted the ring into an Octagon. He topped that off hiring a coupla UFZ has-beens to run classes and rented out the cage for one-on-one training sessions the rest of the time.

"Do you want me to text you the address?" asked Puma.

"I know where it is," and added good natured, "my memory ain't all shot."

"Just your liver."

"Look who's talking." They shared a laugh. Both used to be quite the drinkers. "Hire a legit fighter to get into the ring."

"Already planning to." If Puma wan't easily impressed, Dusty's bar be even higher.

"What's his name?"

"Nobody'd you know," Puma replied carefully, not knowing where Dusty stood about training a girl.

Sure enough, it caught Dusty by surprise when he showed up. He didn't care if Jenny heard him. "What the fuck, Puma? A chick?"

"Fuck you too!" Jenny got snarky right back. "You've trained so many champs in the men's division that women are beneath you?" She looked at Puma, "You didn't tell him? Why not? Seems like he's gotten no further than you in his career."

"Does your mouth match your talent?" Dusty snapped back.

"Hear me come out, see you, and say out loud to Puma, 'this old fart your idea of a trainer? He looks as washed up as seaweed?'"

"Oh-kay," Puma stepped in, "unbind those panties, both o'ya."

Jenny kept going, "Motherfucker walked in here thinking he's Eddie Fucking Futch!"

"Dusty," Puma continued peacemaking, "when Nunes and Rousey were at the toppa their game, they ruled MMA. The mountain top be the same, men or women."

One corner of Dusty's lips twisted up, "Eddie Futch?"

"Best there ever was," said Jenny. "What? You think you're better than the man who trained Joe Frazier, Ken Norton, Larry Holmes, and Trevor Berbick? Four of the five men to defeat Muhammad Ali?"

"You know history most boxers today ain't even aware."

"I'm not most. Never been. Never will."

"Let's see," Dusty said, then admitted, "but I shouldn'ta walked in with reservations."

"Or mouthed off without first checking out my abilities."

"You're not lacking in confidence, that's for sure."

"I didn't hear an apology," reminded Jenny.

"Show me I owe you one," Dusty replied.

"I'll make you kiss the fucking ring." She punched a fist into her palm.

"Lesson in there for you too, Jenny," said Puma. "Never pridefully allow anger to fester. Blow up, clear the air, move on—that gotta be our working agreement." She gave him a thumbs up. Dusty nodded too. Puma clapped, "Good! Let's go!"

Jenny headed into the cage. Following her in was Ivan Petrov, 30, 5-7, 125.

"A dude?" Dusty reacted, surprised by the unexpected a second time.

"Not any," said Puma. "Won the Flyweight in Dubai four years ago'n done enough since to keep his UFZ card."

Being Russian, he came with macho in his blood, and wan't here to be shamed by a woman. Walking by Jenny, he sneered, "If I crush your dream, don't take it out on all men."

"Have you ever seen Rocky IV?" Jenny shot back. "Stars and stripes never loses to a fucking sickle." Ivan jerked his head with a guffaw of non-comprehension. "Never seen a classic or cracked open a book. That's a dumbass Commie for you."

"Cut the crap," said Dusty. "This a friendly."

"Not for a fucking moment!" Jenny responded vehemently. "This is a real fight."

Dusty looked over. Puma nodded. Cora Felix III headed into the Octagon to play ref.

"Puma said you have to see the promise of a belt. I won't make any apologies if you won't make any judgments about my style, skill, and technique."

"That's what training's for,"

TingTing! Puma punched the bell connected to the big, digital stop clock overhead counting down the five-minute round.

Puma'd always gone with instinct when it conflicted with his brain. With Jenny, instinct and logic concurred. Boy, did she give notice, taking Ivan behind the woodshed from the first strike. OK, younger fighters possessed a strong advantage based solely on age. Gender shoulda equalized that. Plus the fact, he was a six-year pro.

But he was up against a buzzsaw here today.

She quick fired right out of the gate, tagging Ivan with a giant hook that landed flush and wrenched Ivan's head around a full ninety. He never recovered. Jenny dropped a series of thudding kicks and straight punches. Ivan snuck in a head kick to her face, but she flashed that evil smile and went on a spree of strikes, big lefts, hard rights, and leg kicks.

Then, she looked up at the clock as if it was time to end this.

Thirty seconds left.

Puma'd advised her to finish on the ground, if she could. And she did.

She chose a flashy high-risk, high-reward finish—the flying armbar. An armbar hyperextended the opponent's arm. The flying version of it came out of BJJ—Brazilian Jiu-Jitsu. She knew just enough of it to be dangerous. Ivan least expected a low-percentage-small-window move from a green prospect trying impress. Poor bastard didn't know Jenny. Brief be Puma's own acquaintance with her, but somehow he sensed it wouldn't be something simple and effective. *Elton John on HGH—excessive and flamboyant.* She set Ivan up. He bit, extending his arm. She snagged it, mounted him in a flash. Wrapping him, dropping him, and forcing a submission before the bell rang.

Jenny sprang back to her feet, gloated over to Dusty, "Impressive enough?"

Grinning from ear to ear, Puma looked over to Dusty to find him shaking his head, just as pleased. Half an hour later, the two men were sitting across from Jenny at a coffee shop around the corner. She wolfed down a breakfast you'd see in front of fat slobs.

"Where did you learn to fight?" asked Dusty.

"Youtube," Jenny swallowed first, then answered.

"Your parents OK wi—"

"They are dead. Only child. No boyfriend. No record. Let me give a you a skinny of my life, so we can put that behind us. I was born and raised here in the San Fernando Valley—the porn capital of the world. I haven't been in any skin flick, and in the spirit of full disclosure, I've had offers. I skipped a grade, graduated high school, started Pierce College down the street at sixteen, when my parents were killed in a car accident. They left behind a mountain of debt, so the creditors took the house, seized their accounts. Hated the few relatives I knew. Food and a roof became the pressing priority. Since first grade, I was suspended more times than I can recall for fighting. I joined a hole-in-the-wall boxing gym. One of the trainers was a shady perv." She shrugged nonchalantly. "A hand job here, a blow job there, and I got into the fight club circuit on my eighteenth birthday." She winked, "Since neither of you share my universe in the looks department, if you're hot, you play by a different set of rules."

"You can forget special treatment from Puma or me," said Dusty without ado.

"Just for the record," Jenny grinned. "I'll pity-fuck both you geezers."

"So you have nuthin' tyin' you to L.A.," said Dusty, not even acknowledging her innuendo.

"No, why?"

"I work outta New Orleans. If you wanna train with me, that'd be where."

Jenny looked at Puma, "You're willing to move?"

"I just have to lock up the house."

"Gym fees, rent, and food comes out of your pocket," Jenny said, making a spoon out of the toast to scoop the entire raw yolk of her sunny side-up eggs into her mouth. "I need an allowance."

"Four hundred a week's all we can afford," said Puma.

"That's fine, but when the real money starts rolling in from real fights, I don't want to be sewing a vendor's patch to save fifty bucks. Ten percent of the purse for each of you. No siphoning more for incidentals."

"Sounds fair. Puma'll play manager, and I'll be your trainer. My expertise is boxing and Muy Thai. This don't change all the way to the belt, if we get there."

"*When* we get there."

Dusty didn't acknowledge the confidence. "We'll bring someone in for grappling in due course."

"A lotta silver tongues gonna be wagging in your ear," said Puma. "That be nature of winnin'n success."

"Temptation to trade up is inevitable," added Dusty.

"We are going to lock all this down on paper, yeah?" said Jenny.

"Still, I need to hear you say it, lil girl," insisted Puma. "Loud and clear. My word is a promise, I expect yours will be too."

"The no-trade clause cuts both ways," warned Jenny. Then men nodded in agreement. She grinned, "Then, fuck and shit, OK!"

"Now we can shake on it!" Puma grinned and extended his gnarled hand, palm down. Jenny put hers over his, a sharp contrast, with its fair, youthful, smoothness. Dusty dropped his, a wrinkled mess of veins and arthritic fingers, over theirs.

"So, what's your day job, Dusty?" Jenny asked.

Makena Cole: Eyes Only Summary Notes, Mogadishu

These screams were different. They were louder, more fearful, so many, and accompanied by machine gunfire. Cries died only to be replaced by more. Makena, 7, 4-0½, 50, just finished changing into her uniform—white blouse, blue skirt—and slung on a backpack to meet her friends and walk to school. Her awareness leapt far beyond her years, like a lot of children in Mogadishu, who grew up around daily terror and violence.

Born to parents who were notables—leaders—within the Hawaiye, a major clan in Somalia, Makena was particularly bright. She sat on her father's lap, listened, and learned, when his friends came over and they discussed politics over hookah and local illicit rum from sugarcane. Six months ago, on July 13, 1990, President Siad Barre, the country's Hitlerian despot, with an ironfisted hold since he seized power after a 1969 coup d'état, suffered a huge blow following the Stadia Corna Affair. The US had ended aid to Somalia. The Hawaiye, who opposed Siad Barre, instigated protests at a soccer match. Government troops opened fire, killed sixty-five people, and arrested hundred and fourteen notables, Makena's father being one of them. They were sentenced to death, but protestors surrounded the court and crippled Mogadishu. Forced to pardon them, Siad Barre even needed to flee and lay low in his military bunker.

Aslam Hirsi, 30, 6-4, 199, Makena's father, burst in. Slammed the door behind him. Drew the dead bolt. "*Isaga Red Beret ayaa na laaya! Cidna looma badbaadin!*" The Red Beret is slaughtering us! No one is being spared!

The Red Beret was Siad Barre's elite army unit, known for savagery. Aslam never believed Siad Barre had quietly conceded defeat. A civil engineer by day for the city, he warned that any reprisal would begin here in this middle class neighborhood of Mogadishu, where the Hawaiye were concentrated.

Makena shrugged off her backpack.

"Get your purse!" he said urgently in Somali. "Where—"

BangBangBangBang!

Machine gunfire punctured the door with holes. Wood chips exploded like shrapnel! Shot daylight through. Aslam buckled forward, riddled in the back.

Makena screamed!

Sultana Hirsi, 25, 5-4, 135, seven months pregnant, ran in from the kitchen, where she was preparing lunch boxes for the family to take with them. Sultana taught at the local school.

"Break down the door!" barked a gruff voice.

Shoving her daughter in the back, her mother cried, "Makena!

Go, run!"

Crash! Soldiers kicked down the door.

Makena kept running. Sultana did not, turning around to face the soldiers.

"Is there anyone else?" demanded the same gruff voice.

"No one." The last words Makena heard her mother say before Makena emerged into the backyard to pandemonium and terror from neighbors on all sides. The men's shouts cut short by gunfire. Women's screams transforming to wailing shrieks. Soldiers cursing, yelling! Swarming!

Too dangerous to go into the street, Makena ran into the outhouse. Closed the door. There was no place to hide. She thought for a moment. Opened the door, then retreated back inside, and climbed into lavatory hole. As her feet sank, piss and shit climbed up her body. She held her breath for as long as she could, but had to let go and inhale the stench.

She threw up loudly!

A soldier came outside. Walked up to the outhouse.

Makena gagged herself even as her chest convulsed.

Leaving the door open worked. He returned to the house.

Makena threw up a few times before her brain and body accepted the grossness and smell. She stayed in the lavatory, hour after hour, trying to shut her brain off from the raucous laughter of the soldiers over screaming women. Including her mother's. She felt relief when explosions— Red Beret lobbing grenades and Molotov cocktails and helicopters dropping bombs—drowned out the terror-stricken cries. The gunfire, almost continuous throughout the morning, became sporadic, then died completely when the sun set, except for an isolated staccato.

The soldiers left, but Makena waited till dark to climb out and enter her house. Her mother lay on the floor. Naked. A bullet through her skull. As young as she was, seeing Sultana's spread-eagled body and blood between the legs, Makena knew what her mother had endured. Makena wept softly beside her parents' bodies. Eventually, she peeled off her sewage-sodden clothes, washed, changed, and found the purse her father asked her to grab before the massacre. She kept it under her mattress, so she could get to it in a hurry.

It contained money, papers, and a phone number.

Spending a few more minutes mourning the death of her parents, Makena finally mustered the courage to leave the house. The streets were littered with bodies—men, women, and children. Not everyone died from gunshots. Many were brutally stabbed, cut, even decapitated. The silence and smell of death pervaded the night until she turned a couple of corners. Slowly, like an ebbing tide, signs of life gradually appeared, first as men, women, and children, weeping and mourning beside the dead. Then she saw refugees of all ages—most with bags, some carrying the elderly and babies—headed out of the city.

BoomBoomBoomBoomBoom!

Cannon fire from the sky!

A helicopter emerged like a ghost out of the starry night and thundered across, Siad Barre's gunners hanging out from both sides lobbing grenades and strafing down. Makena ran for cover.

Thuthuthuthuth!

Bullets stitched the ground inches from her. She dived into a ditch. The helicopter melted disappeared. Gunfire and grenades receded.

Astutely realizing the refugees'd be targeted as long as they trekked across open ground, Makena reversed direction, got to her school. One side of it—where the classrooms were located—had been shelled. Black soot smeared across the walls, swaths of it still smoldering. The offices remained intact. The slaughter began so early this morning, not a single kid or teacher had reached school. Makena entered the principal's office.

She knew it contained the only phone. Picked it up. *It works.* She opened her purse, extracted the phone number, and dialed. Holding her breath, hoping and praying the call would be answered, it was!

"Hello?" said the deep, male voice.

"Sharif Hirsi?" she asked. Silence answered back. "*Adeer, kani Makena. Gabadha walaalkaa ah.*" This is Makena, your brother's daughter.

"Makena!" her uncle recognized at once, asked in Somali. "Are you all right?" After Makena told him what happened, he said, "Smart girl. Hide where you are. I will call you back." About an hour later, he did. "Can you get to the dock before daybreak?'

"Yes."

"Go to Pier Fourteen."

Anchored there, a wreck of a boat. The captain was expecting her. The crew comprised two other rough looking Somalis. They shoved Makena in a cramped engine room misty with diesel fumes. Locked the hatch. She fell asleep, jolted awake when the engines fired. The boat began to move. Heat and smoke almost suffocated her. She pressed her nostrils to the gap between the planks of the hatch to breathe. When they were in open sea, the Captain let her out. He returned her purse without the money and they fed her scraps left over from their plates. They sailed down the coast to Mombasa, Kenya. The five hundred and thirty-three nautical miles took two days.

On the pier, stood a giant of a man she'd only been introduced to in photographs by her father as his older brother, Sharif Hirsi, 35, 6-7, 299. She'd never met anyone more intimidating. His face melted and he scooped her up in a bear hug. They stayed three days in a cheap Mombasa hotel, waiting for forged papers, then got on a plane to Baltimore, USA.

Sharif legally adopted Makena, and soon, bright as she was, she figured out how he'd engineered her escape and arranged for her citizenship. He served as muscle for Mr. Knight, an up and coming drug lord in the process of building a Cartel in Cherry Hill. She came of age about the time it did—ruthless and notorious as it was deadly and dangerous. Sharif's position also meant Makena was off limits, especially when he observed intelligence and maturity an entire cut above kids her age. A strict parent, he made it clear she was going to get a college education.

While attending Baltimore City Community College, Makena recognized a young, black, and brash nineteen-going-on-twenty dealer from her neighborhood. He introduced himself as

Tavon Cole, then surprised her and endeared himself when he confessed he also aspired for a way out, but knew to play by gang rules during the day and attend school at night. They fell in love, but Tavon needed Sharif's approval, and got it.

Makena married Tavon, mainly because he knocked her up. They never told Sharif, who assumed his grand daughter was born four weeks premature. Then, Tavon's day job came calling. A fatal bullet found his street manager during a disagreement. Tavon'd paid his dues, shown loyalty, and had collected enough street cred to be next up. He didn't want it, neither did Makena or Sharif. They also knew he could not say 'no.' Being the smartest one in the room, Makena suggested Tavon enlist. Sharif, now a person of influence, helped sell it, saying the kid was drunk when he walked into the recruiting center, bragging he wanted to kill turban heads. Coming right after 9/11, Tavon's enlistment looked like an immature, reckless, spontaneous decision.

There wasn't retribution but repercussion. The cartel found Makena a job as a bookkeeper for a shipping company in Baltimore's inner harbor. Makena didn't mind—looking at it as white collar crime. So much better than Tavon leaning into cars to exchange cash for crack, not knowing if a rival would pose as a buyer and kill him. But, on the last day of Tavon's tour, driving to Kuwait to fly back home, Tavon died. Ambushed.

It devastated Makena. She flew to Dover Air Force Base to receive his body, where she met Nigel Hansom and instantly felt a kinship, especially when he wanted to keep a promise he made to Tavon to take of her and her daughter, three at the time. Not the type to accept charity, she refused. But they kept in touch. Got close.

A year after Tavon's death, Nigel called her. He was in Baltimore. Asked her to dinner. She was puzzled when he brought up his trucking business. "We'll be covering Canada to Mexico," he said, "and I want someone I can trust."

"I'm just a bookkeeper," she smiled, flattered.

"Exactly," he smiled. "From Cherry Hill." Then, explained the offer.

Although everything about her job was on the up-and-up, it wasn't hard to connect the dots. Working as a bookkeeper in Baltimore harbor couldn't be just fortuitous or an accident. Not for a girl from Cherry Hill—a major narcotics hub—whose uncle ran security for the Cartel.

"I have to ask," she said with a wan smile.

"Of course."

She spoke to Sharif, who took it up the chain. That very night, they were summoned to The Mansion. Cops to crooks, everyone in Cherry Hill knew it to be the Cartel White House. The few who'd been inside didn't even dare describe the furniture. Walking in, the décor surprised Makena—not gaudily pimped out at all, but restrained and classy. Makena wondered if the Jean-Michel Basquiat—a Haitian black artist who commanded a hundred and five million dollars for one of his paintings—on the wall, as you entered, was an original. *Probably.*

Sharif and Makena were led into a library. She wore a conservative business suit—knee-length skirt, collared blouse, and sensible heels. Sharif put on a suit.

Mr. Knight, 51, 5-10¾, 210—Makena knew him only by name and notoriety—walked in a moment later. No one knew if it was his first or last name, or dared to ask.

"Sit," he gestured to the couch. Sharif and she took the three-seat sofa and Mr. Knight sank into the single. "I remember Sharif bringing you to Baltimore. Watched you grow up, marry one of our own from Cherry Hill. Tragic, Tavon's death. You have been a very good bookkeeper. Sharif outlined the details, but I want to hear from you."

She didn't expect to him to so soft spoken. A measured calm tone encapsulated every word—each overtly innocent, all the implication hidden. Mr. Knight hardly looked like a gangster in the white Untuckit shirt over dark trousers and brown slip-ons without socks. No jewelry, none whatsoever. He'd be mistaken for an academic, which he may have been. He had a degree in religion and theology, Uncle told her. More myth than facts surrounded Mr. Knight's rise to become the most feared and powerful crime boss in the northeast.

Makena spoke. He did not interrupt. Makena figured Mr. Knight'd already turned over Nigel's life and dug into Easy Trucking's business down to the last detail. After she finished, he nodded and played with his lip with his thumb and forefinger.

"Let's start small, build trust," he finally said. Then laid out the numbers and the tiny wiggle room she had in her negotiation with Nigel. "That percentage in the wiggle room, whatever you can save, is yours to keep."

Makena held back her smile. Sharif'd been doing this too long to even react. The wiggle room could add up to millions if she and Nigel grew the partnership. *I'm thinking too far ahead.* She nodded. "Thank you."

Mr. Knight stood up. Extended his hand. Makena took it. He put his other hand over hers and grimily added, "If we meet again, it means things have gone very wrong."

Makena's heart climbed to her throat. *Price of doing this kind of business.* She called Nigel as soon as she got home. "I'm in."

"There must be details to iron out."

They met the next morning in his penthouse suite at the hotel for breakfast. Makena conveyed the lowest number of the deal, then lied, "Anything else, I have to get approval."

She knew he didn't want this to go back and forth, but get cash flowing ASAP. Also, he couldn't buy smart, and she was that. Makena made no mention of the wiggle room, the entirety of which she claimed, when he agreed to her first offer.

When they raised their orange juice to toast the deal, the attraction that'd been building exploded like an IED. They forgot breakfast. Nigel slammed his lips upon hers. Such was the intensity, urgency, and force of his kiss, their teeth knocked against each other. He reached down and cupped and squeezed her crotch. Nails of her left hand dug into his skull while the right unbuckled his off-white slacks and pulled down his black briefs He roughly spun her around. Hiked her pleated flared skirt. Ripped down her lace panties. She felt the warm tip of his swollen penis enter her. She hadn't been with a man since Tavon and pent up sexual desire consumed her body, greedily thrusting backward to feel more of him inside her. Instead, he pulled away. She turned around, breathing hard.

Read his expression. Understood at once. As cliché as the adage was, it was also undeniably true.

Don't shit where you work.

"This is not a good idea, is it?" she panted.

Both realized the enormity of the agreement they'd struck. She'd rocket up from a low level drone manipulating manifests to the point person for distribution across North America. Together, they could grow Easy Trucking into the biggest conduit for Cartel products. He nodded. She reached up and kissed him. He kissed her back. Their lips stayed fused. She felt his erection between her legs. They clung to each other, enjoying this, their last intimate act, for as long they could. Then, they pulled apart

The partnership worked out like a dream.

Makena moved into the fancy 'burbs of Locust Point. Hotter than every white housewife, she opened the supply route to the party circuit of the wealthiest of the wealthiest. Mr. Knight loved her for it. Makena became Nigel's muse, sounding board, his closest confidant. As Easy Trucking burgeoned into the colossus they envisioned, theirs became an incredibly entwined relationship—some might say internecine. She knew every aspect of his operation, as he did the Cartels'.

If one went down, the other would sink too.

Following a trucking convention in Atlanta, Nigel ran an idea by Makena. Like a wife giving in to her man's midlife crisis and letting him have his red Ferrari, she said, "Run with it."

According to Dusty Saldana

Ripley came up suddenly along a desolate stretch of the I-10, west of San Antonio, Texas. You'd pretty much guess it was a ghost town if you paid any heed to the sign when you passed it on the freeway—rusted, bird pooh all over, missing rivets that left most of the regulation green iron sheet bent and flapping in the wind.

Ripley used to service a quartz mine. When the stone ran out, so did the citizens. About fifty people lived in Ripley now. A gas station remained—didn't look like it did much business. How it stayed open, I don't know. A restaurant, more dive than eatery, stood between shuttered stores. At the corner, just as I pulled around, a chubby leather-faced old timer, 60, 5-11, 140, appeared behind the glass. Wrinkled, sunburned, a Ripley die-hard, looked like. He turned the sign around from 'CLOSED' to 'OPEN.' If he hadn't, I'd've figured it was another bankrupt business. A liquor mart. *Of course.* I swung my eyes back front.

Google Maps on my burner took me right to the big grocery store—venue for this I-10 fight. This was my sixth, since Nigel hired me three months ago. I was getting used to the several hundred miles of travel from New Orleans to these godforsaken towns. I didn't have one of 'em talking GPSs. I used to. But not after National Public Radio said your GPS collects Big Data—first time I'd heard that. *As scary as it sounds, trust me.* Big Data be info the GPS computer in your car collected, you know, like where you go, what roads you take to get there, how fast you went—basically your every move. Car companies then sold that info, which explained how advertisers knew to send you all the right kind of junk mail and robocall you. For an old coot, I was tech savvy enough to deduce you might as well be wearing an electronic bracelet. Hell, what if there was a spot I didn't want people to know I was at? Sure, I could get one of 'em tech support Indians to find a way around. *Easier thing to do?* Getting rid of the damn GPS and that's what I did. It's also the reason I never bought a fancy Smartphone. Always used a new burner every month. Drove Nigel crazy.

The grocery store belonged to a big name chain that upped and left, probably well before the working stiffs in town knew about the coming layoffs. A couple of letters were gone and another dangled loosely. The neon inside them been looted likely the day after it closed. Paint peeled. Missing roof tiles. Basically, an abandoned building. Half-assed graffiti. Rural rednecks lacked the urban artistry of black and Latin kids.

I bumped my seventeen-year-old, gray, Toyota pickup over the cracked curb into the large parking lot. There were a couple of forty-foot eighteen-wheelers with Easy Trucking logos. They transported the fighters.

My first fight for Nigel been an eye-opener. It wasn't in a ghost town like this one, but coulda been—so damn shitty and poor. West of Mobile, a dump called Carville. They hated Mexicans, blaming them for coming via the Gulf and taking jobs on the oils rigs. But Nigel'd greased the local Sheriff and KKK. If you're wondering why he didn't just move the fight, then you're probably a nine-to-five drone wallowing in the middle class. Who in the right mind would look in Car-fucking-ville for illegals, and even if they did, who in their fucking mind would dare come and bust the fight? Nigel was always smart but he'd evolved to shark smart. Unscrupulous.

Anyways, what I was trying to say about the first fight being an eye-opener be how a dump that looked DOA—dead on arrival—transformed in the space of an hour from a racist hell hole to a hopping fight night. White, black, brown, yellow, they all walked on the same side of the street. Shops came alive. Cars and trucks parked bumper to bumper along Main Street. The local school gym hosted the Octagon. For the next four hours—and only for those four hours, mind you—skin color didn't matter, only the green of your betting money did.

The I-10 fighting corridor was something else. I'd heard about it, but never in a million years'd've figured Nigel created it. *All thanks to me starting an itch in him for competition.* To dovetail it with his business was all you needed to know the kinda crafty sumbitch he'd become. The freeway skimmed the southern border across these entire United States. He already had cops in his pocket—an inescapable necessity of running a trucking business. The cops helped him bring in crooked BSF—Border

Security Force—agents. They in turn opened the door to ICE—Immigration and Citizenship Enforcement. Nigel diligently built a rep of transporting only fighters across the border in his trucks.

I got outta my truck. Locked it. Started across the parking lot, nodding to Nigel's lackeys and heavies—the advance team that prepped the arena. Cables snaked from the electric pole outside to juice up the fluorescents inside and out. I walked into a derelict warehouse-size space, where remnants of shelves of the old store been shoved against the wall.

An Octagon, to MMA specs, been erected in the middle. The office and other rooms in the back became lockers, where the next couple of hours just flew by as I prepped my fighters, telling 'em in Spanish to fight their hearts outs. "Just 'cause you live and work out together don't mean you should show each other mercy. Beating down your friend shows the promoters you got a killer instinct."

I wrote down the number, you know, what the bump in pay would be if they got picked, on a piece of paper and had them pass it around. I kinda knew whose eyes would light up, but that didn't mean shit 'cause only getting into the ring would reveal if they possessed fangs. Some were born with just gums.

Then, it was time.

A rowdy, standing only eclectic mix showed up. Rednecks, blacks, Mexicans, Asians, cops, BSF, ICE, government officials. Almost all male. Some were still in uniform—showed you how deep Nigel kept the law in his pocket. Suited and booted in his 'occasions only' attire, he milled around, a regular social butterfly. Girls in short tight skirts—hauled out from New Orleans in one of the eighteen-wheelers—carried trays loaded with smokes and booze to cater to every taste. They had instructions to make sure they kept the cups refilled.

WhamWham! Right off the bat, with a nasty right-left combo of strikes, Zapeda, 23, 5-6, 150, his body chiseled like a sprinter, put the hurt on Alfredo, also 23, 5-4, 148, thick. Alfredo had feet slower'n molasses. He didn't backslide them or sidestep fast enough, even though he saw Zapeda coming with an outside trip.

It didn't make Zapeda a better fighter—in fact, it probably set off warning bells for any scouts watching. One, Zapeda shoulda concealed his intention till the last instant. Two, and worse, Zapeda was a boxer. In his best interest, then, to keep as much of this upright. Instead—

Bam! Zapeda's power head strike sent Alfredo to the canvas hard, but Alfredo also knew what came next. Zapeda pounced and landed in Alfredo's wheelhouse. You see, Alfredo wanted to be a WWE wrestler, but lacked the flamboyant personality or looks that'd play on TV. Grappling came naturally to him. Like a snake, he methodically began to work his arms and legs into wrapping up Zapeda, who now had to figure a way back onto his feet. Unfortunately, Zapeda became a lamb in a python's wrap, getting into a worse bind with every wriggle. He lost the use of his left hand. The strikes he land with his right be weak and ineffective.

It was my job to evaluate the strengths of every fighter Nigel brought in, then create a regimen to show them off. All through training, I dinned it into Zapeda that he should fight on his feet. He clearly didn't hear me, more likely thought he knew better. Alfredo, awfully slow as he might've looked at the outset, put Zapeda in a rear-naked choke.

When I made this pairing to be the first fight, I did it with good reason. Neither threatened to be a serious prospect. Still, I had to at least make the pretence of selling 'em as such. As boxer and wrestler, Zapeda and Alfredo were just about good enough to work as a warm-up act while the scouts, bettors, and spectators got their drinks, pressed flesh, traded news, whispers, rumors, and gossip from the circuit, and settled in. Regulars to these shindigs knew the good match-ups started around the fight #3. Nigel continued to work the room—man had a natural charm and an unbelievable memory for names and family details to make every conversation feel intimate and personal.

The ref circled over to make sure Zapeda had a chance and wasn't hanging on outta pride or bravado. Zapeda realized it wasn't his night and tapped out with almost a minute to spare in the first round. It came as no shock. These were three-round affairs and the first couple usually lasted one. So, this followed the script.

The fighters got out and headed back. A lackey wiped down the canvas. I noticed Nigel wandering over, tapping out a cigarette from a pack, and I drifted to meet him halfway. But then, a couple of lawmen stepped in between and I pulled up when I started to overhear it was business they wanted to discuss. I knew when to turn my ears off and go deaf. That don't mean I didn't listen in—just that I'd never recall the details if someone asked me.

"An FYI, Nigel," one of the uniforms was saying. "It's about Crispin Martinez."

I recognized the name. Crispin Martinez, 21, 5-6½, 141. A DACA kid—Deferred Action for Childhood Arrivals—you know, brought to this country as a child, going to school and college and pretty much American in every way except being legal. Crispin wasn't a fighter, though he'd tried out to be one. Neither was he, I was learning now, as clean cut as I thought.

The uniform's voice dropped and I couldn't hear the rest. Judging from the way Nigel's eyes went dead and his face tightened, the news came as a shock. Nigel liked Crispin. Treated him like a first among equals. Trusted him as only one of three drivers to smuggle fighters across the border. I didn't have a clue about the nature of Crispin's transgression, but the way Nigel then said, "I'll take care of it," made the hairs on the back of my neck stand. Crispin had it coming and it wasn't going to be pleasant.

"You should," said the lawman grimly, "don't want others getting ideas."

"You're right." Nigel hadn't lit his cigarette, that's how upset he was. It took five years, Nigel said, to build the I-10 circuit to what it is today. *His baby, end to end.*

He owned it, controlled it, and now that I worked for him, knew for a fact that poachers paid the price with their lives trying to claim even a piece of it.

The uniforms walked away. Nigel stood for a moment, not

hiding the betrayal on his face. His eyes met mine, the expression unchanged. I didn't know whether to go over. Thankfully, the crowd erupted, inviting the next two fighters. I had an excuse to look away and gladly did, stopping them before they climbed into the Octagon. I put a hand each on their shoulder and said, "This is what you've been working toward." I nodded first to the strawberry picker-turned-boxer, 24, 5-5, 147, "Hector, this is your last shot. So, fight like your life depended on it."

Nigel gave every fighter three shots and six weeks to be picked up. Hector was headed back to farming and I think he knew that, but you never knew. One fluke remarkable fight, which could be tonight, someone might see potential I missed, and take him. I been wrong before, not often, but enough to know not to make definitive pronouncements that could humble me.

Then I looked over to the cocky, jacked up Julio, 19, 5-7, 146, hopping like a kangaroo on roids, "Calm it down, Julio. Your problem always is your intensity, which leads you to breathe hard and fast at the start, then you run outta air by the end of the round."

Both were boxers, so this could go a couple of rounds. And if there was a pattern in how much most of 'em weighed in at, it was 'cause Featherweight (145-155 lbs.) was far'n away the most popular of the twelve men's MMA weight classes. Names everyone knew, like McGregor, Aldo, Yamamoto—they were Featherweights.

Bam! Julio stunned Hector with a wicked strike thirty seconds in, followed it up with a right high kick, and then unloaded a barrage. I counted about ten power strikes in the next minute and a half. Julio went on to land about thirty in all, missing five. Hector reeled, backpedaled, but he'd read the book on the younger fighter. More important, he listened to me about surviving the first half of the round 'cause Julio started running outa gas, just like I warned him. The kid probably figured he could force the older Hector to submit early. That didn't happen. Hector found his range. So, even if Julio was the more skilled fighter, Hector's staying power became an equalizer. He took

Julio behind the woodshed.

TingTing. The bell saved the kid.

"If you don't listen, you won't win," I told Julio, when he sulked over to his corner. "People watchin' have their ears open too about you willing or unwilling to take instruction." While the lackey cleaned him up, I walked over to Hector, patted him, "You're playin' it perfect, but you need to land some strikes early. Julio can get lucky with a strike and lay you out. "

I shoulda bought a lottery ticket 'cause I was a fucking savant. *Pow!* Julio lifted Hector off his feet with an uppercut. A strike with his very first swing of Round 2. Hector fell flat on his back and lay there for the long term. The ref called the fight for Julio, then looked over to the lackeys, "Help Hector outta here. Next fight!"

Julio strutted off. There was something to be said about raw talent. The kid had it, but so did a lot of others. Still, only one in fifty harnessed it, and half of those, probably less, succeeded up to the next level. One in ten outta that group got a shot in the big leagues—auditioning to just get in, not fight, mind you.

Proof I could be wrong bore out in the third fight, the only Heavyweight card of night, when Javier, 21, 5-9, 265, quick as a gnat, but undersized, landed a roundhouse that hit at the right time, right angle, right place. Like a hole in one by a long shot amateur golfer playing his first round ever. His opponent, Victor, 23, 6-2, 271, taller than I liked in a fighter, but with arms that extended below his knees. He didn't have a chance to show that reach. Victor flew backward, hit the ropes, then the canvas. Concussed.

The ref saw no point even counting. "Next!"

Applause and boos canceled each other out 'cause this contest lasted all of thirty-eight seconds, and one I really thought would go three competitive rounds. Nigel looked none too happy. Quick rounds akin to quick ejaculations—a source of embarrassment.

Luckily, the next fight featured evenly matched Featherweights and it went the distance. Meaning, the clock turned off in the third round. The "no mercy" rule went into effect. The fight ended with a tap out, precluding the ref from stepping in and calling it. The finale, I prayed'd cap it all off.

These were a couple of good looking Welterweights—arguably the second most popular weight class. Manuel, 23, 5-7, 157, jumped up and down. Dominico, 22, 5-8, 156, punched a ghost. I explained, "Both you about even. Manny, you got reach. Dom, you got reflexes. Both of you're equally strong. I'm relying on you to bring out the best in each other and make this the fight of the night. I got my money on both of you bein' gone tonight. Make it true. Don't hold nothing back."

They headed into the cage. Ref shut the gate. Nigel came up to me, "Swing by the house tomorrow around five?"

"Sure," I nodded.

Ting! There wasn't time to ask him why and I forgot about it.

The guys jumped outta their corners. Manuel came out punching with speed and landed several stiff shots that surely must've rung Dominico's ears but he weathered this early barrage, then landed a straight right that turned things around. I realized Dominico'd paid heed to my instructing him about putting together combinations 'cause he unleashed a strong salvo of heavy shots to Manuel's body.

Manuel was a wild, free-swinging brand of fighter. He also remembered that I told him he had arms longer than most others and to use them, and he did, delivering some serious blunt force trauma that opened a nasty gash on Dominico's forehead. But a debilitating kick laid Manuel on the canvas. He turned just enough to avoid his ribcage being crushed. Both could grapple. So, neither could defend subs and maintain top control long enough for a submission. I told Nigel to make this the last fight for a reason. When the bell rang to end Round 1, even I couldn't take a side. I scored a draw, though if you gave it to Dominico by a whisker, I'd have no argument.

The crowd couldn't wait for the next round, and most important, the scouts and promoters crowded the cage. Manuel came out strong and nearly ended it in the second frame, firing a potent left straight into Dominico's mouth. Dominico came right back with a single-leg takedown and an armbar. I'd told the ref at the start of the night to give them space. Sure enough, given time, Manuel used pressure and slick grappling to not only get outta the jam but nearly finish a *Kimura*—a double armlock that put painful pressure on the opponent's shoulder. Named after Masahiko Kimura, who came up with it to defeat one of the founders of Brazilian Jiu Jitsu, Helio Gracie. Dominico's reflexes saved him, effectively bouncing elbows off Manuel's face.

Ting! The round went to Manuel, no question.

So, there'd be no clock running for Round 3 for the second fight in a row. I caught Nigel's eyes and he look stoked. Manuel saved the best for last, using his reach for a spinning back-kick that launched Dominico into the chainlink. Dominico called upon his reflexes to duck outta a follow through strike that coulda finished him. Not only did he recover—

WhamWham! He delivered back to back elbows that bruised Manuel's cheeks. Manuel staggered. Dominico snapped a left hook and a dropped monstrous overhand right. *Crash!* Manuel's spine pummeled into the cage. Dominico swung and missed 'cause Manuel sidestepped right, then planted, turned, and looped his right leg. Perfectly placed—by accident, more likely. A stunning shot, regardless. Struck Dominico smack in the middle of his face. Knocked him back and down. Manuel pounced and plastered Dominico.

When blood started to spray, the ref stepped in and called it.

The place went wild. This'd played out like a real pro fight. Buyers crowded Nigel. When it was all said and done, the two Featherweights, Manuel, and Dominico got picked up. One more than the worst we'd done on any fight night since I took over. Before me, Nigel said some nights had zero sales. Past month, I felt job security for the first time, but knowing Nigel, he was a 'what've you done for me lately' kind of guy.

I'd set a bar and now there were expectations.

I found Hector with his head in his hands. I said a few nice things—all canned. He knew that 'cause he'd seen me give it to other three'n outs. I handed him an envelope with his severance—a grand in cash—and a choice, "I can put you on the next truck headed to Mexico, or we can forget we even know you ever come across the border and you just walk outta here."

"Maybe I go to L.A," Hector said. Most fighters preferred to take their chances as illegals staying in the US. He opened the envelope but didn't count the money inside, having known me long enough to trust me not to shortchange him. He just rippled the bills with his thumb.

"Perfect city to blend in." I patted him on the back. "Good luck to you."

I'd forget him, his face first, then his name, or the other way around. Didn't matter. Empathy only kept you hanging onto memories that did nobody no good, most of all me. You only got depressed about another dream—however improbable and foolhardy—being crushed. *Hell, I'm still writing that book.*

I went about wrapping things up, making sure the guys and equipment all got loaded up. About two hours after the final fight, the last of the trucks left for New Orleans. The unsold fighters got paid when they reported to the gym and resumed training after a day off. Load their wallet tonight, and they could do something stupid here, where Nigel didn't have the same pull or muscle he did in New Orleans. Plus, there wasn't a rock he couldn't turn over in Louisiana to find someone who bolted without fulfilling his contract fighting three matches.

"It's happened," Nigel told me.

I bought it. Nigel did the heavy lifting, paying off the authorities to sneak these prospects over the border. Like any sport, there was only so much talent. Understandably snakes slithered in with promises of greener pastures. Fighting was a dog-eat-dog world, ruthlessness being part of doing business, especially in the underworld of the sport. Nigel could hold his own. I recalled his killer instinct just as a lifter at LSU when he three-peated. A rare trait. You couldn't teach that, or acquire it. *You have to be born with it.*

I got back to my place around 5 AM, hit the sack, and went

dead to the world. I slept till lunchtime, then woke up, and cooked some canned crap. With everyone enjoying the day off, I lounged and loitered until it was time to head over to Nigel's. I'd never been to his home, believe it or not. He lived in Carrollton, specifically Audubon—a ritzy neighborhood in the classy part of New Orleans. I pulled up at a ten-foot high gate. The intricate ironwork probably cost more than my rent for the year.

The fence on either side was a sold brick wall at least eight feet high, with broken glass pressed into the cement cap on top. I wasn't surprised. In the little time I worked for him, I surmised Nigel be a kingpin of sorts. Easy Trucking couldn't have rocketed to the top transporting lettuce and lumber. Shit, if he had the gall and gumption to risk his trucks to traffic fighters, he gotta be moving other things not entirely legal and far more profitable. I ain't no rocket scientist, but neither did I have to think too hard what demand he be satisfying, Mexico to Canada.

I punched the keypad and looked up into the security camera. The gate opened. Smooth. Noiseless. *That's what dough buy.* A maintenance dude getting paid to show up often enough to oil this thing.

The half-mile driveway had neatly trimmed trees on both sides. Only after you took that curve you saw the house—make that a mansion. There were a couple of black gardeners tending to the yard the size of a football field on either side of the house. Heavies, all white, sauntered like sentries back and forth, a couple on the roof. They weren't armed but I wasn't buying that they weren't. Prestige and respectability likely demanded they conceal their weapons. Think back to 'em Civil War movies and how'n where the biggest, baddest plantation owner lived, then update it with security cameras aplenty and for all to see—that painted an accurate picture of this place.

I pulled up, got out, and started up the three front steps. A woodworker clearly spent time customizing the oversized solid wood door, then polished it like a mirror. The fancy glass on either side must've cost a fortune too. Everything reeked of money and care. I didn't have a chance to knock. *Oh, good.* The brass handle of the old world knocker didn't have a smudge. The door opened and I stared at a stern'n squat black maid, 60, 5-5, 150, wearing a pressed white apron over a floral dress. *Like I said, plantation.*

"Mr. Hansom will be with you," she said and clicked the door shut softly in my face.

OK. I'm not allowed inside. One thing about Nigel—punctuality. Seconds later, the door opened again. Nigel had his arm around his wife's waist. He pecked her on the lips, "I should be back in a few hours."

I only knew Kamryn by name, rep, and pictures. She hadn't lost much of her Miss Louisiana beauty, having aged well—that likely thanks to the Hispanic in her 'cause white chicks mostly don't—and could still turn heads. She must've had work done, but she'd done it right. Not hiding her age, rather working with and around it. Nipping and tucking with discretion, unlike a lotta rich broads who walked around with a forever smile and plastic skin. Married to a piece of ass like this at home, I couldn't for the life of me understand why Nigel wandered for poontang. He didn't introduce me to her and she didn't spare me even a glance. I wasn't there as far as she was concerned.

"Hey, Dusty." He shut the door. "We'll take your truck." I'd parked it right under the stately porch on fancy pillars like the kind outside the White House.

"Where we going?" I asked, rounding over to the driver's side.

Nigel didn't answer. One of his heavies appeared outta nowhere. *Clang!* He dropped a tire iron in the flatbed. The obvious question started to form in my throat, but my brain smartly stepped in and shut it down when I noticed the heavy wore gloves. A hole opened in my stomach. It took all I had not to let the angry surprise I felt about not being given a choice. *What'll I've done with one? Say no?*

What made it crazy surreal was Nigel behaving like we were just driving to get a drink or something. In between smoking and shop talk about the fighters in the fold and what was in the pipeline, he gave me directions. Loyola Avenue, Nashville, South Claiborne, and onto I-10 East. My stomach started to tighten again with premonition. When we hopped off the freeway and took St. Bernard Avenue, my fears came to pass. *Oh, fuck.*

We headed into the Seventh Ward—an infamous neighborhood that was night to Audubon's day. You had a one in ten chance of being victimized. Not surprising, if you looked around. Closely packed crappy homes, broken windows, littered yards and sidewalks, junky cars, hookers. Then, there was that dead giveaway—the demo. Mostly black, some Latino. Not being racist. I hated rednecks with equal passion. Also, I trained mostly Latinos, some black, but these fuckers, hanging about idly curbside, swigging from booze bottles wrapped in brown bags, hardly fit the neighborly working class type. Truth of the matter—cops didn't even bother showing up here unless a shooting turn into a riot. Not a bad idea to let the gangs settle their differences without wasting tax payer money on arrests, trials, and prison time, only to have the cycle repeat when they got out.

I couldn't pronounce the Frenchie name of the street we entered an hour and change into our drive from Nigel's house. The sun'd long since dropped outta sight.

"Turn off your lights," said Nigel.

I did. For a couple of seconds I couldn't see nothing. Didn't help that none of the street lamps worked, save one at the far end, having fits, desperately flickering to stay on. My pupils dilated to whatever light spilled outside from the homes on either side. A rap song blared outta one so loud, the bass physically vibrated the air. In the Seventh Ward, you'd be out after dark only if you were up to no good or had a death wish. Not a coincidence Nigel timed it so.

"Pull up here," said Nigel.

I killed the engine. Coasted to a quick stop. Nigel climbed out, reached into his pocket for a pair of blue surgical gloves that clung like a second skin. *OhfuckOhfuck.* I didn't know why it came as a surprise after expecting this outcome the entire ride over.

I been in and around enough dicey situations to be trained to keep my expression the same. Never thought Nigel got his hands dirty. But then it made sense. Nobody could finger him, but him. *So, why bring me along?*

"Stay here." Nigel retrieved the tire iron and walked up the drive past a black Lexus, which looked pretty new. Outta place in the Seventh Ward. Whoever lived here was doing quite well. Maybe too well. Lights were on in one of the two windows facing the street. Nigel climbed the coupla the steps and knocked using the tire iron. I recognized the kid who opened the door.

Crispin Martinez.

Of course. In the back of my mind, I suspected it all along. *So why is my stomach knotting up?* It hit me. I was afraid for Crispin. The way his face cracked with a smile that mixed fear and surprise all the same time—*he knows.* He started to say something but never got past the first word. I don't think he saw the tire iron, let alone what hit him.

WhackWhackWhack! Nigel pummeled Crispin's ribs, once, twice, three times. I could hear the bones break. Dull, distant, but it was a special sound. Unmistakable. Sickening. *Shit.* I realized why Nigel brought me along. Being a witness made me an accessory, tied my tongue, and assured him of my loyalty with few avenues to get out. Not without turning into a snitch, and Nigel knew me to be old school. No rat.

Crispin hollered and fell backward. I looked around to see if anyone heard. No caring or concerned neighbors here. If you grew up in the Seventh Ward, you went about your own business. Got through life one day at a time—the first rule of survival in a jungle. This was the worst kind. One populated by the most evil of all predators. Humans.

When I looked back, Nigel'd shut the door. He was inside. I could see through the window, though. Not Crispin—he lay on the floor—but Nigel. Tire iron raised and resting on his right shoulder. Delivering an enraged message, spit flying! His voice reached me, muffled, incomprehensible.

Then, he swung the tire iron like a lumberjack who'd

lost it. Not content just cutting wood, but pulverizing it. *WhackWhackWhackWhack!* I oughta be hearing nothing, not through a closed window and sitting in my truck twenty feet away. But I could. Thought so, at least. More likely 'cause my brain filled in the gaps, made up the sickening sound, having heard it up close and personal from inside the Octagon all my life. Metal meeting flesh and bone. Only, blood didn't spurt up like it was doing now, splattering Nigel. He didn't even notice. If he did, he had to be enjoying it. He didn't pause to wipe off, just kept swinging the tire iron.

I'd seen Nigel angry, but not like this.

My heart was beating around my throat somewheres. Any doubt not to be afraid evaporated, as also any notion of turning against him to ever cross my mind. Nigel hadn't built the I-10 circuit being Gandhi. This was an integral part of what kept it going—one that I needed to see for myself. *I'm right.* Me sitting here was no accident. This was as much about sending me a message as it was incriminating me up to my eyeballs. *Crafty bastard.* I shoulda known, but if I was being honest, I did know deep down when I took the gig. I'd knowingly made my bed and I was getting fucked in it. *Story of my life.*

Nigel disappeared, walking deeper into the house. He returned a few minutes later with a big-ass knife and a plastic grocery bag. *What the fuck?* He stood over Crispin, speaking with a smile? *No!* Crispin's still alive! Nigel dropped outta sight below the window.

I heard a guttural scream!

Muted by distance and the walls of the house, but distinct. Still aroused no curious lookie-loos. The scream died. Whatever Nigel did next took a full five minutes. He emerged outside with the tire iron in one hand and a grocery bag, knotted at the handles, in the other, which caught the light from the house and glinted. *The big-ass knife.*

Nigel walked unhurriedly down the driveway. I reached over and opened the passenger side door. He dropped the tire iron, grocery bag, and knife on the floor between his legs. His gloves looked as if they been dipped in red paint, which glistened, indicating it was still wet. That didn't stop him from lighting up. I said nothing. Kept the headlamps off till we turned the corner, and then really didn't have to turn it on.

Whooom!

Fire erupted into the sky from the back of Crispin's house and quickly became an all consuming inferno. Nothing stopped cops and forensics dead in their investigation as definitely as a charred out crime scene. Don't matter that arson started it. You only had to turn on the stove, strategically spill some burnables, like booze and cleaning supplies, from the stove to the floor and walls. Then, it just became race against time. Not really. These houses were old, combustible, and fire trucks never rushed over to the Seventh Ward. NOPD Detectives would show up, take notes, and toss them in the bottom drawer 'cause somone'd just taken a dirt bag off their plate and the street. A win all around without lifting a goddamn finger.

Nigel looked out the window, "When we get home, pull around the back. One of my guys will bleach your truck while you wait."

I didn't say nothing. Just nodded. Turned again, switching on my headlights.

"Crispin was in business for himself," said Nigel all on his own. "Moving contraband, cartel mules, ordinary illegals. Violated agreements I have in place, creating an unacceptable risk for Easy Trucking."

I swallowed. Kept my trap shut. Mainly 'cause nothing came to mind.

"Do you know what *Hadud* is?" he asked.

I shook my head, "No."

"It's Arabic. Translates to boundaries. More in the sense of lines you cannot cross without consequences. I first heard it when I was deployed in I-raq. I was intrigued, then fascinated, then became a believer. It refers to the Islamic system of crime and punishment. Whatever you may think of Muslims, I'm quite the fan of their justice system. Simple, logical, no leeway."

Nigel lifted the grocery bag. It was soggy and red. *Oh, god.* I started feel queasy about what part of Crispin was in the bag, but uncertain and afraid at the same time why I needed to be educated. Nigel turned on the light inside the truck.

"In Crispin's case, you don't compete with your boss while you're on his payroll," he said as he untied the handles of the grocery bag. "And use my resources to do it."

He opened and tilted it toward me so I could see inside. Good thing I spent a lifetime repairing open wounds and broken bones, or I would have hurled for sure.

"That's stealing," said Nigel. "Times two."

Inside, were both of Crispin's hands, cut off from wrist down.

"Jesus," I croaked, unable to stop myself.

"*Hadud* mandated punishment," Nigel added without acknowledging my shock. "Stop."

It took me a sec to react, then I pulled over. Nigel picked up the knife, turning it toward me, grasping the handle in a way you would to stab. My entire manner tightened. *I'm fucked if he wants to kill me.* He outweighed me two to one. The spot he'd picked was ideal to dispose my body. This deserted stretch of road ran right alongside the Mississippi. He didn't even have to carry me. Just open my door and yank me out. I'd slide right down the embankment and wash downriver. *Why will he?* I done nothing wrong.

Tossing the cigarette out the window, he smiled full of admiration, "So, what do you think?"

I realized he was talking about this Islamic justice. I mustered, "Effective."

"Isn't it?" Knife in gloved hand, he asked, "You want to tell me about the girl out of California you're training on the side in Baton Rouge?"

"Hi. This is District Attorney Arlen Taylor. Boz—can I call you Boz? I'd appreciate it if we could meet, say around seven, after you get off? I'll text you the address." Nothing cryptic about it. Except, it was left on his personal cell, with the emphasis to come after work, he'd never met the man, *and how the hell does he know to call me Boz?*

Boz knew Arlen's face. Passed his giant picture at the end of a long line of his predecessors every time he went into the 'OFFICE OF THE DISTRICT ATTORNEY.' A modern concrete and glass box on White Street. Boz mostly dealt with one of the boatload of ADAs—Assistant District Attorneys—handling his case. ADAs did all the work—paperwork to litigation. The DA played overall boss, publicly elected and "committed to advocating for crime victims, protecting public safety, defending the interests of the State of Louisiana, and upholding justice in a firm, fair, and ethical manner." That's when you threw up or laughed, depending on which side of corruption you occupied.

Boz saw no harm in taking the meeting. The address he texted took Boz to a hole-in-the-wall deli, *Tremayne*. Barely fifteen feet across, it ran about thirty feet deep. A handful of bulbs in recessed cans. All working but dim. The first couple of tables were taken.

They'd never met, yet the owner, 60, 5-7, 230, long, sallow face, pointed him to the back. Maybe because Boz looked like a cop through and through. Aided by the fact, being so hot, he wore no jacket, and his badge and piece hung around his belt.

"Something to drink?" asked Sallow Face, as Boz walked by.

"Beer. Anything dark," Boz said without breaking his stride.

Even though Boz never called back to say he was coming, Arlen waved from the last booth in the rear as if he expected the detective to show. Boz's guard went up the moment they shook hands. One reason, Arlen acted with easy familiarity, the diametric opposite of Boz, who preferred being distant, using dry, stern-faced humor to make people wonder.

"Are you operating on some sort brightness quota?" asked Boz, when Sallow Face brought over the beer.

"Customers choice." Code for discrete, shady, call it what you want. *So that's how this place stays open.*

"The current Mayor is retiring, if you've been following the news," Arlen opened. "Made the sudden announcement after he was diagnosed with prostate cancer. So, there is going to be a Special Election next March—two Tuesdays after Mardi Gras." Pause. "I'm running." That would explain the outgoing demeanor. Arlen sipped what looked like gin, then continued, "So is the Chief of Police. He's already thrown his name in the hat." Boz knew that. "I haven't, not yet, and it depends, not entirely, but in large part, on how our meeting goes."

"You haven't heard, then," Boz replied. "I operate on an island. Solve the cases assigned to me alone, show up in court when I have to, and don't give a flying fuck about squad room politics since I've plateaued myself out of promotions. I'm radioactive. My Commander knows better than to even assign me a partner. Guilt by association is a real thing if you're looking to climb the civil service stairway."

"Well, then, now I'm certain I have the right man."

"I occupy rock bottom."

"So the only direction available is up."

Boz smirked, "Tossed that ladder a long time ago."

"OK," Arlen laughed. "Let's finish our drink and call it a night, then"

Boz recognized the bait. Obliged the DA. "Shit, Arlen. I drove all this way. Might as well find out why someone, with the smarts to pass the bar and cut enough throats to become District Attorney, reached out to a pariah."

"You don't think I did my homework?" Arlen said smugly. "I have access to every personnel file and I have kids on my payroll who can hack into any system if I need more. You graduated from the Academy tagged 'most likely to go all the way.' A huge deal, since your father, his, and his, goes back generations, were cops here in New Orleans as long as we've had a force. They all served with distinction, but never cracked a promotion beyond Commander. You, with your good looks, were going to be our first made-for-TV Chief of Police. Then all the promise went to hell in a hand basket."

"At least I didn't lose my good looks."

"Another reason I called you. There are a whole lot of corrupt NOPD cops who can do what I want, but they all have faces for radio. I'm in need of a good looking asshole."

"I am that."

"Sorry," Arlen chuckled, "and as insensitive as it may sound, I mean it sincerely, I am so glad you made a mistake at every turn of your police career. Starting with a routine traffic stop that killed your partner."

"Internal Affairs couldn't pin anything," Boz quickly clarified.

"You were hitting on the eighteen-year-old hot driver instead of frisking her. She was a nut with a gun. You were a rookie, so you got a pass. Two years later, you took up with your lieutenant's college freshman daughter. Not an offense, but poor fucking judgment, when you refused to accept she was in it only as a summer fling between semesters. Stalked her. Broke into her room. Avoided charges by accepting a transfer from the First Police District to the Fourth along with a 'watch-him' notation on your file. Remarkably, you stayed out of trouble long enough to pass your test and get promoted to Detective."

"I scored in the top percentile," said Boz wryly, "if we are rehashing details."

"Yet cursed with an uncanny knack to step in it. A twenty-year-old woman was murdered. Little doubt who did it—the boyfriend, who had a history of domestic abuse. He accused you were sleeping with the victim. Probably why he killed her."

"A junkie's word against mine."

"But you put your hands on the suspect, forgetting the interrogation room has a camera. He walked. After the bad press, Commander shipped you off to where you are now, the Third Police District. IAD moved your file to the top drawer because it would only be a matter of time before you invited them back.

And you did. The boyfriend turned up dead six months later."

"Unsolved to this day."

"Due to the fact the murder followed the CSI handbook." Arlen snapped his fingers for a refill.

"I was never charged."

"You were not exonerated either."

"I passed every lie detector test."

"You like your women young, don't you? And have a hard time moving on." Arlen threw up his hands. "No explanations necessary, Boz." Sallow Face stopped three yards away. Arlen nodded. Sallow Face stepped up and refilled the DA's glass. "I brought it all up only as an FYI. I read your file cover to cover and let me reiterate, I'm happy you're a fuckup. This assignment can be redemption."

"Am I'm looking for one?" Boz didn't even waste a smile. Signaled he did not want another beer. Sallow Face left.

"America is all about second chances."

"No need to sell me, Arlen. I'll vote for you. I don't give a fuck who is Mayor."

Arlen moved the folder, sitting all along in front of him, a few more inches closer to Boz. "Interested?"

"With my uncanny knack to step in it," Boz threw Arlen's words back at him, "I need to know more."

"Of course." Arlen gulped down a chunk of his drink."The current Mayor is going to endorse the Police Chief, who has more than twice the deep pocket donors I have." Arlen became deliberate, pausing for punctuation, "But there's one mega-donor, if taken down, could dry up the rest." He leaned back. "See, what rich fucks fear most also, guilt by association."

"Who is he?"

"I need a hard yes."

"Am I going by the book?"

"Book isn't even in play, since it will be off book. The Police Chief can and will shut it down if he as much gets a whiff."

"What about my Commander at Third?"

"He recommended you for the very qualifications that

make you radioactive," smiled Arlen, sitting down. "Also, he knows I think so highly of him, he'll be my first choice to be the next Chief." The casual and genial tone of this conversation minimized Arlen's ruthlessness. *That's a damn good politician.*

"Now that we've covered the back scratching and back stabbing—"

"Think scorched earth with this takedown," Arlen waited a beat before he filled the void of Boz's deliberate incomplete thought. "It'll disgrace the Chief and expose corruption in every branch of law enforcement across Mexico, the US, and Canada."

"Well, fuck, now I'm too intrigued to say no."

Arlen held out the folder.

Boz opened it. "Nigel Hansom."

According to Dusty Saldana

"Power ain't talent," be the first thing I said to Jenny when she showed up at the gym Day One.

"You say that," she replied, "but Puma only noticed me because I kicked my opponent's ass to Tuesday."

She was right about that. I tilted my head, arched my brows, neither here nor there. We headed over to a bag I'd moved to the far corner, away from the regulars, young'uns among them unable to stop and stare as we walked by. This kinda joint saw few chicks, definitely never one in the gorgeous category. Jenny didn't notice, cared even less, by the rubbernecking. Having grown up looked at all the time, she took it for granted. More likely, expected it, and perhaps was pissed if guys didn't pay her heed.

I'd set up a camera on a tripod and hooked it to a laptop on a stool. "Everything you do, we gonna put on tape. We also gonna study Dempsey, Tyson, Andy Souwer, others. Break 'em down. See what make them great. Most trainers don't care for numbers.

I do. When MMA start, you fought standing up 30%, but now that's how long you're on the ground. Everyone's a headhunter, eight outta ten punches being thrown at your noggin."

"I can attest to that."

"But it also be the one you miss with most. If you can land three outta ten, you're better than 80% of the fighters. Four outta ten top 90% of fighters."

"Shit, Dusty, I came to train," Jenny rolled her eyes. "Not write a fucking paper."

"Oh! God forbid." I wanted to nip this in the bud and stepped behind the bag. "So show me what you can do with your hands'n legs."

"Prepare to be impressed," Jenny nodded.

Approximating the real thing, I'd divvied up the punching bag, front and back, into three sections, and scrawled with thick sharpie: *Head, Torso, Legs.* I turned the bag a couple times around the chain. "The bag gonna swing and spin. You got sixty seconds when I say go." I held up a stopwatch. "Go."

I shoved and released the bag. Stepped back. The clock started ticking down. The bag moved side to side, unwinding.

Jenny started with a one-two combo to the 'head' that rattled the chain, then threw a knee to the 'body' that left a deep dent in the bag, four more more punches, and showed off with circling around for a kick to the head again.

"Time."

Jenny grinned, all cocky, "Questions?"

"Just one," I could be quick with smartass comebacks too. "Ask me what you did wrong?"

"Nothing?"

"Almost every fucking thing." I went blunt with her, "You landed eight shots, about two less than the average ten per minute at the UFZ level. Your feet might as well been bolted down when you throw punches. Your roundhouse at the end look pretty but take so long even an old fuck like me coulda jerked off and finished."

"With or without a blue pill?" she smiled.

"You can spurn or learn?" I was done with her not taking nothing serious.

"You should that put in a Chinese cookie."

That's it. "Pack up. Fuck off." I slapped the laptop shut. "I'm done."

"Shit, Dusty, I was kidding."

"You probably used to guys swallowing everything you shovel 'cause their dicks are calling the shots. You want this to work? This is a holy fucking church. What I say, you accept as honest to God truth. No games, no attitude, no room for interpretation. Save your joking, shut your face, do as I say, or get the fuck back to la-la-land. I'm OK returnin' to living a life of low fucking expectations. Ain't the first time Puma gonna be disappointed neither. And you can return to thinkin' you can fuck your way into the big leagues!"

"Oh-kay." Jenny threw up her hands. "Don't get bent out of shape. You're the boss."

Not a scintilla of humility in her tone. She simply wasn't capable. Didn't offer no apology neither. I didn't expect her to. Part of me liked the unrepentant bitch in her who cow-tow to nobody. I'd never have to worry about coddling and babysitting her for the malady afflicting a lot of fighters—insecurity and self doubt.

"You're nasty hip'n above," I conceded, "no question."

I walked her over to the wall, marked her height head to toe, then her wingspan, fingertip to fingertip. Then we measured both.

I double took. "Holy shit. I knew you had big hands and long arms at first sight, but," I wrote on the wall, "Sixty-eight inches tall, and a wingspan of eighty! That's 1.2 ratio. Making you a rare freak. More'n even Ali and Jon Jones."

Jenny smiled, "A compliment."

"Don't get used to it. Bringing us to reach advantage. If the other girl's the average MMA Bantamweight, which is usually the case, standup fighter like you should win three outta four with your wingspan."

"I have no intention of losing even one."

"Then we need to get you strength trainin' twice as long to get you equal strong, hips down." I sauntered over to the laptop. "Your legs right now ain't up to par."

"Guys I fucked would disagree." Then right away, threw up her hands, "Sorry. It's reflex. I'll work on it."

"I ain't asking you to lose bein' sassy." But she needed to learn to save her bravado, mean streak, and inability to feel sorry for anything, anyone, for when and where it was needed—in the ring, during a close fight, when the last card to play was simply the will to win.

"That is one thing I don't need training for."

"Believe it or not, that part of your charm."

"I know, right?" Jenny teased.

"First off, you need to add to your strikes per minute be it punches, kicks, knees. That'll come once you clean up your feet. From the punches you just show me, you squared up. Nothing wrong—there a time'n place for going dead-on. But when I see you doin' it, seem like it come natural. That make it a bad habit you need to rid. Don't, and you open yourself to all sorts of damage."

Jenny nodded, attentive and serious.

"You do everything right handed, I notice. Write, eat. But you fight southpaw."

"You know about the PFL fight where I was demolished? I read about the southpaw advantage and decided to give it a shot—I was a decent switch hitter in high school. I went underground for six months. Retrained myself as a leftie. Never looked back."

A quick learner. I didn't tell her. It'd take off to her head first. "Southpaw advantage's a real thing when you go up against an orthodox fighter. Stats show better accuracy, more takedowns. But! Against another southpaw, it's the opposite."

"Simple solution—I fight righties only."

I didn't merit that with neither smile nor response. "Punchers not necessarily born, most definitely made." I ran my forefinger and thumb on the laptop. Brought up a bunch of thumbnails. I clicked on one. "Mike Tyson. Watch how he throw punches" I played a clip from a fight against Evander Holyfield. "Whatja see?"

"He springs forward into his strikes."

"Break it down even more and you'll see are four parts to every punch he throws, which is just as strong Round 1 as it's in the last. Graspin' that concept will making you judicious about exerting power in, power out, every punch, which, in a fight that go the distance'll tire you out. Come Round 4 and 5, what you land'll get weaker'n weaker. Follow what I do."

I demonstrated. "One, your feet, everything start there—and yours? Calling it shitty be a compliment. You just stand still lead-footed and swing. You gotta fall it forward. Decisive. Two, then take your weight one leg to the other. Three, turn your hip deliverin' the blow includin' whippin your shoulder to the core. And four, lunge up'n finish off transferin' the weight."

I watched her, corrected her, and made her do it over'n over, the rest of the session. "It should come as second nature, then squarin' up become a tactic you toss in as a surprise that sign the other girl's death warrant. OK, until you get to ten strikes a minute with your hands, feet'n head right, we ain't trainin' on nuthin' else."

When we broke for the day, Puma thumped over with his cane. Jenny and he'd made the trip together from L.A. to Baton Rouge in his Ford 150. He allowed her to park her stuff and 1999 Chevy in his garage in case the dream crumbled. By the time they arrived, I'd already set them up in separate, one-bedroom, fully furnished apartments. I rented them on different floors, so there'd be no privacy issues. Puma looked at Jenny the same way she did back at him. Her face always softened for Puma, and *only* toward him. *OK, she's genuinely fond of Puma, trusts him.* At least, as much as she trusted anybody, which, from what I seen, was absolutely no one.

I pulled out a dog-eared paperback, *Championship Fighting*, by Jack Dempsey. "You ain't just muscling up, you're gonna work that brain of yours too."

Jenny couldn't believe it, "Reading?"

"Fightin' smart is just as important as fightin' hard."

"I thought I'd left books behind when I quit school."

"Think of it as college you didn't finish. Because I got a lots more homework as we go along."

She snatched it. Unhappy. "Is there goin' to be a quiz?"

"No need. I'll know you ain't done your reading the way you move your feet and strike." When she got to the door, he warned "I know, soon enough you're gonna want fuck buddies and explore the French Quarter up in New Orleans. Just saying, use protection and a good head."

"Don't need one if I just do the other." Jenny winked.

Puma chortled. I smiled too. *She's a handful.*

"I'll be an angel, papa." She left, the door swinging shut behind her.

"Fiesty'n a vixen."

"Ain't the worst thing in a fighter," Puma grinned.

I left to drive eighty miles and an hour'n change—New Orleans was the next major city over—to work with Nigel's fighters. The schedule worked out as if the good Lord intended. 'Cause Nigel liked to show up after his nine-to-five obligations at Easy Trucking, I'd set the start time for training at one in the afternoon and we worked till 9 PM. The fighters liked sleeping in. That opened up my mornings. More important, since Nigel had no cause to pry, I did not have to come up with evasive answers what I did every morning.

Jenny didn't complain neither. Turned out, in L.A., she always woke up at 5 AM to run. She made it a point to show me her fitness watch to prove she'd put in the steps I insisted. I didn't doubt her. Her eyes were dead dedicated. She showed up to train by 7 AM. Never late, her apartment being around the corner from the gym, whose owner I knew from the circuit. Puma did too. An ex-boxer, Stan Kelly, 68, 5-8½, 168. Good guy. Irish to the bone, Stan languished in the bottom drawer. Gave up trying around thirty, like yours truly. He smartly banked most of every purse, unlike yours truly, and found a government gig in Public Works. After he put in enough time to make his pension the same as his take-home pay used to be, he retired and opened this place. From the scant membership I'd seen, Stan broke even, just about. Most fighting facilities, love of the sport kept 'em open, not profit.

Puma arrived around 9 AM every day with breakfast. Jenny never grumbled about the strict diet I imposed like the law. She could go off it every Friday night and Friday night only, I warned her. If she cheated, I'd find out when when we measured her body fat. Meaning, she'd have to run and burn it all off before we'd resume training. She lifted every day, and about a week later, threw her head back and roared when I said we'd be doing yoga too, which she came to appreciate after intense sessions I rode her to brink. We always finished up watching tape of her from the morning. I pulled up previous days and showed where'n how she'd improved.

She soon understood why I harped about studying stats. "Next level up, in the UFZ, judges keep tabs, jabs to power strikes." Jabs helped measure reach and range, be a distraction, or set up something more lethal. What followed the jabs won you points and matches, none more important than the power head and body strikes—punches, kicks, anything and everything that landed where you intended. "Going to the head, jabs and power strikes about even. When you target the body, you can double the strikes with only half as many jabs, and they are about third to the legs. How can you use those numbers?"

"Use body blows to set up a KO to the head."

"Someone done her reading."

I had to hand it to her. Once we squared away boundaries and expectations between us, she took to training like a junkie to sugar. One plus of graduating high school and a few months in college, she'd watched all the right Youtube videos to get into the cage. Anderson Silva, Edson Babros'n the likes for Muy Thai. Demian Maia for BJJ—Brazilian Jiu Jitsu. Daniel Cormier, Randy Couture, for wrestling. Boxing with Conor McGregor.

She understood the complexity of MMA. You had to be good at multiple styles because there was no telling your opponent's forte. She be ahead of the curve there, but nowhere near starting one when it came to breaking down what made those guys so good.

"You never watched any women," I noticed.

"They are good within their own league," she replied, "but side by side, they are a universe below the guys. I think."

"'Cause girls don't have the muscle strength for some things."

"Tell me something I can't do, and I'll show you I can."

I left that alone. "You can get good at any style with practice, but the trick be to creating lethal combos for everything you get throwed in the Octagon. Most times on the fly."

"Isn't that your job from the corner?"

"I can scream what you gotta do till I'm blue in the face, but showing patience and stickin' with what you ain't comfortable with—now that separate the great from the good."

"Message received. Here and now, I'm committing to be great."

"Let's not get to the end of this book," I put the kabash on getting ahead of ourselves. "We barely outta chapter one."

"Just spoiling the ending for you," she winked, unfazed. This girl didn't lack confidence. Misplaced or not, the jury still out. Being a smartass came natural to her, which I started to cotton to, even laughed with her sometimes.

As for the jocks in the gym, they gave up in short order. She emasculated them in a way they'd never heard, "Show me your cock. Let me see if you're worth my time." "Foreplay would be searching for you dick." "Fucking me is special. So I have to castrate you after because I can't have that penis reused."

This guy, 24, 6-1, 163, inked only where a suit'd cover, pulled up in a shiny white Mercedes. One of 'em on-and-off regulars neither I nor Jenny'd seen before. Nothing subtle about him—aggressive, thanks to being rich, entitled, and good looking, you know, the formula for arrogance and unable to grasp rejection. Poor bastard made the mistake of stepping in front of her when she entered. "Hi, I'm Dean. You're just, shit, wow!"

"I know, right?" Jenny's catch phrase before she flung acid. His smile widened. She looked at his crotch. "Hmm. Is your junk missing? Or do you have a cunt, not a cock."

Laughter erupted. Dean's face turned red. Likely spoiled his entire life, always getting his way, he lost it, spat, "You fucking bitch."

"Really, Dean?" Jenny said, awful calm, and I got nervous. "You hit on me first. Now it's my turn." Addressed the others, "Only fair, right guys?"

She dropped her bag and slapped him across the face. Dean didn't expect it. Fire leapt into his eyes. He had gloves on and raised them to retaliate. A mistake he regretted the next second. He didn't stand a chance of even laying a hand on her, regardless of whether he planned to hit back or not. I saw Jenny's entire manner transform. I never seen a monster, but she turned into one. And the way she beat him had to be a felony.

"I'm sorry!" Dean pleaded. "Sorry, stop! Please stop!"

Jenny laughed. When the guys on the nearby bags started to move forward, she snarled at him, "I will put you cocksuckers down too!"

By the time I got over as fast as I could, it looked like Dean needed plastic surgery. His face was a bloody mess. He curled up to protect himself from the vicious kicks that rearranged his kidney and juiced his nuts. Jenny saw me and stepped away. Her demeanor changed like she flipped a switch. Became the Jenny with a mouth I been training the past three weeks.

Casual like, she crinkled her nose, "Damn. I may have squared up again."

"Walk the fuck away," I said sternly, my mind racing how to clean up this mess.

Jenny strutted off shaking her ass like a hooker sure of business.

Stan came running out, asking, "What the hell happened?"

I helped Dean to his feet. Broken nose, cut lips, chipped teeth, probably black and blue bruises under his workout clothes—

nothing not salvageable, ego to injuries. Of course, he went to the go-to line for rich fucks, "I'm going to sue!"

I held up a hand, quieting Stan, whose face understandably dripped with concern, and took charge. "You don't wanna do that."

"You think I'm joking! Maybe I'll call the cops too."

"Then we have to give a statement. Guys here'n I can't lie. You made the first move. See, Dean, this a gym to work out, but you chose to pick up a date. And the way you did it seemed clear, if you ask, a girl should just happily hike her skirt." Doubt crept into Dean's eyes. No one jumped in to deny the facts I laid out. "You're welcome back if you just wanna train. Make a federal case and I swear it'll turn into a public embarrassment that dredge up other past sins I know pricks like you have aplenty." Dean said nothing, which I took as acceptance of my terms. "Stan'll fix you up. Go to a doctor, don't, that up to you."

Jenny looked over as if nothing'd happened when I got there. Something needed to be said. "He punch a bag to be fit, you train for a living. Hardly a fair fight."

"So, I could've killed him," she said, dead serious, making the hair on the back of my neck stand, "and I didn't."

"He was begging for you to stop."

"Not his call. And my prerogative entirely, once he opened his pie hole." Then she laughed, "Kind and merciful, fuck, Dusty, you know that's not me. Never been, never will. Building on the wisdom of Hall of Famer, Terrell Owens," an American football player legendary for his ego and antics, "I love me a whole lotta me!" Then she threw up her head and shouted, addressing, "Under Armor! You should endorse me! I protect this house!" Under Armor was an apparel company with the tag line, 'protect this house."

If she intended to make me wary of her, she sure as hell succeeded. *Is the contract we signed even worth the paper it's written on?* Puma gave me some solace. She'd never fuck him over. *Or, will she?* That fear became moot, when Nigel dropped the bombshell at knife point, three months into training, "You want to tell me about the girl out of California you're training on the side in Baton Rouge?"

It took a second to sink in. We were stopped alongside the Mississippi, coming off Nigel just murdering Crispin Martinez. Fear had a chokehold on me, under the circumstances.

"Jenny Sharp, nineteen," Nigel added, knife ready to plunge. *How the fuck does he know?* "Bantamweight. Virgin fighter." Meaning, she hadn't stepped into an UFZ ring. "Built up quite the rep as a badass bitch. Hasn't lost a single fight club match."

I didn't mind he kept talking. Gave me time to carefully choose my words. *Less is more.* I swallowed, said, "I'm training her on my own time."

"Young, beautiful, white—how likely is it she'll stick with you if you can't get her into the UFZ, and how likely is that, what with you suspended for six more months."

"She's not going to be ready for six more months, the earliest," I blabbed like a condemned man trying to talk his head outta the noose. "'Sides, it's not like trainers and promoters were lining up then, or now. She was wiped out in the one PFL fight she bought her way into. Her manager, Jenny'n I have a deal in writing she can't fight without me in her corner."

"Come on, Dusty," Nigel scoffed. "There's no contract money can't break." He jabbed that knife back and forth at me, "Why would you hold out on me anyway?"

"Bluntly?" I needed to show some spine, as foolhardy as that seemed, what with my life on the line. "We aren't looking for a partner."

"Shit Dusty," he shook his head, "I'm the only one who believed in your ability to train again." At that point, I thought I was going to take his grim disappointment to my grave.

Fuck it. I should grovel. Justified why my life should be spared, "I'm grateful and I'm showin' it by working my ass off with your fighters. Number of 'em you've been able to unload's jumped tenfold since I started. You said so yourself."

"UFZ is a mountain everyone wants to climb. You have a fighter with promise."

Will he kill me right here and now if I decline? I couldn't be sure. More likely than not, I revised.

Then, he didn't ask, but simply decreed, "I want in."

I gulped and nodded. After what I seen him do to Crispin Martinez, I knew to take him serious.

"Excellent!" he beamed as if *he* gave *me* a chance of a lifetime.

Nigel climbed out of the truck with the grocery bag containing Crispin's decapitated hands. He tied the handles to the tire iron and knife to weight it down to the river bottom when he tossed it into the Mississippi.

Splash! As they sank, my relief surged along with apprehension.

When I told Puma—leaving out Crispin's death by unnatural causes, of course—he took it better than I expected. I'd driven directly here to Baton Rouge after dropping off Nigel—that how much I was rattled. I wrung my hands, paced around, "We are in his city, his state—if there's a Mafia here, he's it."

"Seem like he give us no choice," said Puma, calm, which I ascribed to him being sleepy and not grasping the gravity of the situation.

"You OK with it?" I was surprised.

"We have to be, no?" He sat with the cane between his legs. Sage like.

"I guess."

Nigel walked into the gym and Puma cordially shook hands saying, "Your rep precede you, Mr. Hansom."

"Some of it good, I hope," Nigel smiled.

"Fuck, no. We wouldn't be here if any of it was."

Nigel roared, and Puma with him. I smiled thinly.

I decided not make a stunt of this by inviting a guy into the ring. I found a female fighter, Stefani Alameda, 29, 5-6¼, 135, Brazilian. She'd racked up a 9-7 record in a bunch of UFZ approved leagues overseas. She happen to be training in New Orleans. Agreed to show up only after I assured her, no, she wasn't gonna be a sparring dummy 'cause I'd insisted to Nigel, "If Jenny don't pan out, don't say we misled you with a patsy."

He bankrolled the Brazilian. She came without fanfare and

just as quietly got into the Octagon. She looked and behaved like a pro, jiving with what I read about her online. I'd cleared out the gym. Stan knew Nigel, and not in a good way. I appreciated his honesty. He left to take a long lunch. 'Twas just Nigel, Puma, myself, Stefani, and her trainer.

Jenny sprinted outta the lockers. I saw Nigel's face light up. *He loves her already.*

"Jenny Sharp. I'm Nigel Hansom."

"Prepare to be impressed, Mr. Hansom," she flashed her teeth and jogged into the Octagon.

"One five-minute round," I announced, stopping at the gate "Stefani's trainer will ref this."

Stefani's trainer, 46, 5-9¾, 171, New York attitude and accent, walked in. I shut the gate. Stefani extended her hand for a prefight fist bump.

"Oh, fuck off," Jenny sneered. Nigel beamed.

That disrespect set the tone. Tension became a physical thing between the two women as they walked off to their corners. Neither'd seen the other fight. That being the case, Stefani was trained to do what I'd taught Jenny this past month—use setup jabs to test the opponent's reach. The way Jenny come outta her corner, like a maniac bull that seen red, distancing didn't even come to play. Pummeled in a significant strike—a straight left which snapped the Brazilian's jaw. *Genius.* Stefani was expecting a 'spotting' jab from Jenny's right.

On her heels with the first punch, Jenny landed two power head strikes. *PowPow!* Right-left. Almost identical force, one hand to the other. Even if Jenny wasn't a true southpaw, her training to become one—partly also being more ambidextrous than she gave herself credit—made both her arms equal strong.

Whabam! Jenny unleashed a perfect high leg kick that had to've released shockwaves inside Stefani's skull. Her knees buckled. Jenny brought hers up, connecting this time square under Stefani's jaw. Like a door flying open, slamming a wall, and return bouncing, the back of Stefani's head contacted her spine and return-jerked up.

I knew how Jenny's mind worked. She didn't want Nigel thinking she was only sensational on her feet. She covered the open canvas in the blink of an eye—made me swell proudly 'cause we'd worked on quickness—and wrapped her hands around Stefani's legs for a shooting upper body takedown. Judges in a fight would have recorded it as a 'slam' on account of the bone-crunching force with which Jenny drove Stefani into the canvas. *Game, set, match.* It was over.

Fran Shamrock, who'd recorded the first slam KO way back in '98, would've been proud. Jenny stood up and looked down, striking the same iconic pose Muhammad Ali made famous when he wasted Sonny Liston. I'd played Jenny the video a while back. I shoulda known she'd take away celebration before technique.

"Holy fuck, Dusty!" Nigel slapped me between the shoulder blades so hard, I stumbled forward. I never seen Puma stretch his lips that far to his ears'n flash so many teeth.

Jenny, true to form, pranced over to Stefani's trainer. Shit, his face coulda been in an illustrated dictionary to describe disbelief. He'd likely be still processing the demolition on the drive back to New Orleans. Jenny gloated, "Did she forget this was a fight, or is she just that bad?"

"Jenny!" I snapped. "Be a sport. Help her up."

"Sorry," she apologized insincerely. Almost distastefully, I'd say, she yanked Stefani to her feet, and the devil surfaced yet again, "Quit the Octagon and spit out babies. It's that time in your life and career."

The Brazilian didn't respond, likely still surfing stars.

"Show some class," scolded the trainer.

Jenny gave him the finger, emerging from the Octagon. Nigel fawned over her, Puma proudly in tow. At least one of us should be courteous. I patted Stefani, thanked her, and pointed the trainer to the back of the gym, "Lockers are back there. First-aid kit. Need anything? Holler."

"Your girl's a shitty piece of work," he said bitterly and they walked off.

"That was beyond impressive," I heard the last bit of Nigel's flattery as I sauntered over. *Don't feed her ego no more.*

"I know, right?" She shamelessly self-promoted, "Sir, you didn't think I'd let you come all this way and be disappointed?"

Crafty bitch. The 'sir' lifted Nigel's adulation into a hard-on.

Puma sprinkled more fairy dust. "That's with just a month of training. Imagine where she be after six?"

Nigel looked at me. "I always said you're a helluva trainer, Dusty. Now that you have talent to work with, you are proving it. This is going to be LSU all over again, coach."

"Before Dusty says it, I will," said Jenny, "I'm nowhere near ready. I still have a long way to go."

Fucking chameleon. Add that to the list I'd started about her, sly and manipulative being at the top of it. Her tone right now, shit, that was honed by a girl always scheming to get ahead in man's world. *Look at Nigel.* As accomplished a businessman as I ever knew and a ruthless killer, she had him eating outta her hand.

"I know you haven't stepped into an UFZ Octagon," he smiled like a prospector who'd struck the vein of gold he been searching all his life. "but I can't help make the comparison to Rousey and Nunes."

"That's flattering, Mr. Hansom," said Jenny. "But I have my sight is set on being used for comparison and not being compared to."

I had enough of this back and forth stroking. "Jenny, change and come back."

"Don't talk business without me," Jenny said, changing gears again, her tone all shop and no nonsense.

"Yes, ma'am," Nigel nodded. *Respect.*

She flashed a million dollar smile and hurried off.

"What she's got, you're only born with," Nigel gushed. "God given raw talent."

"Sometimes raw remain just that," I cautioned. "Raw. For every success, there's 99 athletes experts swore was the sure thing but flamed out in the pros."

"That would be on you then," Nigel's eyes went flat for just a moment, then sparkled back up, "shit, you turned me into an

Olympic gold medalist and world champion twice."

"Fighting's a little more complicated than heaving weights over your head," I said.

"Come on. You're licking your chops too."

"I would be too," Puma kept laying it on thick for Nigel. "Even I'd look like a genius, harnessing just a fraction."

"Instead," I said, having had just about enough, "just so happen, you think of me right after I started working for Nigel here."

"What are you gettin' at?" Puma's eyes flashed.

"You think it's a lucky coincidence that the three of us are standing here? Slick planning's more the way I see it." From the moment Puma shook Nigel's hand, an ink drop of suspicion been oozing and growing. Now, it was a dark splotch of certainty beyond reasonable doubt. "I shoulda seen it when I told you Nigel wanted in. You went, 'oh, well.' Matter of fact. Calm. Too calm. You! A paranoid bastard who didn't trust his own mother shunting you outta her womb in nine months. Stupid me, I didn't put it together till Nigel walked in and you started lap dancing him like he was waving C-notes."

Nigel's eyes narrowed. "You want to fill me on what the hell is going on?"

"Ready to cut the bullshit, Puma?"

"Bullshit?" Jenny appeared. She'd changed into sweats. "Is there a problem?

"Fuck yeah," I said angrily. "Trust, or lack thereof."

"Dusty thinks you brought him in to get to me?" ventured Nigel.

"Yeah," Jenny shrugged, "so?"

I accused, "I shoulda known you'd be in on it."

"It's not a fucking conspiracy, Dusty," Jenny sneered. "Know how many promoters and scouts wanted me? I turned them down because they could only offer me nothing I couldn't already achieve on my own. Unless Puma could come up with something more concrete than a fucking pipe dream, you think I'd have hitched my wagon to two geezers—one who's been off the grid for a year and can barely walk, the other a blackballed trainer?"

"Promise of another bottom feeder made the difference?" I was pissed, but that don't mean I didn't immediately regret them right after the words spilled out. If nothing else, I discovered the meaning of a 'pregnant' silence.

Puma's face tightened like I never seen. Even Jenny knew I'd mebbe gone too far.

Back when Nigel hired me, I'd shot my mouth off without thinking, tarnishing his I-10 circuit. When something's said spontaneously, he said, it's the truth you feel and believe. I had to soften the blow. "No offense, Nigel."

Bastard knew how squeeze blood outta stone, and did, with this silence. He let it go for a beat longer than needed to make his point that he could take it personal or turn the other cheek. Finally he laughed, "I call it good business acumen and planning on their part, targeting me as their end game. Who's going to give you a fight that'll qualify her for UFZ? I have the kind of money that'll kick open doors."

"So, why haven't you, all these years?" I'd burned half the bridge, so what the hell?

"I'm a businessman. I need to see viability."

"I'm guaranteeing nothing."

Jenny stepped in. "I will." She looked at me, "So, the pressure is on you, Dusty, if you are as good as Puma and Mr. Hansom seem to think you are."

Sly bitch. She lobbed the ball into my court. *How badly do I want this?* I been waiting all my life. Walking away'd make me a chicken when it come time to deliver.

"The four of us, we are a motley quartet of low lives, you know that?" I said, being brutally honest, since I was well down that foolish path.

"More like a nest of rattlers," said Puma "Living cozy and entwined, but respecting each other's bite and venom."

"Trust Puma to find the perfect analogy," said Jenny. Then grinned, "Works for me." She looked at Nigel. "Now that we have a venture capitalist, a new deal is in order. Starting with a move to New Orleans."

"No!" I nixed it at once.

"Why not?" asked Jenny, "Aren't you training fighters there already?"

"We stay here," I said firmly. Looked from her to Nigel. "She's a legit fighter, taking a legit shot. I don't want no risk of cross contaminating, if you know what I mean."

"It's not like Puma and Jenny are unaware about the I-10," said Nigel.

"I wanna keep us separate," I said firmly.

"OK," Nigel gave in.

"Let's talk numbers," said Jenny.

"Mind if I smoke?" Nigel asked. All of us knew it was rhetorical because he'd already pulled out a half empty pack and lighter.

Puma and I agreed to the industry standard—ten percent of every purse. Nigel added a weekly wage, which was sweet. We could stop emptying our nest egg, like we been, paying Jenny and Stan to rent the gym. Jenny, shit, she didn't kid around money. Asked for and got a grand week, on top of rent. Nigel threw in a car with a gas card until she could afford both. Since Nigel was footing every expense, they went back and forth, and settled on a 50-50 split of the remaining pot. *He's going all in and all out.*

"One last thing," Nigel said in all seriousness, looking from Puma to Jenny, "Since you brought me in, eyes open, I'll insist you keep a lid, L-I-D—loyalty, integrity, discretion."

"I came out of fight clubs, where they just plagiarized the movie, rules one and two being, you do not talk about fight club." Jenny smiled, "I like keeping a LID better. Fucking clever." Seriously, "That said, I'm assuming the punishment is unpleasant. Perhaps harsh, since you have more to lose—stature, infrastructure, investment."

Nigel smiled crookedly toward Puma, myself, "I should name her my heir apparent."

Everything was working out hunky dory, yet I couldn't shake

an itch I couldn't justify. *Is it the mega-shadow Nigel cast?* The real threat of harm he brought which wasn't there with just Puma, Jenny, and I? That I never suspected Puma's ulterior motive? *Is Jenny the real deal?* Or, how everything just fell into place?

If it's too good to be true, it usually is.

Puma Song: Recollections from River Road, New Orleans

Whack! Jenny swung from a squared up stance and connected. *Whoom!* In the next cage, to her left, Nigel, puffing a cigarette, swung and missed. *Clang!* Nigel's ball struck the iron netting. *Whoom! Clang!* Dusty, who stood to Jenny's right, not only missed, but toppled over. He staggered back up just as the next ball came whizzing at him. *Whoom! Clang!* He tumbled back awkwardly with a cry.

Throaty laughter erupted. It came from chubby midget, 39, 4-1¼, 120, Puma observed sidle out of the night. His long sleeve Nike jumper came off the kid's rack. Light stubble, sad but engaging eyes, wide flat nose, and long hair tucked behind the ears. If he weren't an adult, you'd push the kiddy swing for him—he had that kind of genial face and manner. No disappointment, none whatsoever, being little. On the outside, at least.

Dusty, Jenny, and Nigel occupied the first three in a row of five batting cages. A yard behind each, bolted to the ground, were metal benches, dark green paint peeling here and there. The midget leaned over the first one, behind Dusty. Puma sat behind Jenny, cane between his legs. The hearty laugh be Pint Size's first move to introduce himself. He wan't fooling Puma, who'd inhabited cesspools long enough to see the runt for what he was right off—an artist who'd spotted four easy, marks. In the con game, this be called '*The Put Up*.'

"Shit, Dusty," Puma played along, "you got Pint Size here laughing like you the main-act freak at the county fair."

"No, no, no sir," Pint Size objected, his voice as disproportionately deep'n loud like his laugh. "You couldn't be further from the truth." *Well spoken little shit.* "More like watching Charlie Chaplin slapstick."

Puma laughed. Like any huckster, making effortless conversation came easy to Pint Size. Dusty stumbled back to his feet, leaning back to avoid the next ball whizzing by.

Pint Size roared again. "Oh, come on now. That was vintage Dick Van Dyke!"

Onto ingratiating himself. That be '*The Rope*.'

Jenny took the bait, looked over. Her lips cracked in a wide smile. "You are adorable! Always wondered how it would be to bone a dwarf."

Pint Size opened his short doughy arms with a big, harmless grin, "Wonder no more."

That tickled Jenny even more. "Stick around. I may carry you home with me."

It wan't that late, 'round 9, Friday night, about when festivities got kicked off in New Orleans. But then, they'd started eating'n drinking at 6 PM in a restaurant called River Road, on account it being addressed along River Road, which snaked right along the edge of the Mississippi. More a sports bar than a fancy joint, but nice enough for Nigel's stature. Of course, the manager knew him, and tucked them, exclusive like, in a corner with a waitress more or less dedicated to their table. Patrons talked loud, laughed loud. Drinks flowed freely. As dinner progressed, the noise and slurring volumed up all around, not just at their table. By 8 PM, the four of 'em were smashed, having their glasses refilled non-stop with every kind of booze, which began sedate and polite, with beer, when they sat down, and Nigel toasted, "Look at us. As ragged a group of oddballs as God ever thought fit to assemble. But it's working."

"Chemistry's like shit," said Jenny, clinking her glass. "It just happens."

"Nothing just happens," Dusty piped in, utterly disdainful. "What unite us is failure and unfulfilled dreams." Clinked his glass next "Damn you, Jenny, for cursing us with that poison called hope."

"Trust you, Dusty, to suck the air out of the party." Jenny tapped her glass last.

"But misery always perks me up." Dusty chugged down, kicking off the drinking.

Gradually, the talk made less'n less sense as they got more'n more bat-shit sozzled, combining all sorts of hard liquor together into cocktails that was never meant to be. Around 8:45, they walked across the street to the batting cages, which were closing up, but Nigel made it worthwhile for the twenty-something custodian to stay longer. The kid hustled up four scamps, 12-15, 4-9 to 5-5½, 78-118, who looked straight out of the projects nearby, to play ball boys. Nigel promised them twenty bucks each—more'n they probably handled, except by dealers they had to pass everyday coming'n going from their crappy public school. Puma knew 'cause that was his childhood in South Central L.A.

Pint Size's idea for an easy score likely snapped on same time as the cages lit up.

Whoom. Nigel missed again. *Clang.* "Aargh!" he yelled angrily. "These balls are all outside the strike zone!"

Whack! Jenny connected again.

"That's a varsity stroke," Nigel observed, "if I've ever seen one."

"Played all the way through the high school," Jenny replied. "Named best short stop two years running."

"That position all about hand-eye coordination," Dusty piped in. "Honing that at next level will make you a killer in the Octagon." *Whoom. Clang.* Dusty swung and missed, turning a full circle.

Pint Size slapped his knee, cackling.

"Maybe I'm more of a bowler," grumbled Dusty.

Whack! Jenny met the ball with the meat of her bat.

"Shit, girl," Puma admired. "You're on fire, even drunk." He turned and said to Pint Size, "I discover her."

Pint Size casually tossed loose change—a quarter, a dime,

and a nickel—up into the air and juggled them adeptly. There it was, '*The Con.*'

Whack! Jenny winked toward the good looking black kid, 14, 5-0, 105, street written all over him, picking up loose balls gathering around Nigel and Dusty. He grinned back, all smitten. She smiled back, "What's your name?"

"Kewan," he replied.

"You've been staring at me like candy you want to taste," Jenny said.

"Sorry," Kewan became all awkward.

"Shit, no, Kewan. I enjoy being looked at, so, don't you dare stop." *Whack!* "I like boys, Kewan. Do you like girls?"

Whoom! Clang! Nigel hollered, "That pitching machine is rigged!"

"I seen this game," Puma said, after watching Pint Size juggle for a minute. "I'll bet a dollar."

"Bet a dollar on what?" asked Pint Size, brows arching, all puzzled.

"Which hand's holding the dime when you stop juggling—isn't that the hustle?"

"Hustle? Come on now. I have legs barely eighteen inches long, bowed at the knees and wider than a chick in stirrups on a gynecologist's table. Which takes running away off the table, which in turn makes being a crook a bad idea from a business and personal injury standpoint. But yes. I do juggle to pick up extra cash from tourists in the French Quarter. Not in the way you're implying, you know, the crooked, sleight of hand, Three-Card Monty on a street corner crate."

"Really?" Puma asked skeptically. "How often do you lose?"

"Enough, believe you me, to make this only a part time gig. Only crate I use is the one I stand on all day behind the reception desk at the Best Western." *That explain his silky speech and manners.* "This is not a guessing game. It's a fair and square contest. Your vision skills—good eyes, keen observation—versus mine as a deft and speedy juggler. I'm not a hustler, shit no. I couldn't sleep at night, worse, look Father O'Donnell in the eye every Sunday at church."

Puma slurred extra for effect, "I'm old, I'm cynical, OK?"

"You should be in this day and age. Also, it's 'spot the quarter.' Being the biggest coin, it further shifts the game in your favor. Also, I myself have no idea into which hand the coin falls." Leaning the odds toward the sucker be '*The Tale*' in con lingo.

"Ok, quarter it is. Let's go."

"Oh, no. No. I can't in good conscience take your money. No offense, but I see the cataracts in your eyes."

"Shut the fuck up, Pint Size, let me play!" Puma insisted angrily. Being drunk made the outburst adamant. "I ain't going to the poor house losing a buck."

"True," Pint Size backed off, raising his shoulders. "One game, no more."

He showed Puma the three coins, the quarter in his right palm, the nickel and dime in his left. He dropped the quarter into the left hand. "Ready?"

"Go for it," said Puma.

Puma chucked them in the air. Not too high. They rose barely a foot. *Pint Size be good, very good.* He clearly'd been at this a long time. His hands circled, crossing and uncrossing with the same blazing speed that the coins rotated up'n down, in'n out of his palms. You couldn't make out which one was the nickel, dime, or quarter. Just silver streaks.

"You tell me when to stop," said Pint Size. "That way you're in control, further eliminating any charges of hanky panky on my part. Like I said, I don't know myself until I open my hand."

"You speak good," Puma squinted suspiciously. "Shyster like."

"Shit. You're close. I tried and failed the L-SAT twice. Lucky guess, I hope," Pint Size raised an eyebrow, smiled, "or you're the one hustling me."

Puma didn't laugh. "Stop."

Two coins fell into Pint Size's left hand, one into his right. Then, he turned 'em over, knuckles to the sky. Puma slid his eyes left, then right, back left, not letting on that he knew Pint Size'd rigged the game before the first coin even flew.

"Cataracts affect my sight, you said," sneered Puma. "Let's see about that." Puma tapped the right hand. Pint Size turned it over to reveal the dime and the nickel.

"Shit!" Puma looked away in disbelief. "I was hundred percent certain. OK, again!"

"No, nonono!" Pint Size shook his head vehemently.

Whack! Jenny continued her hitting streak.

"Good thinkin', Pint Size," Dusty said from the cage. *Whoom! Clang!* The ball went by well before his bat arced embarrassingly slow. "Walk away. Not 'cause you're a buck ahead, but 'cause Puma not been entirely upfront. A few casinos banned him for countin' cards as fast the dealer shuffle 'em."

"Shush, there!" Puma slapped the air with his palm, all the while winking at Dusty with the eye Pint Size couldn't see. Dusty grinned back. "Those sins belong to my youth, long time ago."

"I dunno." Being the good actor every con's gotta be, Pint Size brought on a doubtful expression. This part, treading reluctantly on the part of the artist, called '*The Breakdown*,'' tap into the gambler in everyone—the part where you thought you'd surely do better the second time.

"Come on, Pint Size," said Puma, "you've gotta give me a chance to win my money back."

"OK," Pint Size relented after deliberating for a long beat.

Little fucker milk that well. Puma clapped his hands like a kid, "Yes!" He pulled out a crumpled note. "I wanna bet five!"

"Five? I have to check if I can match that," said Pint Size, reaching for his wallet. *Oh yes, you can.* Puma let Pint Size keep up the charade, turning a listenin' ear to Nigel and Jenny, leaning on either side of the chainlink separating their cages, while they waited for the kids to load up the pitching machines.

"Some guy sponsored you for a while?" asked Nigel, crushing out his cigarette.

"Fucked me, sponsored me, tomato tomāto," she smiled like she gotten away with something. "If I'm being honest, I walked into that one with my eyes open. Being hot is one thing, but if you're also intelligent enough to realize guys and dicks are inseparable, it can be a way up and out. But I wasn't ready and he knew nothing about the Octagon. After I got my ass handed to me, I told him we were done. I had sense to cut my losses. Took six months off before I went back to fight clubs, but smarter for the experience—I wasn't going to shack up with the next guy with money, a cock, and nothing else."

"I can cover it," said Pint Size, waving a ten dollar bill.

Puma nodded, "Let's go for it."

Pint Size went through the same routine as the first time. Puma kept one eye on the flying coins and one ear tuned to Nigel and Jenny.

"I'm sure he made you sign something," said Nigel with a tinge of anxiety.

"Yeah," Jenny dismissed. "Don't worry. Nothing that he's going to come back for."

"Wasn't he a lawyer?"

"Yup. So he knows better. I told him that I'd tell the cops he drugged me and raped me," she said with a proud smile, "then sex-slaved me into a fight I'd no business being in. Also, that I'd saved every condom he used to prove the number of times he fucked me." She threw her head back and snickered, "Fact is, I love sex. He came with a cucumber for a penis. We fucked all the time and everywhere. Just think, if I cry as I tell it, that paints a completely different picture. Cops'll see a thirty-two-year-old sex maniac repeatedly assaulting an eighteen-year-old." She looked up and hollered, "Thank you, MeToo!"

"Ready!" hollered the kid from her pitching machine.

Whack! Jenny got right back in rhythm.

Apprehension, doubt, and thoughts you don't want to see creeping in, showed up in Nigel's eyes and stayed on Jenny.

"Ready!" The kid at Nigel's machine shouted. Couldn't have come soon enough.

Puma swiveled back to the juggling. "Stop."

Pint Size turned his hands over. Puma picked the left hand. It contained the nickel.

"Fuck me silly!" Puma threw his head back, all drama. "I

thought I had it! You're right. My eyes be shot. I'm done. Shoulda listened to you in the first place." Glancing away, he noticed, "Where's Dusty?

"Crapper," Pint Size nodded to the Men's Room.

Dusty emerged, pale, under the weather, wiping his mouth.

Whack! Nigel finally hit a ball. Barely. Bouncing it a yard behind the machine. "Finally! A pitch over the middle of the plate!"

"Sorry, Nigel," said Dusty, "most o' the food'n booze you paid for now gracing the drains of New Orleans."

Puma teased, "You used to be able hold a full bottle of Jim Beam."

"That's a shame! Telling you right now, I can't be toasting with mineral water when I claim my belt!" Jenny mocked between pitches. "So, Dusty, if you can't drink, you're fired! Unless you have a better reason to keep you on as my trainer."

"I'll stand up for coach," said Nigel. "Thing about Dusty? Once he believes in you, he becomes a full service support system. In college, at LSU, he banged my Spanish teacher so she'd give me a C to stay on the team." *Whoom! Clang!*

"That'd count as a sacrifice only if the room couldn't be dark enough," said Jenny. *Whack!*

"It's a sacrifice, him pooning anyone," Puma interjected. "All the years I known this sumbitch, granted, I still ain't sure he got a working piston 'tween his legs, but boxing be his wife, his mistress, kids, family, what he eat'n shit. He probably squirt in his pants thinkin' up a new combo."

Everyone laughed, none louder than Pint Size, "Are you the most interesting man in the world, or what?"

"For the record," Dusty said, "The Spanish teacher was a hot jalapeno. I was happy to do her."

Whoom! Clang! Nigel shouted at the machine, "I wasn't in my stance!"

"Seriously," Pint Size said to Puma, "before I leave, I feel morally obligated to give you a chance to win your money back."

"A night of revelations," Dusty smirked, flopping down on

the bench behind Nigel. "A righteous midget."

"'Double or nuthin'," said Puma. Or, '*The Send*.' Upping the wager to extricate yourself outta the negative side of the ledger.

"You don't play around, do you?" Pint Size said. "The math is entirely in your favor. You now have the law of averages working for you."

"I'm done." Jenny tossed her bat. "I gotta piss. Kewan, want to watch me"

The kid didn't know how to react. "Jump at it, boy," Pint Size opined with a lascivious smile. "She could go to jail just offering you this opportunity."

Jenny grabbed Kewan and kissed him full on the lips. Fluttered her eyelids. "I'm afraid to go in there alone."

She crooked her arm into his and walked him into the Ladies Room. If his tongue hung out, he'd be the puppy on a leash.

Puma chuckled, "I love that girl even if Satan reside in her."

Whoom! Clang! Nigel tossed his bat in disgust. "That's it." Nigel hollered to the kids at the pitching machines, "Shut 'em off, boys!" He wandered around to the benches. Lit up again. No nonsense when he said, "Jenny comes with scary dark baggage, the kind you have to watch."

"Before indicting just her," Dusty said, "we're not without rap sheets either."

"At least we have scruples," said Nigel. "She has none."

"Really?" Dusty bristled. "I thought Puma was a friend when he approached me. Mothafucka was just conniving."

"Cry me up a river!" Puma reacted. "You'n I met, counting ringside and bars, about half dozen times in twenty years. Apart from knowin' my wife's name'n how much I loved her, you know shit about me, and I less about you."

"All I'm sayin's let's not give ourselves angel wings and Jenny devil horns."

"And all I'm saying, only one of us is writing the checks. I won't hold it against you if it is money well spent." Nigel then went no-nonsense to ominous, "But if it's something you should've told me and didn't, I will be pissed." Switched up into a smile, "I'm feeling generous tonight. If that happens, I'll give you a running start."

Puma smirked, "Won't do me any good."

Nigel guffawed, and still flashing teeth, "But I fucking mean it. Things better not sour with either of you to blame."

That's fucking chilling. Nigel made the hair stand. Puma noticed the same trepidation he felt on Dusty's face.

The kids approached. Nigel distracted, warming his smile. Opened a bulging wad of tens, fives, and ones. "Time to settle up, huh, boys?"

"Ready whenever you are," interrupted Pint Size, whose eyes gleamed sliding toward the kids collecting. Found Puma staring at him and laughed, "Kids made out quite well. Good for them." He dropped the coins into his right hand and showed them to Puma.

Puma ratcheted up his naïveté, "Third time the charm. I can feel it."

"You got this one." Pint Size tossed up the coins.

"Puma, were you a fighter?" Nigel asked, still paying out.

"As a pro, for about ten seconds. But growin' up in Compton, protectin' yourself start about the same time you stop suckin' your mama's titties." Chuckles rippled. "Fifteen or so, when I started cleaning blood off fight club floors, then holding a spit bucket in corners to working them corners. Shitty fights. Never got much better, save some, but so few I can count 'em'n have fingers left to shake your hand. Hang around enough, you realize talent always jump out, you know, like a good singer. Two bars in, you know if they got the pipes, but more important, they gotta have that somethin' to sing in tune. I come across a few with potential. Don't matter their skin color, but mine they mind. Bein'a Korean nigga somehow don't fit, preferring a white asshole to manage them, no offense." Nigel got it. "Say what you want about Jenny, that girl never show no judgment from moment one." He waved his cane. "Stop."

Pint Size stopped juggling. Let the coins drop.

"OK!" Puma rubbed his hands, not hesitating as he pointed

to the left hand.

"Shit." Pint Size's face turned south.

Puma beamed, pretending that Pint Size's disappointment was caused by the fact maybe he'd picked correctly. Pint Size opened his palm. In it, the nickel and dime. Puma threw his head back like a diva.

Pint Size dripped crocodile tears, "Aw man! I thought you'd nail it this time. I'm so sorry."

"That's it!" Puma declared. "Don't try to talk me into another game." He counted out five singles and gave it to Pint Size.

"Of course not," said Pint Size. "Hey. I didn't want you playing in the first place."

Puma addressed Nigel, "Jenny pull you up on the computer. You were a weightlifter who win Olympic gold and coupla worlds."

"But I tanked royally as a pro," Nigel confessed, paying the last kid.

"And I hitched my entire wagon to him succeeding," said Dusty. "He made out nicely and I joined the ranks of has beens before ever having been."

"Never heard failure put that way," chuckled Pint Size, still with them. *He isn't done yet.*

"Yep. I shoulda been a fucking poet."

"A career which requires you to die to make any money," said Nigel.

"Will I ever catch a break?" Dusty at his bitter best.

Of course, Pint Size roared. Jenny appeared. Winked wickedly, licking her lips, "Kewan needs a minute."

"You didn't!" Dusty shook his head.

"Get off your high horse, Dusty," Jenny dismissed. "It's just a BJ that'll remain the greatest highlight of his life. You think he's going to meet a girl in my league?"

"There he is!' Puma grinned. Kewan emerged, smiling from ear to ear.

Pint Size started clapping. "The hero of the night!"

Kewan's stride become a strut. "He deserves an additional

five, Nigel," said Puma. "Put it on my tab."

Nigel peeled off twenty-five dollars.

"Let me tell you, Kewan is little Denzel fucking Washington," Jenny grinned and threw him a high-five. He met her palm like he just won the lottery. Which, Puma figured, he had. Metaphorically.

And who sees that too? Pint Size.

His eyes got beady and greedy. "Kid, is this your luckiest day, or what? I'm probably going to regret this, want to double that five Puma added?"

And there it is. 'The Fleece.' No explanation necessary.

'Twas the reason why Puma let himself lose money and allow the con go on. He knew from the start, Pint Size's target wan't the four drunk adults but the four gullible kids. '*The Play*' and '*The Rope*', which conmen used to gain trust and empathy, Puma reversed 'em, making Pint Size buy '*The Tale.*'

"No guts, no glory, Kewan," egged Jenny. "You have balls. I've seen them." She bit her lower lip, naughty like. Of course, that changed everything for the kid.

"Fuck, yeah," Kewan said right away. Put the five down.

Everyone gathered around.

"Eight pair 'o eyes on you, Pint Size," warned Puma.

"That would make a hustler nervous," responded the midget. "But this is a game of skill, like I've been saying. Ready whenever you are, Kewan."

Kewan nodded, beaming.

Pint Size opened his palms to reveal the coins. The quarter rest in his right, the dime and nickel in his left. He closed the right palm, turned it over to drop the quarter into his left, curling his fingers in the same time to hide all three coins,.

Before he tossed all three into the air—

Whack!

Puma's cane struck Pint Size's left hand! He cried out sharply in pain! The coins fell to the ground.

Two nickels and a dime.

"Where's the quarter, Pint Size?" Puma asked.

The color drained from Pint Size's face simultaneous with

his scream, which concurred with a sickening, crunchy *whack!* Metal to tibia. Puma's cane to the shinbone below the knee cap.

WhackWhackWhackWhack!

Puma struck without respite, his cane flying back and forth. This horrifying violence against the midget was misplaced, he knew somewhere in his subconscious. An utterly disproportionate response, unconnected to a five dollar con.

Rage, he didn't want to control, exploded.

Pint Size, who hopped after the first couple of hits, fell, and received the brunt of Puma's fury. The sharp cries of pain turned into sobbing screams, which, combined with Puma's incoherent yelling, rent the air with a cacophony of agony and fury. Puma didn't stop. Sprayed saliva.

The kids stared, jaws unhitched.

"Looks like Puma's working some things out," said Dusty.

"I know, right?" Jenny shook her head.

"Poor bastard," added Nigel. "Wrong place, wrong time."

Puma finally ran outta breath. Spit dribbled down his chin. Pint Size wept loudly. Puma reached down and emptied Pint Size's pockets of the swindled money and gave it to Kewan. "Share it equal and don't spend it all in one place. Now, git!"

The scamps fled.

Puma'd exclusively targeted the midget's legs. The cane etched slish-slashing cuts, all bleeding profusely, some so deep, the shin bones lay bare. Where there was flesh, bits of it hung loosely. A weaker stomach'd've turned.

Pint Size groveled, wailing like a flayed pig, when they left.

"You said, you're investigating a murder," said Dusty, who started to get a little twitchy, wondering what this was all about, where this was all headed. Boz offered no clues at all if they were midway or close to the end of the questions. "Whose murder?"

"If you don't know," toyed Boz, "there is nothing to worry about, is there?"

"I'm thinking," Dusty suddenly defiant, "I need a fucking lawyer."

"Sure," shrugged Boz readily. "Of course." Boz swept Jorge's pictures into the folder. "Then we have to take this to the station. Read you your rights. Make it formal. Put you on camera and on the record, while, this here, it's you and me just talking. Nothing admissible." Boz straightened the folder upright and tapped it on its end to line up the papers inside along the bottom edge. Boz leveled his eyes to Dusty's. "Is that what you want?"

The bastard glowered back. *Fucker will blink.* And did. Literally. Dusty defensively reiterated, "I got nothing to hide."

"Then you have nothing worry."

Boz put the folder back down. Reopened it. Turned Jorge's pictures over, face down, to the left, so he could leaf lower down the docs on the right. He kept his eyes down, turning the pages deliberately. Let Dusty stew. Allowing the gears in old codger's brain to engage, slip, and stall. Work through combinations of words, emotions, and expressions to use to keep the law on the other side of the door. Boz pulled out the Driver's License photo of Crispin Martinez.

"Know him?"

Dusty hesitated. Recognition flared in his eyes, leaving admission as the only way out. Surprised Boz when he shook his head from side to side. "I don't know him," Dusty began, then sensibly turned that around, "but I seen him around. He may be a driver for Easy Trucking."

"He is. Nigel got him a green card. Was a DACA kid. Know

that is?"

"Parents bring him as a child to the US."

"Do you know his name?"

"No."

Boz placed another horrific crime scene photo in front of Dusty. His head went back just a fraction. The corpse was mostly skeleton poking out of charred flesh. "Notice, he's got no hands. Coroner said they were hacked off while he was still alive."

Dusty said nothing. Looked up from the photo.

Boz asked, "Anything you want to add?"

"Shit?" Dusty didn't smile.

Neither did Boz. "His name is Crispin Martinez. Sure you can't tell me more?"

Dusty shook his head, pursing his lips.

"A neighbor saw a grey Toyota near the house."

"I drive a Lexus."

"Not always," said Boz. "I checked the Office of Motor Vehicles. You owned a gray Toyota almost seventeen years, before trading it in for the Lexus after you took Jenny on."

"Gray Toyota as common as dogs in a dog park," Dusty retorted quickly. Too quickly. "But I can categorically deny it wasn't me or my gray Toyota."

"I haven't even told you when or where."

"Don't matter. I ain't ever near the man's home 'cause I don't know him or where he live."

"Nigel ever a passenger in your truck."

"I don't recall he ever was."

"The neighbor also saw a driver in the truck."

"Moot," Dusty's bristled, "if I was never there or Nigel never ride in my truck."

"The neighbor swears," Boz read from the report, "his words, 'this really fat fucker—coulda killed someone just sitting on you—got into the pickup on the right side and the truck drove away.' That's Nigel to a T." Dusty just raised his eyebrows, his skin crinkling up a couple of furrows end to end on his forehead. "Do you deny being the driver?"

"Asked'n answered," Dusty said. Short. Then elaborated. Boz let him. "First of all, you think a zillionaire like Nigel would risk everything to commit murder of some driver, an employee to boot? Second, you think he be dumb enough to take along a witness?" A general rule of thumb—perps are lying when they say more than the question demands. As if throwing in an explanation sealed their innocence. Worked to do opposite. Usually meant accomplices worked on their stories together, or they were laying the groundwork for plausible deniability. You know, so they could say, "you misunderstood me" or "that's not at all what I meant."

Boz ignored Dusty's exculpatory hypothesis. "Where were you on the night of May 3rd?"

"Almost a year ago? Sorry. Thanks to the amount of booze I imbibe leading up to this point of my life, not to mention significant strikes to my noggin, I can barely remember what transpire last week. Likely, I was right here, drinking."

"It was a Sunday night."

"Probably, right here, then. If your next question is, was there anyone with me? Probably not. If there was, I absolutely don't recall."

"That answer right there is why Nigel's a fucking mastermind. You're his alibi as he is yours. He kills, but as an accessory, you can't sell him out." Boz laughed, "Maybe you didn't know the purpose of his visit, when he got in your passenger seat, and once you did, it was too late. You knew you were fucked. But I'm shocked you two haven't discussed your whereabouts."

Dusty laughed right back. "You can keep accusing me all you want, but I don't know Crispin more'n a passing knowledge that he worked for Nigel. Didn't even know he was dead, let alone murdered. FYI, Nigel don't involve me in nothing but the fighting part of his business."

"That's just it," Boz retorted. "Crispin belonged to the fighting part of his business. He transported the illegals across the border."

"We are going round and round here."

Yes, I'm circling the drain, motherfucker.

According to Dusty Saldana

"Boxing, kicks, elbows—they are your bread'n butter strikes standin' up," I explained to Jenny, "and the surest way to get a KO or TKO, but account for only a quarter of outcomes in Bantamweight. Equal number end on the mat with a submission. When you look at individual matches, sure, you're on your feet 70%, but it don't matter shit if you tap out during that 30% you're on the mat. You ever win grappling from the bottom position?"

"Never had to," Jenny dismissed. "I've always had top or side mount position. Haven't faced anyone who put me down on my back."

"UFZ have a much higher caliber of fighter. 'Sides grappling's what created this league."

Jenny's parents were probably kids themselves in 1993, when the very first MMA tournament aired on TV. Quite the spectacle. Brazilian Jiu-Jitsu master, Royce Gracie, showed up clad in his *gi*, to fight Art Jimmerson, a big ass boxer, with a 33-18 record. You see, Art entered the Octagon, already nervous, wearing only one glove, so the ref could see him clearly tap out with his naked hand, which Art did in a panic, seconds after being planted on his back. People then didn't even have a name for the simple mount Royce used for the submission. Since then, Brazilian Jiu-Jitsu been as much a part of MMA as flying kicks and knees and elbow strikes made knowing Muy Thai and boxing mandatory to survive, let alone win, in the Octagon.

"So," I pointed behind her, "let me introduce you to Kevin Yang."

Jenny swiveled around, unaware Kevin, 38, 5-7¾, 144, been standing behind her this whole time. Shirtless. In his shorts. Muscles that looked like coiled wires. A dragon, breathing fire, tattooed on his clean shaven head, its body snaking down his spine. That be just the most striking artwork on a torso otherwise inked head to toe.

"Shit, Kevin," Jenny launched into him at once, "how long have you been admiring my ass from back there."

"Shit, Jenny, I'm still looking for it," he could be sassy right back. Puma and I had a buncha prospects for this gig, but knew we needed a horse wrangler unafraid to use a whip.

Jenny roared. "You come forewarned."

"About your mouth, not your talent."

"Those who can't, teach."

I put an end to the back and forth. "Let's get to work. Kevin's part of the team."

Having Nigel as a partner allowed me to hire an instructor Puma and I could never've afforded. Kevin come outta Chinatown in New York, worked as a foot soldier growing up for the Shadows, one of the local gangs. He found Jesus in jail after being ratted out and sentenced to eighteen months for extortion. The prison pastor counseled Kevin to turn his passion and love for MMA into a way outta crime. Upon his release, Kevin dropped off the grid and resurfaced five years later in the Octagon in Brazil—one of the Big 5 cages, second only to the US in MMA. Turned out, he immerse trained in BJJ in some way out temple known only to the absolutely serious. He won his first fight, then traveled wherever the UFZ let him fight, running up a decent 10-8 record. All his victories came with submissions from the ground game, and all his defeats standing up. I worked the corner a couple of fights against him. Folks, familiar with the nuances and beauty of grappling, unanimously consented Kevin was a ground'n pound fiend. Pity he never could master standup and put it all together—he coulda been elite.

"I have seen tape of you," Kevin spoke with a thick New York accent. "Most of your work's on your feet. Your opponents are pretty much done for when you get them on the ground. Didn't see a single escape. My job's to seriously up your grappling skills. Teach you to not just escape, but win off every compromising position you might find yourself on the canvas."

Jenny liked to learn. Read all the books and watched all the tapes I given her. Nothing went in one ear and came out the other. She absorbed information like a sponge and hoarded it like a shylock. Ever since I told her, on day one, she needed to work on her legs, she never stopped, staying late almost every day. 'Twas why I waited until she developed lower body strength to bring Kevin in. Now, his drills'd be worthwhile.

Having her train with a man a full weight class higher toughened her to the talent jump she'd see in the Octagon. In fight clubs, you overcame the disadvantage by clinching your opponent in the middle of the mat or against the fence to mitigate blows, buy yourself time. Not in UFZ, where the clinch occurred for less than a fifth of every round. Judges weren't impressed by the strikes—which were weak, at best—thrown by embracing fighters, and also 'cause they rarely, if ever, ended a fight. The only exception being Anderson Silva, who brought his Muy Thai skills to secure a record never surpassed—more knockdown wins than anyone. He couldn't do it today. Fighters'd come a long way in quickness, strength, endurance, and skills.

"Wrestlers in the MMA," Kevin said, demonstrating upper and lower body takedowns from the clinch, "try to put stand-ups like you on the ground. Because she's on top doesn't mean she can win, just as all is not lost if you're on your back. It's about who's controlling who."

And where TIP— Time in Position —became as important as a pulse for life. Where grappling elevated into an art and a skill, costing you a match regardless of the fact you were T-fucking-Rex while you were on your feet. Unless they were power head strikes, body shots didn't count for much even though they were 80% accurate. Mostly 'cause, they were usually weak elbows, since winding up and landing a fist took time and lose you your position. Didn't matter if you were on the top or bottom, judges favored the fighter they thought was dominating. The fighter playing defense had then better damn well find a way to minimize TIP. More and more, with MMA athletes getting adept at escaping, maintaining position got shorter'n shorter.

"This where you need to get skilled in every kind of choke, armbar, and lock," said Kevin. "Rear naked choke may be the most common and boring, but it's delivered the most submissions. Come Round 4 and 5, and you can't get the fight upright, injuries and fatigue will become a factor, doesn't matter how well conditioned you are. So you need to learn to use your legs for more than splashy kicks."

The next three months blurred by.

Between training Jenny and Nigel's I-10 boxers, I went home exhausted every night. My hands curled into claws. I sat with my bare feet soaking in Epsom and warm water. I could barely grip the longneck of my Corona. On the other hand, for the first time, I felt good. A feral cat, Jenny displayed the same claws inside and outta the cage. Kevin couldn't stop praising her. Puma treated her like a doting father. I'd never seen Nigel smile so much.

Why couldn't scouts see her talent? It nagged me, despite her claim she was picking who'd take her to the next level. I asked around discreetly, making sure it didn't get back to Puma, and especially Nigel, who wouldn't take kindly to me not voicing my misgivings. I came up empty. Nobody outside the L.A. fight clubs heard of her, and even those inside only remembered her as a showboat and unfriendly. They confirmed that she turned down their offers to sign her—never politely neither. I tracked down the PFL fight she lost, and found no record of it, then discovered Nigel had her only loss expunged. A crafty, ruthless businessman, he doubtless'd asked questions too and dug quietly in the dark to verify the authenticity of his purchase before he shelled out a dollar. Obviously he came away satisfied. *Maybe it's just me.* Deprived of hope and luck my entire life, I was simply incapable of accepting my dream had a real chance with this girl.

"Goddamnit!" I lost it. Jenny staggered backward like she been hit in the head. At least she gave me something to complain about. "How many fucking times we gone over this! You squaring up!"

Jenny wore wraparound 3D VR—virtual reality—Goggles. I could see her and her opponent on the big screen TV I'd upgraded to in our training corner. I might have no GPS in my car and own nothing but burners, but I been itching to work with this technology ever since an unknown Flyweight, Charlie Diego, 23, 5-6, 112, put the goggles on me. I was up in San Jose a few years ago, working the corner for a low rate match. Never'd heard of 'virtual boxing' until that night. A couple college braniacs from Stanford'd come up with the idea. They recruited Charlie to test it, hoping to sell it as a training tool for boxers.

Shit, even Angelina Jolie climbing into bed buck naked could'nt've given me the hard-on these goggles did. But I had to be real with these Stanford kids. It'd be a hard sell. Trainers were curmudgeons like me—old school, clinging to tradition, trusting only living, breathing sparring partners. Also, most fighters couldn't afford it.

A year later, I saw they put out a money-making video game version. I heard the kids'd succeeded selling a training version to some top notch fighters, which could be custom tweaked to mimic any opponent I wanted. I never had a prospect worth the expense, until Jenny. As quick a learner as she was in every UFZ style and skill necessary, she drove me up the wall unable to shake her habit of opening her face. Having switched stances to go southpaw, I deduced her brain was inclining her to her natural side as a rightie.

I hoped a virtual boxer programmed to exploit this weakness'd cure her. I approached Nigel, who was impressed right away, same like I was. Told me to go for it. It came with a sensory plug-in, punishing you with a nasty buzz that reverberated between the ears.

"Maybe the first fight you get away with it," I said. "Your opponent after that now have tape on you, then what? They'll make a target outta your face and it take just one significant strike to lay you out. Happen to Tyson, it can happen to you."

Jenny nodded. Went at it again.

"Stop!" I got after her five minutes later. "Shit, girl, we been at this now six months! Angle, angle, angle!" I hollered. "Let's go again."

I noticed Nigel walk in and walk across. He had a broad grin on his face, and I suspected what'd come outta his mouth. "Moment of truth, Dusty. Three-round, six-match Friday Fight Night sponsored by UFZ. Win and you get into the big league."

"Where?"

"San Paolo, Brazil."

"No wonder you left that part out. Let me guess, her opponent is local."

"So?" Jenny peeled off her goggles. "I'll fight anyone anywhere."

"And," Nigel said, "you're the main card."

"Fuck yeah!" She high-fived Nigel.

"How did you manage that?" Being hard enough cracking the UFZ door open, let alone get a foot in. "A no-name, no offense Jenny, on the main card?"

"Money and circumstance." Nigel hadn't stopped grinning. "Remember the very first *Rocky* movie? Apollo Creed, looking for a patsy, picked Rocky."

Jenny clenched her fists, threw up her hands, and danced like Stallone, singing '*Eye of the Tiger*.'

"That was the sequel," I said.

"Yeah," Jenny replied. "The movie in which Rocky won. Six months I've been sparring, hitting bags, and virtual boxers. So, I'm also a caged fucking tiger, dying to hunt and kill."

"Brazil's notorious for judges already picking the local as the winner."

Nigel finally lost his smile. "Then you have your work cut out."

"Shit, Dusty, don't you like a challenge?" Jenny couldn't be contained. "I do." Bringing the smile back to Nigel's face. I wondered if he be this proud when his daughters was born.

"Just so you know, Jenny, there ain't gonna be no three-man posse in the corner on fight night. Just me. So there is just one voice in your ear from the moment we leave here until the end of the fight. I can catch things from the corner you cannot, especially when matters go to the canvas. Also, I can watch the other corner, which way the judges're leaning, things like that."

"What about Kevin?" Jenny pouted toward him.

"My work ends in the gym," replied the man himself. "Dusty's magic when it comes to in-fight strategy and tactics, upright or on the ground."

"Wouldn't you like to wipe me down between rounds, Kevin?" Jenny seduced. "I'll be so hot." Kevin smiled blandly, unmoved. "Carry my spit bucket?"

"I'd tell you two to get a room," I said, "but you're in it."

"Ooohh!" went Jenny. Nigel and Puma O-ed their lips.

"OK, that's enough," I told Jenny, "Back to work." To Kevin, "Teach her acting skills to throw wool over her opponent."

Nigel turned toward me, all business, "All this corner talk will be moot if you can't be there."

Xavier White: Anonymously Sourced UFZ Hearing Notes, Las Vegas

Xavier White, 41, 5-9¼, 225, placed his briefcase on the table, adjusted the lapels of his glistening suit, and sat down. He glanced over, offered up a perfunctory smile, "How are you this morning?"

"Nervous," whispered Dusty.

"Don't be. We got this." If Xavier had been white, he'd just be an ordinary looking, blue-collar lunch-pail. Hardly worth a second glance. Being a very dark African American, with a couple of diamond studs in his ears, a ring on each pinky, plus a blingy wedding band, he received double takes, thanks to good ol' fashioned profiling. Jewelry, his skin color, and stocky stature compelled people, especially guys—and Xavier could actually see their brains straining—to match his face to a professional athlete. Was he a linebacker at one time? Fullback, maybe? And if they ran into him again inside the courtroom, the looks ran the gamut—surprise, curious, you name it. *He's an attorney?!*

"Yep," smirked Dusty. "What can go wrong?"

Xavier didn't laugh. "As long as you haven't violated any of the terms of your suspension, they have no cause."

Dusty looked uncomfortable in the ensemble he'd picked as his Sunday best, none of which should have been worn together. Plaid blue shirt, polka dot tie, and khaki slacks that likely came from his closet of sparse formal wear. Then, he made it worse going to *3-Day Suit Broker* to pick a coat that belonged even less. Awful color and fit. Drooped an inch off the shoulders. On the plus side, it fit Dusty's rough and tumble personality.

A self confessed flashy dresser, Xavier liked silk and gloss—his caliber of client associated that with sharp and slick.

"You haven't?" Xavier repeated, as a question. "Violated any terms?"

"Shit, no," Dusty replied vehemently. "I been a model fucking citizen. Stayed away from the circuit entirely. Kept my head down and my nose clean. Not even a parking ticket. Piss I submitted'll come back cleaner than the Pope's."

"Good."

Xavier was a military kid, born at JRM—Joint Region Marianas—Naval Base in Guam. He covered the globe from Japan to Germany with stops in South Korea and Saudi Arabia before he turned ten. His parents divorced and he moved with his mother to her native Tucson, and never left, until he passed the Bar after graduating from the James E. Rodgers School of Law at the University of Arizona, when he started as a junior in a Las Vegas firm retained by every major Sportsbook. Married a Latina ex-stripper-turned-bail bondswoman. Mutually referring clients, they made quite the decent living. Dusty came via a referral from a fighter who'd needed their services both to make bail and plead out without jail time.

"However much you are inclined to speak," as a trial lawyer, handling criminals from the lowest denominator with little or no education, he used the universal language of clarity, "shut the fuck up."

Dusty nodded.

"Let me do the talking," Xavier wasn't done instructing. "If they ask you a question, don't answer. Look at me. Answer only if I nod. Be brief, to the point. If the answer requires only a 'yes,' 'no', or 'I don't know,' then just say that. Don't elaborate. Any question that needs you to jog your memory, or you have the slightest reservation or doubt, say, 'I don't recall.' Here they come."

Three suits entered via the back door. They were all gathered at the UFZ's Sin City corporate HQ, which was designed with every plug-in money could buy. Quite the impressive multi-acre complex. Designed to serve fights, fighters, training, media, and humdrum admin staff. Disciplinary hearings, however, belonged in the back of the house, off a sterile corridor, in a room deliberately Spartan and stern. Scheduled start was 1 PM, still, Xavier asked Dusty to arrive the night before.

"A flight delay, and you're not here when they are, they'll dick you around months for another date," he told Dusty when they met up for dinner last night at *The Wynn*, where Dusty was staying. Being the middle of week, rooms enjoyed deep discounts.

Xavier adjusted his tie, twisted his neck once back and forth, to loosen it from the collar. More a mannerism than anything else. When Dusty started to push his chair back, Xavier put a hand on the trainer's shoulder, "Stay in your seat. This isn't a court, they aren't judges."

The suits barely looked at the pair while they took their seats. Xavier did not expect they would, busy emptying their briefcase or satchel. Folders appeared, opened, papers shuffled. Nameplates in front identified them left to right: *Randall Goeffrey*, 43, 5-11, 196; *Alan Genova*, 52, 6-3, 211; and ex-ref *Trevor Ross*. All three looked every bit the rule enforcers the UFZ purported them to be.

Xavier wanted to smile, but checked himself. The stenographer, 49, 5-5, 145, came in. She'd been at this a long time, you could tell, arriving with her own table, chair, steno machine, and the quickness and familiarity with which she set herself up to the side.

Dusty should thank his lucky stars. Everyone on other side wasn't just white, but buttoned up white, and his attorney was not just black, but pimp black. They had to be extra careful not let their first impressions of Xavier in any way slip out as words that could be mistaken for prejudice or stereotyping.

"Good morning, gentlemen," said Alan, seated in the middle, and leading this proceeding.

The other two looked up, Randall friendlier than Trevor. Xavier said cordially, "Good morning, hope you are all doing well this morning."

"First, some housekeeping." For the record, Alan identified himself, the suits on either side of him, Dusty, Xavier, and the date, time, and purpose of the hearing. Then, he extracted the folder halfway down the stack of about six, maybe, and opened it. "I'd like to just review why Mr. Saldana was suspended—"

"With due respect," Xavier—a trial attorney, he appeared in courts with overloaded dockets and jaded judges, who only responded to aggressive lawyering—interrupted sharply, "this is a reinstatement hearing. Details of the why, how, when, and where of the suspension are irrelevant since a punishment was already handed down."

Alan was a retired judge and Xavier expected he'd behave like one. "Neither I nor Mr. Ross were part of the first hearing," Alan said firmly. "We didn't receive the transcript till last night and have not had a chance to fully review it. If you want, we can set a new date."

"No," Dusty interrupted at once, standing up."I'm fine to tell you what y'wanna know."

Xavier snapped his eyes over, glaring at the old trainer.

"You can speak sitting down, Mr. Saldana," said Alan.

Dusty sat down, leaned over, and whispered, "Sorry, but I need this done today."

"OK. I'll take it from here then." Xavier looked at the suits. "Mr. Saldana was hired—"

"We'd like to hear directly from your client."

"I object."

"You can't," snapped Alan. "If you're uncomfortable to let Mr. Saldana speak—I don't know why you'd be, if he is repeating facts already on record—we can adjourn till we familiarize ourselves with what happened—"

"I'll tell you," Dusty piped in again.

Dusty stood out as the alpha in this room that wasn't lacking testosterone to begin with. He continued like he was instructing from the corner. Unapologetic, sounding a little angry even, as if he shouldn't be here having to explain himself. *Lack of polish may work out better than legalese.*

"I got nuthin' to hide," said Dusty. "Johnny Cortez—he go by his fighting name, Muerte Cortez—hire me for a UFZ approved fight in Oklahoma City. I came on just a week prior to his match against Rubin Hovick 'cause I worked the corner for Rubin six months prior. Muerte wanted me to prep him—you know give him my first hand knowledge of Rubin's tendencies'n such. Rubin still won. KO'd Muerte second minute of Round 3."

The staccato of the steno machine played like background music. Instead of typing words letter by letter, each key represented a sound, and that's how the stenographer kept up.

"He gave me an advance when I arrived," Dusty continued, "with the agreement I get the balance after the fight, win or lose. I showed up in his locker to collect and he welshed. We had words. I walked away. I get to my truck, Muerte's trainer come runnin' and have the audacity to ask me to treat the mothafucka's cuts. He was bleeding pretty bad, havin' taken quite a whuppin' for most of the fight."

"Where was the arena physcian?" asked Trevor. Xavier had backgrounded him. Upstanding, respected, without an even an inkling of dirt, his career as an UFZ ref ended with an induction into the Hall of Fame.

"They couldn't find him," replied Dusty.

"Should have come up in the first hearing," said Alan, the ex-judge.

"It did," Xavier took that one. "The physician testified he called Muerte's locker room. Nobody answered. So, he left."

"Did Muerte's manager confirm that?"

"When the UFZ's investigator reached out to Muerte's manager, he said he didn't remember."

"The physician's phone records could've easily confirmed if he called or not," the judge in Alan kicked in.

"Sir!" Xavier raised his voice, exasperated. "We are not retrying Mr. Saldana today."

"He used the venue's intercom," explained Dusty. "Cell phone service not the best in 'em basement lockers."

"This is all ground that was covered and considered when the UFZ suspended Mr. Saldana," Xavier added, his patience running thin.

"Phone likely rang," interjected Dusty.

Shuddap! I'm trying to end this. Xavier couldn't glance over with withering eyes. The suits might take it the wrong way.

Dusty went on, "But it got pretty loud 'tween Muerte and myself. His manager maybe ignore the phone when it ring, concerned with keeping the argument to words not fists."

"Was it coming to that?" asked Randall, speaking for the first time. A career nine-to-five pencil pushing Human Resources rep, Xavier had Randall's card from the first hearing. Randall's job entailed risk management, getting ahead of any blowback.

"Muerte'd just lost," Dusty said. "He was pissed. Fighters never blame themselves for being shitty. They got too much ego for that. Of course, who he gonna point the finger at, but me. So, yeah, he was looking to kick the shit outta me. Even hurt as he was, he still be a heavyweight, thirty years old to my fifty, forty-nine at the time, with arthritis. I could tickle him, max."

Xavier chuckled. Nobody else did.

"You agreed to treat Muerte, then?" asked Alan.

"Didn't want word to get around I refused attention to an injured fighter and cost me gigs. I always bring my corner tote, regardless this fight I worked only as a consultant. So, I went back and treated the bastard outta decency. The audacity then of

Muerte's daddy to file a complaint I wan't as diligent as shoulda I been. UFZ took his side, ignoring the fact I was there voluntary and did his sumbitch kid a favor. Anyway, I left after I treated him."

"Quite a few omissions in your story there," said Trevor, hostility rising.

The ex-ref has a beef. Why? Xavier spoke up at once, "Those are the main points. Muerte hired Dusty. Muerte refused to pay Dusty. Yet Dusty put that aside and treated Muerte. In fact, before he left the second time, Dusty wished Muerte a quick recovery."

"You can check your papers," Dusty said. "I shook his hand and I said, 'no hard feelings. Thanks for the opportunity. We'll settle up one way another. Good luck and good night.'"

"By settle up one way or another," accused Trevor, "you meant laying in wait and assaulting him in the parking lot."

"The police would've charged Dusty, don't you think?" argued Xavier.

"There were no cameras in the parking lot."

"In fact," Xavier added, "the detective indicated Muerte's habit of not paying bills had earned him lots of enemies and any one of them had motive to put him in a coma."

Alan sat up, "Coma?"

"Yeah," Trevor replied. "Muerte never came out of it. He died a week later. His father, Hector Cortez—part of the first class of MMA refs, consensus Hall of Fame inductee after he retired—never got over his son's death. I knew Hector. Mentored me into the ref I became. He died three months after Muerte did." Resentfully direct to Dusty, "Nothing wrong with him, doctors said. Just couldn't live with the grief."

"That is tragic," Xavier took a grim tone and the attention off Dusty, "but unfortunately not in any way relevant to this hearing." He swept his eyes from one man to the next, "To be blunt, all of you are here only to verify that my client has fulfilled the terms of his suspension.".

"UFZ has confirmed that Mr. Saldana has," said Randall, the

HR drone, looking over to Alan and Trevor. Not concealing he wanted nothing more than to stamp 'CLOSED' on this report and bury it—after all, Dusty and Muerte were a couple of unknowns.

"OK then," said Alan. "All in favor of reinstatement."

Randall raised his hand. So did Alan. Trevor, Xavier anticipated, would not and did not. Mattered not. Dusty only needed two of three.

"Mr. Saldana, you are reinstated, effective immediately," pronounced Alan.

Dusty smiled, not toward the suits, but Xavier. "Thank you. I brought my check book."

He reached into the inside pocket. The suits gathered their stuff.

"Promise me you'll toss that jacket on your way out," ribbed Xavier.

"After using it just this one time?" Dusty responded. "Hell, no. I'm returning it for a refund."

Xavier laughed, sliding his invoice. "If you have a social conscience you'll destroy it."

The suits left while Dusty cut a check. "I need to hit the head."

"Me too." Xavier tucked it into his wallet, which he slipped into his back pocket.

They headed into the Men's Room, tiled in all white. Found it empty, the doors to the two crappers ajar. They took the urinals on edges, keeping a vacant one between them.

"You flying back out today?" Xavier smiled over.

"Yep. I'm prepping for a UFZ authorized fight in Brazil next week. That's why I needed this taken care of today and why I be eager to speak up."

"You did all the work, I got all the money."

Dusty laughed. "You wonder why they say killing a lawyer ain't a crime but a good start."

Xavier roared.

The door opened opened. Alan and Trevor walked in. "No way he could've knocked Muerte into a fatal coma," Alan was saying. "You saw him, he's fifty, an arthritic alcoholic—"

Alan broke off, seeing Xavier and Dusty turning, zipping up.

"Don't for a moment think this is the end of it," Trevor launched in. "I didn't mention it out there, Hector and his wife were like family. Muerte was my godson. I held him when he was baptized. Take this to the bank, I'm going to make damn sure every UFZ judge and ref knows what you did."

Xavier shook his head imperceptibly, signaling Dusty to keep his cool.

"I think the arena physician was probably on his way," Trevor accused. "You intercepted him, poisoned his mind, and told him turn back around, knowing the manager would then be forced to come for you to treat Muerte. Manager was the one who found you and hired you in the first place, right? After Muerte passed away, y'all three covered for each other. Low life cretins rather collect favors and IOUs, not be ostracized as rats."

"Fact you stand up for a scumbag like Muerte," Dusty spat. "mebbe there's dirt to be pulled out of your self-righteous Hall of Fame ass."

"You scumbag piece of shit!" Trevor advanced angrily.

Dusty put up his dukes, "Bring it on mothafucka!"

"Trevor," said Alan grabbed the ex-ref. "Don't waste your breath."

Xavier shepherded Dusty, "Walk away, Dusty."

"You weren't there to stop the blood," Trevor wouldn't stop, raising his voice as Xavier opened the door, shoving Dusty out. "You doped him through the open wounds, then waited in the parking lot, and put him in a coma."

Xavier shut the door. Kept hustling Dusty forward. "Unable to control yourself," said Xavier, "and saying more than you should is how you can trip yourself up. You don't have Double Jeopardy protection. UFZ can reopen the case."

Dusty nodded. Pulled himself together. They made the final turn to the main lobby.

"I have to admit, that was a good theory," confessed Xavier. "Do you have one?"

"Remember O.J. Simpson?" An African American football star accused of murdering his ex-wife and a waiter back in 1995. Sparked a sensational trial in Los Angeles. Xavier'd been a kid, who didn't much care or follow it. In law school, though, he learned how years of misconduct by a racist white LAPD and black rage acquitted OJ, despite overwhelming evidence against him. "I'd refer you to the book he write coupla years later. *If I Did It.*"

The automatic sliding front doors opened.

"Goodbye and good night." Dusty smiled, winked, and walked away.

According to Dusty Saldana

I yanked off Jenny's robe. The crowd, who'd loudly booed her swagger down the aisle, turned it up times ten. Jenny circled the Octagon, gesturing them to bring it, even put a palm to her ear, like they weren't loud enough.

"I love that girl!" Nigel hollered in my ear. He flew in this morning. Dressed to the nines in a suit that probably cost what all the people in the bleachers here earned in a week.

Puma did a jig, waving his cane, egging the crowds dislike.

The Mayor of San Paolo, with ringside seats behind the opponent's corner, stood up, plucked the microphone tossed to him outta the air, pressed it to his lips, and yelled into it. Not that anyone noticed or cared that static wrapped his greeting.

"*Olá, Olá, Olá San Paolo!*" Portuguese for 'hello, hello, hello San Paolo.' Silence ebbed down in dying waves. "*Você está pronto?*" Are you ready?

The crowd emptied their lungs for mebbe two full minutes, before the Mayor signaled them to quiet down again. The cheering subsided for a Brazilian fight night tradition.

"*Uh vai morrer,*" the Mayor chanted into the silence. "*Uh vai morrer.*" You are going to die. You are going to die.

The audience joined in, one section at a time. Like it was choreographed. I knew it wasn't. I been in arenas all over Brazil. These fans grown up knowing the rules of this ceremony. It started with the power of one, multiplied exponential from there.

Within a minute, 21,000 fans chanted as one, "*Uh vai morrer! Uh vai morrer!*"

Jenny loved it, danced to the center of the cage, and threw up two middle fingers. Nigel, in the front row, stood up and cheered, circling his fist over his head, hollering, but looked like a silent mime. We been here a week and Jenny made sure she climb to Public Enemy #1.

This fight topped all trending on all of social media. I can't deny I loved the attention, having labored in corners so anonymous they coulda been in Witness Protection. It began with Nigel. He distributed her picture that made a plain Jane outta even a stunner like Rhonda Rousey. Throw in, him reaching out to his nefarious and powerful 'you-know-what-I-mean' partners, local TV showed up the morning after we landed.

Jenny was doing laps in the pool, which I made mandatory almost right after we began training together. Swimming increased endurance, cardio stamina, lung capacity, core strength, but importantly, worked joints and muscles to reduce injury long term. Jenny being Jenny, and Brazil being the home of Gisele Bündchen—you know, supermodels and naked sunbathing—she come outta the pool dripping wet and nude, head to toe.

It didn't surprise Puma and I one bit, familiar now that inhibition be forbidden from her dictionary. In fact, we put over-under money how long before she pulled her first antic.

We simply leaned back and enjoyed the show.

Jenny played to the rolling cameras, sexily toweling herself and slamming her opponent.

Within the hour, the internet blowed up.

Nigel called me, elated. *Is it even possible a 323 lb. man can jump up and down?* Sounded like he was doing just that. Euphoric, mebbe a better word. He said UFZ blogs stateside gone crazy.

Jenny Sharp? Who is she?

In the five days that followed, her name spread like that Covid-19 which shut down the whole planet. Nobody be immune. The craze as much about her Playboy act—that being pretty much global—but here in Brazil, how dare she insult the hometown favorite she was fighting?

Who presently made her entry.

Sienna Venâncio, 26, 5-7½, 133, aka Cyborg II.

The chanting switched to feet stomping cheers, so raucous I coulda been standing at the epicenter of an earthquake. Just as flamboyant as Jenny's entrance been, Sienna flapped her shiny cape—the Brazilian flag—and strutted down the catwalk, turning full circles, throwing kisses back.

If I'd just walked in, you coulda fooled me we were half hour behind schedule into the second hour of Friday Fight Night and the final bout of six cards. The decibels slapped you in the face, such was the bursting force of this energy, all pent up with anticipation, unleashing like this was the first event after a drought of boredom. They remained revved up through the announcements, then went a notch higher, if that was even possible, when the fighters left their corners.

Powpowpowpow!

Jab-jab punch-punch. A quick opening exchange, equal strikes on both sides, kicked it off. None of them significant. Both girls were jacked up. Neither wanted the other thinking she was going to let this fight last longer than a round. They stepped back after this volley.

"Pay attention to her leg!" I yelled.

Jenny didn't hear, likely didn't listen. Too busy twisting up a disrespectful grin into her face, beckoning Cyborg II to give it her best shot.

Whabam!

Based on the set up left hand jab, Jenny expected a right fist. Cyborg landed a lightning left leg kick to the right side of the head instead. Jenny never moved. Never saw it coming. The crowd roared. Cyborg II closed in a flash for a shooting takedown.

Down they went.

Fuck! Sixteen seconds in and the Brazilian'd taken the fight to the ground, where she'd made her name like her idol, Cristiane Justino Venâncio, aka Cyborg—the original one—a Brazilian powerhouse from the Chute Boxe Academy, an MMA nursery for several homegrown big names. Sienna came outta the Chute as well. Coincidence, not family relations, be the source of her last name, but modeling her style after the original was no accident. Inevitably, fans saw her as the second coming of their most famous female star and dubbed her Cyborg II.

She ended up on top in full mount—the 'layup' of all grappling positions, where Cyborg straddled Jenny. I caught Jenny's eyes, waved three fingers frantically, shouting, "Go now, go now!"

Cyborg II launched into knocking the living daylights outta my girl, every contact the judges likely counted as a significant strike. Jenny heard me. Squirmed, trying to turn around as if to avoid the fists of fury raining down on her face.

Cyborg II's lips twitched.

I recognized the Brazilian's thought process. *The American rookie is panicking into a rollover.* A no-no in grappling 'cause Jenny'd be letting the Brazilian take her back—meaning Jenny'd be face down with Cyborg II rodeoing her into submission. Cyborg II eased up to allow Jenny dig own her grave, but kept landing punches. Nothing as damaging as the moments prior. Even though she was giving up TIP, Cyborg II knew, once she took Jenny's back, the American loudmouth was done. But then—

With no warning, showing acting chops of a magician who has the audience distracted one way to sneak a rabbit into the hat—Jenny reversed direction in a flash! Cyborg II, her eyes and mind looking ahead to where she thought she'd be reading Jenny's last rites, was completely duped.

Cyborg II's knee, loose off the ground, lifted completely.

She lost leverage.

And just like that Jenny advanced into a side mount.

The audience gasped!

"Lil girl!" Puma shouted, grinning, working to his feet. Swung his cane. "Lay the fucking wood!"

Crack! Jenny's bare knuckles flattened Cyborg II's nose.

Our first significant strike.

The Brazilian didn't faze, Jiu Jitsu being her style of choice. Jenny wanted the judges to have to give her TIP love, but we'd talked about it. She wan't gonna win by decision, not here, not even if she dominated Cyborg II, who'd paid her dues for a ticket into the UFZ. At the time of the pairing, I reminded her what Nigel said—this fight been set up as a mere formality.

But that changed on the way to the party. Jenny stormed up a PR hurricane and made this a spotlight match. Losing it would not only negate Cyborg II going undefeated this past year, but seriously damage her credentials for admission into the big league.

Still, I was the one worried.

The bout so far been fought on Cyborg II's terms. On the ground. On average, grappling produced two submission attempts per round, but only 20% of them succeeded. So far Jenny'd proved the stats right, escaping Cyborg II's first try. On the other hand, nobody come close to getting Cyborg II tap out, and the likelihood of Jenny being the first seemed remote. Leastways, right now. Only 'cause Brazilians be born learning Jiu-Jitsu. Before Cyborg advanced guard—shifted Jenny to defense—Jenny had the option to bring the fight to her.

"Stand it up!" I said.

Jenny heard me. Sprung to her feet.

I don't think Cyborg II expected it, took a second to reprocess, not much more. In MMA, defeat came outta a millisecond of hesitation and victory by less than a millimeter of accuracy. As Cyborg got to her feet, Jenny was not just already on hers, but had completed two of the four components of a Thai-style whipping kick. One, her lead foot was turned toward the Brazilian, and two, hip thrusting and leading the kicking leg. Three and four were fucking poetry. Cyborg II came to her feet to glimpse Jenny into her hip turn that provided maximum force. Jenny crunched her abdomen to tie her core to the strike.

Whabam!

Cyborg II's mouth O'd to funnel out air ejected from her lungs. She suffered another break—a smaller rib, from the sound of the hard bone of Jenny's shin caving into Cyborg II's chest just above her belly.

Clang! Cyborg crashed into the fence.

The crowd subsided. Tasting blood, Jenny closed in for the kill, and learned her first lesson. Cyborg II ain't the patsies in fight clubs that Jenny usually at this point finished off with an upper or lower body slam to the canvas. The Brazilian recovered. Dawned on her, maybe for the first time, she had a fight on hands. She clinched Jenny, and the proximity didn't permit neither any power strikes.

The ploy allowed Cyborg II catch her breath and catch fire.

They seemed disinterested in defense, and enjoyed only brief seconds—yep, seconds—of control. Things being even, Cyborg would take this round. *Who am I kidding?* She'd take it even if they weren't. Home cage advantage was a real stat.

I looked at the clock. Two minutes to go. At least they're standing up. I jinxed Jenny simply thinking it. Cyborg II surprised my girl with a flurry of lightning quick hands, elbows, and knees— post-graduate BJJ. Nothing we seen.

It knocked Jenny on her back.

The crowd leapt to their feet.

Cyborg II pounced. Not fast enough. Seemed like Jenny, with her gloating gestures whenever she had a bead on Cyborg II, was a bad influence. Cyborg II used a second to run a taunting finger under her bleeding nose and spit out blood. Cunning the way Jenny used antics—they never cost her nothing other than infecting the opponent's head.

The Brazilian trainer lost it!

The mere second Cyborg II expensed jeering—completely outta character for her—allowed Jenny to not only recover, but regain advantage with full guard—on her back, her legs locked around Cyborg II, whose only play now—start throwing punches. Sure, she threw some of her hardest in this fight.

"*Parece bater em um búfalo com um taco de beisebol,*" I heard the TV analyst say as I circled the Octagon. Sounds like hitting a buffalo with a baseball bat. That was simply positive spin by a hometown voice who earned his paycheck from the local league.

My chest swelled. Proud. Jenny barely smarted, absorbing the beating, focused instead on attempting a submission from this rare offensive position on her back against perhaps one of the best grapplers. Neither gave an inch.

Jenny remembered what Kevin dinned, day in day out—legs the last to tire. Unlike Cyborg II, who went fist wild, then fist weary, and unable to ground and pound past Jenny's guard. Again, the surprising resistance from this unknown Yank took Cyborg II outta her game. Never one to show the least hesitation or lack of confidence while grappling, Cyborg II did what she never done in her career.

She glanced to her corner for a way out and forward.

Jenny saw the eyes slide off her. Cyborg II's rhythmic hammering missed a beat. In MMA, where speed of thought governed reflexes, Jenny had a lifetime. Shot an arm around past the hesitating hand and around Cyborg II's neck, yanked down the same time her legs slid up.

All working together into a triangle choke hold.

"Godamn yeah!" I shouted and never knew Puma could jump to his feet.

He did, hollering, "Go Boston Strangler, lil girl!"

This being an educated crowd, the noise dipped so far, Cyborg II's trainer's voice came audible, loud and clear. "*Levante sua cabeça!*" Lift your head!

As did mine, "Close it out!"

"*Levante, levante!*" Lift it, lift it!

"End this right here, right now!"

My eyes rose to the clock. Exactly a minute left in the round.

I had no worries about Jenny's lockdown strength—she packed Strongman power in her arms. Her legs, however, which she been bulking the past six months, be what she must subpoena if she wanted to make these last sixty seconds a countdown to victory.

Puma knew it too. "Squeeze 'em legs, lil' girl! Squeeze the shit outta them!"

"*Ascensão, ascensão!*" Rise, rise!

The Brazilian corner looked up at the clock, same as me. Forty seconds. Cyborg II had one shot to survive the round. Powerbomb Jenny—put every ounce of everything she had left to lift and slam Jenny back down to loosen the choke.

Her trainer began waving his arms up'n down, imploring the crowd to catalyze their girl, and they obliged, "*Ascensão! Ascensão!*"

Nigel responded, climbing to his feet. I couldn't hear him. From the way his mouth moved, he was shouting, "Finish, finish!"

Every fight Jenny'd won in fight clubs, they come mostly by laying 'em out cold, and if they were still twitching, she only had to put the finishing touches on the ground. Never had she done it on her back and entirely on the ground. Ask any fighter, there no greater satisfaction than a triangle choke.

Cyborg II was trying, God bless her heart. Her face grimaced with strain same time as the color drained 'cause Jenny'd cut off the blood, which likely barely trickled, neck'n above, when the Brazilian needed it to be pumping. Known in judo as *sankaku-jime*, this figure-4 vice squeezed the carotid shut. It came closest to a most enjoyable murder by strangulation. You were draining the life outta your opponent inch by inch while delighting in the visceral gratification of extracting life ounce by ounce.

Twenty seconds.

Jenny knew she had this. That expression came on that I seen when she wanted to end her opponent. I had to step in or she'd be serving consecutive life terms for remorseless multiple slayings of her sparring partners.

The crowd's chant lost its unison and conviction. So, I heard him, when Puma hollered into the cage, "Call it, call it!"

I looked at the ref. *They'll lynch him if he does.* The ref looked at

Cyborg II's trainer, who shook his head firmly. No!

Cyborg II's eyes glazed. *Tap out, bitch!*

I'd taught Jenny how to hone her internal clock. Great fighters knew, give or take few seconds, where the round stood time-wise. We had a signal.

Bam! Bam! I double-hammered my fist.

She knew my metronomic thumping here on out started a ten second countdown to the end of Round 1.

Bam! Bam! Bam! 10, 9, 8…

Jenny's mouth twisted. A homicidal grin, if I ever saw one. Synchronized to her hand and legs wrenching tighter. Crowd didn't think she could go any tighter. Neither did I. But she did. I rarely caught my breath loudly. I did.

Never seen anything like it.

Only had a notion of it—the psychological line called *breaking point*. You know, that final turn of a vice which cracked open a skull and the primeval reaction it evoked. I felt it, only imagining how satiating it must be for Jenny.

At ground zero, Cyborg II's head straightened sharply like someone had caught her attention ahead. Her glazing eyes widened in absolute agony. And pure life threatening terror!

Bam! Bam! Bam! 7, 6, 5…

If you thought standing fifteen feet away was bad, even up in the bleachers, you felt the crushing, suffocating pain'n suffering Jenny was dispensing to their girl.

Bam! Bam! 4, 3…

Cyborg slapped her palm to the canvas.

The ref leaned down. Cyborg II's nod was small but perceptible. She wanted out. Now!

The Ref slashed his arm, ending the the fight.

Cyborg II's trainer threw his head back in disgust. As rabid and loud as these 21,000 people had gotten, now they dropped their asses back into their seats. Stunned. Polite applause sprinkled between boos, neither enthusiastic. Cyborg II's head collapsed down to the canvas after she crawled out on her hands and knees from Jenny's grasp.

Nigel orbited over and pumped my hand. "That was awesome! She was awesome!"

"Holy fuck, lil girl!" Puma banged the cage with his cane. "That final corkscrew was fuckin' badass bat-shit-bitch crazy! Wooo!"

The Ref raised Jenny's left hand, pulled the microphone that lowered down from the rafters to his lips, and announced dully, "*Vencedor por submissão dos Estados Unidos da América, Jenny Sharp.*" Winner by submission, from the United States of America, Jenny Sharp.

Bloodied, with bruises already turning an ugly blue-black, she showed no trace of pain. Her lips stretched from ear to ear like a possum who done eating a second helping of stolen taters. Cyborg II's trainer hurried past her. The ref let go of the microphone.

Jenny grabbed it, circled Cyborg II, pointing down, and sneered to the crowd, "*Se ela é Cyborg, eu sou o maldito Terminador!*"

If she's Cyborg, I'm fucking Terminator!

I shoulda known. She probably learned that phrase the night she landed and was just itching to unleash it. The confidence in that girl. Sure, I'd met cocky bastards but none who walked the talk like she just done.

Puma continued to yip joyously. Boos rained down, along with beer cans and assorted crap. Instead of ducking, like Nigel, Puma, and I were doing, Jenny broke into a dance around the Cyborg II and the trainer. She still had the microphone. Her cackles reverberated down from the speakers across the arena.

She took her disrespect and gloating to the press conference after, Nigel and Puma told me.

I didn't attend 'cause I went back to the arena. I always did, for what I called my Buddha moment. To slow-mo rerun moments that coulda cost us the fight in my mind's-eye.

One specifically.

WHABAM! Based on the set up left hand jab, Jenny expects a right fist. Cyborg lands a lightning left leg kick to the right side of the head instead. Jenny never moves. Never sees it coming.

The fight led off *SportsCenter.* The World Wide Web blew a fuse, the most popular parts being Jenny's antics before'n after the fight. Her lack of sportsmanship and decency drew more kudos than scolding. Not since Ali, there been anyone beloved for bad.

UFZ called Nigel in the air that very night.

We were all on the private jet he'd rented to come down to Brazil. He didn't fly commercial no more, having long ago risen above that. One thing about UFZ brass—they jumped on a good thing pronto. You had good lady fighters currently on the circuit, but none shown the star power draw of Rhonda Rousey and Amanda Nunes. Rousey was smoking hot and a beast. Amanda Nunes was a beast and smart. Consensus being, two outta three, was rare. But Jenny was all three—hot, smart and a beast. That was beyond rare. *That's generational.*

UFZ wanted her to fight the AFC champ in Kansas City in two months. Nigel didn't even wait, grinned, "Yeah!"

Amazon Fighting Championship came to be in 2012 to promote and feature only female MMA fighters—not surprising, considering 'amazon' meant warrior woman. Trust and respect, thanks to a history of quality recruits, earned AFC champs premium slots on UFZ cards. *Just in her second fight?! Shit, that has to be some kinda first.*

"Pull off an AFC win," I said, after Nigel hung up and we whooped and hollered, celebrating, "your third fight'll be an UFZ headliner, and your fourth likely for the fucking Bantamweight Belt."

"It better be," Jenny said, all cocky. "Brock Lesnar got a title shot in his third fight even after being one-and-one coming in."

"He was a WWE legend," Nigel tempered. "UFZ recognized he'd be a ratings goliath."

"I'll be just as big," Jenny bragged. "And that's not just my opinion."

She held up her phone. A sports page headline, all caps, declared: 'A STAR IS BORN.'

Boz singled out a key from a bunch that he fished out of his pocket and inserted it in the lock of the nondescript door in the middle of a gloomy hallway. As promised, District Attorney Arlen Taylor provided Boz a secure room away from the precinct in the basement of his office building, with instructions to use the rear service entrance.

"I have to assume," Boz told Arlen, when the DA asked him to begin a clandestine investigation of Nigel Hansom, "IAD is watching me via stool pigeons in the squad room."

Boz's track record warranted it. They probably snooped and sniffed through his desk afterhours. Making sure to nip an embarrassment before it became one. Also, according to the dossier Arlen gave him, Nigel owned every cop for sale, and over the years, had infested every government agency, New Orleans to Washington DC.

Boz kept how far and deep he'd gotten even from Arlen. That is, until he realized the door was unlocked. *What the*— his hand immediately went to his piece. *Click*. Unbuttoned his holster. Boz knew he wasn't followed here, being extra paranoid, logging out of the precinct using the pretext of following up a lead on one of the other shitty cases on his plate.

He stepped in, drawing his Browning, and pulled up, relaxing abruptly. "Arlen?"

District Attorney Arlen Taylor stood before an oversized combined map of Canada, the United States, and Mexico. A thick yellow highlighter line traced the entire length of the I-10, Los Angeles, California, to Jacksonville, Florida. Strings connected thumb tacks, pinning down pictures and neatly handwritten *Post-it*s and 3x5 cards. The central attraction was Nigel's photo located at New Orleans—the tarantula at the heart of this web.

Boz used red twine for the I-10 operation, to the left, linking Nigel to Dusty and Puma. Inside the triangle they formed—Jenny's photo. On the same side, above them, Boz implicated Nigel in the death of Jorge Vargas, the victim in Mexico, but included Dusty in Crispin Martinez's murder. Both victims were identified via their DL—driver's license—and a gruesome crime scene photo.

To Nigel's right, his drug operation. Blue twine led to the abbreviation, '*CPA*,' scrawled on a *Post-it*, that connected to a dossier-sourced mug shot of his army buddy, Tavon Cole. Beside Tavon, a DL of his widow, Makena. Between them and Nigel, three handwritten lines on a cue card: *Canadian Cartel, Cherry Hill Cartel, Mexican Cartel.* Central to the two sides of Nigel's business, right above his picture, an Easy Trucking postcard.

"How long have you been a cop?" Arlen asked rhetorically. "Drug busts never usually net the kingpin, let alone the fact it'll take years to even build a case that more often than not falls apart in court because a key witness disappears. Please tell me that is not your strategy because this wall screams long-play FBI-DEA operation."

Boz hated having to explain himself. "You can't attack weakness if you don't know the stress points"

"He cannot see us coming."

"He won't."

Boz took a personal day from work and got on the first flight to Newark, New Jersey. Arlen's campaign picked up the tab. Boz rented a low key Honda Hybrid. He punched up the address on the GPS, which took him ten miles west of Manhattan to the middle of suburbia—modest homes and small businesses—in East Rutherford. Nothing identified his destination, a concrete and glass structure protected by a black fence and shielded by landscaping. Utterly nondescript to the constant stream of traffic along Route 17.

Until you wanted to turn into the address, 100 Orchard Street.

Twin, oversized 'STOP! DO NOT ENTER!' white on red signs, one for each lane, stood in front of a blockade stretching sidewalk to sidewalk. Boz had instructions to go around the block and enter off Hackensack Street.

"Detective Bostwick Oswald," he introduced himself again at the front desk after going through a lengthy and intense security check at the guard station outside, which included surrendering his weapon, frisking nonetheless, a K-9 search, etc.

The receptionist, 45, 5-6, 140, graying, plump, government lifer by the looks of her, picked up the phone. Following all the stringent guidelines for federal government signage, the discreet insignia on the wall behind her read in all caps: 'EAST RUTHERFORD OPERATIONS CENTER, FEDERAL RESERVE BANK OF NEW YORK.' Known among insiders as—Boz found this out when he began looking into it—EROC.

An executive, 44, 5-7, 139, stepped out of the elevator a couple of minutes later and advanced, extending a hand, "Lucy Stetson, EVP, Financial Services."

She couldn't be mistaken for anything but a banker. Stylish prescription eyewear. Blonde-brown hair fell straight down to the shoulders. Custom cut conservative gray pant suit over a white blouse, top button undone, not that it was sexy or revealed anything. Black pumps with modest, practical heels. Name and photo on the security badge at the end of a retractable lanyard around her neck.

"Detective Bostwick Oswald," He shook her hand. Soft palm of an upper echelon executive, not that he had anything against them. He preferred tougher women closer to street level. "Call me Boz."

"Lucy. I thought it'd be more informative to tour and talk."

"Sure." He clipped the visitor's badge over his front pocket, falling in step.

Almost every door required her to swipe her badge. "Few people know who we are, what we do," she began. Formal, by the book—her entire demeanor. She has to be, being on the top floor of the Federal Reserve, the mother of all banks. "As the financial nerve center, secrecy and the heavy security are necessary. All checks, wire transfers, and transactions, from and to citizens and corporations, pass through here, along with the world's most important commodity—hard cash. Every denomination of new and used currency." They entered an immense three-story cavern. "This is the vault, which can hold about sixty billion dollars."

There wasn't a soul on the floor. "No people?"

"Only observers." Lucy pointed to a glass enclosed, high-tech, control room populated with men and women vigilantly watching video surveillance and computer screens. "All money is counted, bundled, packed, and moved by robots." Storage and retrieval vehicles hefted shrink wrapped bills onto pallets, which were carried off on conveyer belts.

"Removes temptation," observed Boz.

"Also allows to more easily scan, audit, and track every bill that comes in for destruction or leaves this facility for circulation."

"So, what happened on June 22, 2004?" asked Boz.

"We processed the largest single order of currency for distribution," said Lucy. "Almost two and a half billion in hundred dollar bills. I wasn't here and I couldn't find any employee with direct knowledge, but we maintain meticulous records, and I can only tell you what transpired here."

"I'm following money, Lucy," said Boz. "It's rare I can start where the trail begins."

"The twenty-four million notes weighed thirty tons and needed forty pallets, which were then loaded onto a tractor trailer truck. Tracking information showed the truck left our lot and turned onto Route 17. We have an exact time stamp when the driver merged onto the southbound lane of the New Jersey Turnpike and the precise hour, minute and second, when the money arrived at Andrews Air Force Base. Two Treasury Department officers broke the seals, verified the money count, and loaded the pallets onto a C-130."

"Bound for Baghdad?"

"Once the Treasury Department took possession, our responsibility ended. Where the money went, I can't speculate," Lucy smiled, "but there's enough out there, corroborated in public hearings and news reports by politicians and others with direct knowledge. So, I don't have to confirm or deny your suspicions. I pulled all the relevant files." She reached into her pocket and gave him a flash drive. "It's all on there."

Lucy walked him to the door and stepped outside with him,

where she dropped all formality without any warning."The money was to jump start the Iraqi economy by giving it directly to the people. They didn't get a fucking cent. Crooked soldiers stole millions, US contractors got kickbacks, Iraqi and our own politicians lined their pockets. Perhaps the biggest heist anywhere in the world, certainly the most unconscionable." Lucy ran out of breath. "If you're able to nail even one of those bastards, it'll be worth it. Even if it is almost two decades later, because Iraqis have never recovered from what we did to them over there."

"I hit a wall with the Defense Department," Boz said.

"There's someone you should talk to. He was there, saw it all go down, and took down names."

Lucy's lead took Boz to New York. Bedford-Stuyvesant. Top floor of a three-story street corner tenement. Boz parked a few blocks away, not out of choice. He had to be buzzed in. No elevator. The stairs creaked. Walls needed paint, floor a scrubbing. Most definitely rent controlled. So, understandably, the owners let everything go to pot, while attrition—tenants moving out or dying off—emptied the units. Then the landlords could gentrify and cash in.

If Boz hadn't climbed six flights, he wouldn't have known he was on the third floor. Same kind of dilapidation. Four doors, affixed with unpolished brass numbers from a time and craftsmanship bygone, led off the windowless hallway. He knocked on '3D.' Heard at least two deadbolts draw back, then the security chain.

Drew Mastiff, 48, 6-1, 152, swung the door open.

Boz introduced himself.

Drew walked with a stoop he probably didn't have when he enlisted. He pointed to white cartons stacked six high in the hallway, "I started downloading records as soon as I figured what was going on. When I got back, I printed them out."

Through the handle holes Boz made out folders. Every carton carried a distinct number neatly written with a red sharpie. A filing system of sorts. There were more boxes in the single bedroom and the surprisingly spacious, single, open living-dining-kitchen.

"How much money are you trying to locate?" Drew pointed to side-by-side chairs in front of a computer on the only table in the room.

"I don't know."

"I also created a database of names. As you might have guessed, I've had some time on my hands. Beer?"

"Sure."

Drew opened the old fridge and pulled out a couple of Sam Adams. "I didn't have to work when I quit, thanks a decent monthly payout. Disability benefits, pension'n such. I don't feel one bit guilty working the system, not after the kind of highway robbery I saw. "

"You enlisted after 9/11?" asked Boz.

"I was already in the army, maybe six years by then. Enlisted when I turned eighteen." Drew handed Boz the beer. They twisted open the caps together. He sat down. "Being computer savvy, I moved to logistics, and stayed out of combat my entire time in Iraq. Upfront warning, being in the military doesn't mean I walk around wrapped in red, white, and blue."

"I'm just looking for evidence."

"What do you know about the CPA?"

"Coalition Provisional Authority. Created to be a temporary US-led government right after the invasion to provide security and aid and find WMDs."

"Googled it, right?" Drew guffawed. "Taste the *Kool-Aid* as you were talking?"

Boz smiled. "Dug deeper. Shit, whadya know."

"Whadya know is right." Drew continued, "The White House created this agency with basically unlimited powers and no oversight. Being part of logistics in the Green Zone," the four-square-mile center of US occupation forces in the Karkh District of Central Baghdad, "they asked me to be part of it, and I was, from day one. Initially, it seemed well intentioned. The first shipment CPA received was twenty million in one, five, and ten dollar bills that locals could use. None of it got to them, of course. Vanishing into the pockets of middlemen tasked with giving out the money. In that first year, we received twenty-one shipments of cash. All stored in the basement of Saddam Hussein's palace, which served as our headquarters in the Green Zone. The Program Review Board, made up of CPA officers—they competed to out-crook each other—authorized withdrawals. Ten, fifty, hundred thousand, even a million or two sometimes. Few or no questions asked. The cash was taken out of the vault into what we called a 'secure room.' We piled the money on a table. Only an AO—Authorized Officer—was allowed inside and sign for it, stuffed it in whatever he brought down with him—garbage bags sometimes—and took it upstairs. Handed it off to whoever wanted this cash. Got a signed receipt, filed it, and that was the end of the money trail. Because nobody followed up what it was for, where it went. Or, if it ever got there. Nothing. Who are you investigating?"

"A marine. Nigel Hansom."

"Why does that name sound familiar?" Drew was already typing.

"He worked for the CPA."

"Oh, yeah," Drew had Nigel's picture on his screen. "He was an AO." He clicked on a tab to identify the box of records. "86." He stood up, first checking the boxes in the living room. "I should arrange the boxes chronologically. Then I thought, why bother?"

"You were the whistleblower."

Drew headed into the hallway to look. "An early one. *New York Times*, *Washington Post*, *Vanity Fair*, they all did really good, in-depth pieces. Forced Congress to order a hearing. Records showed the money, most of it, went back to the Iraqis. Bullshit! Blackwater, Halliburton, other coalition contractors—they were paid for services rendered and OK'd by the Iraqis, even though it was a fucking shakedown. Then, Paul Bremmer, who ran this whole operation, testified it wasn't American tax payer money, it was Saddam Hussein's oil money that we froze, and so we were in no way accountable. Nobody cared after that. The whole thing died. Ah!" He slid out a carton from under the two above it, removed the top, and rifled through the folders. "Got it."

Drew dropped it on the table. The tab read, "Hansom, Nigel."

He removed two stapled sheets, flipped from Page 1 to 2. "Look at the number of times he took money upstairs. And he was just one of a dozen AOs. Gives you a sense of the scale of the corruption."

Boz scanned down the first page, flipped it. Caught his breath, "His last withdrawal." He showed it to Drew.

"Eighteen million? That can't be right." Drew's fingers flew across the keyboard of his computer. "What's the date on it?"

Boz read off, "June 21, 2004."

"Of course." Drew leaned back. "That was the last week of coalition control. I remember now. It was moved forward from the thirtieth to the twenty-eighth—the day the US handed the government back over to Iraq. CPA emptied the vault in hefty, daily chunks. To Iraqi coffers, if you believed the authorizations."

Boz flipped his own note pad. "June 21st was also Nigel's last day of his tour in Iraq. You said he takes the money upstairs and hands it over."

"Let's see who signed the receipt?" Drew opened the folder again. "As unaccountable as the CPA was, we had to scan every transaction. Outside of here, the only other copy is buried in the basement of the Pentagon somewhere, never to be found." Drew found the receipt. "Phil Brevin and Russell Talbot." He returned to his computer. Name searched. Swiveled with a smirk. "Blackwater contractors. More like, mercenaries. Nobody made out more than Blackwater in Iraq."

"Any contact info for these guys."

It took Drew just a second to shake his head, "KIA." Directed Boz to the date. "June 21, 2004, in an ambush on Highway 1 en route from Baghdad to Kuwait."

"Same day." Boz sat back. "Nigel's Army buddy, Tavon Cole, discharged with him, died that day too. How fucking convenient."

So, that's where Nigel got the capital to expand his fleet, vaulting Easy

Trucking to the top overnight. Better yet, Boz now held an information grenade he could detonate without Nigel even realizing the pin had been pulled.

"Hmm," Drew pointed to his computer. "Quite the deadly day for Blackwater on Highway 1. Three other contractors were found dead. Shot." Paused. "And burned."

According to Dusty Saldana

I didn't see Jenny for a week after we got back from Brazil except on TV. She basked in the attention. I kept my fears about sensation and money from Nigel and Puma, but they were confirmed, when she pulled up for training in a shiny yellow Porsche. Two hours late. Puma'd gotten here before her. She looked like she'd climbed outta bed, climbed into her car, and driven here. I held my tongue, cutting her slack, being her first day back.

"Angle, angle!" I snapped when she squared up, ten seconds into taking on the bag. Retreating beside Puma, I couldn't help being snide. "That car must've put her back eighty grand, likely more, knowing she the type to splurge on every show-off accessory. Put down a chunk of what she made, loaning the rest, I'm figuring."

"Ain't the first athlete who blew their first check on wheels," shrugged Puma.

We'd split the $300k purse four ways as agreed. That was Jenny's cake. Despite her bad behavior, they had to award her the SOTN—Submission of the Night—bonus. $25k. The icing. Puma and me, our eyes be on the belt more'n the money. So we didn't object that Jenny—crafty knowledgeable about the extra perk checks on fight night—negotiated keeping it all when we agreed to new terms upon Nigel coming in.

"What's wrong?" I reacted sharply, seeing Jenny lean up against the bag, outta breath, after just fifteen minutes.

"Nothing," she said, smiling crookedly. "Late night."

"Booze, drugs, partying?" My blood started to boil.

"Come on. I been drinking and snorting since I could spell both. That shit doesn't tire me out." Jenny wasn't it taking serious. Not one bit. "Sex does."

I restrained myself from blowing my top. "You didn't run or swim this morning, did you?"

"I just told you, I was fucking all week, up, and until this morning. For someone into books, Dusty," Jenny went mock earnest, "you should know there's no cardio better."

"How's it working out for your legs?" She had me fuming.

Jenny grinned, "Touché, sir!"

"Get out!" I lost it. "Come back when you're serious! Better yet, quit now! That way, you can go down as a one fight wonder!"

"Surely you have a stat!" Jenny retorted back.

"Yeah! Zero! The number of trainers and promoters who want you!"

"Like you're on every short list!"

"That's enough," Puma stepped in. "No need for either o'you saying somethin' that you need to walk back. Dusty, her personal life be her own. Lil girl, Dusty got a point. You need to get back to the intensity that make you a winner."

"The fight is seven weeks away," she said sullenly.

"Just enough time to get ready," I retorted. "Body and mind!"

"Only by putting in a full day every day," added Puma. "This like the playoffs, lil girl. Every fight from now get bigger and tougher, demanding you work longer and harder."

Jenny nodded. I cautioned, lowering my voice, "Not to mention we also struck a deal with Devil. Nigel don't take kindly to losing, especially if you dunnit to yourself."

"Back to the old regimen, agreed?" said Puma.

"Would be so much easier if we trained in New Orleans. All my business is there now."

"Oh, all your business?" I rolled my eyes back into my head. "This girl is fucking impossible. Didn't realize one win and one week'd made you into Elon fucking Musk!"

"Walk away." Puma poked his cane into my chest. I did. To Jenny, I heard him say, "Go back to hitting the bag."

She didn't let up on the bags, flushing her technique down the toilet, punching square up. I was too mad to correct her.

"If anything," I whispered to Puma, who knew I was sadistically letting her kill herself trying to prove the week off and whoring it up all night was no big deal, "it reinforces what I love about her. She can will herself past limits."

He smiled. I went over when the clock ran out on the punching part of her session. She was drenched, heaving. I'd cooled off but showed her no kindness.

No apology in her eyes neither.

"Take ten." I said, tossing her the VR Goggles. "The AFC Champ's standup skills are programmed in. FYI, she won a kickboxing championship in Tokyo against Bruce Lees. Came back to get a decent BJJ degree. So, she's equal good upright and on the mat." Five minutes into Jenny's bout with the virtual boxer, I was screaming, "Get off your fucking heels!"

The rest of the session became all friction.

When it was time for me to leave, I jabbed, "By the way, Kevin still waiting on a grateful thank you for preparing you to win on the ground."

"Should I address him as Mrs. or Ms?" Jenny taking shot at Kevin being so girly sensitive.

Puma laughed. I didn't crack a smile. *Bitch.* I'd have loved spit that at her.

"OK, again, both o'you," Puma stepped in once more, "stop." I reached the door and she stooped to pick up weights. "Y'two shitfucks sleep this off. Tomorrow mornin', I better see so much friendliness, tonguing each other be only thing left to prove this spat is over."

I put the the whole bad morning behind me by the time I got to New Orleans and felt the difference with these fighters. They were so grateful, always trying to do more than I asked them. What they lacked in talent, they made up with effort. *Why does talent only ooze outta assholes?*

Nigel came by around his usual time. We discussed the next I-10 fight night in a coupla days in Lizzy, Alabama, population 123, flew Confederate flags, and barely showed up even when you max magnified Google Maps.

"We should be able to unload four," I said, "six, if Perez and DeLeon have the night of their lives."

"Something I want to talk to you about," Nigel broached, a smoke between his fingers, grabbing a beer outta my RV-size fridge tucked under a counter, upon which I'd stacked first aid, gloves, paper-work, you name it.

We were in my office, if you could call a closet-with-a-door one. I shouldn't complain. Nigel'd created a pretty sweet training facility in this huge warehouse barely fifty feet from the Mississippi. Equipped it like a state-of-the-art gym—weights, bikes, an Octagon to UFZ specs, everything you saw in glossy fitness magazines. Facilities formed one arm of an L along the far wall—lockers, crappers, showers, medical tables, even a spa. A doctor and a therapist showed up when needed. The other arm contained my office and a row of eight-by-five feet quarters furnished with a cot and mattress. An 8 AM-to-8 PM Mexican cook prepared and served meals in a large common area with tables, chairs, kitchen, and a bigscreen TV.

Next door, a gated parking lot, with a workshop, housed Nigel's fleet of trucks. Past that stood the mint—Easy Trucking HQ. Employed about thirty-eight desk jockeys. Nigel located his office at the front corner overlooking the river. Not accidently. He could see who come in and go outta all three adjacent properties he owned.

"Jenny should start training here," he said, chugging down.

That she-snake! I shoulda known she'd've already slithered behind my back and coiled her charms around Nigel. Mentioning it to me this morning was after the fucking fact. I let Nigel finish. "I am concerned, not so much you driving two hundred miles every day—you're mature and careful—but she's twenty, now drives a sports car."

"Why is she coming to New Orleans every day?" I asked.

“Companies are knocking on the door for a piece of her.” Shoe makers’d called, I knew. Looking the way she did, apparel and cosmetics must’ve too. “The kind of crossover hype she’s generating doesn’t come along often. We have to capitalize. I hired a publicist and a social media team.”

Jenny open this can. “It’s one fight, Nigel, one upset win. The AFC champ will be a whole ’nother level up from Cyborg II.”

“Yes, an all-American matchup that Pay-Per-View is salivating over.” He completely ignored my caution. “That girl is savvy. Knows it’s out there for the taking— money, publicity even more.”

“Exactly.” *I’m going to pull out the worms.* “Do you want her bringing attention to your gym? The I-10?”

“She knows to be discreet,” said Nigel. Went off topic eagerly, “By the way, I’m installing a cryo chamber.” To treat injuries with ice. “Should be in by the time Jenny starts here.”

What the fuck? “So Jenny’n you already finalize moving here.”

“Is that going be a problem?” Nigel’s tone changed.

Mine did too. “Due respect, Nigel. We brought you in. So, I expected a discussion not a decree.”

“An unhappy trainer, I can work around.” Nigel went dark. “An unhappy fighter, I cannot replace.”

“Sounds like you just draw a line.” My eyes glinted. “Expendables on one side.”

“We have a good thing going, Dusty. Don’t fuck it up, being stubborn.”

Jenny’d played her cards shrewdly and won his ear. Not that Nigel didn’t know. He recognized her game, but by giving in to her, he astutely shifted the power dynamic in his favor. Plus, he had the pockets, and if Puma and I wanted to keep our hands in them, we now had walk in step with him. “Just sayin’, if you keep givin’ in to her, she’ll keep asking for more.”

“You have to coddle talent.”

“Not with all this outside shit.”

“It keeps her relevant. She understands it. Why can’t you?”

I’m pissing in the wind. “It’s hurting her focus.”

"You're her trainer. So, get her attention."

I did not have to. She got what she wanted, and just like that, went back to being Jenny From The Block. Kevin showed up to resume her BJJ training. Wearing a sports bra and Spandex shorts, she gave him a tight hug and kissed him on the lips long and hard. Then, she handed him a thick wad of cash in an envelope. And just like that, all that hurt he was whining to me about vanished with a blushing grin.

Jenny looked over to me. Winked. *That shrew.*

"She may be difficult, bull-headed'n a pain in the ass," said Puma, giving me that look like I may've jumped the gun with her. "She good people too."

I reserved judgment. One act of kindness didn't a Mother Theresa make.

We decided to move to New Orleans the upcoming weekend. Puma and Jenny found rentals. I helped him with his—a one-bedroom apartment three blocks from mine in the Warehouse District. I'd picked the area to be fifteen minutes from work. I found out later, I'd moved into a trendy address.

Jenny rented swanky digs on the top floor in a modern glass affair on Canal Street in Iberville, a YP—short for young professional, I learned—neighborhood, right adjacent to Downtown on one side, the French Quarter on the other. I wasn't surprised but I sure was nervous. Excess and outrageous oughta been her middle and last names. How they'd rear their ugly heads, I didn't know yet, but it was just a matter of time, what with cash popping every which way outta her pockets, and living proximal to party and booty.

Puma tried to soothe me, "She's a minx, I know that. Can you blame her? Needing to survive on her own, her parents dying in an accident when she barely sixteen."

"Did you ever check that out?" I asked.

"Why?"

"Knowing as much as you do now, you never consider she might be lying?"

Puma shrugged. "Does it matter they real dead or just dead

to her?"

"Find out, can you?"

"And you call me a bleak, untrusting sumbitch."

Nigel Hansom: Hearsay from New Orleans

"Estás aquí ilegalmente." You are here illegally, Nigel began the spiel he gave every new batch of fighters. Five arrived last night. Dusty'd lined them up in the Octagon, Nigel continued in Spanish. "While you are here, I am paying for everything. So, I own you. You have no rights, even fewer options. Stay in and lay low. Disobey, and I will not wait for ICE. I'll kick your fucking ass back home myself. Are we clear?" He raised his voice sharply when nods weren't forthcoming. Happened with every batch. "Are we clear?"

Now they wagged their heads front to back, mumbling, "*Sí, sí.*" Yes, yes.

Dusty stood behind him. Other fighters kept working out—they'd been there, seen that. Out of the corner of his eye, Nigel noticed Jenny'd stopped boxing to watch, Puma too—they hadn't.

Nigel went on. "If you're not in pain, you're not training hard enough. If you are not sweating, you're not training hard enough. If you're not bent over puking, you're not training hard enough. No booze, no drugs, no women, no parties! You have only six weeks and three fights to be picked up. No exceptions. After that, whether you go on or go home, your time here never happened." Now came the part where he needed to convey fear. "Say nothing, forget everything. I hate rats, I kill rats. Are we clear?" This time nods came swiftly. "You have a choice. It's one or the other. I can be your best friend or your worst enemy." He gave that a long beat to sink in. "Good luck."

He left the Octagon, lighting up.

"Your Sergeant Hartman moment?" Jenny asked. *Trying not crack up?*

Nigel let it go because he was more surprised and impressed. Arched his eyebrows. "From Stanley Kubrick's *Full Metal Jacket.*"

She manly voiced from the movie, "I bet you're the kind of guy that'd fuck a person in the ass and not even have the goddamn common courtesy to give him a reach-around."

"It set the tone for the rest of boot camp."

Jenny pulled back on the laughter, not the mockery in her smile. "The barking drill sergeant—oh-kay."

Nigel went dead serious, "Worked for me in the Marines—hell, it works for the entire US military for that matter, and has for two hundred years—effectively conveying respect and expectation for authority, discipline, and obedience."

"You could post a white guy with a gun and save yourself the theater," she said, then winked, "but you get off on the power trip, don't you?"

As prized as she was, Nigel didn't care for the disrespect. "Never had anyone stray."

Jenny laughed. "So, you never had anyone with balls."

"Stay in your lane, Jenny," Nigel bristled and walked away.

The increased daily exposure to Jenny made him realize she really respected nothing and no one. But, Dusty reported, her intensity and motivation returned with the move to New Orleans. She ran, swam, and showed up at 7 AM sharp. Didn't cut corners during standup and grappling practice and drills. After workouts, she visited with the social media team—authoring every tweet and post to enhance her brand, all the while taunting her AFC opponent to keep the fight as one of the top trending topics.

"Every now and then, I need to holler at the illegals to quit gawking at her," Dusty joked. "Funny thing, she treats them the exact opposite of the guys in Baton Rouge, who she routinely belittled." Jenny's Spanish was decent, having studied it in school and smartly kept up with it, Nigel discovered.

He showed up at least twice daily now. Breakfast, around 9 AM, to eat with Puma, Jenny, Dusty, and the guys. Before quitting time in the afternoon. Sometimes a surprise visit in between, depending on what was going on with Easy Trucking.

Dusty came around too, reluctantly appreciating the move to New Orleans. He admitted he didn't miss the trek to and from Baton Rouge. Now that he could shuttle between Jenny and the guys in the same gym, he didn't have to work from dawn till midnight, burning both ends of the candle. Everyone kept regular banker hours.

"With no cause to complain," Dusty confided, "I worry." Nigel laughed, but Dusty was serious. "Shit, it's nerve wracking. Never had a hunky-dory run like this. I wake up every morning waiting for disaster to strike."

Just so happened, Dusty just got the time of day wrong.

Nigel pulled up with a squeal of tires. Livid! Friday night—make that Saturday, around 2 AM. Nothing legal or pleasant happened, none that he knew, at this hour. He plowed into the parking lot between the warehouse-gym and his office. A private security firm, known for discretion, remotely watched the cameras and motion detectors monitoring all three properties. Per his instructions, the firm called Nigel, not the police, and sent him a link to the video footage.

"I got this," he replied, indicating he'd take over. No guard needed to be dispatched.

Eighteen-wheelers, some with a cab, mostly not, stood parked five and six deep around a central workshop. You could run a thread from end to end, side to side, and these containers on wheels looked like they could square up and line up both ways. Nigel's size allowed him only a few inches of clearance on either side. Still, he advanced like a battlefield tank about to lay down some serious fire. Which he fully intended to do.

Music with Spanish vocals became audible, grew louder, tracing to the forty-footer parked bang in the middle, far enough away from the street to be out of sight. He recognized it as the one modified to smuggle in illegals. Back door rolled up, a couple of hurricane lamps, crudely strung to the ceiling frame, splattered mood light, so to speak, for this unauthorized shindig.

What the fuck? A party with drugs, booze, and whores—his four absolute don'ts.

Nigel stepped onto the loading ramp that was lowered half way to serve as a step, then grabbed the dangling rope, and heaved himself in. One of the fighters looked up from snorting off a splatter of coke.

"*Aqui para unirte a la fiesta, jefe? Es el cumpleaños de Jenny.*" Here to join the party, boss? It's Jenny's birthday.

Fighters recognized him. He counted eight of the ten. Empty Tequila bottles and beer cans lay scattered all over the floor around cartons of takeout and remnants of a devoured cake. So, they'd been drinking for hours, smoking weed, and snorting coke. Now barely able to even slur a greeting, let alone be afraid of him for breaking the unbreakable rules he'd laid down. A few danced—the way they were grinding crotches with naked and near-naked whores, they could've been fucking, standing up. There was actual fucking going on too. In all the years he'd brought and trained fighters for the I-10, not once had anyone dared to bring even a six-pack on the premises. Hell, no one looked him in the eye. Keeping his distance elevated the unspoken fear, intimidation, and dire consequences of crossing him. A whore giggled and rubbed herself against him.

He shoved her away roughly, growling, "Fuck off!"

She didn't take it personally. Probably been treated worse by johns.

What looked like the front end of the container was actually a disguised accordion-style slider, set three feet in, to create the space necessary to transport his human cargo across the border. A quarter of the way open, Nigel shoved it aside to discover the remaining two fighters. They meant nothing, not as much as the instigator.

Jenny.

She was on the floor, naked, in lip lock with Ecuador, 23, 5-7, 156, ripped, his hands all over her tits. Hers in his hair. Tongue-dueling. Her legs were locked around another fighter who was mining her crotch. She saw Nigel, yanked Ecuador up off her mouth.

"Nigel!" She sounded just a little tipsy, but hardly as drunk and high as she should be. "Didn't invite you because I didn't think this party's in your wheelhouse. Pretty clever, this smuggle cabin. I didn't even know it was here until the guys showed me."

Nigel grabbed the guy between her legs.

"Come on," Jenny drawled, disappointed. "I was almost there."

Clang! Nigel rammed him into the side of the container. The back of his head struck a ridge of the evenly spaced serrations. Knocked him out cold. Now that he could see the fighter's face, Nigel recognized him as Cesar, 21, 5-7½, 159, one of the newcomers.

"That was a bad business decision," Jenny said, sitting up. "He had promise."

Dusty thought so too, Nigel recalled, and turned his attention to Ecuador. The crack of Cesar's skull brought a fleeting moment of sobriety into Ecuador's eyes, and with it came fear. Dusty graded Ecuador an average Lightweight in every stat—accuracy, strikes, skills. He'd been in two fights already without drawing interest and now faced a make-or-break third. Ecuador was too far gone to react as Nigel swung his leg across, his heel passing inches above Jenny's face.

Wham! Buried the toe of his insanely expensive John Varvatos leather shoe under Ecuador's chin. The Mexican's naked ass lifted off the floor and landed a good yard back. Hard! Jarring his spine, hip to neck. He cried out!

Jenny sat up. "What the fuck is your problem?"

"Get dressed." Nigel stepped over her.

"I'm not done fucking yet," Jenny lost her temper. "So fuck you!"

First, Nigel grabbed Ecuador by the hair with one hand. Ecuador barked. Did the same with Cesar and he groaned back to his senses. Nigel dragged them both out. Jenny'd picked the two best looking pieces of ass for her pleasure. He dumped them out of the Smuggle Cabin. The other fighters looked over, eyes glazed. Puzzled. Nigel turned, spit foaming at the corners of his mouth. This kind of anger usually ended in a slaughter.

"I told you to put on some fucking clothes," he snarled.

"Why?" she sneered back, standing up, not in the least shy she was naked. "See something you don't at home?" Reached between her legs.

Nigel almost lost it. Took a threatening step. "Never go there."

Jenny didn't flinch. "Where to do you get off telling me what to do?"

"I warned you. Stay in your lane."

"I did. This is it. I drink, I snort, I orgy."

"Keep it in your fucking house, but don't bring it into mine!"

"It's my birthday, Nigel. Join the party or fuck off!"

"What did you say?" Nigel took a threatening step.

Jenny didn't balk. "You heard. We're having a good time."

"If they wanted one, they should've dropped themselves off at Tijuana."

"Tijuana?" Jenny laughed. "If you're such a badass, you say TJ."

Nigel went over the edge. "You think this is funny?"

His hand darted up, fingers curling to wrap around her throat and choke her. He glimpsed her knee crook and rise with a quickness only a fighter could manage. She froze it from his balls the same the time he stopped short of her throat. He clenched his teeth, restrained his rage. She reeked of booze. Her nostrils were red. Eyes dilated. *She holds her liquor and coke better than any man.*

He backed off. She dropped her knee.

Her lips curled up one corner, "Not funny. Tragic. Out of your stable of ten, only Cesar, whose skull you may have cracked, has an outside shot. Maybe Rodriguez, and that's it, if Dusty was honest with you. Three are headed into their final fight, and most definitely off your payroll. So, I gave them something to remember." Toothy grin, "Ecuador and Cesar, a little more than others."

Infuriated even more she wasn't quite grasping his

seriousness, Nigel poured iron into his voice, "So there is no misunderstanding—I was a Marine and I built the I-10 ground up like it's a battlefield. No mercy. You kill or you die. Same rules of engagement have kept my circuit going without as much as a whisper. I also pay a shitload of money to cops and politicians, who have an even lower level of tolerance."

"And I cut my teeth in fight clubs, as dark, or darker, than your I-10 'battlefield'." She made mocking quotes with her fingers.

"Are they attached to a billion dollar business? Check those whores for a wire?"

"They are fucking naked!" exclaimed Jenny with a snort, then picked up a grocery bag. "And I took their cell phones."

Expression to tone, Nigel became granite, "I mean it. Don't mistake my friendliness for weakness. This is my only courtesy visit. Next time, it'll be police tape and another unsolved homicide. You know how many of those there are in New Orleans?"

Detective Bostwick Oswald: Off Duty Notes

Up and out. Down and in. Parking for Dummies. Since he faced uphill, Boz twisted the steering of the budget friendly Toyota RAV4 away from the curb along this narrow, winding residential street of fancy homes. That way, if the car slid backward, the twisted wheels'd bump the curb and stop even if the parking brake failed. Boz'd flown in this morning to LAX—Los Angeles International Airport. Arlen's campaign again foot this day trip. Took him an hour to get to Hollywood Hills on this wet and dreary Saturday. Ironic—it should be raining in New Orleans, instead the city cooked in triple digit heat. Sunny Southern California, meanwhile, soaked in unprecedented rain. Naturally, he wasn't dressed for this weather. Didn't even pack a jacket.

Boz slipped on the tie he'd brought with him, climbed out, lowered his head, and hurried up the driveway toward a sleek and contemporary home, one of several he passed. Square lines, fixed glass panels, a mixture of exposed cement and wood slats. The awning over the frost glass front door extended far enough to get him out of the downpour. He caught his reflection—the tucked in blue shirt, slacks, and recently added tie made him look official enough. He rang the video doorbell. Said he'd show up around 10:30 AM. Looked at his watch. Fifteen to eleven. He assumed people in LA accounted for traffic delays.

The door opened and Boz knew at once he was looking at Sid Rosen, 32, 6-0¼, 177, jet black hair slicked back like an Italian mobster, but Jewish to the bone. The aggressive demeanor of an attorney jumped out from the moment he opened his mouth and invited Boz inside. Boz politely stamped his feet on the doormat and entered. Looks to speech, an oily motherfucker. Sid couldn't hide he was a sleazeball even if he body-snatched Jimmy Carter. He made small talk about the weather. Boz grunted back monosyllables.

"My maid doesn't show till noon on weekends," said Sid, gesturing Boz to a black and chrome sofa. "I can open a fridge and pull out a soda—and there ends my hosting skills."

If he expected a smile, Boz didn't oblige. Growled, "I'm good."

Does this fucker even live here? The interior décor looked out of a catalog—pristine. Everything dusted, positioned, and untouched. Maybe the place was a front. *Won't surprise me.* Held meetings here for appearances sake, then crawled back into a serpent hole to be with his kind.

"You're a long way from the Big Easy, Detective." Sid sat down, stretched an arm along the backrest, and crossed his legs like a lady. "You didn't say much on the phone?"

"I didn't want you tipping off anybody."

Sid laughed. The nervous kind. Anyone could spot one of those. The humor just wasn't there. Just teeth showing out of a fake smile he was trying to make look genuine.

"The DA out here was real helpful," said Boz. The four-hour flight and drive put him in a mood. "Your practice is built on defending dealers, mules, basically any low life on the wrong side of the war on drugs."

The indictment didn't bother Sid one bit. "I fill a need."

"Where does Jenny Sharp fit in?"

Sid arched his eyebrows. "Who?"

"Who?" Boz repeated, forcing a humorless smile. "Shit, Sid, if only I had a dollar every time a perp said, who? You want to amend that response."

"If she's a client," Sid persisted with his unawareness, "I have to pull up my records. You can swing by the office, Monday—"

"I have already spoken to and have a sworn statement from another sewer rat you're acquainted with, Gavin Lobo. He runs an underground, completely illegal fight club in Long Beach. You want to take it from there?"

"OK," Sid dropped the charade. "I dated her for a bit."

"Do better than that."

"I fell for her. I asked her out. Turned out she was psycho. I ended it."

"Really, Sid? You ended it? At what point in this conversation, will the truth be the first thing that comes out of that forked tongue of yours?"

It got a rise out of Sid. *Good.* Went to Page 1 of the Lawyers' Playbook. "I can end this interview right now. I only agreed to meet you as a matter of courtesy, Detective."

"Then do me the fucking courtesy of being honest."

"I don't know what she told you, but that's what happened." Sid gleefully added, "Is she in trouble? It was just a matter of time before shit caught up to her."

"By that you mean—" Boz left it hanging.

"Probably fucked over the wrong guy, am I right?"

Boz left Sid guessing. Followed his tactic of switching up. "All you two did was fuck's what you're saying?"

Sid shrugged, "Pretty much."

"The DA's office hates what you do, who you defend. FYI, they've signed off." A lie, but Boz's grim demeanor allowed him to bluff perps into believing he was delivering the word of

God, "I can cuff you and extradite you right now. You'll be in New Orleans by day's end, where you'll get your phone call, and Monday'll be the first opportunity to get in front of a judge—someone I probably know. What do you figure your chances are of leaving Louisiana for the foreseeable future?"

"On what charge?"

Boz laughed. "Really?"

Some of the cocky left Sid. His throat rolled nervously. "OK, she saw me as a sugar daddy. Moved in the morning after our first night. She was eigtheen, with no reservations," Sid curled up one corner of his lips. "But she's cold. Heartless cold. Which made her an even bigger turn on, what can I say? I like cruel women."

Boz could identify. "Get to it."

"I saw her fight in the Octagon when she first showed up. She was vicious. I couldn't get her out of my mind. I knew Gavin—common business interests."

"Drugs," Boz surmised loud.

Sid didn't bite. "He introduced me to Jenny. We hooked up. I knew going in there'd be a price to pay, and I honored it. Put her in a PFL fight. She lasted seconds."

"You left out the detail of a contract you made her sign first."

"You can't make Jenny do anything. It's usually the other way around. She called it a twenty-five thousand investment in her—that's how much I shelled out to get her in. I remember her saying 'just so you know, nothing is free,' before she opened up," he grinned, "if you know what I mean. I already had a no-going-back hard-on, I said sure. Sex meant nothing to her. Just a means to an end."

"She walked out on you and the contract."

Sid's face tightened, "Yeah. I knew she would, deep down, but she was so fucking hot and nuts, I refused to accept it."

Boz baited, "It must eat you up, looking at her now."

Sid bit. "I recognized her talent before anybody did." His resentment grew. "Of course, I'm pissed off, wouldn't you be?"

"Do you know Nigel Hansom?"

And grew some more. "I looked him up. A redneck trucker?

And two old nothing-names—"

"Dusty Saldana and Puma Song."

"I heard they've been around so long, they were just bound to bump into talent. Like a stopped watch, the correct time is inevitable twice a day. They get to cash in?"

"Your deal with Jenny? Is it still valid?"

"It's in writing. Just because she broke it doesn't mean it's terminated." Sid snapped, his anger in full bloom, "To answer your question, is it valid? Fuck yeah!"

"You've never been tempted to demand what's yours?"

"Right place, right time," Sid seethed. "I'm in no hurry."

"Nigel Hansom is more than a trucker, but you know that." Boz came here to sow seeds. "You can't just walk up, show him a contract, and claim a piece of Jenny Sharp."

"He may be shady," Sid said between clenched teeth, "but I can be fucking darkness if I don't get what's mine."

According to Dusty Saldana

Nineteen thousand fans unleashed boos almost equal to the downpour of cheers. As white a crowd as I ever seen. We were in the Event Center on 14th and Grand, the Missouri side of Kansas. A serious upgrade from the 3500-seat Memorial Hall, where the Amazon Fighting Championships usually held their fights. Once again, the PR juggernaut called Jenny Sharp up-valued tickets to must-see premium and skyrocketed PPV numbers. First fight I saw celebrities ringside. Not summer blockbuster stars, Grammy singers, tycoons, and do-nothing socialites that showed up for Vegas marquee bouts, but B & C League camera hogs all dressed up in the colorful crazy you saw at the Kentucky Derby.

Jenny did her usual dance down the red carpet to the Octagon. Playing up what she, her publicist, and social media team'd come up with and hyped all week—that being a catch phrase, which she plucked the dangling microphone and yelled out, "You love to hate me, don't you, Kansas?"

They expected it and they roared.

"FU too!" she shouted back disdainfully. Took the noise to a whole another level.

It grew from there, when the AFC champ appeared to a dark arena with strobing lights and heavy metal. Nadia Kelly, 27, 5-5¾, 134, more ruddy than white. Powerful broad, body and legs. Hopped up and down the aisle. She called herself "global down to her DNA," claiming Ireland to Russia and every country in between in her heritage. Of course, Jenny turned that around and called her a world class mutt.

Entering the Octagon, Nadia drew her hand across her throat. Jenny got off her stool instantly, gesturing the champ to bring it on. I calmed her down. Grabbed her by the chin, "Time now to move the yap to your fists!"

"I got this, Dusty."

She stood up. I removed the stool. Headed out the same time Nadia's trainer exited. The fighters walked to the center for the prefight handshake. Nadia extended her hands, palms down. Jenny took hers forward, palm up. A goodwill two-hand slap. A second before their palms met, Jenny pulled away, and turned her back on Nadia. The crowd erupted—cheers and disapproval running equal. Sparked Nadia's fuse. She lunged and shoved Jenny in the back.

Jenny swung around.

Slap! She delivered an open faced palm across Nadia's cheek.

I threw my head back. *No!* Puma went ecstatic, as did Nigel, who showed up with Kamryn. AFC, being an all-chick league'd pussy-whipped him, since husband and wife came dressed by a loud fashion designer, looked like, who thought this be the moment and occasion to brag. Kamryn just gasped with a shocked smile.

The crowd shot to its feet and, for the next minute, I couldn't hear myself think.

Ref Zaire, 48, 6-2¼, 239, stepped forcefully in between. Big, burly, a light-skinned black, he towered over the girls. Quickly imposed martial law, shoving them back, thwarting a pre-fight brawl. He said in a Barry White baritone you'd expect to go with that imposing physique, "I'll disqualify the next one who throws a punch that's not between bells!" He dragged Jenny over to me, "You're already on thin ice, madam!"

Jenny pulled out her mouthpiece. "That was the plan, sir! I like fighting from behind!"

Zaire slashed his arm down. Kicking off Round 1 of five. The Timekeeper slapped his countdown clock to tick down from 05:00:00. Judges straightened.

Jenny hopped forward, and right off, underestimated Nadia's speed and accuracy, both of which she knew to expect since I'd programmed it into the virtual boxer. The real thing, as always, was faster and sharper. Nadia landed a dozen strikes—two significant, that I counted—in the first minute to none from Jenny. It didn't help that Jenny, after the first few, squared up like she always done under adversity.

I screamed into deaf ears, "Angle! Angle!"

The TV color analyst observed with a Country singer twang, "Nadia looks like she's done takin' guff and deliverin' some of her own in the form of a beatdown.'"

I couldn't argue with that. Nadia found Jenny's weakness—not seeing what come from her right fast enough. And brought a high left leg kick. *Wham!* Jenny eyes didn't even move. Then, Nadia walked Jenny all the way to the chainlink, dropping some absolute bombs.

This place went off.

Nadia was local, sort of. She come outta Nebraska, Kansas's neighbor to the north. Farmers for parents. Flag waving Republicans who loved guns. Local media painted Jenny a left wing liberal, who supported killing babies and protecting illegals.

The clinch may have declined, sure as hell saved Jenny. Also, it was our strategy. Nadia made her name as a pure distance striker. Close range, her power decreased drastic. But time was short.

Suits upstairs had standing instructions for refs to pull fighters apart quicker 'cause it stagnated fights, fizzled energy in the arena, and TV hated a break in the action. Jenny remembered, starting with an upper cut, that moved Nadia back just enough for a Thai Plum—where you wrap your hands around the opponent's neck. Kevin worked with Jenny on this as a real maneuver in this fight. Nadia's back arched to escape the clinch, opening up torso space for Jenny to land vicious knees!

"That's it!" I yipped.

"Break her fuckin' heart!" Of course Puma had a money line.

Nadia staggered backward. Jenny lunged for the first takedown of the match.

Wham!

Sitting next to Nigel's wife, I saw her wince. Nadia's head bounced on and off the canvas, once, twice. She recovered, too skilled to allow a fight ending half-guard or side-mount. Neither earned TIP points, but Nadia paid for it. Jenny went old school with her ground and pound inside Nadia's guard, trying to get to the premier grappling position—back control. Nadia absorbed the beating, refusing to allow Jenny to pass guard, escaped submission attempt after submission attempt. *Tough, tough broad.*

In the end, stats ruled. In the modern MMA game, grappling your way to a victory'd died with the last dinosaur. Jenny'd done it in Brazil. *Can lightning strike twice?* Fluke or not, Nadia landed a laser right, flush to Jenny's chin, to engineer her escape to her feet.

"Don't square up!" I shouted as the two girls practiced distancing.

This time Jenny had an answer for everything. Blocking punches, checking kicks, and landing her own hooks and knees. Nadia'd likely trained the entire time leading up to this fight to neutralize Jenny's southpaw advantage. It was a whole another story coming up against it. Jenny and I'd practiced making Nadia get fixated on the left hand to unleash a flurry of shattering knees. When Nadia quit thinking about the southpaw, Jenny came like a thunderbolt outta the blue with a significant left hand strike.

Whabam!

For a moment, Nadia became Galileo, looking at stars.

Jenny jumped in for a head-and-arm throw. Shaking off the cobwebs, Nadia would've none of it and tried to take her back. Jenny secured top position, then side control, all the while bloodying Nadia. Round 1 went the distance, into a stand up again, and ended in a clinch.

I hurried in. Put down the stool. Sat Jenny down. Washed her mouthpiece and wiped her down. "Fight going exactly like we played out it would, except for you facing up."

"And she still hit like a girl," denounced Jenny, gargling, wincing because of the Listerine in the water. It closed and cleaned any cuts, removing any excuse for the physician, who could be from the Midwest too. Best remove all risks.

"She gone five rounds once before," I cautioned. "So, tiring her out ain't a working strategy."

"Five rounds? Shit, Dusty, Round 3 isn't even on my agenda," she began seriously, then smiled lopsided, "I have early dinner plans." Her eyes lifted, said, "A lady doc," to the arriving arena physician, cutwoman, whatever, 50, 5-3, 130. I figured all-chicks-all-the-time was AFC company policy. Jenny joked, "I got no business for you tonight."

Apart from some bruising, nothing caught the doc's attention. She arrived and left all in the same breath.

Puma pressed up against the cage. "Lil girl, word be all three judges scored the first round a draw."

"Just pick up where you left off!" I said. Nigel remained in his seat, reserving judgment, or putting up a dignified front for his Mrs. I had no time for his beef or manners, whichever one it was. "Don't think they haven't seen your tendency to square up. But they also seen tape and know you have a thick skull."

"Shit, Dusty," Jenny laughed. Only she could, in this calm eye of a stormy fight. "Are you knocking my brains or admiring my bone density?"

I had to smile. "Both." She punched me in the arm. "Seriously, look for her to come out intent on givin' you a facial—the kind that rearrange your jaw. And nooo-body wanna fuck Mrs.

Frankenstein."

"Shit," Jenny perked up, "if I can't fuck I'll eat the gun." Jenny planted a kiss on Dusty's cheek.

Crowd went "Oooh!"

Jenny grinned, "I love you, Dusty Saldana, you get me!"

"Now, go plant the bitch!" I ordered.

Nadia never expected what came next. Jenny came outta her corner in a blazing sprint! Covered the distance between them in the matter of a second. Left the canvas, feet first. Taking a page outta a WWE takedown.

There's your advantage being a newbie. There was scant tape, but the one on Nadia, however, was a whistleblower—her corner always played it safe, going back to what worked in the prior round, the thinking being, let the opponent find a way to stop you. Playing it safe won her the AFC belt two years running. Jenny appeared vulnerable against her distance striking and I figured Nadia would try to control range. Being truthful, Jenny come up with this tactic whilst we were studying. Said she'd pulled it off a couple of times in fight clubs. I insisted she trust me if and when to make the call, our code being, "Plant that bitch!"

Success came with four caveats. One, surprise—at this level, fighters were lightning quick to react. Two, a high-jumper's skill and control to elevate only as high as Nadia's neck. Three, arriving horizontal at that altitude. Four, counting on Nadia's muscle memory to dictate her reflexes, head snapping to the right—her natural side.

We nailed the first three. Failed on the fourth.

Nadia took a step back, not right. *Shit!* I never heard a crowd lull down in the matter of a second. But you coulda heard a pin drop, it seemed like, compared to the frenzied cries from a moment afore. Jenny channeled Michael fucking Jordan!

Adjusted in midair!

And turned over too. Face down when her feet whipped on each side of Nadia's neck. Scissoring full circle, when she locked her ankles. Yanked the champ off her feet. Jenny fell back first, Nadia plunging down on her side with no control on the landing.

Whabam!

For the second time in this match, Nadia's skull bounced off the canvas. This time though, it didn't simply hit, but smashed down. The definition of an MMA 'slam!' Nadia faced me and I saw her eyes almost leave their sockets. Her cheeks fluttered like the skin was cheap plastic confronting a gale. Jenny stood over her, one arm up, forefinger extended and circling.

"What are you waiting for?" I hollered.

Jenny had the pick of submissions to finish this off.

"What the fuck!" Nigel hollered, drawing a sharp look from his wife, who didn't know MMA. So, she didn't get that her husband was dismayed that Jenny let Nadia stand, be it on butterfly knees.

"Jenny being Jenny," I yelled back, suspecting she'd found this fight boring so far.

To be honest, Nadia'd fared better than the stats for an orthodox vs. southpaw in accuracy and head power strike share. Jenny, for her part, fulfilled the metric of takedown success and ground advances. Jenny declared winning by the numbers was a good way to be forgotten quickly. Defying them set you up to be the GOAT—Greatest Of All Time. Big talk for a young pup—like it or not, but that's where her head was at. Always been. Sometimes I wondered if she'd rather lose trying the exotic than use what won 80% of the time—the armbar or choke.

Nadia got halfway up. Jenny wrapped Nadia's neck in a guillotine. Nadia slipped her head by Jenny's hip and grabbed Jenny around the middle. *Nadia shouldn't be thanking her lucky stars but asking why Jenny let her off the hook.* Nadia continued to set up to drive Jenny to the chainlink. Jenny was off script, not without reason, for a change. I knew she had a crazy idea. Whether she could pull it off was another thing. I—hell, everyone in the arena—got their answer.

She did something nobody had done before to Nadia.

Hoisted the AFC champ clean off the ground!

Jenny loved to lift—I never seen anyone add reps and weights almost daily. Waist up, she was Hercules, but not the heroic kind.

She pulled out her inner Daikaiju. That wasn't astonishing. What came next blew my mind. *Holy fuck!*

I thought it. Puma yelled it, "Carousal guillotine!"

The crowd—they were educated and blew up. Shocked, amazed. You couldn't tell who screamed with what emotion. *Who cares?* I bet the arena never seen the noise meter stay sustained red as long as it did.

Jenny helicoptered Nadia around!

Once, twice, three times. Remember watching *Star Wars*, *Transformers*, *Matrix*, or *Avatar* that first time? And having your mind blown away? That's what her finger twirling all about. A telegraph of the carousel guillotine, imitating that hitter who points where the home run gonna be headed and sending it there. Jenny released Nadia like a discus thrower.

Whabam!

Nadia hit the fence. The cage coulda been manufactured outta elastic, the way it bubbled outward, tattooing Nadia with the chainlink pattern. Boomeranged back in, sinking Nadia. She and this canvas now'd become more than just good acquaintances, this being her third up close and personal contact.

Jenny gloated to the crowd.

Ref Zaire circled over to the champ, treating this Nadia-canvas kiss as *finito.* But her corner clapped. Elated! Even Ref Zaire blinked. Stunned.

"She ain't done!" I hollered to Jenny, directing her eyes back to Nadia.

Never-say-die been Nadia's rep all career and, sure enough, she refused to die. Ref Zaire stepped back, turning down Nadia's corner for time. *Mothafucka's fair.* A novelty for me. Jenny had a window yet again for a pick of submissions to finish this off.

"Stop playing!" I heard Nigel yell, still standing.

His wife didn't know if she should smile or be embarrassed. The woman dripped so much class, she probably turned on the radio when she peed.

My ears hurt from the deafening cries. Again, you couldn't tell who had the upper hand, supporters or detractors. Regardless, no way in hell this decibel level sounded legal or safe. Nadia staggered erect. Jenny landed a strike that defined significant—a lead-leg head kick that come outta the instruction manual. Caught Nadia flush. *Bam!* Made the fence her blood relative. In the time it took the chainlink to retract, thrusting Nadia forward, Jenny repositioned herself.

Nadia had a straight shot at going low at Jenny. She did.

I knew Jenny hoped Nadia would.

Brilliant! Spectacle and spectacular's how Jenny acquire all this notoriety. *Here it comes!* I blamed Kevin, 'cause he opened this can of worms. *Pull this off, Jenny'n you'll be etched forever in MMA lore.* So would the carousel guillotine. Shit, the entire last minute of this fight'd go down as the Eighth Wonder of the World.

Nadia sprawled. Jenny worked into an over-under position—forcing Nadia down on her elbows and knees. Jenny's arms slipped on either side of Nadia's neck for a gable grip—which was locking up her wrist with her other hand. Drew her left leg over Nadia's neck, pulling down Nadia's head, all the while tightening up the chokehold. Jenny smashed her ass down hard! Swung her outside leg over Nadia's body.

Mind you, all this transpired in mere seconds with Nadia flopping like a slippery fish that just come outta water. But Jenny'd set this up perfectly and used the few initial moments of Nadia being slow and dazed to work into position that rarely—almost never—occurred to allow this submission to work. No wonder then, it be done just once in history—when CB Dollaway used it to crush Jesse Taylor. Now Jenny was one move from being only the second. Here came the *pièce de résistance*, pardon my French. Jenny tightened her arms into a noose.

Make that, Peruvian fucking Necktie!

Known more as crank than a choke, it came outta, yep, Peru. The brainchild of Anton Nicolas de Souza, who created a style called Cholitzu—combining the ethnic Amerindians, or *cholo*, and BJJ.

Ref Zaire leaned in. Nadia was a penny from passing out.

Gave the tap.

Jenny kicked the champ loose. Sprang to her feet and circled the Octagon bathed in cheers. Even the boo birds marveled the finish. One judge did the unthinkable. He stood up and clapped. Nigel forgot his wife. She looked lost, on her feet, smiling and politely clapping like she be at the Queen's dinner. Never seen Nigel move as fast as he did to the Octagon. He hugged me. I hugged Puma. We were jumping up and down, no matter that us ancients risked tearing our ACL.

"That was fucking MMA Picasso!" Puma nutshelled it.

"Poetry!" Nigel shouted into my year.

"She something else, ain't she?" I yelled back, never so elated.

The next fifteen minutes just became an ecstatic blur with the Ref Zaire declaring Jenny the winner, Jenny holding up the belt, and finding a way to destroy sportsmanship by waving it in Nadia's face as her corner helped her out. The crowd ate that up. *So, what do I know?*

Nigel went over and bear hugged Jenny. Their first interaction since Jenny'd broken his four cardinal rules two Fridays ago. He didn't give me all the details when he called me Saturday—the morning after the crime—and asked me to go down to the Easy Trucking parking lot and report back that Jenny'd cleaned up the mess like he warned her to, *or else.* I got there, extracted the skinny outta one of the fighters. Jenny'd complied. You couldn't tell there been an orgy till the wee hours.

I figured Jenny got Nigel's message loud and clear, but that turned out to be a pipe dream. She remained unapologetic when she came in on Monday. Poor Ecuador and Cesar took home gifts of scars for Jenny's birthday bash. Simple fact—she forced guys to think with their dicks and they ended up payin' for it. But I got through to them. Not just that it was dangerous and wrong, but disrespectful to Nigel. More than the money, he gave them a shot at a dream. It wasn't a hard sell, since remorse and fear been building all weekend.

Nigel did not show up for breakfast, but stopped by in the afternoon. The guys did not dare to even look up, the bees knees the way they kept punching and training. Usually he greeted them.

Not that Monday. His face set in stone, we talked logistics about our next I-10 stop. Jenny, in her corner, fought the virtual boxer. Puma wisely stayed outta the picture. Once we done talking, I signaled the guys with a nod. They stopped working out, came over, and apologized, most of them with genuine tears. Being a businessman, invested in these dumbasses, he softened. Forgave them. Slapped Ecuador and inquired after the back of Cesar's head. Mind you, he did not smile once through his pardons.

Then, he looked over toward Jenny, who'd stopped to watch this apology tour. Their eyes met, she pulled her 3D Goggles back on, and resumed training.

"I told her just mouthin' sorry won't cut it," said Puma, limping over. No saying if Nigel bought it. I didn't. Puma had her back. Always. "She needs to find a way to show it."

Nigel simply nodded and left. *Fuck, he's not risking his business for a belt.* Looked like we'd be hitting the end of the road with him shortly, not unless Jenny backed down or Nigel backed off. Neither showed any inclination to reach for the white flag. They said not a word for the two weeks leading up to this fight.

Those two weeks, though, were the best training Jenny ever put in. I made sure Nigel knew that. Maybe Puma'd advised her right. Nigel didn't pull the rug, but I woke up expecting it every day. I also couldn't imagine the tension when she went next door every afternoon after practice, what the with social media team and publicist parked right outside Nigel's office. Didn't seem to affect her creative juices, authoring a Twitter storm with, "You love to hate me, don't you, Kansas? FU too!" Nothing got to her. If Nigel dumped her, she'd care less. She'd just move on. *This girl ain't just a survivor, she survives and thrives, one adversity to the next.*

All that receded into the rear view now.

Nigel and Puma, as usual, went with Jenny to her post fight presser. I headed back into the empty arena for my recap. Nadia exploited Jenny's bad habit but once. *Nadia's brings a high leg left kick. WHAM! Jenny's eyes don't even move.*

If the next stop was UFZ, I had to get this Achilles outta her heel.

The love fest between Nigel and Jenny that began in the Octagon and carried on in the locker room and presser, now continued in the private jet back to New Orleans. *Winning cures everything. Ain't that the truth?* With Nigel's wife being on board, Jenny didn't misbehave.

"Mrs. Hansom," she leaned and whispered, but everyone could hear, "You're so classy, I can't bring myself to even say hell, let alone fuck."

Kamryn laughed. A good sport. You could see we were the help from her vantage. But being Southern, she showed grace and graciousness. That aside, she still put two rows between us when we began another round of drinking and patting ourselves on the back.

"How about I show up at the next I-10 event?" Jenny suggested to Nigel. "I can grip, grin, and hype the bubble prospects you otherwise couldn't unload."

"I don't know," I said. "Nobody'd be watching the fights if they are too busy kissing your ass."

"Exactly."

It was Nigel's call. His ear to ear beam said it all.

Puma Song: Recollections from New Orleans

Puma saw Jenny as a breeder would an untamed, Arabian thoroughbred. Unbridled and savage accounted for all the beauty and charm. If the aftermath of the Brazil fight set a bar, the glitz following her claiming the AFC belt—nobody done it without working up its ranks—climbed outta this world. Stratospheric, that the word. So many morning shows called, she did it like the President—be on all of them at the same time from her apartment by having Nigel dispatch a crew from the local station and have the big shot TV folks ask her questions from their studios.

'Round midweek, Nigel summoned Team Jenny to his office. By that time, New Orleans, hell the entire state of Louisiana, claimed her as their own. Governor down to the Mayor tweeted out congratulations. City set up a ceremony for this Friday to present her a Key.

Nigel's announcement did not come as any big surprise. "UFZ called. Ever since Jenny blew up MMA, they were holding back announcing who'd fight Bella Haroon to earn a spot against the Bantamweight champ in Vegas this Summer."

"Bella Haroon," said Dusty, looking at Jenny. "African. They call her the Black Widow."

"I've heard of her," knocked Jenny, unimpressed. "Been close. Twice. Failed to get into the title fight both times." Twisted her lips, deriding further, "Third time's going to be the curse."

Puma loved it. "Tweet that out!"

Nigel laughed too. "Guess the venue? Irvin, Texas, Cowboy Stadium!"

"Holy shit!" Jenny high-fived Puma. "That holds a hundred thousand fans, give or take! Glad UFZ is bringing it up to my level."

"Bella's paid her dues and to die hards, you haven't," said Dusty. Puma didn't expect him to partake in the joy. Finding sumthin' to poke at instead. "Expect bad blood."

"Perfect!" replied Jenny. Snapped her fingers. "I know! I'm going to address her as Ma Bell in every post."

Nigel and Puma laughed whole heartedly. Dusty didn't. *Of course not.*

UFZ's President made the announcement. The reaction came instantly via TV and social media. There was as much outcry as cheering. Mostly reporters, who never even landed a fist into a feather pillow, condemned UFZ for selling out to money, ratings, and the TMZ demo. Fans knew better, indicating if the previous two fights turned out chart toppers, this'd fucking bust Billboard. Nobody talked about nothing else for a coupla news cycles.

Jenny, of course, celebrated like it was 1999. Curmudgeon Dusty disapproved, "I hear her apartment become party central."

"She twenty years young, rich," said Puma. "Not like us at at that age barely scraping by."

"Force us to drive harder."

"To nowhere."

"Booze, drugs, cock—you can survive one, not all three."

Dusty wan't wrong, but Puma didn't want to admit it. Whatever the reason, he looked upon Jenny like his own child. She showed him respect she showed no other. "She broken every prediction, and so my money on her coming out ahead of this one too."

"*Vogue*'s asked for a photo shoot," Jenny said, Friday morning of the brouhaha outside City Hall to hand her the Key to New Orleans.

They hung together in the area where VIPs mingled between the microphone and five rows of folding chairs ten across. Dusty'd grabbed a corner seat in the back row, looking for an excuse to bolt. Shit, a crowd of coupla thousand showed up. Puma and Dusty received passes they slung around their necks to be allowed inside the velvet rope.

Puma never bought *Vogue*. "I flip through it in the airport," Puma said. "They notion that shiny paper and guesswork lace somehow make hoochy tasteful."

"What's wrong with that?" she laughed. "About time I classed up my tits and pussy, don't you think?"

Nigel pressed flesh, milling between politicians, the Mayor, other big looking wigs. The Police Chief and DA—both running to join the rogue's gallery as next Mayor—worked the crowd line on opposite sides. The election was in three months, around the time of Jenny's match against Bella, and pundits proclaimed the Police Chief had this in the bag. He probably—no, make that most definitely—was already on Nigel's payroll. For the obvious reasons. No doubt Nigel'n his rich cronies likely also'd already handpicked who'd take over the NOPD.

"Bostwick Oswald."

A good looking blue-eyed, blond in a suit and tie snuck up from behind and extended his hand to Jenny. Puma saw the badge in his belt. His hackles rose. Immediately suspicious.

Jenny's face cracked wide. "You better not be married."

"No, I'm not," he smiled politely. "Just wanted to say hello."

"Fuck," Jenny, like she always done, "I'd like to do more than that, Bostwick," almost made him blush.

"Boz," he recovered with an uncertain smile.

The loudspeakers whined when the Mayor tapped the microphone to kick off this affair. "Good morning, New Orleans!"

"Give me your card, Boz." Jenny aggressively put her hand out over the applause greeting the Mayor. Puma'd narrowed his eyes and kept 'em fixed on Boz, who reacted, surprised, but pulled out his wallet and gave her one. She looked it."I won't be calling you on official business, Detective Boz. Write your personal cell."

Boz smiled. He pulled out a pen and obliged.

Jenny stuffed the card in her bra. Winked.

Boz retreated. Puma watched him pull outta earshot and disappear behind crossing bodies. The Mayor, meanwhile droned on, thanking everyone from Jesus on down. Puma leaned into Jenny's ear, "Why'd a cop come up to you?"

"He wants to fuck me, Puma, why else would any man approach me? But I'll ask."

"I don't trust him. Be careful."

"What are you? Channeling Dusty sitting over there like he can't move his bowels." She slipped her hand into Puma's arm. "I want you by my side."

"Lil girl, I ain't exactly enhancing your image."

"Don't sell yourself short," she smiled. "Old, black, Asian, crippled, you check a lot of boxes."

A bit later, Jenny took the microphone, holding up the oversized golden key, "I'm fighting Ma Bell, y'all know. I'd like to say I'll send her career to an early grave. Hell," Jenny be crafty and sly, never needing to be bleeped when she play directly to the public, "that would mean two things, she's young, and she has a career!"

The crowd roared. This kicked off her relentless attack—with Jenny, it was equal portions personal and professional. She ordered her social team in Nigel's office to troll Bella relentlessly. The Black Widow refused to be drawn in, taking the high road in her responses. The media chose to plug Bella. It created a sympathy wave. Which suited Jenny fine.

Storm clouds gathered when Jenny returned to training after a week off. Dusty didn't look happy with her effort. Puma asked him to lay off for a day or so to let her work off the banquet circuit since dethroning Nadia.

"Open your eyes, Puma," Dusty angrily whispered, watching Jenny struggle at the bag. "The cancer commenced with her win in Brazil. Now it's full blown rot of conceit." Still, Dusty acquiesced to Puma. Waited three days. Come Thursday, when she couldn't break out of a routine lock while grappling Kevin, Dusty walked over, "Kevin, take five."

"Don't look like it's just cock, but sugar on top of it," fumed Dusty. The harshness and bluntness caught Puma's attention. It took Jenny by surprise too. "Is that the story?"

"Yeah, why?" Jenny stood up. Her retort come swiftly, "You want to see how it's done?"

"I ain't one who likes to repeat a conversation we already had."

"So, I'm enjoying my success," Jenny remained unrepentant. "Not my problem if you don't know how."

"Success?" Dusty laughed, looked at Puma like the girl just cracked a joke. "What success? You win two fucking fights and still two from the title!"

A few illegals, working out, looked over.

"I know," Jenny started caustic, "that looks like a long way off to you, Dusty, what with you waking up looking in the mirror, morning after morning, and seeing only disappointment," then unleashed, "for thirty fucking years!"

Jenny raising her voice drew the attention of the rest of the illegals. Kevin started to advance. Puma signaled with his eyes for him stand down and stand back. Jenny and Dusty were once again approaching the line. Puma interrupted, "Come on, now."

"Shit, Puma," Jenny laughed cruelly, "that's ten years longer than I've been alive!" To Dusty, "And you're telling me how to live my life?"

Dusty let her insult roll off his back, railing "I don't give a fuck how you spent last week. But now, here, this, it's business hours, been since Monday, and seems like you still on vacation."

"How many hits have you taken the past two fights, huh? I'm the one absorbing the pain and recovering from injuries. Cock and coke are my release."

"You want goddamn release, shove your hand down there!"

"Looks like you're the one who needs to jerk off, you old fuck!"

"Guys, we all on the same side, same purpose—" Puma tried to usher peace, but those two, they were too far gone to turn back. Now every illegal'd turned into a spectator.

"You have no idea what it takes to be a champ!" Dusty bellowed.

"And you do?"

"You ain't even close!"

"There!" Jenny pressed her head up against his face. Her nose an inch from his. Spit flying out. "You just got close to one! You can die now!"

"Get the fuck outta my face!" Dusty shoved Jenny.

Jenny swung back, reflex instant.

Pow! Struck Dusty's jaw. Sent him reeling. Kevin caught him. Dusty shook him off angrily. Lunged back.

"Come on!" Jenny beckoned him, disparaging. "I dare you!"

"Enough!" Nigel's voice shot across like a cannon.

Everyone froze.

Dusty worked his jaw,, "I should cut you ear to ear."

"Thank Nigel for his timing, or Puma'd be dialing 9-1-1 right now," hissed Jenny, not about to let Dusty have the last word, "reporting an unable to resuscitate."

"Shut up, both of you," Nigel walked over. Jenny and Dusty remained angry. "Make up, or I'll get involved, and you don't want that."

Puma shoved his cane in Jenny's back toward Dusty.

"Sorry," she said sullenly after what seemed like an eternity of glaring 'tween the two. "I know you have my best interest."

"I'm old school," Dusty grumbled back, like a kid needing to be dragged 'cause he refused to move his feet. "I know only tough love."

They got through training with no further flare ups.

Puma played elder statesmen, "This be like 'em four-by-hundred relay races. Jenny, you running the anchor leg 'cause only you can bring it home. Setting you up in the best position to win—that's Dusty, Kevin, Nigel, the early runners. Sometimes, early runners stumble, or the baton exchange ain't smooth, but you don't blame, don't give up, because all that matters is crossing that finish line number one."

"How long have you been waiting to drop that?" asked Jenny, drawing smiles, which was Puma's objective. *At least, that ends the day light-hearted.*

It took Jenny another couple of days before looking 'fighting' fit. Her focus returned. Bella Haroon, she found out combating the virtual boxer, was a beast. Bella taken out every opponent in her career in two rounds or less. No one else on the circuit came even close to this remarkable record.

Jenny knew she had to seriously raise her standup and ground game. Started pumping 'em weights. Delved into the archives for Ali, McGregor, Cena—you know, every champ, boxing to MMA to WWE. Forced Kevin and Dusty to study more too.

Puma attributed this sudden diligence to the last thing Nigel said after Dusty and Jenny reluctantly apologized following their blow up. "I'm out coming up on a quarter of a million dollars. Blood will spill, should my investment go south."

Nigel said nothing about Jenny being there until she just walked out between the first two fighters. The room dropped quiet for a moment, then went off like a gas explosion, with crazy loud whoops and hollers and clapping. Rednecks to the law, and every one 'tween, they reacted identical. The attention whore that she was, I thought Jenny'd get into her prefight antics, but she was restrained, just waved, raising an arm of each of the guys she escorted into the Octagon. *That girl never ceases to surprise.* So self-confident in her own glamour and fame, she conceded the limelight to the fighters.

"Hey, hey, hey!" she shouted and subsided the room. "Don't see any women. I love it! Means I have my pick of the men who are ready and willing to cheat on their wives and girlfriends!" The way the guys tried to out-cackle each other, you'd think it was a contest with the heartiest going home with Jenny. "But this isn't my night. It's yours! Yeah, yours! To find the next Jenny Sharp! Trust me! These guys all have potential! You just have to recognize a diamond in the rough like Dusty and Nigel did in me." She pointed to me'n Nigel. *She's just stroking our ego.* So, I forced a modest smile, but Nigel bought her snake-oil and beamed and waved. "OK! Shall we get the ass whupping started?"

And with that responding roar, the first card got underway with a couple of forgettable Flyweights 'cause I figured Jenny'd garner all the attention initially. I put Ecuador into the second match. With that boot to the head, Nigel gave him a concussion. Cesar too, marrying his skull to the steel wall of the container, which knocked both outta the previous I-10 stop.

Tonight, we were in Vulture City, Arizona. You could find a needle in a haystack easier. Fifteen years ago, the military built a silo—inside which we were fighting, a pretty damn cool setting, if you asked me—then, had second thoughts, and just left. The town that sprung up during construction discovered a strain of gold, which brought in prospectors, and hope surged that VC'd survive. Turned out, the quantities're so scant and scattered, mining it took more effort than it was worth. Most prospectors fled. Diehards stayed behind and formed a community of 38—no joke—around a gas station, which also stocked grocery, drugs, hardware, tools, you name it. You didn't need another store, not with Amazon Prime.

Those who'd seen Ecuador didn't bother watching. Newcomers to the party paused. Cut like he was, kid looked like a fighter. But that attraction faded fast, when Guido Hoya, 22, 5-7, 148, scored an early head kick, added a question mark kick, and followed that up with a wheel kick. Guido'd turned out to be a sleeper in training. Quiet, understated, respectful. He exposed Ecuador's lack of speed. Matters went to the mat. Ecuador survived an armbar and the round.

Guido's skills turned heads. A lackey cleaned up Guido at the other corner. Not that he needed it. He was barely touched. In the other corner, I grabbed Ecuador, "Guido took the first. You gotta go for broke in this round." The lackey and I switched places. "Guido. Do what you're doing and you'll be on your fucking way."

Interest heightened in the second round, when I saw Jenny grab the chainlink and pay attention. This coaxed promoters to watch. The rest of the crowd—mostly bettors—kept their eye on the fight only 'cause they had money.

Desperation made Ecuador reckless. Guido force fed him right hand after right hand. Ran Ecuador to the fence and continued to score with power punches. Guido, who dropped outta high school in Monclova, Coahuila, Mexico, showed off his wrestling chops, when he knocked the feet out from under Ecuador, then used an active guard from the bottom and pulled off an omoplata submission—a sweet looking BJJ shoulder lock done from the bottom.

I caught Jenny's eye. She winked. This pairing was her idea.

"Guido'll look so dominant," she said," someone will bite." Three did, and set off a bit of a bidding war. Jenny may have fucked Ecuador, but to get back into Nigel's good graces, the girl had no conscience fucking the Mexican over.

Next card featured two heavyweights, Rodrigo, 22, 5-9¾, 268, and Ortiz, 22, 5-10¼, 270, both with boxing backgrounds and we worked on their limited grappling skills. Rodrigo been a quick learner from the moment he got off the truck and it came through, diving for a kneebar. Remarkably Ortiz, not only stuffed it, he managed to end up on top in half guard. That turned out to be his last successful act. Rodrigo stood the fight back up and found a home for a barrage of power head strikes, then landed a thudding left hook. Dropping Ortiz, Rodrigo landed on top, gained top mount, and hammered away.

"End it now!" Jenny hollered, looking up at the clock. Forty-five seconds remained.

Her jumping in set off the crowd, buyers to bettors. I looked at Nigel. *Shit, we never had participation like this.* When Rodrigo threw down a gruesome armbar that'dve broken bones in a lower weight class, the crowd began a ten count led by Jenny. Another first. Ortiz tapped out when it got to five. Heavyweights, being rarer than hens with teeth, Rodrigo attracted more than one suitor and went to highest bidder.

Jenny also had the law eating outta her hand. They fawned over her. She touched them just so, circled a hand around the waist, playfully slapped them—all manipulative to the core—that they likely believed they'd fuck at some point tonight.

A couple of Welterweights I had no hope for, went three rounds and two extra savage 'No Mercy' minutes to decide a winner. One sported a crimson mask, but sliced open the other with an elbow. Finally, a head kick put this to bed. Both ended up going, I seriously think, 'cause Jenny circled the cage, doing my job, yelling instructions.

"This is a meat market," she whispered, "without a single prime cut. Fortunately, none of these fools are butchers."

I had to smile.

The final match—a battle of Lightweights—featured Jenny's other honey, Cesar, against Zappa, 20, 5-8, 162. Jenny stepped up with a couple of buyers to my left.

"Cesar is a star in the making," Jenny promoted. "Zappa is

a grinder. I sparred with them both. Neither should be headed back to New Orleans, am I right, Dusty?"

"Ain't my job to sell 'em," I smiled, 'cause that was Nigel's rule. "But Jenny's been with them where it matters—in the Octagon."

After a quick exchange of jabs and leg kicks, Cesar landed a punishing power head strike. Zappa lost his balance. Cesar went in like Nazis into France, chasing Zappa with significant strikes, taking him to the canvas for more abuse. *Survive the round!* I wanted to yell, but I didn't have to. Zappa escaped to his feet and refused Cesar's takedown attempts.

"You got heart, Zappa," I said, between Round 1 and 2. He was badly hurt, on shaky legs. I fed him some smelling salts, and while the lackey came over to clean him up, I jacked up Cesar, "You had Zappa on the ropes the entire round. But you didn't finish!"

Zappa came out a different fighter—a jackrabbit on 'roids—and landed some solid strikes with his legs and fists, then judo-tossed Cesar to the floor.

Jenny got everyone going again.

This shaped to go three rounds and did. In the 3rd, Zappa opened with a straight right. Cesar found his range, began peppering counter strikes. Zappa came with forward pressure. Cesar showed his superior footwork, pushed the action. In the final minute, he dumped Zappa on the mat, scored with short punches, and with a body triangle, forced Zappa to tap out.

"Wooo!" shouted Jenny. "Some fucking way to cap the night!"

She left Nigel to conduct his business. I hung around answering character and work ethic questions about the guys moving on, tips on their strengths, weakness, anything else the buyers wanted clarified. Overall, the sentiment was this was the best crop Nigel'd put out. I disagreed, but kept my trap shut. Cesar, Rodrigo, and OK, Zappa, shoulda been the only three purchased. On the rest, Jenny put lipstick and nobody saw the pig. She forced the buyers into thinking with their smaller head.

I-10 have no 30-day return policy, so shit, I don't care.

I headed outside. Nigel had rolled in two RVs to serve as the locker rooms and toilets. I caught up with the fighters. Everyone came packed and I congratulated the five who were moving on, shook their hands, counted out the cash owed, and wished them good luck. Three were coming back with me to New Orleans, to train and try again. I had to cut two loose, one being Ecuador.

"Where's Ecuador?" I asked.

"Jenny came by. Took him outside."

She's pity fucking him. I couldn't be angry, I wasn't pleased either. *How the fuck isn't she afraid of HIV, crabs, all kindsa STDs?* Not like Ecuador came here with a wallet full of condoms. Sure enough, both of them came outta the equipment truck—the eighteen-wheel behemoth that transported the Octagon and everything that went into setting up these fights.

"Oh, don't look so fucking judgemental, Dusty," Jenny smiled. She kissed Ecuador hard and long for one last time. "*Llama a Gavin. Puedes comenzar con su club de lucha.*" Call Gavin. You can start in his fight club. "Have you seen Cesar?"

"RV." I tilted my head toward the one I just left.

"I'm not going to fuck him," Jenny laughed. "He'll have his share of tail, now that he's moving on." She walked away, looking back to Ecuador. "*Cuídate.*"

"You too," he said in English and whispered to me, "*Ella es alguien con quien follas, no te casas.*" She is someone you fuck, not marry. So much for me worrying about him being heartbroken. I gave him the usual goodbye kiss. Didn't bother asking if he wanted a ride to Mexico since he'd decided to head to SoCal and try the fight clubs.

Jenny flew back with Nigel outta Phoenix. Since only three headed back, we paired up in the two RVs for the trip back. Arrived in New Orleans the next night, make that midnight. I hit the sack and didn't get outta bed till noon.

I met up with Puma for dinner. He didn't make the trip, but was prideful Jenny helped move the bubble fighters and pleased she got us back on the right side of Nigel's ledger. I had money on a week, before she did something to end this truce. Puma had money on "not going to happen." To affirm his confidence in her, he added, "Her parents? Killed in accident like she said."

Makena Cole: Eyes Only File Summary Notes, Baltimore

Makena pulled through the gates of The Mansion, her heart and mind racing.

"If we meet again, it means things have gone wrong," Cherry Hill drug lord, Mr. Knight, had warned Makena the night she brought Nigel's offer to use Easy Trucking for Cartel business. Shown into the same library, she searched for the reason for these summons. Worrisome also—he asked her to come alone. *What's gone wrong?*

"Makena," Mr. Knight greeted. She whirled around, her throat rolling fearfully. "Sit," he gestured to the three-seat sofa. He took the single across, like last time. He looked distinguished in a three-piece suit. She wasn't sure if he was headed out or coming back from an important meeting. Dressed business-casual—ankle length slim fit pants, conservative blouse, and stilettos—she crossed her legs and clutched her purse in her lap.

Makena wanted to speak. *No. Let him.* What she might suspect as the reason could be something not even on his radar.

"Business is running fine," Mr. Knight said. "It's not about that."

Makena almost sagged her shoulders in relief. He probably did not remember his warning. She blinked attentively, relaxing the nails that'd been biting into her palms.

"Nigel uses his trucks to smuggle fighters in from Mexico. You didn't tell me."

"It did not concern our business," Makena replied carefully. She'd OK'd Nigel's vanity foray. *Not something I want to admit.* "And he is more aware than us about keeping it separate. I monitor as well. There is no overlap. He uses one specific truck for this. It's not used for our product. Besides, Easy Trucking is his company. I didn't want to make it an issue until it became one."

"Have you been following his new fighter, Jenny Sharp?"

"Yes. He thinks he's got a champion."

"Good for him. What about us?"

Makena did not understand. *Does he want a piece?* "I don't think there is enough money to go—"

"No," interrupted Mr. Knight. "About the spotlight she's shining on Nigel and his business."

Makena thought quickly on her feet. "It cuts both ways is how I look at it. The high profile only makes it highly unlikely anyone will suspect he or his company could be doing anything illegal."

Mr. Knight pursed his lips, curved it down at the corners, and went, "Hmm." Like she had a point. "Pay him a visit." He stood up. Makena followed. *And say what?* He read her mind, "Express my concern."

Nigel was no fool, she knew. Her sudden call to schedule an arrival meant a Cartel message came with it. The flight from Baltimore landed at 3 PM. Nigel sent a limousine as always. She pulled up in front of Easy Trucking's offices at 4:30. The driver opened the door for her, then ran ahead to hold the front door too. She hadn't been to New Orleans since Jenny'd signed on and so'd never met her. But Makena followed Jenny on every platform. Even though she was familiar with the outrageous taunts, insults, and jokes—some laugh-worthy—it didn't prepare Makena for the real thing.

Jenny emerged from Nigel's office with Dusty and Puma—Makena knew who the two men were because she made it her business to familiarize herself with everyone close to Nigel.

"Makena," Nigel smiled, surprised. "I thought you were coming later tonight."

"I found an early flight." She embraced him.

Nigel's smile faltered. Recovered, "Jenny, my CFO, Makena Cole."

Jenny smiled and went, "Wow! And I thought I was fucking pretty!" Makena laughed modestly. She'd let her hair down. Light linen skirt, soft belted at the waist, and buttoned up front over her right leg, which created enough of a split to tease her thigh. "Your name's even prettier. Makena."

Jenny's handshake was firm like a man's, and Makena returned the compliment, "I have heard nothing but championship talk about you."

"All true, even the bad stuff. Makena, later tonight, let's get a drink and—hell, I won't pussy foot." Winks. "We can go up to your room and I'll swing all the way over for you."

Makena smiled uncertainly.

"Jenny is an acquired taste," joked Nigel.

"Dusty, Puma," Makena shook their hands. "Nigel mentioned you two as the brain trust."

Slam!

The front door opened hard! Hit the doorstop, bounced back violently. They all looked over as one. A distraught, handsome blond, his tie loose around the collar, stormed in.

Makena's eyes went to his belt-bound badge and gun.

He advanced angrily, "Jenny!"

Jenny inquired with casual curiosity, "Boz?"

"You are carrying my baby!"

Detective Bostwick Oswald: Off Duty Notes

Meeting Jenny Sharp the morning she received the Key to New Orleans was no accident. District Attorney Arlen Taylor got him VIP credentials, so Boz could approach Jenny to recruit her as a CI—confidential informant. Ideally, without her knowledge. Meaning, Boz should use his good looks, get close, and pillow talk her into spilling secrets about Nigel.

"Remember I said I wanted a good looking cop?" reminded Arlen.

Boz'd been quite the ladies man, still was coupla times a month. He lost the dour cop act and easily picked up the girl he targeted for a one night stand. Seeing Jenny alone with her black manager, Puma Song, he went for it. He was as taken as taken aback by the way Jenny looked at him like a piece of meat when he extended his hand and introduced himself, "Bostwick Oswald."

Jenny's face cracked wide. "You better not be married."

"No, I'm not," he laid on the charm with a smile. "Just wanted to say hello."

"Fuck, I'd like to do more than that, Bostwick." She came onto him and made no bones about it.

"Boz." *This is gonna be easier than I thought.*

Then, the Mayor started talking.

"Give me your card," she said genially. He did, happily. "I won't be calling you on official business, Detective Boz. Write your personal cell."

Boz flashed his best smile, pulled out a pen, and wrote it on the back.

Jenny stuffed it in her bra.

He left. Buoyant, not so much by how that went, but by the breath of fresh air—that's what Jenny's lack of reserve or filters felt like. Not ever did he look forward to a woman's phone call like he did hers. She rang him. Around 5 PM that same evening. Asked him to come to her apartment with dinner.

"Stop by the drug store," she said, "and stock up before you show up."

She was wearing a sports bra and cutoff jeans. In her defense, it was hot and humid. But she'd also turned on the AC in her apartment down to about 60°C. Her nipples were threatening to puncture through. Anyway, Boz had never seen a girl as fit. Not an ounce of fat anywhere. She didn't need any makeup, didn't put on any, and still looked sensational. She let him in. Closed the door.

"You aren't wearing a badge tonight, are you?" she asked.

"Not if it's a date," he replied, aware where this was headed.

"Then, this is a date."

Her apartment was plush—designer furniture and furnishings, nice stuff all over. She probably had a cleaning service because the place looked vacuumed and dusted. He put the food down on the dining table. Turned around and saw her snorting up one of five lines of coke she'd cut on the coffee table. *What the hell?* He went over and sniffed up the second.

"What's your story, Boz?" she asked.

"I've to admit. Not a big fight fan. I haven't seen a single match of yours. DA gave me a pass, I saw you, and thought, shit, she's seriously gorgeous."

"Ditto, when I laid eyes on you. Now, I just hope we don't disappoint when we fuck." And just like that, she straddled him, her lips crushing his.

They were naked within seconds. She looked down and smiled, "Size does matter to me."

He ran through all the condoms. After intercourse on the sofa, they ate dinner, sharing whiskey from the bottle. She didn't keep any other booze, bought it by the case, he noticed. They did some more coke, then he bent her over the kitchen sink. Finished up the remaining lines of coke, started for the bedroom, but never got there. Her legs wrapped around his hips and he pounded her against the wall standing up. The nightcap ended in bed, missionary style.

Boz woke up. Daylight streamed through the window. He swung out of bed, dressed softly. He usually left with just a cordial goodbye after his one night stands, not even that sometimes, slipping out while she was still sleeping. Also, he never fucked the same woman twice. He stared down at Jenny, who slept on her stomach. She'd tossed off the sheets. He couldn't take his eyes off her—a fully nude work of art. Beyond that, her rawness—personality to beauty—had him *smitten?* He was. After just one night. Nigel never came up. Hell, they were so high, he didn't remember what they talked about. Or, if they even did. *Do we even have anything in common?*

"Hey," Jenny turned around, waking.

"Good morning."

"Duty calls?" She stretched.

"It's Saturday." He was getting aroused.

"Shit. Is that what comes after Friday?"

He laughed. I haven't done that—laughed spontaneously—for a long time. "I'm off weekends, but I thought I'd be a gentleman and leave."

"If I wanted a gentleman," she grinned sleepily. "I'd have insisted on a top hat and a tux."

"Can I interest you in breakfast?"

She wisped hair off her face. "You don't have to show me morning-after courtesy, Boz."

He laughed. *Again?* "I really don't want to leave."

"Stay, then," she raised a leg, "unless you want to waste a perfectly good boner," and caressed his bulging crotch with her toes.

What the hell. He dropped his knees on the bed. Her legs opened. Then, they showered together. Had coffee and coke, then went out to breakfast around the corner. The restaurant knew her. Sat them in a booth. A few people recognized her, stared. A couple of teens came over for an autograph.

"If you're not a fight fan," asked Jenny, "why were you at the ceremony?"

"Plainclothes police presence," he lied easily. "Just in case." The waitress brought over coffee and took their orders. Boz decided dive straight in. "You find Nigel Hansom or Nigel Hansom find you?" Smiled with his quick follow up, "City knows him as a business mogul. Had no idea he funded fighters too."

"My trainer and he go way back," she said. "So, give me some dirt."

"On Nigel?" Boz blinked, puzzled. "He's a state hero—"

"I can Google too, Boz," Jenny interrupted. "What's not there? Money—like the kind he has—is usually built on piles of dirt." Grinned mischievously, "So, what's the dirt? May come in handy when it's time to re-up my contract."

She's pumping me. Boz needed to turn this around. "You have daily contact with him, you probably have more."

Jenny's eyes narrowed and asked with a sly smile, "Are you looking?"

"I'm a cop," Boz knew he was treading on thin ice. "I'm always looking."

The waitress interrupted with their breakfast. "Anything you want," she said to Jenny, "just holler."

He didn't go back to Nigel. Neither did she. So they talked back story. Sounded canned both ways. They ate, snorted, drank, fucked—just not in that order all the time. Sunday night, she said, "Boz. I have to be up early. Resume training. Fuck off?"

"Can I call you?" he asked, not offended, familiar now with her bluntness.

"No need. Just come by around eight. If I'm not fucking someone else, we can, or we can make it a threesome."

He laughed. She kissed him hard. This girl did nothing in half measure. He walked away, wondering if she was joking about sharing her with another guy. When he met up with Arlen Taylor, the DA gave him that grin men reserved when another got lucky, "Boz, you horn dog."

Boz'd have none of that. "She's sharper than a surgical blade. Doesn't give a shit how Nigel makes his money as long as he sugar-daddys her championship run."

"First time I seen you without a scowl. You're not falling for her, are you?"

"I've never met anyone like her. Hell, I don't think there's another like her."

"Fuck, Boz. That's the only genuine compliment I've heard that's not sarcastic or backhanded."

Boz hadn't been able to get Jenny out of his mind all day and couldn't wait to get this meeting with Arlen over with and head to her apartment. She let him in. Boz went back Tuesday and Wednesday. He hadn't felt like this toward anyone. A schoolboy crush on the prom queen, who gave him the time of day and nobody else—only, it wasn't a crush. On his way to the precinct on Thursday, he stopped at the newsstand and bought *Sports*

Illustrated to gawk at her fight in pictures. At work, he went online to take in some more.

He'd fallen for her. *Shall I tell her?* Tonight, he decided.

Then, his phone rang.

"Boz." It was Jenny. He felt his heart palpitate. "Dusty chewed me out. All the fucking's wobbled my legs".

He laughed. "Of course. The weekend, then."

"No, Boz, we're done," she said bluntly. "It was fun. Surpassed my expectations. Now, it's over. Lose my number."

She hung up. It took several seconds before it hit him. A hole opened in his stomach. *What just happened?* He pulled out his cell. Dialed her right back. It went to voice mail. He didn't leave a message. He called four more times. Gave up. *I'm heartbroken.*

He just had been in an emotional vacuum for so long, she clicked with him in ways no one else did, and he mistook it for love. Went overboard. Made up a romance that never was there. *I was her fuck buddy.* He shoulda known. She'd done the same thing to Sid Rosen, the lawyer—but Boz considered himself a serious upgrade. Looking back, he couldn't remember a single tender moment. Nothing intimate, personal, or emotional. Why did he think it went deeper? Clearly, it did. *For me.*

Now, it hurt. Wondering how many guys Jenny'd used and abused, a hot wave of jealousy swept through him. Maybe she just found someone else. Someone younger. He was almost twice her age.

He began to follow her.

She trained and did nothing else. 5 AM to 5 PM, sometimes staying later. No men showed up at her door when she got home. A girl with that much sexual appetite couldn't just go cold turkey. Secure in the knowledge she trained religiously, Boz began following Jenny when she left the gym after he quit the precinct every evening. His brain told him this was getting out of hand, but just as a compulsive gambler always thought the winning hand was the next one, Boz hoped she'd change her mind and call.

Arlen's witch hunt ground to a halt, but staking out Nigel's business gave Boz cover. The DA wasn't stupid. Boz's sour and dour demeanor returned. Arlen started showing impatience and displeasure, what with the election closing in, a month away, and Boz with nothing to show.

Friday evening. An eighteen-wheeler pulled out of the Easy Trucking lot, along with two RVs. The trainer rode in the lead. Boz, parked a block down, figured they were on their way to an I-10 fight. The following afternoon—Boz'd begun his stakeout outside her apartment at breakfast—Nigel arrived at Jenny's apartment in a limo, picked her up, and they drove off.

He's taking her to the I-10 fight. Boz fumed, despising Nigel for having money, having Jenny, having it all.

Fuck this! Boz got out of the car, fully cognizant that rational thought was not fueling his actions. This is crazy. He could be fired. He didn't care.

He broke into Jenny's apartment.

Wandered through it, an erection pressing against his fly as he touched, caressed, and recalled every sexual moment. *I'm behaving like a psycho serial killer.* Again, obsession dismissed logic and caution from his brain. He sat on her bed, swept his hands across the sheets. Then, he walked into her closet, smelled her clothes. He opened the bathroom door and his eyes went still.

Resting on the sink counter, a pregnancy stick.

Nigel Hansom: Hearsay from New Orleans

Rarely floored, Nigel was. The time and place sucked even more. Makena stood right there with him, when this crazy barreled in and dropped the baby bombshell. Jenny didn't look surprised. *It's true!* Nigel stepped in the way, looking outraged.

"Who the hell are you?" Nigel saw the gun and the badge after he asked the question.

"Detective Bostwick Oswald. This is none of your fucking

business!"

Nigel didn't dare check out Makena's expression. "Yes it is. You're on private property! And this doesn't sound like police business."

"There's no fucking baby, Boz!"

"You're lying! I saw the positive pregnancy stick!"

"You been stalking her?" Nigel stepped.

"Yeah, *and* he had to have broken into my apartment!" Jenny actually laughed, "You sick, desperate, pathetic fuck."

"You're a liar!" shouted Boz.

"I'm calling your Commander!" said Nigel.

Boz snapped out his gun. "I'll put a bullet into that bald fucking head of yours!"

"What makes you think it's yours?" Jenny asked. "I fuck so many guys, I don't even know."

She's pregnant. Disjointed thoughts popped in and out. Money. The upcoming fight. Endorsements. Media frenzy. Mostly disappointment. Anger. *We were so close. So damn close! Stupid, stupid, stupid bitch!* He expected to see the I-told-you-so look on Dusty's face.

But Dusty was trying to de-escalate the situation, "Put that gun down, Detective."

Boz ignored Dusty, waving his piece. "I've been staking you out."

"You fucking perv!" Jenny spat.

Boz didn't seem to care. "You haven't been with anyone else."

"Yeah, maybe since you and I fucked," replied Jenny, then lashed out with a cruel smirk. "You think I came to you a virgin? Like it or not, I'm a proud, self-professed whore." Then flatly, "Anyway, I took care of it."

The boulder pressing down on Nigel lifted. *Of course she did.* She couldn't care for, or about, another human, and expressed exactly that with a shrug, "So, who cares?"

"I didn't see you go into Planned Parenthood."

"Planned Parenthood? Ha!" Jenny snorted derisively. "I just stuck in a coat hanger, dumbass." She looked at Makena, who's face had gotten so tight, it looked etched in stone. "Done in five."

That stopped Boz cold. "Jesus!"

Whack! Puma caned the gun out of Boz's hand. Dusty grabbed it off the floor.

Boz didn't even care or realize. He lunged, "You fucking soulless cunt!"

Crack! Jenny put an elbow into his face.

He bounced back, his nose bleeding. Boz's eyes blazed. "You just assaulted a police officer! I'm taking you in!"

"Try, motherfucker!" Jenny took a step.

Dusty pulled Jenny back and Nigel stepped in front of Boz, "You bring charges, we will too. You had sex with a girl twenty years younger than you. Stalked her. Broke into her apartment. Then you pulled a gun. Three felonies, and the sex, I'll turn into assault to send you away for life!" Nigel's voice rose, "Walk away now and we won't press charges."

Boz's expression turned murderous, wiping the blood with the back of his hand. He pointed to Nigel, "I'm one cop you don't own."

"If it makes you feel any better," taunted Jenny, "the little bastard wasn't alive," then paused with a pure evil smile, "I don't think."

Boz started forward. Puma raised his cane. "Move and I will cut you down, muhfuh."

Dusty leveled the cop's gun as well.

Boz flung another hate-filled glare at Jenny, "Jezebel. That's you."

"Hey," Jenny grinned, "that's a good fighting name. Jezebel Sharp." Then grimaced, "Maybe not. Bible thumpers won't buy my gear."

"Keep looking over your shoulder, all of you," Boz warned. "This is not over, not by a long shot."

"Get the fuck out of here," Nigel dismissed angrily.

Dusty gave Puma the gun, "You'll get it back once you step outta the building."

Boz headed for the door, Puma in tow.

Jenny had to have the parting shot. Yelled, "I should've saved a piece of the little fucker for you as a keepsake!"

Boz whirled around. Puma crowded him, pressing the gun between the Detective's eyes, "Keep walking."

Boz exited. Puma returned the gun to the detective, locked the door, and started back.

Nigel turned to Jenny, "When did all this go down?"

"We hooked up a few times for a week after my win. I found out before we left for Vulture City and took care of it right after I got back." Jenny was nonchalant. "Performed the self-surgery, drained the tub, refilled it for a nice bubble bath. I could have even fought an hour later." To Dusty, "Kick me in the crotch. Go on!"

"Shit, Jenny," Dusty shook his head. "You reset the bar every time."

Jenny grinned. Looked over to Makena, "You're speechless. I make a living enduring pain, Makena. This was just a sore pussy."

If Jenny flustered or shocked Makena, his CFO did a damn fine job acting, "Did you know he was a NOPD Detective?"

"Of course. I'd never fucked one *and* takes a couple of to-dos off my bucket list." She winked. "I recognize that look. Abortion on a bucket list? I'm sick, crazy. But I live a different kind of life, Makena. Don't judge mine, I won't judge yours."

After Jenny, Dusty, and Puma left, Makena dropped into the couch in Nigel's office. Dazed. "Is she for real?"

He poured her a drink and one for himself. "She can be exhausting," Nigel smiled. Lowered himself beside her. "Early flight? You wanted to surprise me. Surprised?"

Makena did not smile. "Cartels are anxious about the attention Jenny's bringing."

"She came out of underground fight clubs. So she knew about I-10 circuit, and that's the extent of exposure. She knows nothing about our business."

"She brought a jilted cop here, Nigel."

"Again, separate, unconnected."

Makena remained worried. "He can make matters messy. Worse, public."

"I'll make sure this goes no further."

"Then you have Dusty and Puma. They've been around long, if you know what I mean. They can suspect, but they can never know."

"Those two are the last you have to worry about. They are old school, for one, and two, single-minded fighting junkies on the cusp of something only few experience. Coming from where they did—I'm sure you backgrounded them—they know to turn a blind eye and deaf ear."

"Cartels want an assurance you will choose our business over the fighting."

"Of course, Makena," assured Nigel. "Should they look at or listen to what they should not, I will not hesitate, and they know I will not."

"Growing, harvesting, making, packing, transporting distributing, diluting, bagging, and selling—it's an unbreakable chain. An interruption with one disrupts the entire sequence, nothing more seriously than transport because that directly affects revenue."

Nigel nodded. "Jenny, Dusty, and Puma are a world away from Cartel interests in Easy Trucking, trust me."

"Of course, I do," Makena softened. "You and I built this. Sorry to threaten the hammer, but we don't want to ruin what's been a really good partnership. Mainly because we have been low key, operating below the radar."

"This incident stays between us?" sought Nigel.

"Yes," she assured. "As long as you have me on your side, you have nothing to worry about."

The final two weeks leading up to Jenny Sharp vs. Bella "Black Widow" Haroon whirlwinded by, thanks to the intensity of training and media frenzy ballooning daily. Think a loan shark's compound interest. Triggered in no small part by Jenny's almost-daily shitting on Bella on Tik Tok, Twitter, Facebook, Youtube, Instagram, Snapchat, Zoom, you name it. Calling her Ma Bell and old and on the downside of her career, which nobody'd proved. Not yet.

As much of a sensation as Jenny'd become, her bad girl image didn't find universal approval. Particularly purists. Even if they come to terms she was anointed to the main event this night, they felt some of Jenny's rants against Bella on social media went too far. The Widow said little, allowing her record to do the talking. She was good. Damn good. Many called her great. Not me. She didn't belong in the pantheon 'cause she never reached the summit. Great in regular fights, but choked in the ones that mattered for a record of 6-3. Actually, this was the closest she'd gotten. The press glossed over that. Instead, harped on the controversial choice of Jenny for this bout. Nonetheless, the fight's all anybody talked about in the papers, blogs, chat rooms, TV, shit, everywhere. Orchestrating the ol' credo, 'any publicity is good publicity,' UFZ smartly engineered the global interest into that time-tested battle cry.

Good vs. Evil.

A Bella win would represent the triumph of all things sacred to MMA—respect, sportsmanship, reputation, you know righteous crap you want your kid to grow up learning and practicing. The UFZ penthouse didn't write up a memo. That'd be illegal. But the ref and judges watched TV, read the sports page, and understood what crawled 'tween the lines via the press bias. Ain't no accident neither when my past and Puma's convictions got dredged up.

Coming' into the fight, we were tabbed 'The Jailbirds.'

Our poll numbers turned south. Jenny moved them lower, when she picked a fight with Bella at the weigh-in. The Widow kept her cool, not raising a hand, capping two weeks of the media dinning the public with Bella's pros and Jenny's cons. Hardly surprising then, also, a pro-Bella partisan crowd filled Texas Stadium. That the high brass'd hinted down their preference showed up in the prefight hostility toward our corner.

"I can't believe they let you back in the corner," Ref Ray, remarked, all snide, when he walked by.

"I served my time," I snapped. "So fuck you."

I saw Nigel's jowls jiggle, tighten. They jiggled and tightened some more when the three judges took their seats. Every one of them stared at me unfriendly. Then, Trevor Ross, the ex-ref who voted against my reinstatement, slid into the chair behind ours. He glared back, disapproving like the rest of 'em.

Pow! Jenny landed the first significant strike into the middle of Bella Haroon's midsection like a wrecking ball to kick off the match that'd decide who'd go on to fight for the Bantamweight Championship of the World. Jenny stole being the elite boxer that Bella been to open this frame. The crowd went boo. Judges weren't pleased neither. Bella clinched Jenny, who didn't let up. Before Jenny could lock Bella around the knees and plunk her down, Ray stepped in and stood them up.

There was no point crying foul. I muttered, "The fix is on."

"We knew that coming in," Nigel replied sharply.

Ref Ray ignored a low blow by Bella later in the round. Jenny didn't help herself neither, showing incredible strength, then incredible stupidity. Bella landed significant strikes galore. One in particular that everyone in the arena, but Jenny, saw coming. The fight went to the ground where Jenny took charge. The bell saved Bella. She still took Round 1 free and clear.

Round 2 kicked off with a typical Jenny gimmick I thought might work. She crouched deeply as if she was taking a dump on her toes. Then sprang to her feet, catlike, grinned, bowing tauntingly. But misjudged her distance for the double-leg takedown and didn't pay off the showboating. A mistake that could've won Bella the match, then and there, if she didn't do something nobody expected—mimic Jenny's habit of risking everything for a highlight reel. Show the upstart she was capable of going into the history books too. Bella released Jenny to pass guard for a fancy submission.

Pow! Jenny's fist came outta nowhere! Bella's head swung halfway around the Octagon. Jenny took charge again when the girls went toe-to-toe for the next part of this stanza. Fight went so one-eighty, if Jenny could draw enough blood outta Bella's nose and ears, Ref Ray would have no choice but to call the fight. But this wasn't Bella's first rodeo.

Bam! Delivered a knee right into Jenny's privates.

Another low blow Ray conveniently 'missed.' This time, the bell rescued Jenny. The positive that come outta of this round was Bella never fought beyond the second. Vegas, though, had Bella winning by submission in Round 3, and it began with Jenny and Bella distancing.

Nigel leaned over, "The ref's got it in for you." I didn't realize this be his precursor to the bombshell he dropped after Ref Ray looked at the judges, who wanted him to call the fight when Bella spilled Jenny's blood all over the canvas. "Maybe for the championship, you should sit it out."

Jenny got outta that jam a heartbeat before Ref Ray ended it in Bella's favor and promptly found herself in another. Fortunately, the clock hit zeroes. In the nick of time too, 'cause Bella's thighs were tightening like a vice, choking the life outta Jenny. But the bell didn't ring.

"The clock's at zeros," noticed Nigel.

As did Puma. "Hey! What the fuck?"

I shot to my feet shouting and pointing at the giant digital timer. Ref Ray, the timekeeper, and the judges were doing their best to fulfill the Vegas line. That how much this fight stacked against us. *TingTingTing.* Finally.

"Blood'n' guts! You got both in spades and spilled 'em in buckets!"

"Yeah!" Jenny mumbled, jacked up.

"Don't worry about no points! Don't worry about no submission!" I grabbed her by her wrists. "You get outta the fourth and I'll show you how to fuck her up in the fifth!"

TingTingTing!

"There ain't no room for error!" I warned her and sat down.

"Why the fifth?" Nigel asked angrily. "Why not end it now?"

"So you and me are clear," I retorted.

Round 4 got under way, the crowd fully into this one now. Judges weren't smiling.

Bella struck first, planting a left-right-left combo into Jenny's body, then finished off with a dropkick. Jenny buckled. But she used her stumble to trip Bella onto the canvas.

"That's it!" I yelled.

Jenny and Bella grappled, each fighting for some kind of mount or guard, but neither would allow it. Jenny forced herself on top and lay down the law to Bella's head with elbow and fist.

"I won't do it, Nigel. I ain't prepared to play second fiddle. Even for appearances sake. Not after waiting twenty years. 'Sides, you won't even be here if I didn't bring you in."

"You wouldn't be here without me either," Nigel shot right back. "Shit, Dusty, you've been around long enough to know this isn't personal."

"Yeah, it's business," I chided acidly. "Save the clichés." I glanced over. "You're being awful quiet, Puma." Then I realized, "You're in on this!"

"No," denied Puma calmly, "But it ain't a bad idea, now that I hear it out loud. I know it be a long time comin' for you, Dusty, but it's not like none amongst us wouldn't know you deserve all the glory. Especially if it's Kevin. He one of our own."

I rose, "Wrap her up!"

Jenny almost entangled Bella in a half guard. Bella slipped free and took the fight where she wanted—to her feet. Jenny found a second wind, countering Bella's fists with her own, punch for punch.

"Look at her, Dusty," Nigel said, "she can go all the way."

"Yep," I remained stubborn, "and I want the credit for it out in the open. I wanna stand next to the Champion of the World. I wanna know that glory. God knows I've paid more'n my share of dues."

Like Heavyweight was in boxing with Ali, Frazier, Tyson, Holyfield, and *Rocky,* Bantamweight—which boasted Queens of the Jungle, Rousey and Nunes—was the glamour belt in MMA.

Nigel eased off, "Not like I won't make it worth your while."

Of course, he has to play the cash card. But some things were worth more than money. I remained firm, "No."

"Win this one first," Nigel threw down the gauntlet.

"I know we can," I said, then tossed the ball into his court, "I brought her this far, I can end it right here. So?"

Nigel's lips thinned, not used to being cornered. He nodded. *OK.*

Bella bled outta her nostrils, something I don't recall seeing since her early days in the Octagon. Jenny connected on a right, left, and finished with a kick to Bella's calves. The Black Widow stuffed a takedown by backing off at the last minute. For a moment there, Jenny was bent over awkwardly, but Bella stood flat-footed, more concerned with catching her breath than seizing the moment to crash her elbows down on Jenny's exposed spine.

"I can't believe she missed that," remarked one of the TV guys.

My girl wore her down, dumbass. Thirty-two was the tipping point, speaking of age, when fighters declined, but Bella, at twenty-six, and stats reinforced it, should be in peak form. Her side had no excuse, except that she'd had never been this far along in a single fight. Arms go first. The lack of stamina was showing—shouldn't, but it was. Like stealing Church's money—you know, an unexpected freebie—Jenny bull-rushed Bella.

Whabam! Jenny planted Bella.

The collective gasp in the stadium coincided with the tremendous sound of force and impact that rocked the cage. Applause rang out once again without a single boo. Fans realized this now merited a diary entry as a night to remember—like when they thought they were coming to watch MMA legend, Anderson Silva, have another routine victory vs. Chris Weidman, and watched the underdog pull out one of the biggest upsets of a headliner.

This fight vs. prohibitive favorite Bella "Black Widow" Haroon could be only the second such historic upset. Even bigger than Holmes vs. Rousey. *If it comes to be.* I know I shot my mouth off, boldly predicting, we got this, but I cautioned myself, not falling into the trap I never should in the corner, and that's look beyond the next second, 'cause just as the fight'd turned for Jenny in one, it could just as quickly turn against her in the next. Bella still reeled from the jarring shock and pain.

"Get in there!" I hollered.

Jenny's arms triangled themselves for the anaconda choke—an arm triangle from the front headlock position. Bella somehow found enough strength to keep squirming and putting off a submission. It would be an insult on top of injury if she went down to a tactic that required years to perfect and produced only two victories in the entire history of top tier UFZ matches.

"Stay with it!" I shouted, knowing Jenny. *Will she listen?*

I had my answer when I heard Puma groan, "No!"

Jenny got impatient, gave up on the anaconda, and went for a front choke. Bella knew a reprieve when she got one. She been fighting five years longer than Jenny. The Widow tore free, rolled over, and leg-locked Jenny. The girls' faces were inches from each other, eyes squeezed, teeth grit. Thirty seconds remained in the round—an eternity.

I don't know why I looked over to Bella's corner, but I did, and the trainer nodded. Ray moved in front of me.

Next thing I heard was a vicious *crack!*

Bone against bone. Bella broke the law again.

"Head butt!" Puma leapt, always first.

Ray stepped outta the way. Jenny's forehead above her left eye opened. Blood did a starburst!

"You don't see that head butt?" I followed up. When Ray didn't respond, I got in his eyeline and screamed, "Ain't you goin' to call time at least?"

"No!" He waved me off.

The crowd sounded on his side. They loved the dirty shit.

It'd become that kind of fight. Any stoppage'd spark a riot.

Jenny hung tough despite the crimson tide surfing down. Using sheer power, Jenny freed herself from Bella. Wiped the blood off as they climbed back to their feet. So did the crowd, rocking the Jones Mahal yet again with all cheers for the two girls. Jenny squared up 'cause she probably could only see with her right eye, her only good eye. Didn't seem like it. Swung blindly. Somehow she found and clinched Bella. I didn't mind it, Bella being too tired to take advantage, lashed out wearily. Ref Ray pulled them apart. Before Bella reset—*TingTingTing!*

Even though she won this round too, leading the fight 4-0, Bella never looked more vulnerable heading to her corner, head down like a whipped dog, swollen and bleeding. There never been any inkling of any shakiness in any of her prior fights. People were no fools. They recognized this 'cause nobody in the arena sat down, and we were between rounds. I never seen an about-face in crowd sentiment like this, favorite to underdog.

"You feel the love, lil girl?" Puma smiled ear to ear. "Everyone here admire your grit! This fight's playin' out just like *Rocky!*"

Jenny sat down, beaming, even if she looked like she been showering in blood and snot. The kudos was all good and dandy, but now I had fulfill my prophecy—finish this off.

"Bella's tired," I said, staying serious. "Remember what go first. Arms or legs?"

"Arms," panted Jenny.

"Nobody use 'em more'n Bella. That the only way she knows how to make a living. But you! You're versatile." The cut over her eye gushed blood as fast as I wiped off. I nodded to the lackey, "Keep the towel pressed against the cut."

"Dusty," Puma nudged my eyes toward Ray, who looked from the judges over to Jenny, then headed over to Bella's corner. "Muhfuh up to somethin'."

Nigel walked over a third time, heard Puma, and said, "Beating the fix isn't new when you're up against a name fighter."

I knew he was pissed at me. *But shit, this ain't no time to be negative!* I flipped that around into morale juice. "Y'hear that,

Jenny! It's you against the world."

Puma, no fool neither, added, "Yeah! Nuthin' sweeter'n proving people wrong!"

"Shush!" I hissed, seeing Ray and Dr. Ned close in.

"Lookie, lookie," Puma taunted. "I figured why you mothering Bella. Y'be sucking her titties at the Four Seasons, ain't you?"

"I've had enough from you, old man!" Ray retorted. "Address me one more time and I'll have you thrown out of the arena!" He looked toward Jenny. "The bleeding over your left eye, let Ned look at it."

The lackey pulled the towel off—it was soaked in red—and blood rivered out.

"Oh, dear," said Ned and put the towel back on.

"Can you stop it?" asked Ray. "I can't let her fight if she's bleeding."

"I don't know," Ned began.

"I saw you, Ray," I accused, "step in the way to block a view of the head butt. It was planned, so you could swing the fight for Bella's corner."

"You accusing me?" Ray raged.

Despite our beef, Nigel wanted to win too. He stepped in and stepped up, "I'll tell the world in the press conference to go back and check the replays, and also how you and Ned here then conspired to stop the fight from going forward, even though the entire arena gave the women a standing ovation, expecting a fifth round."

"Look around, muhfuh," said Puma, "they still on their feet."

Ray backed off, glowering, "Do what you got to do, Ned."

"I don't know what I can do," said Ned.

"Don't fuckin' lie!" I dismissed. "I know you got Thrombin in your bag." That was a type of cow coagulant which stopped blood quicker than cork in your asshole.

Murder in his eyes, Ray warned, "If that cut opens as much as a shaving nick, I'm stopping the fight."

He turned on his heel and made a beeline to Bella's corner,

likely to inform them we'd tied his hands. He wasn't about to risk his rep and be ostracized from officiating future big bouts.

Ned got to work. It didn't take but moments, that's how fast Thrombin worked. The skin on either side of the cut just fused like someone took a welding torch across. Ned took off.

"This is it, Jenny," I said. "Round 5. When and where champions are made. Bella come close but never made it over the hump. Keep her on the wrong side of it! You find that elation! Make her eat more disappointment!"

Jenny nodded. Reminded me, "You said if I got through the fourth, you'll show me how to fuck her up in the fifth."

"Are you ready'n willing to lay it all out there?"

Her jaw setting, she nodded. I schemed it out for her.

Puma gave Jenny a proper sendoff, hard-selling with an intensity I never seen, "Make history, lil girl!"

I sat back down. Nigel remained ornery. "We can't be fighting the opponent and the system. You have to see that."

I thought we'd settled this. *Mebbe not.* I didn't say nothing. Neither did Puma, who I noticed sliding his allegiance away from me some more. The tension ratcheted up as if someone had sprung walls between me and the two of them.

Jenny came out quick and on the attack. Like I figured, the 4th had taken it outta Bella. Her strikes per minute dipped to around five, half the UFZ average. I banked on Bella and her corner thinking, this being the 5th and final round, Jenny would go for the takedown. Instead, Jenny stayed upright

Wham!Wham!Wham! Left, right, kick. *Wham!Wham!Wham!* Jenny busted Bella with six connects. We fooled them.

Jenny squared up.

Wham! Bella went back to what worked. Using her right to feint and come in with a hard left.

Wham! Another significant strike that delivered serious wood. Bella backed Jenny to the chainlink. Jenny did not allow a direct punch to the newly fused scar line, taking each to the side and back of her skull.

Wham!

"What the hell is your strategy here?" demanded Nigel, openly suspicious. I waved him off.

Wham!

"She's getting killed!" insisted Nigel.

"Sit your ass down!" I exploded. "I know what I'm doing!" I saw the surprise in his face, but he got the message and backed off. I'd never barked at Nigel. It felt good.

"He's over there," I'd told Jenny, nodding toward Ref Ray, "whispering all Bella has to do is open this cut. That was the purpose of that dirty head butt—to steal the win from you. So! Let her think she can. Take the punishment, but to the right side and the back of your head, not the temple. Got that? Protect the cut!"

Jenny did. After four straight, Bella thought she could do this all day. I'd said, "Wait for my signal." I gave it, hollering, "*Now!*"

Jenny turned only her head without moving her feet so as not to tip off Bella, whose left glided by, a hair away from the cut. Bella didn't expect it, caught with the wrong foot forward.

"Then show her the hand of God."

Whabam!

Jenny connected with a left into Bella's midriff that clean lifted the Black Widow off her feet. Jenny showed the pistons that powered her to all those wins in fight clubs.

Bella's back hit the canvas, then the back of her skull bounced.

The logical next step would be for Jenny to jump on her with a high percentage straight armbar, or being the show-off that she was, go back to the anaconda, which would have sealed it just as easy.

I held my breath, 'cause, hell, you couldn't tell with this girl. She was an enigma—the perfect student when she needed to be and a fucking frustrating petulant hot head full of tantrums the rest of the time. Whatever brain chemistry it was that made you act the way you did, it was spontaneous combustion with Jenny. Bitch or pro, one or the other, nothing in between. I guess she remembered the stakes. More likely, Puma saying, 'make history!'

"What is she doing, passing up an armbar or any choke?"

reacted the TV commentator.

Finishing with a flourish, nimrod. Like I said early, she was all about adding to her highlight reel.

Jenny wrapped her legs around Bella's throat instead. Didn't tighten them. Not yet.

Jenny walloped Bella's head against the canvas.

Bam! Bam! Bam!

Dispensing the same nasty medicine Bella had at the end of the third round after the clock ran out. Only tripling the punishment. Tripling it again. *Bam! Bam! Bam!* Jenny kept pounding Bella's noggin, and now began to squeeze the air out of the Widow's lungs while concussing the shit outta her. Ray could do nothing, judges neither, and not for the lack of trying. Everything Jenny did was so legal, even the Supreme Court couldn't overturn it.

Bella hung tough, too proud to tap out, though her eyes bugged outta their sockets. As black as her skin was, you could see the blue washing in from all the air leaving her lungs and none entering. Spit dribbled outta her lips. She tried to crook her legs, wrap 'em, twist her spine, jerk her hips.

Nothing worked.

For one thing, Round 3 on, this fight been foreign country. Second, she went for it all in the first three rounds 'cause she was confident she didn't need more. As a boxer, her arms were her strongest asset, which she overused for four rounds, and they let her down in this, the 5th.

"Give it to her, lil girl, give it to her!" Puma screamed.

Bam! Bam! Bam! If Bella wasn't going to submit, Jenny wasn't going to stop. Bella looked a breath away from passing out. She weakly turned the free palm down to the canvas.

And tapped it.

"Off!" Ray yelled.

Nigel roared to his feet. He heard it before the crowd. Just by a sec. Then, bedlam!

I couldn't hear him but I read his lips as he circled his arms, lassoing invisible cattle, "Yeah! Yeah!"

Jenny rolled off.

The judges stared, their jaws unhitched. Stunned.

Bella still lay on the canvas, groveling like a deer after an unfortunate meeting with the front end of a speeding truck. Not quite killed, but near dead. Her trainer, hell, everyone from her corner rushed through the gate. Ray moved away, taking no responsibility for this loss. He done everything he could.

This crowd hooted and hollered regardless of the fact who they started out supporting. This be Spartacus vs. Spartacus—equal to or better than the best on the men's side. It'd lived up, even exceeded the hype. Jenny cashed every check her mouth wrote leading up, then some, and made that known now, flaunting and prancing around the Octagon, raising the roof, putting a hand to her ear, asking for more noise, wearing the blood and bruises of this five-round beatdown like a badge of honor.

I realized Nigel was shaking my hand with both of his. Just so there was no misunderstanding, I leaned into his ear. "Make no mistake! I'm stickin' around! Like it or not!"

Nigel's face tightened, but had to keep smiling as TV cameras swarmed in.

Puma was the one with a level head 'cause he realized this fight hadn't been officially called yet. He banged the chainlink and hollered to Ray, "You be declarin' a winner or there still room for interpretation?"

Bella's corner still knelt around their girl, who finally sat up, completely out of it from the blanks in her eyes. Ray had to grab Jenny, she be so jacked up. He raised her hand, declaring her the official winner. 125,000 throats exploded and broke the meter.

Nigel yelled in my ear, "What if Jenny dropped you?"

I stared at Nigel. He was ruthless Mr. Money Bags. Jenny had no scruples and no loyalty, not to me, at least, considering our prior blow-ups and differences. But I was no fucking angel either, and made it known, shouting back, "She can try."

When I stepped back, Trevor Ross, the ex-ref from my hearing, stood no more than a foot away. He heard the exchange. *Fuck it.*

In the locker, later, Puma was paying for coming to his feet as often as he did during the fight. He sat in the chair, looking totally pooped. Jenny opened the crapper. Perched on the throne. Naked, of course. "Shit, Dusty, I'm pissing blood."

"Doctor'll be here. But that should be expected, considering the shots you took to the kidney."

"I don't care if I'm dying," she dropped sopping red tissue into the toilet, "but being unable to fuck is unacceptable."

"It'll clear up in a few days. Does for guys anyway."

"That wasn't my question," She flushed and emerged to start dressing.

"Had no long term effect on me."

"That's right, you fucked Nigel's teacher after you quit." Jenny slipped on her jeans. No panties. I never seen her wear a pair. "But only for a C grade."

Nigel barreled in, beaming, "UFZ wasted no time. Title fight. Vegas, this Summer!"

"Woo!" Jenny high-fived Puma. "Fuck yeah!"

The Event Manager poked his head in. Stared for a moment at Jenny topless. "Press is waiting. UFZ President will be sitting with you to announce you'll be in the Title fight."

"Ohhh!!" Jenny pursed. "La-de-da. The man himself."

"A bra, please," I said. "

"Oh, all right." Jenny said disdainfully. Slipped one on, then a T-shirt.

"Behave yourself," Puma grabbed her hand. "No cussing."

"A bra. No profanity. What's next? I can't handjob the UFZ boss under the table?"

Nigel laughed. "Let's go."

Jenny followed him out. I nodded to Puma, "I'm going out to the arena."

"For your Buddha moment?" said Puma.

I didn't smile. At the door, "I told Nigel, no. His move now."

I left. Who should I run into, but Ref Ray and Trevor Ross coming outta the officials' room. Trevor scowled, "Bella should've won."

"Shoulda," I shot back, "what with Ray here and three judges fighting alongside, and still couldn't." I veered off into the tunnel to the stadium.

"You killed Muerte, asshole," Trevor hollered after me, "and you will never live that down."

Why fart into a headwind? I ignored him and turned up the tunnel and back into the stadium. I reached the Octagon. Lights still burned. A cavernous quiet swept across the empty seats. I wandered around inside the cage. Recalling Jenny's mistakes, and how'n why it'd happened. I lost track of time until voices, vacuums, garbage carts, and trucks invaded the stadium. I came outta my reverie. A small army began to clean up and strike the Octagon—chairs, TV platforms, everything brought in for the fight. I smiled and waved, headed back into the tunnel to be immediately confronted by a fracas up ahead.

Raised voices. Security jostled a man trying to get into the presser. I saw Nigel in the middle of it and hurried over. *No.*

"I'm a cop!" shouted Boz, the detective who claimed Jenny killed his baby. He come all the way to Dallas, probably used his badge to get back here. "Get off me!"

"You're drunk," Nigel said calmly, "you're belligerent, and you are violating the agreement we made that you won't come near Jenny."

"Fuck you," Boz slurred and swayed. "I love her!"

"Sure, you do," Nigel mocked. "Go back to New Orleans if you still want to stay on the force."

"You're threatening me?" Boz tiraded. "You fat fuck!"

"Throw him out!" snarled Nigel, losing it.

Security grabbed Boz. Started a forcible escort. Boz shook them off, turned around, and hatefully hurled, "How's this for a threat of bodily harm? Be sure to convey it to Jenny as well. Report it to my Commander or the Police Chief you're bribing into becoming the next Mayor. Won't matter. Corpses can't beat the law, however famous or rich. But I'm a Homicide Detective, I can beat a murder rap every fucking day of the week."

He walked away, security in tow.

My blood ran cold. Sonofabitch meant every word of it.

On the flight back aboard the private jet, Nigel was elated by Jenny's win, but piqued by Dusty's refusal to step back. Sure, they all drank and celebrated, Jenny being the life of the party, as always, but the tension between the three men clung like an undertaste.

Utterly pissed, Jenny didn't notice, her biggest concern being, "I don't have a guy lined up during my time off."

"Just an hour ago," Dusty said, "you said you were bleeding."

"It's an hour later." Cackled.

Nigel had a couple of limos waiting when they landed in New Orleans. Puma helped Jenny into one. Dusty stood at the bottom of the plane steps for a minute after Nigel wished him a curt goodbye and headed for the second limo, firing up a smoke.

"Nigel, wait up," Dusty called out. About to get in, Nigel looked around. Dusty hurried over. "You know, we escaped with a win tonight."

Nigel nodded. "We expected a tough fight. That it was."

"It's a pattern. Three fights now, she reacted slow to the other fighter's left. Squares up right after to compensate, six times, by my count, against Bella. She won't survive the title fight without correcting it."

"You just have to figure it out, then," said Nigel tersely.

"That's what I wanna talk to you about," Dusty replied. Paused. Nigel waited. "There's two kinds of people. Those who have the knack'n all the luck in the world to be at the right place and time. You be one of 'em. Then, there's schlubs like me. Always missing the bus. Anything we touch turn to shit. Even sure things." Dusty laughed, hollow. Nigel stayed dead pan, showing none of the relief he felt. *He's come to his senses.* But let Dusty get to it. *I owe him that much.* "You're right. Jenny's got a shot and I don't wanna jinx it." Dusty paused. Nigel waited to hear the words. "I quit."

"You mean the corner on fight nights," Nigel tried to clarify.

"No. One trainer in the gym, one in the corner, that's a recipe for ugly. I'm walking away complete."

"What about the I-10?" Nigel couldn't deny, since Dusty came on, the circuit climbed solidly into the black.

"That too. A clean break be best." Dusty thrust his hand out.

Nigel hesitated a long beat. Then said, meaning every word, "Shit, Dusty. I never intended for you to leave."

He didn't know if Dusty bought the sincerity. Likely not, considering the old trainer had just buried his dreams. More lip service than anything else, Dusty reciprocated, "No hard feelings. Thanks for the opportunity." Dusty closed his other hand over Nigel's, "We'll settle up one way or 'nother. Good luck."

Nigel forced a smile.

Dusty got into the other limo, and it pulled away first. The goodbye—something about it—troubled Nigel when he heard it, stayed like an itch he couldn't reach. It wasn't until he was halfway home, nodding off in the back seat, half asleep, that he sat up sharply.

Those were his last words to Johnny "Muerte" Cortez!

According to Dusty Saldana

I woke up, rethinking what I done. I wondered if I should've slept on it. Let my anger cool off. My hostility toward Nigel, being betrayed, remained undiminished, make no mistake. Seemed like he won, the way I quit, 'cause I was no fool. Nigel was a dangerous bastard who rarely accepted 'no' for an answer. The best revenge'd be one that he know who done it and but have to just eat it. Nothing untouchables like Nigel hate more than feeling helpless.

I spent the rest of the day just shedding the weariness from my muscles and bones, watching TV. Jenny's fight led off almost all sports shows. Evening arrived, I drank, and fell asleep to gathering sounds of a parade.

Monday dawned with Jenny all over the morning shows. I knew Nigel paid for hair and makeup, and they did a miracle job. You wouldn't know she been in her most bruising match a night and a half ago. I didn't hear a peep from Nigel nor Puma. Come nightfall, I drank myself to sleep to the sounds of celebrations running longer and louder.

Tuesday kicked off with as much about Jenny's upcoming Summer bout for the Bantamweight Title as her *Vogue* spread that just hit the stands. Even an old coot like me, with hardly no interest in chicks, acknowledged that God was inspired building this girl. If only He hadn't slapped it together when it came to values and virtue.

Come afternoon, Nigel still didn't call. I checked the volume on my ringer. Held out hope. *Just a matter of time.* Sure enough, when my cell rang, my gut tightened. "Hello?"

"Dusty Saldana, please." Male. No nonsense. Not Nigel.

"That's me."

"Detective Bostwick Oswald, New Orleans PD." *Not him again.*

Boz hinted not an iota of the anger from fight night. Attire to demeanor, he played it by-the-book official, showing me his badge, asked if he could come in. Once seated, his first question was, "She can try, you said. Recall saying it?"

"Maybe I did, maybe I didn't." I tried to sound neutral.

"You did. It's been confirmed by a credible source."

Trevor Ross. Had to be. Being the only one close enough to hear Nigel and me, and for Boz to add, "Your comment came after he threatened to have Jenny fire you on the brink of your first title shot."

Then, Boz jumped all over with his queries. He thought he was being sly, but I worked all my life in the seedy weeds. I knew how to zig my answers when he tried to zag with his questions. He brought up Jorge Vargas's murder, which Nigel definitely committed—the crime scene photos reeked of tribal justice. Boz beat around the I-10 bush and landed on Crispin Martinez. I played dumb pretty well, even though a hole opened in my stomach, when he said an eyewitness seen my truck and Nigel getting in. Boz never clearly told me why he was here, what exactly he was investigating. Cunnin' mothafucka circle back to ask a question I don't answer before. I may have slipped here'n there, but recovered before I fell on my ass.

"We are going round and round here," I declared, then set the record straight.

CASE FILE: 010146888
Reporting Officer: Detective Bostwick Oswald

"I quit," said Dusty, about forty-some minutes into the interview, "so the exchange 'tween me an Nigel ended with no hard feelings. He wants to win as badly as I do. He saw and I didn't—being in the thick of a close contest—the fight still could've gone the other way on account of the baggage I brought. More'n I realized. It was heartbreaking. Tough. But I knew what I needed to do. Step away and cheer Jenny from the sidelines."

"Quite the selfless gesture." Boz did not hide his skepticism. "Or because you schemed to get your revenge some other way?"

Dusty didn't bite. *Smart.*

"To recap," Boz began, sitting back, throwing an arm along the backrest of the couch in Dusty's living room, "Jorge Vargas—you don't know him, you never thought to ask Nigel about the guy you replaced. You claim you didn't know he was tortured and torched, or that he was dead. Crispin Martinez—you were completely unaware he smuggled in your I-10 fighters, hell, you don't even know those fighters are illegal. You deny being with Nigel in your truck—an old, gray Toyota, exactly like the one you owned at the time—or anywhere near Crispin's home the night he was burned alive after his hands were hacked off." By this time, Boz could not keep the mocking disbelief from his voice and cynicism from his smile. "You went Jesus, the way you unselfishly and nobly accepted Nigel's boot to your ass, kicking you out of Jenny's corner for a greater good. Saying, 'She can try,' was just an empty threat. You meant nothing by it."

"Layin' out and linin' up a bunch of bad shit like you just done?" Dusty protested defiantly, "That's you being clever'n crafty, forcing misleading connections where there nothing to mislead or connect."

"I have convicted people with less," said Boz and meant it.

"Look," Dusty got defensive, "you got your heart broke by Jenny, don't misdirect that toward me."

"And you're not resentful at all?" Boz chose his words carefully, alleging and implying more than anything else.

Dusty smirked, "My skin been thickened over a lifetime of disappointments."

"Still, it must eat you up. Bringing Jenny to the verge—one match away from the glory and recognition you've been scraping and clawing to get all your miserable life."

"Try as you might, I ain't admitting to nothin'."

"Sounds like you're taking the fifth."

Dusty kept quiet.

"Your goodbye kiss for Nigel—the circumstances and words sounded awful similar to the goodwill you expressed to Muerte Cortez, when he screwed you. Of course, we know how it ended for Muerte."

"Police didn't even open an investigation against me."

"They haven't closed the case either."

"You think I'd hurt Jenny?"

Boz tilted his head. "That'd teach Nigel, won't it?"

"You've shown more inclination to!" Dusty went off warmly. "With how you behave fight night back in Texas."

Boz let him vent. Anger undid even the cleverest assholes.

"You probably one of 'em southern rednecks who think a woman should have no fucking choice, hell, not even the right to vote, and Jenny should put her championship career on hold 'cause you were too fucking cheap to spend the extra dollar on a condom upgrade."

"With one dead fighter in your past, it won't be a big leap for a jury, should another turn up dead."

Dusty's eyes narrowed, "Know what? This whole interview, sounds awfully like you're building a case to pin *me* for *your* payback."

Boz took a deep, relieved breath. Stretched his lips in a vile smile. "Took you long enough to get there."

Dusty looked baffled.

"I can offer you immunity."

Puma Song: Recollections from New Orleans

James Brown belted "*I Got You*" from Puma's cell—his ring tone for Dusty. They hadn't spoken since fight night, and he been too spent the next day. Monday come and go, Dusty stayed silent. Puma figured the old coot just be too proud to pick up that olive branch. So, Puma followed Jenny from TV show to TV show. *Lil girl waste no time dumpin' on her next opponent, the reigning Bantamweight champ.* On Tuesday, she called him and stayed on the phone, while they watched the unveiling of her *Vogue* spread.

"You realize how much jism is flying right now, lil girl?"

Jenny roared. "Just as well. That sperm is better off wasted, don't you think? I just saved a generation of retards being born from those peckers."

Puma's turn to guffaw. "You healing OK?"

"Oh, yeah. Toyota and Ford are bidding who'll endorse me."

"Nice!"

"I'm taking two weeks off. Tell Dusty."

So Nigel don't tell her. Puma decided not to either, hoping by the time she got back, this little dustup'd dissipate.

"Nigel offered me his plane to take me to my first commercial shoot down in Miami. You wanna come?"

"Nah," Puma said. "I just gonna sit around and lay in bed."

"Exactly what I did Sunday, Monday. Almost drove to the Emergency Room."

"Sheeuh, you OK?'

"Not really. I was worried that sex never crossed my mind for two days."

Puma chuckled."Had me anxious for a moment there."

"So, after Miami, I'm going to the Bahamas, fuck strangers, and I'll be back for Fat Tuesday next week. Let's get together. I'll text you."

"Sure."

"Bring Dusty. The perennial stick up his ass may just be his dick, and one way to get it out is get him drunk and laid."

"What better occasion than Mardi Gras," Puma laughed. "Be safe, lil girl."

Around midday, Dusty called. Not about Nigel or making peace. But to warn him.

Puma put the phone down, opened the door, and leisurely made his way back to the kitchen. He lived in the corner unit on the ground floor. Decent complex. No trouble with neighbors—a coupla gay kids, thirty-something, lived next door. Coming outta L.A., where social distancing be the norm, Puma got only as neighborly as a wave when their paths crossed. The rest of the tenants, he didn't even acknowledge. Puma fired up the stove, filled the kettle, and waited till it whistled, before reaching into the overhead cabinet for a couple of cups and tea bags.

"Puma Song?"

Puma looked around. "Detective."

Unlike Dusty's place, which was cluttered akin to someone living there for the long haul, Puma'd purchased just the bare minimum. A flatscreen sat on the dining table. Folding chairs provided the only seats. Bare walls. The open door off to the side revealed a single bed on box springs with a pillow and rumpled sheets. No bed frame.

"I'm drinkin' tea," Puma said, pouring himself a cup. He didn't much care for cops."You want some, pour it yourself." Pointed to the other cup and bag.

Boz declined. Puma limped back to a folding chair. Stared like how black people did a white cop. So did Boz. Untrusting both ways. Boz slapped the folder he brought with him down on the table, pulled a chair back, and sat down. He opened it, making no attempt to hide the top sheet, which had Puma's mug shot. *That supposed to intimidate me, muhfuh?*

Boz flipped to the second page. Sniffed before he began, "So, your mother served in the US Army, Major Keisha Johnson, and while she was deployed in South Korea, she met and married your father, Colonel Jun Hee Song, some sort of desk jockey with their military. Divorced him within a year, but he'd knocked her up. She returned to LA single, you in her belly. She quit the Army, but couldn't hack it in the private sector. Remained lower middle-class rest of her life. Moved into the house her parents owned in Compton." He looked up. "You kept it."

Puma wanted to interrupt. *Nah.* Responded instead with stinging sarcasm that roiled from brain to tongue, "Didn't know none of that. Keep going, mebbe all the way back to my grampy'n great grampy, who likely fucked your kin's unsatisfied wives. Save me paying Ancestry.com."

Boz's lips thinned into a humorless smile. "Growing up between South Central L.A. and Koreatown must've been tough, what with you being neither nigger nor gook."

"Sheeuh, Detective," Puma chortled, "never heard a redneck call me a nigga'n a gook." Couldn't help himself, "Mebbe 'cause most o'you white racist muhfuhs come from mamas secretly craving color cock."

"If that was the case, would I be blond with blue eyes?"

"Likely her ho pussy only sized for pencil-thin cracker dick." Puma leaned back. *South vs. South Central.* "I got a million more, we can go all day, muhfuh."

"I don't doubt it, and you'll have the opportunity—when I throw your black ass among some friendly Nazis, thanks to a paperwork error."

"Even in the dumbass South, ain't it the law I can call my lawyer, especially if you chargin' me?"

"If I was, you'd be in cuffs and on your way to OPP. That'd be Orleans Parish Prison, and being a panzy from California, here's the skinny about what to expect at New Orleans's most notorious correctional facility. When Katrina hit, the Mayor, one of yours, mind you, didn't think twice about abandoning the inmates. Figured it'd be public service to wipe them from the face of this earth. The current warden is a friend of mine, who shares my thinking. Best leave the law of the jungle be. You know, allow the gorillas to work it out. Observe stabbings, rapes, and fights. Not stop them. A cripple like you will be red meat." Boz sat back, "Sorry, I get carried away when I talk to perps about OPP. Of course Mr. Song, you are entitled to an attorney. Do you want one?"

Puma refused to be intimidated. Called Boz out. "So you can take me downtown, leave me sittin' on my ass, while you take your own sweet time to get me to a phone, as be your right, till you actually ask me the first question."

"You know the drill then, having been incarcerated before. Twice."

"Only 'cause there ain't too many niggas coming outta Compton without a rap sheet, thanks to your cousins, rednecks that is. Like vermin, they be everywhere. Even infest LAPD." Of course, Boz'd have pulled his record to use as ammo. *Fire away.*

"But A&B?" Assault and Battery. *Ratatatat.* "Both times? Second time, you escaped a manslaughter charge because the victim recovered and became a character witness for you. Notation here says you threatened his family."

"Clearly no, 'cause judge call bullshit and toss it."

"So, Puma—can I drop the formality of Mr. Song?"

"Can I call you dick? Drop the formality of detective."

"You discovered Jenny."

"Yeah." Again corkscrewed in a jibe, "I saw fists of fury. Sheeuh, lil girl got the pussy of a nympho too," Taunting grin, "You know all about that." The skin over Boz's cheeks tightened and his eyes died. *Ooh. He wants to lean over, grab my face, and slam it down on the table till the last drop of my disrespect bleed out.*

"Rage was cited in both your A&B convictions."

"I felt wronged and fought back," Puma shrugged. "Lady Justice see it different."

"And both times in prison—you never got out early for good behavior because you were involved in some fights. Bad ones. They sent me pictures. You put quite the hurt on a couple of inmates."

"Do a stint. You find out real fast khumbaya don't work."

"Fucking vicious what you did, considering what set you off—trivial bullshit that won't even start a schoolyard fight. Shrink at your second joint diagnosed you with IED—Intermittent Explosive Disorder."

"A white bitch," Puma recalled bitterly, "barely outta college, who needed to write something in my file."

"Good for her. Your diagnosis is just the thing for juries and judges down here, who love to hand out the chair. IED symptoms are uncontrollable incidents of rage triggered by pretty much anything, even someone bumping into you. Then, it's like you black out throughout the violent episode, but not really. You are completely aware, but you cannot, or will not, stop yourself. Inmates, who witnessed you, support that finding. They said you went nuts, not just mad nuts, berserk mad nuts. Suffered any such breakdowns recently."

"No. You wanna swab my cane?"

"Looks brand new."

"Figured for the title fight, I should get something shiny."

"Where's your old one?" asked Boz.

"Tossed it in the trash."

"When did you buy this?

"Few months ago."

"You have the receipt?"

"Never keep any that ain't tax deductible."

"Credit card statement is fine too."

"Don't have one o'those neither. My psych report should tell you I'm a paranoid sumbitch of the conviction that credit cards, bank account'n such—they all ways to keep tabs, and I ain't giving cops, feds'n the government the pleasure. So, I only use cash."

"One other thing. I must ask you not to leave New Orleans."

"Someone dead?"

"Why do you ask?"

"In case I have to buy a suit for the funeral."

"So sweet you think a judge will grant you bail to attend one."

"Optimism killed nobody," Puma smiled crookedly. "Can't say the same about disappointment. Jenny blindsided you with one just recently, didn't she?"

Zing! Boz's eyes flashed angrily. "You lied when you said you did not have an IED episode." Boz flipped to the bottom of the folder. Removed a couple of photos that he turned around toward Puma.

Fuck.

"He tried to cash in when Jenny made it big," Boz continued. "Newspapers didn't bite—he was a common criminal. Came to the station to file a complaint with these selfies he stated he took on the night of, hoping to hustle a settlement outta Nigel. Showed up in the morgue coupla days later. Burned crisp."

"It wan't me," Puma said vehemently, "sheeuh, no."

"Your new cane about as old as these selfies?"

The two photographs belonged to Pint Size, the little hustler-juggler, who Puma thrashed to an inch of his life the night he, Dusty, and Jenny celebrated their partnership with Nigel.

"There are witnesses."

Puma threw in the towel. "What do you want?"

According to Dusty Saldana

WHABAM! Bella arcs in a left that everyone in the arena, but Jenny, sees coming. I slowed the actual moment from fight night in my head. The first power head strike Bella delivered. Then I donned 3D Goggles of the virtual boxer, replayed it, being Jenny. *Bella arcs in a left. Impossible to miss.* I angled left, easily avoiding it.

Following every fight, Silicon Valley folks programmed in significant strikes, so we could study what go right and wrong. They didn't know I'd quit and uploaded to the VR box like normal after a fight. I then broke it down for Jenny. I might not be her trainer no more, but it bugged me silly the shots she took from the right that a sloth could check with ease.

Also, it took my mind off the horns of dilemma impaled into my ass cheeks. On the one hand, I was pissed Nigel didn't have the decency to make a follow-up call to at least explore possibilities. No matter Puma and Jenny used me to get to him, I was central to this alliance being born and flourish. Come Wednesday, hope dwindled Nigel'd ever call. My anger festered into resentment. I no longer felt that walking away, like I done, had been a prideful, hasty, emotionally charged decision. Rather, a gut check, now that Boz had me cornered. *But do I have a stomach for it?*

I quick-timed to another moment in the fight. Became Jenny. *Bella strikes with her left.* I easily checked them. During the fight Jenny had no answer. *Bella connects on strikes with her left hand going at Jenny's right. Jenny pays for it again. Courtesy of Bella's trunksize left leg into Jenny's right temple.* Wearing 3D goggles, being Jenny, I easily ducked. *Bella walks in. Left-left-left.* I swiveled and basic blocked them. Jenny took a pounding. Bella walks in. *POWPOWPOW. Left-left-left. Jenny doesn't react to even one of them*

I stared out the window, 3D Goggles perched on the front of my head. Remembering the bunch of other devastating moments Jenny survived from the two fights prior.

"Watch her left leg!" I yell. WHABAM! Jenny expects a right fist. Cyborg lands a lightning left leg kick to the right side of head instead. Jenny never moves. Never sees it coming. In her AFC fight against Nadia Kelly—*not seeing what come from her right fast enough when Nadia bring a high left leg kick.*

Back to the Jones Mahal. *Bella effectively uses her left to go savage to the right side of Jenny's skull. A roundhouse from the right. Jenny doesn't react to the oncoming threat. Then, Bella's head butt. A crimson tide surfing over left eye, Jenny squares up to see with her right eye, her only good eye.*

Doesn't seem like it. Her swings look blind. Somehow she finds and clinches Bella.

I suddenly stopped.

Rewound that back.

Dropped the 3D Goggles down over my eyes. Took up the southpaw stance. My head snapped each time I took the blow exactly like Jenny done in the fight.

"Ow! Ow! Ow!" I reacted out loud, feeling the punishment of the error buzz 'tween my ears that occurred when the virtual boxer connected. I ripped off the Goggles., exclaimed out loud, "No fucking way."

Stunned first, then realizing the consequences, I almost peed my pants.

CASE FILE: 010146888
Reporting Officer: Detective Bostwick Oswald

Boz watched District Attorney Arlen work the room following his Town Hall meeting at the Fleur De Lis Christian Center. Boz sat through all of it, so he'd pass for one of the middle-class attendees when they met up later. As always, with these affairs, plants in the audience tossed softballs to kick it off and interrupted with diversions whenever the questioning got tough and combative. Arlen was a lawyer, with a knack for speaking out of both sides of his mouth, yet sounding as if he was taking a fresh and courageous position.

The Q&A wrapped. Arlen stuck around the juice and snacks, which probably drew most of these hundred-odd voters. Once he ran out of the freeloaders, Arlen gripped and grinned his way around the room to Boz. They put on earnest expressions and smiled intermittently. But there was nothing friendly about Arlen's message to Boz. Other contenders for Mayor had dropped out due to a lack of money or being unable to garner name recognition.

With the Special Mayoral Election set for the week after Fat Tuesday—twelve days from today—Arlen wasn't the last man standing, which, at this point, he'd hoped to be, and also trailed the Police Chief by ten points.

"You were supposed to develop her as a CI, not fall for her!" Arlen said testily.

An elderly lady, 70, 5-2, 115, sprightly, hard edges, walked up. "My pastor says you're a God fearing family man who supports the death penalty. You got my vote."

Arlen switched off his anger and cracked his face in a huge smile. Boz knew it to be fake, but she couldn't tell. Even became tickled pink when Arlen leaned down and kissed her on the cheek, "Thank you! Thank you so much!"

"I'll tell my neighbors too."

"Just so you know, I am pro-life and believe the Second Amendment is non-negotiable."

"A red, white'n blue American," the lady beamed. "Mr. Taylor, can you switch places with my son?"

Arlen laughed, touched her arm gently. She walked away pleased. Never having watched politicians work up close, and with no one else to compare him to, Boz concluded, as a snake oil salesman, Arlen was more oil than snake. A compliment in Boz's book.

"We lost valuable time because you took your eye off the fucking ball," Arlen picked up where he left off.

He's right. After Jenny abruptly dumped him, Boz lost sight of the ball entirely. He reclaimed it the moment she killed his baby. Discovered only a fine line separated love and hate.

It took but a single step to cross from one side to the other.

Vendetta consumed him. A demo plan emerged. It started with Dusty and Puma. "Think of them as the powder. Now it's a matter of lighting the fuse."

"Save the cryptic metaphors, Boz. Can you or can you not deliver? It's a simple yes or no."

"Yes," replied Boz firmly.

"Just before this Town Hall, I talked to Helena Garcia, now Helena-Garcia Thackery, wife of David Thackery, a deep pocket billionaire. I assured her we'd be speaking off the record and her name would never come up." Helena was the Spanish teacher Dusty claimed to have fucked to get Nigel's grade up. "She had reservations about being associated with Nigel. Word amongst old money? His wealth is dirty. But she confirmed Dusty's story."

"How much was your discretion worth to her?"

"Enough to saturate the airwaves with campaign ads, starting tomorrow through election day." Arlen glanced around, then leaned into Boz's ear. "I want to wake up Mayor the morning after the election, Boz. Should that somehow not occur, I will make your life a living hell."

I wasn't born last night, asshole. Boz did not mince words either, "IAD couldn't ever find anything on me for a reason, Arlen. So, do you seriously think I'd come away from our meetings empty handed? Everything said between us is on the record."

Arlen turned into a malevolent statue.

"Cell phones are wires hiding in plain sight." Boz slid his Galaxy out of his pocket to show the DA the red recording light. "I want this as badly as you do, more so even."

Arlen should realize he hired a volatile motherfucker. Something not on his file? Boz's fascination with serial killers. Ted Bundy stood out, the way he operated. Good looks, devious mind, angry killer. Maybe that played a part, inspired and even emboldened him to break in and enter after a breakup.

"I have to fly to Baltimore," said Boz.

Arlen nodded. Squeezed Boz's arm with a smile. "No one makes up ten points, not without the other candidate dropping dead or dropping out. Make sure one or the other happens." His smile turned sinister, "If we are exchanging threats, I can reopen the murder rap you thought you beat." Then, he went from vindictive to amiable in successive beats, when a couple of black voters came up, shook his hand, and he assured them, "Getting guns off the streets is on my Day One agenda."

Boz revised his opinion. Arlen was more snake than oil.

Next day, Boz took the first AM flight to Baltimore.

He didn't make an appointment, just walked up to the receptionist, 25, 5-7, 118. Cute little black thing with braided hair, red lipstick and nails. Boz flashed his NOPD badge, enjoying her expression tighten, and asked to see Makena Cole.

"Let me see if Mrs. Cole is available." She did not use the intercom, getting up and hurrying through the frosted glass door.

"If she isn't, tell her she should just drop everything."

Boz stayed on his feet. Looked around. Easy Trucking rented offices right along the docks in Baltimore. It didn't take long to get here from the airport, being mid-morning. Tasteful décor, but not plush, the only splashy thing being a big screen TV that displayed a map of North America, with moving dots along all of Easy Trucking's routes. The company reached every extremity of Canada, the US, and Mexico. To Boz, it looked like Nigel was a contagion contaminating the entire continent.

"She will see you," the receptionist reappeared and held the door open.

He followed her into a short and narrow hallway, with two closed doors. Ringing phones and muffled overlapping voices, behind the first, suggested drones—accountants, schedulers, and such. The girl opened the second and stepped aside.

Boz entered a utilitarian office. Nothing fancy in here either, except, maybe, the really nice looking desk in front of Makena. The receptionist retreated out, closing the door. Makena did not stand. Just pointed him to a seat.

He got right down to it. "As Easy Trucking's CFO, you must work real close with Nigel Hansom."

"On fiscal matters, yes."

"Do you have a degree in finance?"

"No. I'm just good with money."

"Your husband served with Nigel in Iraq, right?"

"Detective, don't waste my time. Why are you here?"

I'm bringing it up for a reason. He moved on, lifting the folder he'd brought with him off his lap, and removed the Driver's License photo of Jorge Vargas. "Recognize him?"

"No," she looked down, then up. No hesitation.

He slid out Crispin Martinez's DL picture. Placed it next to Jorge's. "Him?"

"No."

Then, he laid out two gruesome pictures of charred remains and put them next to their mug shots. Makena drew her breath in sharply, recoiling.

"Jorge had his balls and tongue removed. Crispin's hands were cut off. Done while they were alive. Probably conscious when they were burned." She looked up at him. He drilled his eyes into hers. "These are Nigel's fighters. Both murdered."

Makena met his eyes evenly. "I'm not involved with that side of his business."

"Good answer. It would be illegal if you were. What do you know about the I-10 circuit?"

"I have no clue what that even is."

"No?" Boz raised his hairline. His brow furrowed horizontally. "Nigel created it. Underground fight clubs up and down the I-10 freeway. He's using Easy Trucking to traffic fighters in from Mexico," paused, "among other things."

"I have no idea what you are talking about."

"Now you do." Boz picked up the photos, tapped them down on the table to line them up. "You used to be a bookkeeper for a front —let's not be naïve—for the Cherry Hill Cartel here. Mr. Knight—brutal son of a bitch, according to DEA and FBI files. His MO is to stamp out the smoke. Doesn't wait to see if there's even a fire. I don't have to explain that metaphor, do I? Seeing that working for Mr. Knight was your only job qualification for Nigel to bump you up to the top floor." He put the photos back in the envelope. "Probably didn't hurt you're fucking him on the side."

"If there are no more questions," Makena said, her manner hardening.

"You have a daughter, right?" Boz asked.

Makena reacted sharply.

"Just so you understand, rage, not reason, is driving me.

Nigel's money is fueling Jenny's ambition, and I hold them both responsible for the murder of my unborn child. FYI, Nigel and his trainer, Dusty Saldana—you met him—had a falling out. Dusty's angry now and motivated to cooperate. Puma Song is the other low life with priors. He's involved with a third victim. A midget who tried to shake down Nigel. I've offered Dusty and Puma both immunity."

He stood up smiling. "I wonder how it's going play with Mr. Knight and his Cartel partners in Mexico and Canada. Three messy murders, all personally motivated and completely unrelated to their operation. Dusty and Puma—they've brushed up against the law enough times to know evidence is just optional for cops who have already made up their minds to arrest and charge. One way or the other, I'm determined to fuck everything up, all because Nigel stupidly used Easy Trucking to tie it all together. With Jenny being in the spotlight, when all this hits the fan, New Orleans is going to wake up to a seismic shit storm." He slid his business card over to her. "Have a nice day, Mrs. Cole."

"Next time, call ahead," Makena stayed seated. "I want a lawyer present."

"Shit, yeah, you should." Boz headed for the door. "I'll be reading you Miranda rights which expressly advise you to have one. I also know NOPD is a cesspool. Word of an arrest warrant is bound to get to Mr. Knight before I'm able to fly here and execute it. I may be bagging you, not arresting you."

Makena's expression did not change.

Boz knew she was shitting her pants. He opened the door, stopped, turned. "Oh. One last thing. Nigel was the only one who survived the ambush that killed your husband. Did he ever tell you the two of them were carrying eighteen million dollars in cash? The money was never recovered. Something to think about, huh? You're working for a salary, when maybe, you should own half of Easy Trucking."

Boz exited. Shut the door, and strode off like the cat that didn't simply swallow the canary, but rubbed his belly and smacked his lips afterwards.

Puma looked up as Dusty sat down at the outdoor table of a sidewalk café. A clone of every other in the Warehouse District, yuppie to the core. "Shit, Dusty, look around, together we probably got almost near a century on the oldest kid here." Puma slid a steaming medium sized cup toward him. "I got you coffee."

"How've you been?" asked Dusty.

Puma treated it rhetorical. Shrugged.

The weekend before Fat Tuesday, which was upon them, really started the countdown in earnest. The streets hopped with tourists. You couldn't walk the sidewalk as you got closer to the French Quarter without running into a wall of people. Road closures everywhere. Cops from other Districts.

"Mardi Gras," snickered Puma. "How many 'em tourists you think even know it's actually just one day, Fat Tuesday. Named for the last day of feasting before forty days of Lent."

"Been twenty years since I been here during this time," confessed Dusty.

"Longer, I think, for me."

"Just bigger crowds. But drunks, hookers, dealers, hustlers—same ol', same ol' there." Puma laughed, letting Dusty get to the question he was dying to ask, "How did Jenny take it?"

"I haven't told her," said Puma. "Nigel neither. She took off to Miami to film some shit, then to the Bahamas, and back on Fat Tuesday to partyin'n tossin' beads till she go bare titted. So, I ain't about to rain on her parade. Also hopin' you reconsidered, what with the fight a week in the rear view."

"I ran into Ref Ray and Trevor after the fight and that played into my reason to quit. This girl have a chance. But that in no way reduce my hate for Nigel not valuing service and loyalty. Jenny'n me, you been there. We ain't exactly close. So I got no delusions about who she gonna choose."

"Jenny can surprise you."

"I'm not waiting to find out," declared Dusty. "It's a loada crock, you know, about stickin' with your dream long enough'n if you try hard enough, it'll happen for you. Like Fate's holding a football like that girl, Lucy, do to Charlie Brown in 'em Sunday comics. Entice you into thinkin' this time's the charm, only to yank out the mothafuckin' ball and laugh at you fallin' on your ass yet again. Never happens for some people, however hard they try, however right you go about it. What with the creator, Schulz, dead, never will now. Fuck it! I'm through training. Fuck it! I ain't goin' back to starting over from the bottom. Not that I ever got outta the sewer."

"OK, now that you got that off your chest, I know you don't wanna spend sweat equity getting' her ready, so some fucker agreeable to UFZ hold up the belt. If it's Kevin, then Jenny, Nigel, me, we'd know—"

"Sell that swill to the dump, Puma," Dusty scorned.

Puma left it at that. "So, why you call me?"

"If it was too good to be true, it usually, is," Dusty said, then told him what he'd stumbled upon.

"Sheeuh. Don't you think you shoulda led with it?" Puma asked angrily. "You sure?"

They went back to Dusty's apartment. He held out the 3D Goggles, "I never got around to returning this pair to Nigel. Bella's the virtual boxer in here."

Dusty hooked up the box to the TV. Puma slipped them on. Bella appeared.

"Go into a southpaw stance," Dusty said. Puma swiveled his right shoulder forward. Squinted. "I'm gonna play it slow mo. Wait for her to come at you with her left." Puma leaned back to a right. "Here come some jabs." Puma threw up his right blocked it. "Even an invalid like you duck it and ward off easy. Right? I'm going to rewind it. Now play like you're Jenny."

Puma's head snapped like he took a hit to the right temple. "Fuck!" Feeling the error buzz. Juddered to the multiple strikes. "Ow! Fuck! Ow!" He peeled off the Goggles. Reacted only one way he could—stared down Dusty like he'd been betrayed by a close friend.

"You can't shake a bad habit if it ain't one," said Dusty.

"Sheeuh." Puma needed to sit down.

"With almost more'n fifty years 'tween us, most of it spent among low life fighters who try to pull shit all the time, you think Nigel'll believe we didn't know."

"Sheeuh."

"Jenny play us for chumps from the start."

Makena Cole: Eyes Only Summary Notes, Baltimore

Makena stared at her uncle, Sharif Hirsi, who twirled Boz's business card between well manicured long fingers of his extremely large hand. The pregnant pause between them stretched. After seeing her daughter off to school, Makena had called him over to seek his counsel.

They were in the living room of her super-plush home in an exclusive section of the already exclusive Locust Point neighborhood. Somali artifacts that she'd collected over the years—of value and importance to only a native—were showcased throughout the house. The furniture looked insanely expensive because it was. A live-in housemaid kept the entire place immaculate.

Sharif finally said, "Let's tell him only what he needs to hear."

Mr. Knight gave them an immediate audience. Uncle had that kind of clout. Mr. Knight listened to Makena, then simply said, "End this."

Makena bravely broached, "What do you think about informing Nigel we want a controlling interest in Easy Trucking."

Mr. Knight stared at her, and after a full five seconds—long enough for Makena to fear she'd overstepped—his lips twitched upward at the corners. "I can go along with that."

Makena simply nodded grimly because a smile would play as scheming. She did not mention the company was built on her husband's half share of eighteen million dollars, stolen—

amassed, whatever—in Iraq that Nigel never revealed. *Pocketed.*

"Draw up all the papers in your name, even take a pen with you, so Nigel will know he must sign and on the spot." Then looked at Sharif. "Go with her."

He walked them to the door, where Makena paused with an idea she'd saved for the end, debating in her head, throughout this meeting, if she should present it or not. Sharif'd told her to gauge the mood, then go with her instinct.

"I had a thought," ventured Makena, then elaborated.

This time, Mr. Knight's smile came instantly with a delight that reached his eyes for the first time she'd known him. "Never crossed my mind. It solves so many things." Looked at Sharif, "Iron fist, velvet glove, your niece." To both, "Get it done ASAP."

"Jenny is back in New Orleans tomorrow," replied Makena.

"Fat Tuesday," Mr. Knight pursed. "Fitting. It is the last night to enjoy everything you must give up the next day, Ash Wednesday."

Sid Rosen: Debrief Notes, New Orleans

"You can't make this shit up," Sid addressed a rough looking Rainbow Coalition of G-Men—Black Goatee, 28, 5-10¼, 180; Kung Fu Panda, 32, 5-8, 185; and Big Cholo, 35, 6-3, 238—while they checked their weapons, stuffed spare clips into their pockets, and wired themselves with airpod intercoms.

"Check, check check," said Sid. "Everyone can hear everyone?"

Thumbs went up all around.

Evening died, night birthed. This Sid Quartet was cramped in a shoebox-size, upstairs hotel room on Bourbon Street, ground zero for Mardi Gras. The weather Gods smiled, sort of, for Fat Tuesday, humidity and temperatures in the mid-80s. The partying, which began almost when this day did, picked up by the hour, but still far from its zenith, Sid'd guys told him.

Astonishingly, Sid had never been to New Orleans. Ever. He could only imagine how loud and raucous the music and people must be at street level, considering the volume already bombarding the second floor room. Sid shed his suit for T-shirt and Dockers, a handgun tucked into his belt in the back. His hair—oil-slicked and shiny—reflected the colors of the flickering lights of the street.

He tossed photographs down one at time. "Nigel Hansom—a coyote for fighters, also uses Easy Trucking, to move drugs for the Cartels. Dusty Saldana—low level trainer, just came out of a suspension. Rumor is he doped a fighter, Johnny Muerte Cortez, assaulted him into a coma that he never came out of. Puma Song—a one-legged scout with some sort of rage disorder. You should see his record in prison. Makena Cole—Cartel accountant and CFO for Easy Trucking, Nigel's company. Her uncle, Sharif Hirsi, rose from scary-ass street muscle to head up security for the Cherry Hill Cartel." Sid eased his ass off the granite top of the single-drawer base cabinet suspended below a flatscreen TV bolted to the wall. "All brought together for a Mardi Gras summit by, drum roll, Jenny Sharp."

Sid tossed down the week-old sports section with the all-caps, bold headline, 'NEXT-JEN?' Below it, the snapshot from the fight of Jenny's agonized face turned to camera with Bella's fist connected to her right temple.

Makena Cole: Eyes Only Summary Notes, New Orleans

Everyone had the day off at Easy Trucking. So, Makena texted Nigel when she pulled up outside. Lights blazed in the parking lot. Eighteen-wheelers stacked half a dozen deep as usual. Observing no activity on the gym side, she wondered if the illegals got to go to the parade. Nigel came to the front door to let her into a totally empty building.

Her uncle had come out last night to round up muscle

from the Seventh Ward to keep this cleanup local. Her plane had landed a couple of hours ago. She came with no luggage, intending to leave as soon as all the loose ends were tied up. She informed Nigel not to send a limo. She'd rent a car. It set the tone—this visit was unlike any prior. Tourists overflowed, even onto the lesser traveled roads, which her Waze app directed her to take. Still, she made good time.

They engaged in small talk—distance and tension unmistakable—during the short walk to his office. Even so, her manner betrayed nothing of the heaviness of the hammer she'd come to drop. She sat down, not like always, next to him on the large couch, but across. Makena put down the drink he poured on the coffee table without even sipping it. Doing nothing they usually did to drive home the deadly seriousness. She'd also carefully plotted out an escalating series of revelations, so that the final ask wouldn't come as a shock. *Still will.*

"Dusty and Puma have immunity." She didn't know that, but needed the lie to anchor the rest of this conversation. Nigel blinked, surprised. She nodded, "Yeah. It's that cop who was here. Detective Oswald came to see me."

Nigel shook his head. "I warned him. I'll talk to the Police Chief."

"The Chief'll distance himself." Makena lied again, "They are already cooperating. You, for all charges against them dropped. Dusty was probably easy to convince. And Puma's an ex-con?"

Nigel clenched his teeth behind thin lips. "I pulled those fuckers out of the gutter."

"Regardless," Makena instigated, "they are not going to prison protecting you. But you've also had some serious lapses of judgment. The Detective wants to tie a couple of murders—Jorge Vargas and Crispin Martinez—from your I-10 circuit to Easy Trucking. Brought up a third victim. A midget?" Even though Mexico and Canada remained unaware, she exaggerated, "The Cartels are freaking."

Nigel looked off.

Makena embellished again, "Mr. Knight assured them we'll

take care of it. Tonight." Paused. "So." Paused once more. "Uncle came down with me."

Nigel lifted his head sharply, blinking straight into her stern eyes. His fingers tightened around his drink because he knew Sharif's presence meant one thing. *Body bags.* She never thought she'd see Nigel afraid, but there it was.

He quickly masked it behind bravado. "I've been gold to the Cartels! They never had a continent-wide operation. I made it happen."

We did. Makena let it go. "It's never about yesterday with them, you know that. It's about today and how it affects tomorrow. Remember I assured you? As long as I'm on your side, you're safe?"

"But?"

"Mr. Knight summoned me to The Mansion to convey a decision he and the Cartels reached. Steps you must take. First, the I-10 is done. Shut it down."

"Fine," Nigel nodded. "It's a money pit anyway."

"Second, Dusty and Puma have to go."

"Done," Nigel said without remorse. "Fucking snakes."

"Third, and this one comes at a steep price," said Makena. "To you." Nigel stiffened as if he didn't expect there to be more. She extracted stapled, tri-folded papers from her purse. "I'm taking a controlling interest in Easy Trucking."

"No!" Nigel stood up angrily. "This is my company!"

That you built by stealing my husband's half of eighteen million dollars. Makena so wanted to throw it in his face. Instead, her voice remained soft, assertive. "I'm sorry, Nigel. It's non-negotiable."

"No!" Nigel shook his head. "Fuck, no! Hell if I'm handing over the family business!"

I should own 50% stake of Easy Trucking. Consider controlling interest penalty for lying all these years. Makena succinctly laid out the consequences Nigel faced, which she had rehearsed in her head on the flight over, "So the Cartels will suffer a stoppage. It's not the first time, and certainly not the last. Every time they've found another way. They will, again, without you."

"Fine. They want to walk way? I will too."

"Problem is, knowing what you know about their operation, do you seriously think they'll just leave you be? Or Kamryn? Or the girls? Your family may know nothing, but will the Cartels care?"

Nigel went still. Stared at the pen she held out.

Sign, you sonofabitch.

Ever since Boz told her about the money, Makena's resentment for Nigel grew by the hour. He'd been two-faced from day one. Playing a concerned and caring gentleman, doing right by Tavon, all the while building his business with her husband's blood. Offering her a salaried position may've been rooted in guilty conscience, but shallowly so, nowhere near nine million dollars deep. Actually it was self-serving—to gain access to the Cartels. So, he not only kept Tavon's share from her and used it to add enormously to his personal wealth, he multiplied it with money she brought to the table via the door only she could've opened. *Here I am, all these years, ecstatic with the wiggle room percentage Mr. Knight allowed me to keep.*

Makena swallowed the bile and manipulated, "If Dusty and Puma had not turned, I wouldn't be here."

Nigel sat down.

"Do it to keep your family safe."

He took the pen, picked up the papers, slow blinked, and signed.

"Do you want Uncle to take care of those two?"

"No!" Nigel snapped. "I will."

Makena expected he would. He'd just lost his company and she'd quietly fueled him to dirty his hands once more, cleaning up his own shit.

Nigel stood up. Headed to his desk. "We're all going meet on Bourbon Street for drinks and whatever else at *Ravages.* A yuppie bar."

He opened his desk drawer and removed three guns—a PPK, Glock 18, and Baretta 93R. Growing up in Cherry Hill, with Sharif as her uncle, Makena recognized the firearms. He asked, "What about Jenny?"

"How much does she know?"

"You met her. She doesn't see much beyond herself." He selected the PPK, put away the other two. "She's high profile, and should something happen to her, it'd do exactly what you're trying to avoid. A spotlight on me and Easy Trucking."

"Good point," said Makena. *Uncle is going to kill her anyway.*

They emerged outside. Did not embrace like they usually did. She touched his arm, faking sympathy, and got into her rental. Drove around the corner. Pulled up. Cut the engine and lights. She peered into the driverside mirror. Didn't have to wait long.

Nigel roared by, driving himself.

Headlights snapped on across the road from her!

Her eyes swung forward. An SUV pulled out, slowing as it passed her. Boz looked over at her from behind the wheel, smiled, and pedaled down.

Makena called Sharif. "Nigel has a tail. The detective."

When Mr. Knight walked Makena and Sharif to the door, and she stopped and said, "I had a thought," she had a diabolical payback in mind. "Nigel's wife, Kamryn, will be more than happy being a silent partner in Easy Trucking and maintain her lifestyle with her daughters. So, do we even need Nigel?"

According to Dusty Saldana

Stars and the moon peered down on America's biggest party night getting underway, when the Uber, which picked up Puma, came over to my place. I climbed into the back seat. City lights sparkled like gaudy bling on a gangsta's necklace. You could distantly hear the potpourri of bands from the different parades, big and small, marching through New Orleans. The sidewalks bustled with stumbling drunks already.

Puma saw my fanny pack, asked, "What's with the tote?"

"You're the paranoid sumbitch," I replied. "I can't believe you didn't suggest it."

"Nigel don't know Boz offer us a deal."

"This is his town, Puma. With eyes and ears everywhere, 'specially on the force. Never once his trucks been stopped or seized. That ain't no accident."

"Good thinkin' then," agreed Puma. "better safe than sorry."

"You bet."

Uber got as close as the barricades allowed. We hoofed it the rest of way. By the time Puma and I arrived, Bourbon Street burst at the seams with outta-their-minds tourists packed shoulder to shoulder. Every balcony hopped with a crazy party. Public indecency might be against the law, and strongly dissuaded in the travel brochures, but that didn't stop girls, high as kites, giggling and lifting their shirts. Beads flew. I didn't see a pair of steady legs. Now you add in the noise—competing music with no unity in the cheering, shouting, and singing—the miracle became our ear drums staying intact, not a virgin called Mary birthing our Lord.

Paparazzi swarmed around the entrance to *Ravages*, a club notoriously restricted to moneybags and celebrities. Jenny was both now and she'd arranged the whole thing. The burly security stared at us like we didn't belong, then he saw our names on the clipboard the doorman, all regaled out in red velvet, clutched. They let us into a bar and restaurant crammed no different than the sidewalk Puma and I just left.

Jenny danced—surprise, surprise—on the counter with a four other Coyote Uglies. Obviously, she been here awhile and chugged down more'n a few. A sex kitten just standing still, when she thrust and gyrated her T'n A, like now, the guys drooled as curs with rabies would. Girl could move as gracefully as she could fight ferociously. She wore a tight T-shirt that nicely outlined her bra-less breasts and nipples. Denim shorts. Open-toe, flatfoot, comfy sandals ideal for a long night on her feet. Hair flying, lips pouting, tongue seductively poking in an out, she'd arouse a gay Bishop. The music ended. Hunks, some of 'em familiar faces—

actors, singers, rich bastards I recognized but couldn't for the life of me tell you their names—helped the girls down.

Jenny, true to form, kissed the guy, who hoisted her down. He went starry eyed. She saw us. Dumped his ass. "Puma! Dusty! I got us a table, come on."

Puma slid into the booth. She sat down next to him. I sat across. Her nostrils were already ruddy from earlier snorting. "Hard liquor by the bottle over here!" she hollered across, then looked past me. "There's Nigel!" Waved, "Over here!"

I moved over. Nigel kissed Jenny on the cheek, greeted Puma, then squeezed in next to me, asking, "How you been?"

"Good. You?" The first words we uttered to each other since fight night.

All genial, Nigel asked, "So? How was Miami and the Bahamas?"

"Loved filming," she said, "can't remember the Bahamas." They laughed. Jenny looked over to me. "Word of warning. I have to burn off two weeks of booty, buffet, and booze. Week One is gonna be rough, coach."

"You didn't tell her, Nigel?" I jumped at the opportunity to put him on the spot.

"You quit, you should." He snapped back, breathing fire. *What's he so pissed about?*

I obliged, finger pointing right back, "Nigel here thought you'd be fighting the refs, judges, and the opponent if I worked your corner. So, he thought it best Kevin take over the corner for your title bout."

"Fuck that, Nigel!" Jenny responded, slapping the table hard. "Steeper the odds, sweeter the win. Hey, when we started, Dusty, Puma, and I signed a no breakup clause." She straightened, leaned back. "So! Dusty, nix your resignation. I reject it. You're going nowhere. But I have to pee. When I get back," she pointed a finger from me to Nigel, "I'll insist on you two making out and making up." She left, swallowed from view within seconds by a crowd of patrons.

I did a double take. "What the fuck?"

Nigel's hand appeared with a gun.

Sid Rosen: Debrief Notes, New Orleans

The upstairs room, where the Sid Quartet was holed up, faced *Ravages* from across the street. Jenny arrived first. An hour later, Dusty and Puma. Nigel, a few minutes after, and the way he shoved his way inside caused Sid to remark, "Nigel looks pissed."

Sid didn't order his guys down right away. He expected other players. Sure enough, "Detective Bostwick Oswald, Third Police District."

Sid pointed out Boz wading through the mass of humanity. About the same time, Big Cholo, who stood with Kung Fu Panda at the other window, announced, "Sharif Hirsi. Far end, south sidewalk."

Sharif towered over the pedestrians and bulldozed through.

"Recognize his guns?" asked Sid.

Ahead, Boz flashed his badge at the door. Entered *Ravages.*

"Seventh Ward crew," observed Black Goatee, coming up to peer over Sid's shoulder.

Three black youth—Bandana Boy, 18, 5-8, 177; Baggy Trou, 20, 5-11, 190; Bare Chest, 22, 5-10½, 186—flanked Sharif. Bandana Boy hunched his shoulders and swayed side to side like a cocky gangsta. *Immature piece of shit.* They took up sentry position against a corner storefront at the mouth of an alley one window from *Ravages.*

"That alley does a ninety-degree-curve and ends in a dead end behind *Ravages,*" informed Sid, pulling up the street map on his cell. "Meaning, whatever happens behind *Ravages* stays behind *Ravages.* I like that. Minimal public risk or participation. More important, the parade goes on." Sid clapped, "OK! Let's go! Everyone can die, except Jenny."

I gulped when Nigel waved the gun. "We are going outside into the back alley before Jenny gets back. Don't hold your breath. She's too far gone to miss you two rats."

"Rats? Wo, wo," I realized why he wanted to piss on us and call it rain. "That Detective offer us a deal, sure, but we never say yes."

"Honest to God, Nigel," asserted Puma.

"We would never. No!"

He didn't buy it. "Outside."

Stood up, tucking the gun between his body and the other arm. "In front of me, both of you. Try to be clever in some way, they'll see Puma fall, never hear the shot, and you don't get the running start I promised you."

Puma and I obeyed, Nigel right behind. I felt his gun jab my spine every time a patron jostled by, which was almost every other second. We pushed our way through the crisscrossing men and women. Nigel's girth helped part the crowd like Moses done the Red Sea. We got to the rear. Found a hallway with two johns, and at the end of it, a door crowned by big, red-lit 'EXIT' sign. As I walked by, the 'LADIES' door started to open.

I saw a sliver of a woman. I recognized the clothes. *Jenny!*

Nigel rammed his gun hard into my spine. I bucked forward. He roughly shoved Puma with his other hand. We passed the door, all three of us. I started to turn my neck. Nigel smacked and straightened my head back forward. *She see us? Or his piece?* I didn't hold my breath. Jenny didn't go into the bathroom just to pee. Dead certain to also sugar up some. I leaned into the panic exit device—that press bar on commercial exits which stretched end to end.

The latch released, the door opened.

Heat and noise slapped us. The alley, which dead-ended about thirty feet left of the door, but curved outta sight to my right. You couldn't see it, but the alley looked like it emptied into Bourbon Street. The racket, even rounding the bend, punched through. Two lamps, affixed high up on the back walls flanking the alley, washed yellow pools of utterly inadequate light. A shit load of dumpsters been wheeled in and parked haphazardly, likely by the City, for the cleanup tomorrow.

"Against the wall!" Nigel barked, backing Puma and myself up to the naked bricks like we was facing a firing squad.

"Nigel," I pleaded. "Come on—"

"Shut the fuck up!" Nigel snarled, checking there were no witnesses walking in from the parade.

I know. I'm cynical and pessimistic and hated life, but I still wanted to die from natural causes. Puma looked calmer than the Dalai Lama. *Sure.* He'd lived to almost seventy. Growing up in Compton, probably didn't figure he'd see the day he could vote. *Me?* As scummy be the layer of society I spent most of my life, I never had a gun pointed at me. *Believe it or not. Not once.* Or been mugged neither. This shitless scare, which I thought I'd left behind—Dad, reeking of booze, swinging that first fist at me when I was five—returned like it never left. I felt my fanny pack.

Realized I literally brought a knife to a gun fight.

"Hey, there you are!" Jenny. *God bless her thoroughly smashed heart!* "Shit, Nigel, is that a gun? You gonna shoot them?"

"Jenny," said Nigel. "Go back in. This is between Dusty, Puma, myself."

Jenny didn't listen. *Thank you!* Walked up beside him. She asked casually, "Why are you offing them? Did they snitch?"

Nigel glanced over at her sharply. "What do you know about that?"

"Nothing. That'd be the only reason to kill them."

"They made an immunity deal with that Detective—"

"No!" I said again.

"Boz?" Jenny snorted with laugh. "He offered me one too." That grabbed Nigel's attention. "That's why I kicked him to the curb. Puma and Dusty'd never snitch, would you, guys?"

"No!" Third time hopefully the charm.

"Tell this dumb muhfuh, lil girl," Puma spoke for the first time.

I jabbered for my life, "I covered for you when Boz said an eyewitness see you come outta Crispin's house. More like, I outright lied for you."

"If it's the I-10," Jenny said, "any one of your previous fighters could've squealed. It's not a secret. Every fight club knows. Boz was fishing to get into Easy Trucking's main line of business." Nigel stiffened like someone starched his spine. Jenny remained nonchalant, "He told me. Drugs—you move 'em Mexico to Canada." Her booze and coke tolerance boggled the mind.

"Puma'n I, we know nothing about that," I jumped in. *We suspected, of course.*

"Now you do," said Nigel.

"Aren't you and the Police Chief tight?" asked Jenny. "He knows all about your drug running, yeah? He'll bail you out."

"Bastard stopped taking my calls, what with the election next week. I paid for his house, his kids college, and every holiday."

"We ain't rats, Nigel," I pleaded.

"Will you go to prison for life without parole to protect me?"

"Boz is bluffing," said Jenny. "He's got nothing."

"Not according to my partners," said Nigel.

"Put the gun down, won't you?" Jenny said.

"Shut the fuck up and join your friends!" snarled Nigel.

Jenny shrugged casually, threw up her hands, staggered.

Nigel lost interest in her, turning his wrath toward Puma, myself. "I came here directly after signing over control of Easy Trucking to the fucking Cartels. I was worth more than a billion dollars two hours ago, and now less than half that. Hate to break it you, you low lives are not worth five hundred million dollars. Not to me." Looked at Jenny. "And you! You're much smarter than a twenty-year-old should be."

"I know, right?" Jenny smiled crookedly. High.

Bam! The back door opened. Boz burst outside, weapon at his side. Seeing Nigel with his gun on Dusty and Puma, "I told you two, the motherfucker wouldn't hesitate to kill you!'

Nigel swung toward Dusty and Puma, "You two are wired!"

Wham! Bang! Jenny threw a shoulder into Nigel a moment before he fired. His 323 lb. frame juddered like a battleship broadsided by a swell just strong enough to list. Which was all she needed to do. The bullet harmlessly struck the bricks wide to my right.

Jenny yelled, "Go, run!"

I was hustling Puma already. Nigel never lost his gun. I saw him recover his hold, curling his finger back around the trigger.

BangBangBang!

But his bullets never arrived. Those blasted in from where the alley curved to Bourbon Street. Puma and I scurried behind the closest dumpster, then peered out like a coupla scoping squirrels.

Boz tried to yank at the door to get back into *Ravages*. It'd self locked—one of those security entrance-exits openable only from the inside. He darted and hunkered behind a big, overflowing trash can right by the door.

Nigel vanished.

Where's Jenny? I whispered, "Only way out is to Bourbon Street.

"We don't know if those guns friendly or hostile," Puma whispered back.

"No harm positioning ourselves closest to the only exit."

Puma nodded. Staying behind the dumpsters, we hurried from one to the other.

BangBangBangBangBangBangBangBang!

This time, bullets flew every which way. Boz fired. Nigel, I guessed, owned the muzzle flashes on the other side of the alley. Shooters from the curve went to town like they purchased their clips wholesale.

Puma and I tried to make sense, looking this way and that. Regardless, I could safely put the count at one—that being Jenny—as our only ally.

We continued to duckwalk toward Bourbon Street.

"Stop!" I whispered hoarsely.

A giant—more like Black Godzilla—walked into view. He saw us. Raised his gun toward us.

BangBangBang!

Before he could fire, the ground and wall around him exploded violently. Like the giant Japanese lizard, he coiled outta sight in the blink of an eye.

"Maybe we got a friendly out there," said Puma hopefully.

"Does it matter?" I said. "This alley's a one-trench battlefield occupied by all the warring parties."

Puma replied with the kinda one-liner that produced a giggle in the movies, "So you're saying there's no place to run."

Sid Rosen: Debrief Notes, New Orleans

"Something's up!" barked Sid, when Sharif and his Seventh Ward boys raced into the alley.

The Sid Quartet raced downstairs and crossed Bourbon Street, guns hanging down their side. Nobody noticed, what with intoxication at levels beyond illegal and bodies pressed tighter than an overstuffed can of sardines. They arrived at the mouth, saw the Seventh Ward kids and Sharif firing into the alley at the curve.

The Sid Quartet opened relentless fire. *BangBangBang!* The kids scattered outta sight around the curve like roaches to Raid.

With the music booming and crowd yelling, you just heard pops, if that. The Sid Quartet sprinted down, spread out behind the dumpsters, connected via their airpods.

Sid saw Sharif's eyes freeze on someone inside the alley. *Jenny?* Sid had a clean shot and emptied his clip.

BangBangBang!

Sharif sensed danger by a beat. Dove behind a cluster of dumpsters.

BangBangBangBangBangBangBangBang.

The Sid Quartet vs. Quartet Sharif vs. Nigel vs. Boz became an OK Corral-times-ten free for all. Driven by recklessness of youth, Bandana Boy showed himself like Bruce Willis in *Die*

Hard, rolling and firing. Sid almost laughed at how easily he and his guys riddled the kid. Like a golf ball dying at the cup, Bandana Boy rolled to a dead stop, dead being the operative word. His buddies went crazy, shooting wildly. Hit not a fucking thing. Sid didn't care, as long as everybody stayed put.

His *Mission Impossible*—and he'd chosen to accept it—*keep Jenny alive.*

Detective Bostwick Oswald: Off Duty Notes

Boz didn't budge out from behind the oversized trash can—the smallest cover of all the guns in the alley, but with no covert way to get to him. A place in Hell awaited anyone who dared to step into the open for a clear shot. He couldn't see anybody, though the muzzle flashes and trajectories allowed him to map all the shooters.

There were two opposing forces of four. One of them, he easily spotted—Sharif Hirsi, recognizing him from the dossier he built on Makena. Light on his feet for a man his size, he escaped the rainstorm of bullets, which a late arriving second group unleashed. These guys acted more strategically, unlike the Seventh Ward hoodlums Sharif brought with him.

It puzzled Boz. *Who's challenging the Cartel?*

He received his answer in a sec. *Sid Rosen.* The sleazebag attorney making good on his promise to collect.

The gun battle raged on, inching deeper into the alley.

Boz realized he couldn't venture out.

The wall about a yard from us just started popping holes, bullets plucking out chunks of brick that added up into an approaching dust storm. Froze Puma and I. Looked like Black Godzilla and his crew were being forced deeper into the alley by this new army that'd joined this gun party. I had no clue who was who, who wanted what. Then, you had Nigel and Boz somewheres. With no love lost between those two, we could be moving from one crossfire into another. So we stayed put.

Jenny? Our only friend. *Where are you?*

"Guys!" God never did once, but she answered my prayer immediately.

We could've been Irish Riverdancers, the togetherness with which Puma and I twirled, then chorused, "Jenny!" with the same enthusiastic thankfulness of "Amen!" at a Baptist Church.

She stooped outside a door that stood diagonally across from the back entrance to *Ravages,* and the only one I passed, but also one which I'd already tried. She pushed it open. Puma and I hurried over.

"It was locked," I said.

"Never picked a lock, Dusty?" Jenny asked incredulously. "You are a disgrace to trailer trash."

"We could die and you're goin' for laughs?" I said angrily.

Of course, she thought I was joking. Guffawed. Pushed us in. Jenny swiped at the switch. Killed the fluorescents inside. Younger, her eyes adjusted faster than mine or Puma's.

She took his hand, I took his, and we hurried along one of the myriad of narrow walkways that threaded between big shiny stainless steel silos, drums, vats, pipes, computers, switch panels, and overhead catwalks. The machines hummed, churned, and gurgled.

We're in a micro brewery.

I knew quite a bit about craft beer distilleries, having worked part time in one for almost two years. This one, I guessed, was a seventy to hundred barrel facility. I remembered the storefront sign, 'JUST BEER.' The holler of patrons reached us here way back, meaning, on the other side of closed doors, the bar was packed wall to wall, not unlike every other joint along Bourbon Street.

BangClang!BangClang!BangClang!

Shots, followed by spark-filled metal impacts, erupted near us. Jenny shoved Puma around a big silo, where I'd already parked myself.

"It's that nigga monsta," Puma panted. "The one as high as Nigel's wide!"

"A Black Godzilla."

"Not at all offensive coming from a redneck," said Jenny.

I didn't care, but she was right. With my heart beating a mile a minute, I stated the obvious, "This ain't ending until we die or they do."

"You came up with that all by yourself, Dusty?" smiled Jenny.

"Why ain't you taking this serious?" I asked angrily.

"Look. Weren't for you, lil girl, we'd be dead," said Puma. "Now, but for me, you probably can get away. So, leave me be. I'll make like we all here, buy you two time to get out."

"Fuck, no!" Jenny snapped at him.

I nodded, "What she said! Despite the fact, I can still feel the knife in my back, you going along with Nigel wanting me outta Jenny's corner."

"Get over it!" Jenny said harshly. "You'd have done the same if it was Puma holding us back."

"Never!" I protested overzealously, and knew at once how that came off. "OK, maybe."

"So, the only one with any integrity about keeping our pact sacred was me." Jenny smiled crookedly, "Who'd have thunk that?"

"Concentrate! Please," I implored. "We need a plan."

"Dusty, you were a fighter once. Recall those good times. Puma, play possum, then use your cane."

"How the hell're you sober after all that booze and coke?" I had to ask.

"Like anything else," she said, obvious like, "practice makes perfect. I started around twelve."

"Noon?"

"Years old."

"Where were your parents?"

Her eyes lifted as a shadow darkened her face.

Black Godzilla stepped outta nowhere without so much as the sound of a footfall.

Sid Rosen: Debrief Notes, New Orleans

The shootout raged on around the corner from Bourbon Street, where it sounded like the crowds, high or drunk or both, were reaching fever pitch. Sharif and his two remaining gangsters occupied one side, Sid and his guys, the other. Nigel and Boz could be called the third front deeper inside the alley, but they'd been silent. *Probably waiting for us to mutually thin the herd.*

An access door to the alley opened. Visible only because light from inside outlined the rectangular doorway. Dusty, Puma, and Jenny scurried in. *She is alive and fucking well!*

"Open door, south side!" Sid hollered, reaching all his guys over earpieces. He didn't figure the gangsters thought to come connected via headsets.

The fluroscent inside died. The doorway turned black.

Rrrrrrrr!

Wheels! Nigel propelled a dumpster, Sid glimpsed the fat fuck for a moment. *Rrrrrrrr!* The Seventh Ward hoods did the same. Forcing the scattered Sid Quartet to follow.

Rrrrrrrr! Rrrrrrrr! Rrrrrrrr! BangBangBangBang! Gunfire crisscrossed. Dumpsters ran amok. The clean battle lines disintegrated. Shooters ducked and darted. Empty shells rained like confetti. Sid's guy, Black Goatee, became the first casualty.

Sid saw Sharif slip into the open doorway. *Fuck!*

BaggyTrou started to follow. Sid had a clear shot. Took it! Blew out a good chunk of Baggy Trou's head. *That'll dissuade anyone else from going in.*

"Aahh!" Big Cholo. A death cry.

Sid lost his man to return fire. Sid pinpointed the shooter. *Nigel!* Who retreated, forced back from getting to the door by the firewall erected by Sid and Kung Fu Panda.

Still, Bare Chest snuck through. Once inside the doorway, the Seventh Ward gangster held the door like Horatio.

Detective Bostwick Oswald: Off Duty Notes

Baggy Trou went down. Sid lost a man. Boz saw a fluorescent rectangle open. A doorway. Dusty, Puma, then Jenny entered, then it went black. Sharif followed them inside. Boz stayed where he was, even when the dumpsters started to stampede. He could have picked off a couple of them, but didn't want to give away his position. *Only if I see Nigel.* With bullets flying, Bare Chest somehow darted in.

This created an unlikely alliance of Nigel, Sid, and his remaining two guys, pumping bullets to access the door. Without much success. The Seventh Ward thug held the door valiantly.

For whatever reason, Big Cholo broke cover, sprinting. He went down, spinning like a top. Nigel took him down—the second of Sid's men.

The bombardment, to and from the doorway, went on. Not an inch gained by Nigel, Sid, and Kung Fu Panda. Even less lost by Bare Chest.

Boz decided to play buzzard.

Jenny, Puma, and I stared up at Black Godzilla. The gun battle outside suddenly became distant. Inconsequential.

I croaked, "Oh, fuck.".

While I expressed fear, Puma surprised the man.

Whack! He took his cane to Black Godzilla's wrist. The gun flew with a growl that coulda been a belching volcano 'cause his breath was hot and stunk.

Jenny reacted with Octagon speed and thinking.

Whabam! She took the easiest, most effective power strike—the UFZ-outlawed foot to the balls. A man that big probably dangled down coconuts. Bigger, while better in the sack, also meant more nerves transmitting more pain. Even Godzilla ain't topping that truth. His eyes shut and his face inflated. He doubled over with a full throated howl!

I channeled twenty-three-year ol' Dusty with an elbow to his nose. Blood spurted. Oh, that felt good. Never raised a hand since I quit fighting. *OK, that ain't entirely true.* I did, once after.

We awakened a monster.

One swipe with a hand, bigger than the oar from *Moby Dick*, and *wham!* I flew head first into the scalding mash tun, which be the stage of brewing where barley, rye, or whatever whole grain malt that been milled, was mixed with very hot water. Think stirring up a bowl of piping hot oatmeal, only the temperature regulated to the degree to convert the milled malt into sugars and dextrins. Together, they made up your 'body' of the beer.

"Aaah!" I felt my hair singe, hit the floor, and lay there with a gopher's view of Jenny throwing a flying kick to Black Godzilla's heart. She coulda been a wet twig, the way she bent, and he stood like a mighty redwood, merely grunting from the contact.

He swatted her down.

Thud! She landed hard, nothing but cement to break her fall. He turned his attention toward me 'cause I was getting back up. He raised his foot. I saw it come down.

Oh, hell, my ribcage is chutney.

The death stomp never came.

WhackWhackWhack! Puma brought his cane to bear. He went for the caps of the giant's standing leg. Metal against bone, metal always win, even if he's bigger'n the Hulk. He stumbled, stooped. Jenny actually run up his back, wrapped her legs around his neck, and tipped him over. Being a monster, she got him down only so far as his knees.

I got up and unloaded left-right-left power head strikes. *Ow, ow, ow.* I think my knuckles hurt contacting his skull more than the other way around. It jolted the ogre's brain within.

He swung at me.

Connected square into my belly. Air left me fast and sudden like a punctured balloon. That came with a pain I never experienced even during my worst beating in the ring or Octagon. I screamed shamelessly, careening backward into the lauter tun—which strained out spent grain from the mashed-in liquid oozing outta the mash tun, that I'd head-butted earlier, to create a sugary syrup called wort. Not as hot a silo, but the steel construction just as strong, and so just as painful impacting it. *Wham!*

I slid back down to the floor, groaning.

Jenny launched herself in the air and brought her ass down on the back of his neck. The momentum flattened him face down. *Crunch.* That likely Black Godzilla's nose breaking. She found time to lift and bang his megahead down once more.

Crack! Forehead met the concrete.

Directly under the brewkettle.

I saw an opportunity. Had to move quickly, though. Smarting, I mustered the strength. *Can I get there in time?*

Black Godzilla had Jenny by the hair, pulling her off, rolling over. He pounded her into the stilts upon which the brewkettle was mounted. Lucky for her. it was the stilts, because the brewkettle itself was hotter'n the sun. She screamed! He didn't let go. She struggled, as he wound his arm back to bash her head in again. *Shit, she won't survive.*

Here came Puma, hobbling over.

Crack!

Bullseye! Puma struck and broke the orbital. The ogre howled, grabbing his eye, and dropped Jenny. I scrambled to my feet, aching all over, but terror adrenalized you in ways you couldn't explain. I reached the brewkettle which received the wort from the lauter tun. Hops were added at a boil.

"Puma! Jenny! Move!" I yelled, spinning open the cleanout tap.

Puma stepped back. Jenny rolled away.

Steaming wort gushed out and down.

"Aaaaaahhhhhhh!!!" Black Godzilla screamed, his deep voice deep no more.

The skin on his face evaporated to the bone!

Jenny swept up the fallen gun and pumped two bullets into his heart, ending his misery.

"You killed him!" I gasped. Becoming conscious again of the bullets flying outside.

"And it felt damn fucking good!" Jenny grinned.

Puma poked his cane into my tote. "You forget why you bring it?"

I kicked myself. "Shit! Completely slipped my mind."

Jenny put her finger to her lips. The gunfire outside ceased and enhanced the humming, churning, and gurgling of the brewery. Jenny pointed to a silo. A bigger terror skinned the cauldrons. Wrapping around the stainless steel was a distorted, oversized reflection.

Nigel was in the house.

Sid Rosen: Hearsay from New Orleans

Sid spotted Boz break cover, cross open ground, and vanish behind an angled dumpster. *What is he doing?* Sid nodded to Kung Fu Panda, the last man alive in his crew, to keep Bare Chest occupied at the door. Nigel's whereabouts remained a mystery. The fat fuck stopped firing. Probably oozing around for a way into the doorway. Sid just wanted protect his Kohinoor—Jenny. He circled quietly, pulled up abruptly. Glimpsed Nigel.

Sid veered, lost sight, and when he relocated him—

BangBangBangBangBang!

The night erupted in fresh nonstop gunfire!

Nigel had a gun to Kung Fu Panda's head, marching him toward the doorway, using him as a human shield. Tubby, though nowhere near as big as Nigel, Kung Fu Panda provided enough cover, spasming violently, absorbing Bare Chest's bullets.

The Seventh Ward hood foolishly emptied his entire clip. When the muzzle of his gun stopped flashing, Nigel dropped Kung Fu Panda's blood drenched corpse.

BangBang! Took out Bare Chest with two shots.

BangBang! Streaked out two more skyward. *Fzzzt! Fzzzt!* The pair of alley lights went up in sparks and smoke.

Darkness switched on. Sid went blind. Lost the clean shot he had. In hindsight, he should've taken it, when Nigel held Kung Fu Panda hostage, since his guy was a dead man walking anyway.

Sid's pupils dilated, adjusted.

Nigel barreled through the doorway.

But Boz silently backed up right in front of Sid.

According to Dusty Saldana

"What unites the Cartel and TMZ?" Nigel asked.

Sliding my tote behind my back, Puma and I stared at Nigel fill the narrow walkway side to side, his gun steady in his hand.

"They pay for their intel," he answered his own pop quiz. "So they never get it wrong."

"This time they did," I continued to insist. Nigel advanced.

"Accusin' a Compton boy bein' a snitch," Puma asserted

angrily, "is grounds for fucking murder. So, you better kill me, muhfuh, or I'm gonna."

"Where's Jenny?" Nigel stopped a yard from us. "I would've found a way for her to be in the title fight. Now, thanks to you two, she's got to go too."

"Actually," Jenny's voice answered, "it's the other way around, Nigel. I dragged them into this."

Nigel swiveled sharply, taking his eyes off us. Jenny was on the catwalk six feet off the ground. He angled his head and eyes over and up.

That was my cue.

One step forward was all it took for my range and reach.

Slash! I sliced him with the blade hidden 'tween my fingers.

"Aaah!" Nigel recoiled, his hands going to his neck, where I found the precise vessel.

In a fury, he turned, his gun level to my face!

Bang! I expected to see the light.

Instead I heard Nigel yelp, "Aaaah!"

Jenny'd fired Black Godzilla's gun, emptying Nigel's hand of his. His wrist sprung a bloody leak. I kicked his piece under the machines far enough, so nobody was gonna get it without belly-crawling ten yards. Jenny swung over the catwalk railing and landed on her feet, lithe as a cat, a yard from Nigel.

"That was sharpshooter accurate," I observed.

"They aren't wearing a wire, Nigel," Jenny said. "I am."

Lifted her shirt. A hair run up her six-pack belly.

"Holy fuck," Puma went first with his exclamation.

Unhitching my jaw, "What he said."

Nigel asked the most pertinent question, "Who the fuck *are* you?"

With everyone's eyes and guns on the doorway, Boz broke cover. Soundlessly, he reached the first dumpster without incident, and crouched, then duckwalked between the gaps. He saw a slice of a humungo silhouette—Nigel—wriggle out of sight. *Dammit.* A second sooner, and he could've blown out the back of the motherfucker's head. It may have saved Kung Fu Panda, not that it was going to keep Boz up at night that he did not.

Nigel cold-bloodedly used Sid's plump lackey to storm the doorway. Bare Chest inside ran outta bullets. Stood no chance, trying to slap a fresh clip. Nigel put two lethal rounds into the doorway. War-trained marine accurate. Then took out the lights and plunged the alley dark.

Boz advanced. *Where's Sid?* Assumed the shyster must be making a beeline for the doorway, now that Nigel had cleared it. Boz carefully straightened. Stepped between dumpsters. Ahead, an unobstructed path stretched to the door.

A footfall. Behind him.

"Aaah!" emitted Boz's throat simultaneous with his brain registering a fierce bark of pain, and a final thought. *Sid Rosen!*

Boz's world went black.

He woke up to his cell ringing at full volume. He blinked. Looked around. *What the hell?*

He was in his car.

How did I get here?

Dawn broke all around him. He glanced down at the ringing phone at the Caller ID: *Dispatch.*

He answered, "Yeah?"

"Possible one-eighty seven." Murder. "Harrison Avenue in City Park."

"Ten Four." Boz hung up and felt the back of his head. Smarted, feeling a tender swelling. Sid knocked him out maybe because he didn't want to be a cop killer.

Why did he move me into my car?

It didn't take Boz long, what with the entire city sleeping off its Mardi Gras hangover, to get to the crime scene. This section of Harrison Avenue ran through City Park. Daylight smeared the sky over the trees, brightening every minute. He saw the flashing lightbar atop a squad car at the bridge, where an artificial creek met the road. A single uniform, young enough to've just walked out of police graduation into the crime scene, trotted over.

"Hyatt Lincoln," the kid cop introduced himself and walked Boz along the shoulder. "Body's totally burned." An embankment descended from the road to the creek. "Bones, innards, and not much else." Boz overtook Hyatt, carefully stepped down and reached the bottom. Lowered himself onto his toes.

Boz stared down at the burned human remains.

His NOPD shield, clipped to his belt between the 9mm Browning and cell phone, caught the rising sun and glinted. *Whoosh!* A wind kicked up as if City Park realized it had early morning company, didn't much care for the intrusion, and spat wet odors at them. Bayou St. John flowed nearby. No matter how long you lived here, you never ever got used to that shitty smell of stagnant moisture. Especially when temperature and humidity ran about even throughout an unseasonably hot February.

The body was unrecognizable. Skin and flesh burned almost entirely to the bone. You could see right through where the lungs used to be, the heart a pan fried tomato. Pieces of blackened stomach, guts. Muddy brown shore water of the artificial creek rippled back to reveal only a skeleton, pelvis down.

"The leg bones below the knee," Hyatt pointed, before the water rolled back up, "see how they are striped?"

Like the victim felt the fury of a cane.

Not a tatter of clothing—they'd completely burned away.

"But then," Hyatt pointed to the cracks in the skull, cheekbone, and ribs, "that looks like the killer took a baseball bat."

However, the first thing that caught Boz's attention—a crumpled newspaper stuffed between the victim's exposed teeth in a skull laid bare. Not charred. So, inserted post mortem. Boz carefully extracted and unwrinkled it.

"Holy shit!" gasped Hyatt, rocking onto the balls of his feet beside Boz, who ignored him and stared at the snapshot from the fight of Jenny's agonized face turned to camera with Bella's fist connected to her right temple. The huge type across the top asked: 'NEXT-JEN?'

Hyatt's eyes leapt to the corpse. "Jenny Sharp!"

Nigel Hansom: Hearsay from New Orleans

"*You're a fed!*" Nigel gasped, sharing Oscar winning dumbfounded expressions with Puma and Dusty.

"Sheeuh," breathed Puma.

"I knew somethin' wasn't right with her," Dusty frowned.

"Take her side and you'll be rats forever," said Nigel, realizing this would shift alliances. Just to make sure the pair knew where their loyalty should lie, "I'll take you down with me."

Jenny threw her head back and laughed. "Shit. Who said anything about you even having that option, Nigel? There isn't going to be an arrest, or a court, or lawyers."

"You were going to kill us, muhfuh," Puma snarled at Nigel, making clear on which side of the line he stood.

"Jenny saved us," Dusty agreed. "*And* you wanted me out. So, fuck you!"

"BTW," said Jenny. "Dusty doped the blade to weaken you enough to feel the pain that's coming."

"Sonofabitch!" Nigel lunged at Dusty.

Jenny leveled her gun, froze him. "Let's take this outside," and grinned, "I always wanted to say that. Now that I have, it sounds lame. Why is it every guy's go-to line?"

"Who needs a running start now, mothafucka?' sneered Dusty.

"Let's give him one." Jenny waved the gun. "Outrun us, Nigel."

Nigel stumbled away with one purpose—seize their misguided reprieve. *Mistake!* Letting him go out into his city. Nigel saw a clear path to the door. Hurried.

Jenny's voice trailed him, "Considering the info gold we mined from the bug I planted in your office, there was absolutely no need for a wire. But, shit, if you go undercover and don't wear a wire, did you really go undercover?"

Nigel laughed. *Did I actually?* Were connections in his brain starting to misfire already? Halfway along, dizziness struck. He reached forward. Grabbed a pipe. Howled! It was scalding hot. Recoiling sharply, he almost lost his balance. Regained it. His vision blurred. Sharpened back. The silos warped and waved like the inflatable air dancers outside car dealerships.

"Never figured it'd be so easy." Jenny's voice echoed. "When I engineered our move to New Orleans, you sat me down with the social media team right outside your door. Allowed me to walk in and out of your office."

Music, people sounds wafted into his head. He stepped over a dead body and out the door. Into the alley. He stared down at a chubby Asian's bullet-riddled corpse. It distended, like everything. Shapes became fluid. He heard and saw double.

"Holy fuck," Dusty reacted to the carnage. Blood-soaked victims, all dead, were strewn between the litter of dumpsters.

A shadow moved up alongside! Nigel punched out, then realized it was his own. He blinked furiously. The night suddenly became filled with flashing lights. He was on Bourbon Street already. *How did I get here?* A lucid thought lasered through his head. I can lose them in the crowd.

Nigel energized forward.

When he turned his head, Jenny yelled into his ear. "You demand loyalty but don't show it back."

"You'll pay!" Nigel reacted sharply. Saw multiples of Jenny. Swung wildly. Missed them all by a mile.

"How does it feel to be the one afraid, muhfuh!" Puma snarled.

Whack!

"Ahhh!" Nigel felt the sting of Puma's cane to his ass, then the lingering burn.

Roar! Cacophony of people and music. Seemed like one

moment to the next, when he found himself in the thick of a street party. Drunks bumped into him. Faces, elongated and threatening, came right up and receded. Nigel flailed, trying to get out of the crowd, but it felt like he was just circling in place.

Crash! His massive body overturned a street vendor's cart.

"Shit for brains!" the vendor yelled.

Nigel turned to confront him. Instead, colorfully dressed dancers worked around him. Interspersed between them, he glimpsed Jenny, Dusty, and Puma. He plunged through the crossing bodies. *Why can't I lose them?*

A woman laughed, pitched down beads. He swatted at them, felt nothing, just air. How he got off the curb to walk in front of a float, he didn't know. Chunks of time vanished.

He was blacking out in one place and coming to in another.

The crowded balconies leaned inward claustrophobically, and the people on both sides met at the apex. All screaming down at him. He looked down. Somehow, even though he had no idea where he was going, he sensed purpose and direction. Not free-willed by him, he realized. Imposed by Puma's cane, Dusty's barking, and Jenny steering him around street corners.

Where am I?

With that thought, someone sharply turned down the volume knob. Snapped the focus ring. Closed the aperture. The sound went from deafening to distant in successive beats. The crowds vanished. The lights dimmed.

Silence.

Nigel whirled around.

According to Dusty Saldana

I used enough dope to disorient a horse. There was little chance Nigel'd stop behaving confused and erratic for an hour at least. He orbited, cursed, threw empty punches. Probably 'cause the drug—a decoction from naturally occurring hallucinogens and toxins I learned to make from a Shaman in Tijuana—disabled his sense of distance. I'd tried it. Used it. So, I knew exactly what Nigel was going through.

Time and continuity disappeared. You became uncoordinated. Brain declared independence from the body. Weakness crippled your limbs. You remained completely conscious while every nerve became overly sensitive—meaning, enhanced pain. *Worst part? You're helpless to do anything about these afflictions.*

Jenny knew where we were taking him. Along the way, she laid out the case against Nigel, "Add up drug related deaths over the years and years he's been operating, he's destroyed families and murdered more than the combined casualties of all our wars. Dusty, you witnessed one murder, know of another, but he's linked to eight others—all tortured and burned."

Dusty nodded, "Tribal justice he picked up in Iraq."

We ended up in an alley off an alley. Solid brick walls. Illumination came from just the moonlight and stars. A preselected spot, I realized, 'cause Jenny's yellow Porsche stood parked in the deep shadow. I still had no clue who she belonged to—FBI, DEA, CIA, NSA, Justice.

I had a whole lotta questions, but held off asking them.

"You won't kill me!" Nigel shouted, clear-headed for a moment.

Backing up to the Porsche, Jenny popped open the hood—since this car's engine occupied the trunk—with her remote. *Oh, shit.* I caught sight of a machete and a gas can on the spare, but Jenny's hands came outta the trunk holding a baseball bat. She advanced, sliding it behind her head with both hands, and stretching, then twirling it like a pro headed to home plate.

"You can't!" Nigel continued. "You're a fed."

"You'd be right," her smile reeking of bad intentions, "if my unit didn't operate out of a basement, had an official name, and didn't have the motto 'Better Dead Than Alive' painted on the wall."

Whabam!

She took the bat to Nigel's chest with no warning.

Crunch.

That'd be his ribs breaking. He staggered backward, a cry wringing outta his throat. I took a step back. Shocked. Puma's lips curled up the corner, still harping on bein' called a rat.

"It's only fair we use *Hadud*, your doctrine for punishment. Balls for not showing some to save your friends, hands for stealing your army buddy's money, tongue for lying all your life, and a place in Hell for the rest of your sins."

Nigel's eyes widened with terror. *That's a first.*

"Jenny." The new voice made me and Puma whirl.

"Sid," Jenny reacted.

He melted out of the black with a gun.

CASE FILE: 010146888
Reporting Officer: Detective Bostwick Oswald

"Tape off the crime scene." Boz left Hyatt guarding it.

CSI turned in as Boz turned out of Harrison Avenue.

He drove to Bourbon Street, parked in front of *Ravages*. Street cleaners'd started hours ago, seemed like. Most of the litter filled the dumpsters lined on either side. Boz went into the alley, and found it clear and empty. He sauntered around the corner. No evidence of the gunfight remained, not even a stray shell.

The door to the microbrewery opened and a burly individual, 55, 6-2, 210, wearing a smock, emerged

"Good morning," he said lighting up a cigarette.

"No trouble last night?" Boz asked.

"Nothing to report." He noticed Boz's badge.

"Always glad to hear that." Boz turned and left the alley, not shaken or surprised by the thoroughness of the clean up.

Boz arrived at *Tremayne*, took the usual booth, way in the far back corner. Arlen arrived five minutes later. Boz held up the

Ziplock with the news headline, "It's done."

Arlen crinkled his brow, puzzled. "Jenny?"

Boz held out a flash drive that he found in his jacket when he regained consciousness. "This is from a wire."

"Who made it?"

"Pretty sure it's Sid Rosen." Boz had been connecting the dots on the drive over. "You'll hear Nigel threatening to kill Dusty and Puma. You'll hear Jenny too. Nigel likely refused to pay off Sid's contract with Jenny, so Sid must've leaned on Dusty and Puma, holding Jenny's life on the line. Forced one of them to wear a wire. Anyway, they effectively tag teamed Nigel into confessing pretty much his entire crime operation, including the Police Chief's complicity. Then everything went sideways."

Arlen easily surmised, "A drug lawyer has the connections to leave behind only what needs to be—not that hard since they had all night and the parade for cover."

The perk of dealing with a shark. Boz did not have to explain the rest out loud. Like, Sid planting the flash drive on Boz. Or, the body being dumped in the Third Police District. A Cartel mole in Dispatch ensured Boz was first on the scene, so he'd catch and close the case. That'd be that.

"Sid's revenge aligned with the Cartels' plans to wipe the slate clean," added Arlen, leaning back. "The drug business at the top is a small world—they had to know each other."

"Sid probably came on as added insurance," nodded Boz. "Clean up after the clean up."

"You can start measuring the Mayor's office."

"You OK?"

Boz shrugged. "It's over."

"What do I owe you?" Arlen bluntly asked.

"I'll bank my ask. Becoming Mayor is only a stepping stone, I sense."

Arlen smiled. "Guilty."

"Are you going to give the Police Chief a graceful way out?"

"That would be decent thing to do. So, no," Arlen laughed. "Not with a star for a corpse."

Makena checked her cell again. She paced back and forth. Went to the window of her suite for umpteenth time. She didn't sleep a wink. Ash Wednesday dawned with clear blue skies and the usual race by the temperature and humidity to keep pace with each other. Dark clouds would've better mirrored her mood. She called Sharif, got his voicemail over and over. Texts remained unread. One hand across her chest, the other over her mouth, she stared out.

KnockKnock!

Makena brightened. Only her uncle knew where she was, having left the hotel and room number in both her voice and text messages right after she checked in, around midnight, when she received no news. She hurried across and opened the door.

A complete stranger, shady from head toe, stood outside.

"Hello, Makena," he greeted with an oily smile. "My name is Sid Rosen. Can I come in?"

Makena wanted to say, no, but Sid just walked in. He wore no tie under his unbuttoned suit. Monogrammed belt buckle. Braclet, oversized watch, and multiple rings. The open, pastel pink shirt revealed a hairy chest and the soles of his shiny, gaudy, aligator-skin shoes squeaked.

"You may want to sit down," he said, glancing around the room first.

"Why?"

"Shit, I don't know," he flashed his teeth, which added sly to his sleaze. "That's what you say when you're delivering bad news. In your case, bad news, worse, and the worst news."

Makena's patience ran out. "Mr. Rosen, I have a lot on my mind."

"You mean, where's Nigel? Bad news, he's dead."

Makena caught her breath audibly.

"Uncle Sharif Hirsi? Worse news, he's dead too. Actually, he was shot and killed first."

Apprehension struck Makena like a physical thing. *How does he know Uncle's name or even that Sharif is my uncle?*

"Let me give you a second to digest that."

"Is this a joke?"

Sid's tone hardened, "Here comes the worst news. Do you want to sit down now?"

Makena did not.

"OK." Sid reached into his jacket pocket, pulled out his cell, and played it.

"Mr. Knight summoned me to The Mansion to convey a decision he and the Cartels reached. Steps you must take. First, the I-10 is done. Shut it down."

"Fine. It's a money pit anyway."

"Second, Dusty and Puma have to go."

"Done. Fucking snakes."

"Third, and this one comes at a steep price. To you. I'm taking a controlling interest in Easy Trucking."

Sid turned it off. Makena did sit down half way through the recording. "That's only an excerpt," he said. "I have the whole conversation, start to finish, including every other communication between Nigel and you going back about a year."

Makena played her only card, "If this is blackmail, you couldn't have made a bigger, more dangerous mistake."

"True," Sid laughed, "but my people outweigh your people. You know, like, my dick's bigger than yours—even with you being a woman, that works, because it takes balls to get into bed with Nigel, Mr. Knight, and his partners."

Makena stared back. Expressionless.

"Behind that poker face, I can see your brain working out what this means. A breach that's a mother of all failures, the harshness of the punishment, since bringing Nigel in was your idea. If I was Mr. Knight, I'd just hand you and your daughter to his thugs to do as they please till both of you are dead."

Makena's throat rolled. *He's right.* "What do you want?"

"You took controlling interest in Easy Trucking." Sid reached into his pocket again. "This is a burner." Held out the phone. "My people will be in touch."

"We ain't leaving here alive," I said dourly.

"Sheeuh, you think?" reacted Puma sarcastically.

Last night, Sid pulled black hoods over our heads and heaped us into a van. Despite terror coursing through my veins, being old had its perks. I nodded off during the long, bumpy drive. So, did Puma, 'cause sounded like he was awakened rudely, like I was, by hands grabbing us and hustling us indoors, God knows where.

When the hoods came off, we were in this windowless room, bare, except for a table, three chairs, and two metal cots with thin mattresses. Mind you, the furniture didn't elevate this to even the cheapest room at one of 'em cash-only, podunk motels, which hookers rented by the hour. It felt most definitely like where you was held and interrogated, the dead giveaway being the metal bedposts and bolted rings on the table, you know, to handcuff prisoners.

"Nigel worked for the Cartels," I piled up the evidence for our execution, which would likely be preceded by a fair amount of torture, if the suspicious dark stains were an indication about how business was conducted here.

"But he told us nuthin'," Puma made the case against, even if his heart wasn't in it at all.

"Would we be alive if they believed that?" The exposed, gray, concrete block walls, looked thick and soundproof.

"Hopefully our hearts give out before the pain get too bad," said Puma, fatalistic, joining me in the 'inevitable' and 'resigned' stage of this abduction.

"Jesus, you two!" interrupted a new voice.

Puma and I swiveled sharply.

Jenny.

She came through the doorway with a six-pack of sodas and two bags of Chinese takeout, "Old hens cluck less!"

"I told this old coot you ain't gonna kill us," boasted Puma, doing a one-eighty, suddenly all confident and brave.

Jenny roared, dumping the bags on the table.

"That ain't funny," I bristled, "considering the way we was brought here."

"The Cherry Hill Cartel had a contract on you two. So, until we tied up some loose ends, we had to keep you out of sight and circulation."

"Why the hoods and locked door?"

"Can't have you know where our HQ is, or have you two wandering around. Not yet, at least."

Cooped up in here, 'tween dooming ourselves, Puma kept running his head back to his first contact with Jenny at the fight club for clues. As did I, over this past year, training her. Both he and I came away amazed by this twenty-year-old with the wherewithal, first, to go undercover, and second, fool everybody.

Assured now that I was gonna live, I wasted no time piping up, "Will there be any explanations forthcoming?"

"That tone went from fear to demanding fast, didn't it?" Jenny joked, as we sat down, opened the cartons and divvied the plates and chopsticks.

Jenny'd showered and changed into a black, Indian, hip-length, Kurti tunic with red and gold borders, white slacks, and open-toe heels. This girl not only cleaned up into a supermodel, she displayed no trace of trauma from last night. Puma'n I still suffered PTSD from what went down and how.

Jenny popped open her soda. Vaporized bubbles fizzed up. "Our mandate is justice not arrests,"

"You can say that again."

Talking about the way she copycatted Nigel's MO to kill him.

"You just twenty, lil girl?" Puma asked.

Like I said, he'n I still hadn't unhitched our jaws.

Her viciousness exceeded her beauty. Okay, so Puma and I participated too. He went to work with his cane and I landed my boot into Nigel's head and kidneys. But Jenny raised it to a whole 'nother level. She chopped off Nigel's hands, carved out his balls, doused him in gas, and dropped a match—all the while keeping the bastard alive.

"Why is that so crazy?" Jenny slurped up a mouthful of chow mein. "Last night, Nigel thought I was too smart to be twenty. Well, when people say, fifty is the new forty—it's usually in the looks department. The reverse is even more true when it comes to brains and maturity. Twenty is the new thirty, seeing as boys and girls fuck earlier and earlier nowadays. I reached down between my legs around sixth grade."

"That's it!" I pointed my chopsticks emphatically. "That's how you pulled it off, fooling us all—with your no-boundaries talk'n attitude. Is this the real you or an act?"

Jenny'd only wink and smile mischievously. "Ask me the name of this operation. Dusty, this one's for a stat and book buff like you."

I shook my head, "OK, what is it?"

"Inside Distance." She grinned, "I picked it."

"Sheeuh," Puma posted an admiring smile, shoveling Kung Pao, "A fight that don't end from time running out."

"Why Nigel?" I asked.

"He was a drug distributor with a monopoly like this country has never seen. But it was also clear he would never be prosecuted. Agencies gave up stopping Easy Trucking drivers—they were always tipped off. Too clever, too many informants, Mexico to Canada."

"His I-10 circuit was a way in," I ventured, reaching for some roast duck.

Jenny nodded. "Over time, like criminals usually do, he started to believe he'd become an untouchable kingpin. But six weeks and three fights was too a small window for even James Bond. Intel from the fights, though, revealed Nigel talked nonstop about a fighter who'd open the UFZ door. You were there for the rest."

"That's why you didn't go with any other scout or promoter."

"I was looking for access to Nigel." She shoveled in a mouthful of beef'n broccoli.

"The slick-haired shyster be one of you," I said, tossing the bone into the spare plate.

"Sid Rosen. He's no lawyer. He's my handler. He was in my ear all night. And from the bugs in Nigel's office that I put in, we knew he was coming to off you two. So, you were never in any danger."

"Except when we were facing off Black Godzilla."

"I knew we could take him," smiled Jenny, going for the fried rice. "Want some?"

"Sure." Puma asked, "Why'd you quit fight club for the PFL?"

"Part of building my resume," she replied, serving Puma, "bad decisions that didn't work out. As much for back story as a character sketch. Like knocking the shit out of the asshole in the gym, remember him, Dusty?" Turning toward Puma, "And sucker punching Gavin? I actually did get hurt in that eighteen-second PFL KO. Had to take six months off. Nearly ended the op before it started."

"You wait for me in the parking lot 'cause you called in and they said, sheeuh, Puma know Dusty and Dusty work for Nigel."

"Actually the other way around. When Nigel hired Dusty, we started looking at Dusty's circle of friends who intersected with fight clubs. We planted that conversation about a chick worth looking at."

"Sheeuh," Puma recalled. "Sports bar on Vermont. I was snookered."

"Aren't you glad you were, though?" Jenny paused eating to plant a big kiss on Puma's cheek. He melted as she wiped away the smudge of soy sauce. "You know why I loved you from day one? You never cheated on your wife. So I knew you were decent and honorable."

Ending that love fest, I asked, "All your shenanigans, like the orgy in the container—"

"Collecting evidence while having a couple of hunks go down on me—that's the definition of mixing business with pleasure." Drew a smile from Puma'n me. "Needed pictures of the eighteen-wheeler which was modified to smuggle fighters with Nigel in it. I knew he'd storm in and go ballistic. He did. Said things he shouldn't have."

"Check those whores for a wire?" asked Nigel.

"They are fucking naked!" exclaimed Jenny with a snort, then picked up a grocery bag. "And I took their cell phones."

"You had one in there, recording," I realized, going for seconds. "Now, I get why you wanted to move training from Baton Rouge to New Orleans."

"The pregnancy?" asked Puma.

"We found out Boz was sniffing around for DA Arlen Taylor, trying to connect the Police Chief to Nigel. Amazingly, Nigel didn't know, but it could fuck up my operation. Dossier on Boz had him as a self-righteous, pro-gun, pro-lifer, with a weakness for young women—girls, really. He obsessively pursued a couple. Stalked them after the breakup. Beat a brutal murder rap following the second affair. He reacted exactly the way our profiler said he would. Put Boz on the Nigel's radar. Each trying to out-macho the other, Nigel stepped up to protect his investment—me. Ironic, huh? Took eyes off my op."

"Inviting yourself to an I-10 fight," I deduced, "so undercover agents wired every which way could show up."

"See it now?" she grinned with her mouth full. "A method to all my madness?"

"How the feds find you, lil girl?" asked Puma. "At sixteen? Your parents really dead?"

"You dug into my back story," Jenny wrapped a hugging arm around Puma's shoulder. "You don't think we kept tabs on you two and Nigel poking into my past?"

"Won't the Cartels come after us?" I wasn't ready to exult.

"Why would they risk adding to the body count? Especially someone as famous," Jenny shrugged, "as me. The way the narrative is being handled, " she circled her chopsticks around the three of us, "the Cartel will believe their connection to Easy Trucking was not exposed."

"So you ain't shutting it down?" asked Puma.

"Fuck, no. Easy Trucking is a pipeline into Cartel operations that we've never ever had."

My eyes widened and I stopped eating. "The black chick,

Makena, she from Baltimore. She wan't just Nigel's CFO."

Jenny winked again, nibbling duck meat off the bone.

"You people turned her!"

Jenny smiled.

"But the way you took out Nigel—"

"Will never been known. Public will hear that he died a hero, taking out Sharif Hirsi—your Black Godzilla and Makena's uncle. The Cartels will let the story stand because they don't want anyone one finding out Hirsi was sent to take out Nigel and me, after Nigel killed you two. Since they lost their inside man, the Police Chief, to know exactly what happened, they have to believe their contacts in NOPD, who'll say each killed the other in a shootout. A paperwork error will have both bodies cremated before anyone can claim it."

"And Boz?"

"He'll move on."

"I'd have figured the DA'd want the headlines."

"He did, but my people upstairs suggested—more like decreed—he go along with our spin. Or else."

"Sheeuh," said Puma. "this onion get stinkier the more you peel."

I realized, swigging down soda, "Your cover stays intact."

"Which means you two are new to my inner circle."

"Sheeuh," grinned Puma conspiratorially.

"What now?" I asked.

"We have a Championship fight in three months!"

"We still on?" reacted Puma.

"Fuck, yeah! I didn't put my body on the line and get all the way to the brink to walk away!" exclaimed Jenny passionately. "Besides, I can't let you two geezers die with dead dreams. We are going to win that Bantamweight belt."

"The feds are OK with it?"

"OK? They are over the fucking moon. The mad scientists back at the lab are working on the next black op using my MMA cover. Besides, I have to win at everything I'm into, including going down as a legend when they write about undercover agents."

Puma grinned ear to ear. "Sheeuh, Dusty, we're secret agents." Channeled 007, "The name's Song. Puma Song."

Jenny belted out the Bond theme.

Of course, I broke up the party. "When were you going to tell us you're blind in your right eye?"

THE END

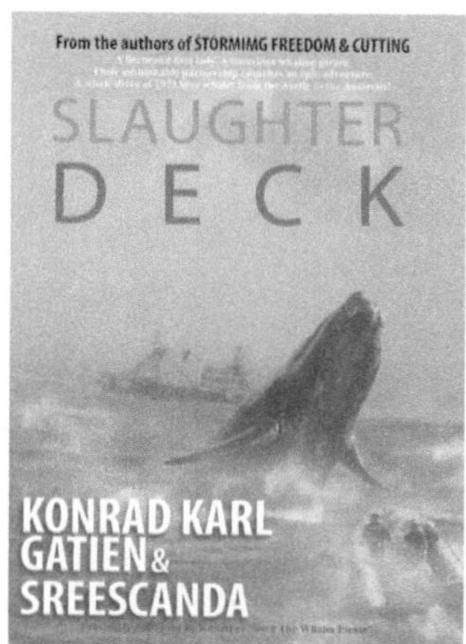

EXCITING THRILLERS BY
KONRAD KARL GATIEN & SREESCANDA

AVAILABLE ON AMAZON, BARNES & NOBLE
AND EVERYWHERE BOOKS ARE SOLD

"A movie between book covers."
Foreword

"A Western on the high seas."
Ventura County Star

In the alleys off San Francisco's Castro Street, young couples are into blood as an aphrodisiac.

It was just a matter of time before someone turned up dead.

Murdered.

Thunder Strike is the first in a series of '*Storming Freedom*' thrillers set in a world beyond and behind the public eye where two families of unlimited wealth, the Ulysses and Hawkes, have battled to influence every President since George Washington.

Thunder Strike begins the sixth generation of this secret feud.

Available in Hardcover, Paperback, Kindle, Nook & other eBooks.

www.ingramcontent.com/pod-product-compliance
Lightning Source LLC
Chambersburg PA
CBHW020554310726
48979CB00008B/1218/J

* 9 7 8 0 9 8 4 5 7 3 0 3 5 *